DIRTY QUIET MONEY

RYAN E. LONG

Copyright © 2014 by Ryan E. Long

Dirty Quiet Money

First Edition — Published 2014

Published by Quality Filth, L.L.C.

ISBN: 978-0-9891175-2-4

All Rights Reserved. Printed in the United States of America.

This book is historical fiction. The well-known (and less well-known) actual people, events, and locales that take part in the story have been accurately portrayed according to available historical research. The remaining names, characters, places, and/or incidents are products of the author's imagination or are used fictitiously. Any resemblance to the name, attributes, or background of any actual person, living or dead, or to any actual event, or to any existing company, is entirely coincidental and unintentional.

Front cover illustration by Mr. Giovanni Ruggiero, Bologna, Italy. Front and back cover design by Ms. Minou Sinios, Brooklyn, New York, Mr. Kevin Robbins, New York, New York, and the author. Photography by Mr. James Bareham, New York, New York.

Special thanks to Chantal S. Long and Adam R. Sanders for edits and comments, and to Mr. Mark Littman of Northern Lights, New York, New York, for help with the book trailer.

To purchase additional paperback copies, please order from Amazon.com, Barnesandnoble.com, or e-mail info@qualityfilthllc.com. To purchase an e-book copy, please go to Amazon.com, Barnesandnoble.com, or I-Tunes.com. For rights and permissions, please contact info@qualityfilthllc.com.

TABLE OF CONTENTS

Chapter 1: Ambush	1
Chapter 2: Silver Spoon	23
Chapter 3: Dirty Face	38
Chapter 4: Like Attracts Like	54
Chapter 5: Appearances Are Appearances	85
Chapter 6: University Of Treachery	116
Chapter 7: Big Bang Theory	145
Chapter 8: Sex, Drugs, & Jazz	183
Chapter 9: Wake Up Call	210
Chapter 10: Action-Reaction	244
Chapter 11: A Woman's Best Friend	276
Chapter 12: Kissing Cousins	331
Chapter 13: Stage Fright To Delight	365

During World War II, my mother's family in Marseille, France, fought in the French Resistance. Their stories inspired me to write *Dirty Quiet Money*.

The Vichy regime and the Nazis considered resistance fighters to be devilish criminals. Some of them were, in fact, crooks before the war. These underworld entrepreneurs sold drugs, alcohol, and/or women to those in France who could afford it. To help the Resistance, they used their vast black market tools to get valuable information from Nazi officers.

At the same time, French collaborators were considered angels. This is so even though they were rewarded for turning in young Jews — in addition to other "undesirables" — to the Vichy police, who were more brutal than the Gestapo. In return, the ruling elite who largely made up the Vichy regime ensured that these "respectable law-abiding citizens" would not have their houses plundered, assets stolen, and lifestyles ruined by the Nazi juggernaut.

The complex story of the French Resistance cannot be neatly reduced to a tweet, nor can it accurately be categorized in the binary "good" vs. "bad." The spirit of resistance is often within those you least expect. And yet in today's scientific world, we are encouraged to believe that complicated human behaviors can be understood and predicted by data mining, deep learning, and/or examining a particular brain synapse.

This is not to say such reduction is never a sufficient predictive tool. It is to say that algorithmic simplification can blind us to black swans — unforeseen events or behavior — because the rational mind often ignores insightful input from the intuitive one. Albert Einstein hinted at this danger long ago when he said: "The intuitive mind is a sacred gift and the rational mind is a faithful servant. We have created a society that honors the servant and has forgotten the gift."

Enjoy learning about *Dirty Quiet Money*.

CHAPTER 1
Ambush

In May of 1963 Sophia, an elegant 52-year old woman, nervously read the following words to me from an old and bloody crumpled letter:

> *My hands splattered with their blood. So I writing this words to you. I not seeing you again after what happen this last night.*

The letter was written on December 5, 1942 by Jacky, a former lover of hers, I later found out. As Sophia's well-manicured hands nervously grasped the frayed letter, tears started forming in her seeming sad eyes. A brewing storm you see far off in the distance but cannot quite make out yet. While I sat in front of her in the middle of her massive Park Avenue apartment adorned with chandeliers, French crystal, and 20-foot windows, I wondered what caused her eyes to tear up.

After all, she had it made. Her son, Otis, recently graduated from Princeton, and her daughter, Etta, was a sophomore at Yale. Plus, Sophia was the head of Veritas, one of the most prominent charities in the United States. According to various newspaper articles I read, she had meeting after meeting during the day, and would see music at night, usually at The Carlyle. I continued to listen to her reading of the letter, and I soon came to understand the source of her tears. They were not so much tears of sadness but more of adoration, just like the brewing storm is refreshment to the dry and parched Illinois prairie.

Sophia continued to softly read from the tattered letter:

> *I not regret nothing. I not perfect. I have done many of the bad things. You knowing this. No matter what I done, I always loved you. I always loving you.*

"Are you alright, Ms. Gordon?" I asked her softly as I leaned over.

Sophia put the letter down for a moment to take a drag off of her Chesterfield cigarette, which was resting softly on the crystal ashtray table next to her. She put her shaking right hand over her right eyebrow like she may not be able to read on.

"Yes, Hank, thank you," she looked at me with a tortured sigh. I could sense reading from the note was both painful and cathartic for her.

I am a 31 one-year-old reporter from Chicago, Illinois, for *The New York Times*. I originally went to Sophia's Park Avenue apartment that day in May to get her input about the new outside garden at The Museum of Modern Art. It was recently built with money Veritas donated. And yet I soon found myself listening to her read from Jacky's letter instead of interviewing her about the donation.

You might ask how?

When I saw an old black and white photo of Jacky and Sophia on the top of her piano, I asked: "who is that?" This was unlike me. I am usually very private. I do my day job. I don't ask questions unrelated to my job. That's how I was raised. I am a good boy from the Midwest. But something in that picture made me want to take a detour. How big of a detour I didn't know — yet. After she started to explain who Jacky was, I started asking more questions, which eventually led to her pulling out the letter.

"If you want to read more, I'd love to listen, Ms. Gordon," I said.

"Thank you, Hank," she took a long drag off her cigarette and then read:

> *I needed to write so you not worry. I not sent to a camp like the others in the group. No. This not my fate. I also need to let you know what happened.*
>
> *The club is been making very much money. German officers been coming in and out every since they coming to Paris. They buy our booze, our women, our drugs. They let us do what we want to do. It is great way of getting the information. Our girls is the best at this.*

I had no idea what Jacky meant by the "group." I softly put my hand out towards Sophia's so as to interrupt her reading to ask a question.

"Excuse me, Ms. Gordon," I said nervously and feverishly, "but what is the group he is referring to?"

She put the note down and looked at me with her soft blue eyes.

"It's quite alright darling," she said with her left wrist bent towards me, and her gold signet pinky ring shining my face. "The group is the French Resistance."

"World War II?" I asked.

"Yes, darling."

"So Jacky was in the Resistance?"

"He was one of their best allies."

I smiled nervously. I am from an Irish working class family in the South Side of Chicago. Yes, I attended the University of Chicago on a scholarship and I work for the *Times*. No, I am not of Sophia's class and don't have her wisdom, regardless of what school I went to or what paper I work for. She is as good as a foreign object to me. So I didn't want to eat my words or ruin the interview by saying something stupid.

"Thank you, Ms. Gordon," I smiled impishly.

"My pleasure darling," she said with a glamorous smile that mirrored Grace Kelly's. She finished her cigarette and stared at the note for a moment.

"Please go on, Ms. Gordon," I said reassuringly.

"Thank you, Hank," she said as she stared at the note and then read:

> *But the things go wrong last night. 5 German SS officers coming into club. They always doing this. We greeting them, giving them their favorite seats, and then Henri, the server, bringing them the fine bottle of the champagne.*

I interrupted her to ask:
"Ms. Gordon . . ."
She interrupted me:
"Please call me Sophia, Hank."
"I'd be pleased to," I said nervously.
"So your question?"
"Why was Jacky giving them a fine bottle of champagne? I mean, they were occupying France at the time. I would think Jacky would want to give them anything but a fine bottle of champagne."

As we spoke, I heard the loud roar of sirens on Park Avenue through the slightly open window in Sophia's living room.

She smirked a devious smirk. I could tell she liked my curiosity. I probably wouldn't have asked so many questions during a regular interview for the paper — but this was no regular interview, and this wasn't for the paper.

It was for me.

"Let's just say he scratched their back when they had an itch, and they did the same for him."

She leaned over closer towards me and then said softly, with her fine pink lipstick lining her thin lips and with one eyebrow up, "do you catch my drift?"

"I think so," I nodded uncertainly.

"Well," she paused as she moved back away from me, "you'll get it sooner rather than later the more you sit here in front of me," she smiled contently as she lit another cigarette and continued to read the note.

> *After Henri leaving this champagne, I looking over and seeing this motherfucker SS officer. I know this face. His name is Gustav Franz Wagner. I hearing about this man. They calling him the 'Wolf' or 'Beast.' Our Krakow people telling me that this man ordering ripping the Jewish babies with the bare hands. I telling you this so you understanding what happening.*

Sophia stopped to take a long drag, and kept reading:

> *Wagner is the devil. I remember he had the good looks of the devil son: square jaw, slickly styled curly blond hair parted on his left, the pinkish color lips like the pretty perfect Aryan baby, no? He sitting with other SS officers, all wearing their uniforms — black boots up to knees, black riding pants, black hats with skull crossbones next to SS*

> *eagle, black jackets with a belt, two white leaves on their lapels, long swords for their rank.*
>
> *These sons of bitches taking off the hats like they was the gentlemen.*
>
> *The rest of officers was also the Aryan models — blond, tall, thin. They perfect candidates for cabaret of the gay men about to start doing their version of the Rockettes, no?*

Sophia looked up at me and smirked as she read this. I thought to myself: Jacky is a first class smart ass. The SS, or schutzstaffel, was a special protection squadron of the Nazis. Their specialties: security services, death squads, and concentration camps, just to name a few things. Dancing like the Rockettes was not one of them.

"Oh how do I miss his sarcastic sense of humor," she smiled and continued:

> *They into their second or third champagne, we sending our girls over keeping them the company. It about 11:00 at night, and the girls sitting on the officer laps. You know our girls — tall, thin, stylish, flapper looking. Our classy pussy keep the officers come back for the more, and we getting more and more information. Our girls is the such good cash machine that we taking good care of them: expense accounts for clothing, shoes, jewelry, hair care. But you knowing this, I think.*
>
> *These SS not having the respect for our pretty pricey pussy like they usually having. I finding out why later in night. Wagner start the pulling Julie's hair, the brown longhair from Lyon. She scream with the pain. The other officers laugh at what Wagner doing, start doing same shit with*

other girls. One trying to strip down the dress of Pauline, this red head with the color hazel eyes and this freckled skin from Bordeaux. These fucks not paid for the women and, no matter what, they knowing no rough play.

So Pauline started yelling, "no, no, no," as this officer taking her dress to make her show the tits, and I taking notice. This bad for business — customers not like this anger in the place of the secret petting of the nice pretty pussy.

It was a warm summer afternoon in New York and I knew that the conversation was making Sophia feel dark. She constantly wanted to look out through the window towards the sun. I didn't really understand why she felt comfortable with me at the time — but I did as I got to know her better. And yet I felt like I was one of the few people who she had a chance to talk to this about. She lightly grabbed my hand as I lit her cigarette with my Zippo, and then, once it was fully lit, she looked up at me with her stunning blue eyes:

"Thank you, Hank."

I nodded as I put the lighter back into my jacket pocket.

She puffed the smoke out as though she was sitting in a sauna and thought out loud.

"SS always dressed in black. They wanted to be equated with death. Sometimes, they didn't wear these outfits, but that was only when the SS officer was a member of the police, say the Gestapo, who were basically plain clothes SS officers."

Sophia put some cigarette ash into the crystal ashtray, continued to drag, and kept reading:

I watching this German bullshit through my cigarette smoke from the bar. I seeing that these horny nasty Germans is too much for the customers, cause they looking and not buying the pussy, I putting out my cigarette and wave my right hand over to Mickey. You know him — he the tall Irish man with the long beard like the Afghan poppy dealer we do the business, he always wearing this big black sunglass — even in the nighttime, you remembering him, our head muscle?

Mickey make the nod to Jacques, Artur, Charlie, Richard, Alex Marinko. These our best men. They mean looking fucks. Scars on faces, hands, arms. They packing the .45 pistols — the Germans knowing this.

I lighting up another cigarette at bar and waiting for Mickey to do his work. The next thing I knowing, the girls got off the officers and I seeing Mickey pointing Germans to front door. Wagner start the pounding of his fist on the table. He yell in loud voice — "nein, nein, nein," like the big spoil baby with the shit in the pants. You know this "no, no, no" in the German, and you knowing I love when you saying the "yes, yes, yes" when we in Deauville all night long, remember this?

He make such big loud bitch voice that I hearing it over the jazz band's play of Miller's "Tuxedo Junction" on the stage. I loving this song.

Mickey and boys pull out their pistols out and cocking them. Things about to getting ugly, so I walk with the slow pace like the snail over and part the sea of my men who circle the Germans. My men is doing the hovering behind me, I look at Wagner:

"Jacky," I hold out my right hand as my cigarette hanging from my mouth.

Wagner not hold out his.

> *I getting in his face. I blowing my nice cigarette smoke in his nice blue eyes as I staring at him. I smash the cigarette into ashtray on his table. He make almost the I want to fuck you stare at me whole time, but I not want to fuck this homosexual in the closet who live the fake life — I only love the staring at you.*
>
> *I telling him and his fucks: "No rough playing with the pussy, even if you paying for the pussy. Yes. You can nicely pet the pussy, kiss the pussy, rub the pussy. But not playing the rough play with this nice pussy cats, especially this one that see Monsieur Himmler. He not like that now?"*

Himmler was the CEO of the SS, kind of like Frank Sinatra of the German killing machine.

"May I have one of your cigarettes please?" I asked Sophia.

"Help yourself, Hank," she held out the box of Chesterfields for me to take one. I picked one from the box, took out my lighter, and nervously lit the cigarette.

"Thank you," I said.

I started feeling more relaxed as I blew the cigarette smoke up towards the twenty-foot high Victorian engraved ceiling, and then asked:

"Did Jacky always write like this? I mean did he always write letters to you?"

"When I first met him, he loved to read and had been keeping a journal but he wasn't a big letter writer. He secretly wanted to be a novelist his whole life, like an Albert Camus. So a lot of his diary entries, and even the letters he started to write to me, were written like a novel. Plus," Sophia took a long drag off her smoke, "Jacky's family always did business with associates from New York, Chicago, and New Orleans. He grew to love

America — the ideas behind it — but he had never been to the States. So the closest he could get to the country was writing in English."

"How did he manage that?" I asked surprised.

"He picked up the language, he told me, by listening and speaking to these Americans since he was a teenager. Started practicing his writing in his entries — especially after delving into some grammar books on his private time. He was self taught. It was his little secret escape from his grim and dangerous life."

She took another long puff off her smoke.

"Don't get me wrong, Hank. His only reason wasn't just to be like an American — it also kept his words from being understood by the prison guards while he was in jail. I made a point of encouraging him to keep writing because I felt like it was a good outlet for him. I remember him describing events with words that a poet would use, but his writing needed a lot of work. He often left out nouns and other words, which made his writing choppy. We used to go to Café De Flore, one of the oldest cafes in St. Germain-Des-Pres in Paris, have coffee, read *Le Figaro* or other papers, and compare our journal entries," she said remembering those sweet times.

She took a longer toke off of her cigarette.

"Oh Hank, I used to love going to that café. We would sit outside with all of the bikes parked, people walking by, people smoking their cigarettes, wearing berets, looking at each other, wondering what people were working on when they were writing, wondering who people were kissing when they were kissing — lover, mistress, husband? And then there were the dogs — people brought in their dogs from all over, and so the place turned into this eclectic zoo full of these characters — human and canine!"

She smiled as she reminisced.

"How long have you been keeping a diary?" I asked.

"Since growing up New Orleans. Like Jacky, I secretly have wanted to be a novelist, at least since I was in college. I used to love Virgina Woolf. And so I practiced my technique in my diaries, with dialogue, characters, you name it."

"Eventually, he started writing more and more in his journal. He actually grew quite a love for it. It's funny how much potential there is in some people. Sometimes it takes just the right person to bring that potential out into the light of the day, and to see it bloom."

"So Jacky wasn't educated at all?" I took a slow drag off my smoke.

"Some high school, but he soon dropped out to work for the family in Marseille," she paused as I lit up another of her cigarettes. "And yet I always think he regretted not having that side of him developed. I think he felt like being book smart was forbidden fruit — none of the family encouraged him to read or write. But he loved to do it once he learned how."

"I see," I said as I looked outside into the shining New York City summer light. I was starting to get a glimmer of a picture of this Jacky fellow. And yet there was so much more to know. I was only seeing the tip of his iceberg. I looked back at Sophia, "please continue," I nodded towards the letter in her hand.

Sophia started reading again:

> *I telling Wagner, "If you putting worm in Himmler's apple, how you thinking he going to eat it?"*
>
> *"I not expecting you to answer this question," I says to him, "but you must respect this house and then you is respecting Himmler."*
>
> *He looking at me with the anger and then he says: "I know who you are. Is a house rule hiding a pretty Jewish bitch?"*
>
> *I just looking back at him. He thinking I help you getting away. You and I know I did.*

"At least she pretty," I smile back at him.

"So you don't deny?" He showing his teeth.

"That she is pretty?" I says.

He look over at others, and then back at me with anger in the eyes.

"Who else but you knowing our mistresses?"

"Their mothers, no?" I says back at him.

"You ordered those photos delivered that day. That's how this Jewish cunt getting away, isn't it?" He said.

"Well, if you talking about a cunt, I not mind so much she is away. Would you mind if a Jewish cunt left?"

Now I understanding why they roughing up the girls. But I not allow it. I could not allow this. If they doing this, then all of them shits thinking they could do this. And then the business is done.

I smirk again. He knew, I knew, that I spit on all of them. "You must leave," I finally says.

"I not banning you from here. This too much. After all, I am the businessman. Businessmen have the reason. I like having your money. But there is lines, and you cats crossing them. My men is the experienced guides," I looking over to Mickey and the boys, "they showing you the front door," I said to Wagner and his fucks.

They stare at me.

They not moving.

"If you not move, I call Himmler and tell him what you doing to his girl, or my boys can making you disappear in the acid, yes?"

Mickey make the sizzle stovetop pan noise in the background with his mouth.

> *I finished: "but that not needed. You have given the easy thing to do: exit that door over there," I point to the front.*
>
> *The bastards all looking at Wagner.*
>
> *He stared into my eyes for a few seconds.*
>
> *I not blink — he do the blinking.*
>
> *He nodding to his men to leave.*
>
> *They getting up. Mickey and the boys walking them out of club.*
>
> *Mickey walking close behind these fucks, and he winking at me as walking by.*
>
> *I looking into Mickey's forest green eyes behind his black sunglasses. "This not the end of it. Get Gabriel on phone," I says with the quiet voice.*

"Who was Gabriel?" I asked Sophia.

"I never knew him. I never met him," she looked at me with an unknowing look, "but he was one of the main enforcers for the organization. I don't think Gabriel was his real name. He was, as I recall," she paused to look up at the ceiling as she smoked her cigarette, "an expert at explosives, hand-to-hand combat, sharp shooting," she puffed some of her cigarette smoke out towards me. She adjusted herself in the turn of the century looking couch.

The contrast between what Sophia was saying and what she looked like could not have been greater. She spoke about experts in death, and knew their dirty tools. And yet she looked so very clean and proper. She wore pearl earrings and a necklace along with an elegant pink dress by a designer named Valentino, who is reported to be the main designer for the president's wife, Mrs. Jacqueline Kennedy. As I got to know Sophia better, I found out she knew the intricate details about the dirty money that was behind her pristine Park Avenue address.

"So I guess Jacky meant business when he put this Gabriel character on notice?" I asked Sophia.

"More than you would expect, Hank," she looked at me somberly.

"So what happened next?" I asked her.

Sophia continued to read:

> *All quiet until 1:00. I was drinking the coffee, looking over receipts, ready to make a report for headquarters in Marseille. And then a quiet knock on the wood that is my office door I heard.*
>
> *It was Mickey.*
>
> *"Wagner is at front door," the sweaty Irishman says with worry in his voice.*
>
> *"What he want?" I knew what he wanting.*
>
> *"He not alone," Mickey saying to me through the cigarette smoke.*
>
> *"I come out," I say.*
>
> *Nobody knowing that I make the big plan with Gabriel over phone. I feeling that something go bad. You always trust my instincts. And so I did.*
>
> *I put out cigarette, lock up all of the paperwork into vault under the toilet, make my tuxedo tie tighter.*
>
> *"They asking for this shit," I saying to myself in mirror.*
>
> *As I walk out of office and into club, everyone staring at me with their big eyes — these dames drying glasses was staring; the women on the horny men laps was staring; the horny men was staring; the bar boys was staring; the boys all lined up next to front door, was staring, too.*

Ambush

> *You know I always love music. I remembering that band on stage was playing Armstrong's 'You're a Lucky Guy.' The band know this my favorite song. You remember when we listen to this song in Deauville before you leaving?*

Sophia looked up at me with happy sad eyes, and then continued reading:

> *Mickey asking me as I walk out: "you want us to come?"*
>
> *"No, you boys staying here," I say as I pat him on shoulder. "I make the plan with Gabriel," I say with the smart boy in class grin.*
>
> *I push open red color wood doors and exit to the street outside. There is was wall of Germans: Wagner and 50 of his SS and Gestapo maggots.*
>
> *The night wet, cold. I see the German breaths coming out of mouths. MP 40 submachine guns, or the Walter PPK pistols, by their sides like the little girlfriends. They the strangers to the warfare of the guerilla, and so they make the line like the toy soldiers.*
>
> *Me, I no stranger to the guerrilla war ways.*
>
> *I walk to Wagner. "Come to chat about women's fashion?"*
>
> *I staring at him.*
>
> *He glaring at me.*
>
> *He not sure of whether if I insane, brilliant, or maybe a mix of the two cousins.*
>
> *"We here to take you Jew nigger lover bottom feeders in. Get them at once!" Wagner says with his jaw clinched.*

> *He not have his gun out — yet.*
>
> *I look over his shoulder at SS men. "That is not going to happen," I shake my head in the fake disappointment.*
>
> *He shifting his head to the left: "oh, and why is that?"*
>
> *"My bottom feeders, they play the card game, and then they got the business to do later. I have date later on with the pretty black doll face, but first I have to cut my finger nails, too, they getting long." I take the long stare at my fingernails — doing the calm fashion diva bitch exam of them in front of this piece of Nazi shit. "Plus, those Berlin politicians inside," I point behind me, "is busy loving our women."*
>
> *Wagner put his hand on the pistol.*
>
> *"Can't we just be friends?" I says playfully.*
>
> *"With a Jew lover?"*
>
> *He start pulling it out.*
>
> *He start to pulling out his gun — not the other long thing in his pants.*

Sophia looked up at me with a smile and then continued:

> *I snap my fingers in air.*
>
> *Ten loud clicks from rooftops above was like the sounds of first rocks from the rock slide.*
>
> *The clicks was from Browning .50-inch machine guns. Gabriel and his men putting the guns on this tripods in windows and rooftops around us.*

I touched Sophia's right arm to interrupt her: "Sophia, what is a Browning like?"

To my surprise, she knew exactly what it was like:

"A mean American machine gun. The infantry used it in gun battles, but it was also used as an anti-aircraft gun."

She paused to think.

"I think it weighed about 82 pounds, was 65 inches in length, and had a rate of 450 rounds per minute. Those things were ready to slaughter, Hank," she looked at me grimly and continued to read after I took my hand off of her:

> *Wagner is the German devil caught in Jacky's trap, and see the trap around him like the vice grips on the balls, yes?*
>
> *He look back at me.*
>
> *"You fool!"*
>
> *"Maybe this true," I shrugging and looking again at my long fingernails that need the manicure, "but I am the fool with the big guns, see?" I looking around at my pretty guns.*
>
> *I put my hand out for Wagner to shake it. "We stopping this now?"*
>
> *He staring at me.*
>
> *"Nein!" The stupid fuck is saying.*
>
> *He started to pulling out his pistol. His men starting to raising their guns to me.*
>
> *I taking the steps back as machine gun bullets from above rip their bodies into the pieces for the fish. Some of their blood sprayed all over my tuxedo shirt, face, and hands.*
>
> *Fuck! I thinking to myself. I have to buy the new shirt.*

Sophia looked up at me and smiled a bright smile. She then read:

> *On top of this shit, my enemies frame me to be with the Nazis. I caught between the Germans and Allies. I need to go into hiding for the long time as I on the death list of both sides now.*
>
> *But I needing to write this letter to you before I do the disappear act for the ever. I love you more than anything I love in my life. You help me love who I am, and to love the pretty things in the life like you. You always next to my heart, in this life and the other side.*

Sophia had raindrop-sized tears dripping onto the floor below now.

I held out a tissue.

"Thank you," she said as she wiped her eyes. She read:

> *I know my New York people been taking the good care of you. I giving you my heart and all of my love. Yours always, Jacky.*

Sophia put the note down on the coffee table. Her hands were shaking. She tried to light up another smoke. But she couldn't hold the cigarette still.

"Here, let me help you," I said softly. I grabbed the gold plated Tiffany's lighter from her hands and lit the cigarette for her.

"Thank you," she said as she inhaled the smoke and closed her eyes in the nicotine oblivion.

"When did Jacky write that letter, Sophia?"

"It is dated December 5, 1942. He probably wrote it in one of his safe houses."

By this time, it was early evening. I took a peek outside. The summer sky had turned to a cobalt blue. Stars started to appear. As I sat there in my thoughts, and as Sophia sat in her couch emotionally shell shocked, her butler, Winston Fermor, interrupted:

Ambush

"Excuse me, but may I offer you an evening tea?" He said with an English accent. He leaned over to catch our attention with a silver plate. On the plate were two cups of Earl Grey tea.

Winston was wearing a crisp tuxedo. I had seen him smoking a cigarette outside when I first arrived. I remember loving the way he kept the cigarette balancing on the right corner of his mouth, as though the cigarette was high up on a tightrope doing a balancing act. He did the tightrope act with his cigarette as he spoke to a flower shop delivery person.

"Yes, thank you dear," Sophia endearingly said as she took one of the cups of tea. I could tell she was fond of Winston, whose tuxedo was kind of like the one I imagined that Jacky and his men wore that night so long ago.

"Thank you, Mr. Fermor," I said as I took the other cup. His hair was grey, slicked back, and he wore round tortoise glasses. His bone colored 60 year old or so skin complemented the angelic white of his shirt and the black of his tuxedo.

"Please, call me Winston. I don't want to feel like that clock over there," and then he pointed to the antique looking grandfather clock in the corner. He seemed like a sweet albeit wry man who had seen tough times in life, but didn't show or talk about it.

The tall clock he was pointing to clicked quietly in the background as I heard the flow of rush hour traffic on Park Avenue below. Winston walked softly away into the faint light of the kitchen in the background, leaving Sophia and I there in the ornate looking living room.

We sat in silence for about a minute before I broke it:

"The tea is lovely," I said to make conversation.

"Yes, it is," Sophia agreed as she sipped more holding the cup with her left hand.

"May I ask you something?"

She nodded with a small smile.

"Do you have a diary of your own? I mean, you mentioned that you kept one when you were younger in New Orleans."

Dirty Quiet Money

"Yes," she nodded.

I gathered my composure.

"I wanted to see if I could perhaps review your and Jacky's diaries. There is so much more I want to learn."

"What will you do with what you learn, Hank?" It was an unexpected philosophical question from her.

"Change my life for the better?" I shrugged uncertainly about what I was saying. I never opened up to someone like this before. "And I don't know if I can do that all by myself. I mean, they say there are two ways of learning, one . . ."

She sharply interrupted:

"Through your own experiences, and through the experiences of others."

"Right," I nodded with a smile.

"I understand, Hank. I understand all too well."

She paused to consider what she was going to say.

"I don't have a problem loaning you the diaries." She lit up another cigarette. "You remind me of my son, Otis. You are earnest, inquisitive, shy, open-minded," she said smiling as she put her hand over mine.

Did she just say: "open minded"? I never thought of myself that way. Maybe Sophia saw something in me that I didn't see in myself. I have always felt closed to the world, in my own thoughts, and afraid to engage uncertainty. And yet meeting Sophia has been a good influence on me. She makes me want to open up more. She makes me want to change.

Sophia got up from the couch and walked over to the old English black secretary desk. It was against the wall between the massive windows overlooking Park Avenue. She opened one of the cabinets and pulled out a large black book. She walked back over to the couch, sat down, and handed me the book. Written on the front in handwriting: "Sophia Low Gordon — New Orleans, Louisiana."

"These are my diary entries from when I was growing up in New Orleans."

I opened the book and started flipping through it. Each page was meticulously written and, as Sophia had said, some of it was written in a novelistic fashion, whereas, at others, it was in a narrative. The diary had photographs of different sizes in the pages.

"I suggest you start reading that. It will give you an idea of my breeding, and just how improbable my feelings are for this man."

After I flipped through the pages, I looked up and started to say to her: "It will give me an appreciation for the impossible..."

"Becoming possible," she smiled broadly as she finished my thought. "And when you are done, we will have another visit together and I will give you the next entry. I think you will find many surprises, and that not everything is the way it seems," she looked at me like how I imagined Jacky knowingly looked at the unknowing Wagner that night in Paris twenty years ago or so.

"Thank you, Sophia, thank you so very much," I rubbed my right hand on the cover of the book. I took my hand off to go and shake her hers. She got up off the couch and offered me a hug.

"I think you and I have grown closer today, Hank, than would be represented by a mere handshake," she smiled tenderly. We embraced in a soft and caring hug for a few seconds.

After we broke our embrace, I said "I'll be in touch this coming week. Can we talk about your donation to MOMA then?"

"Whenever you are ready. Please take your time with the diaries," she responded as though she could care less about talking to me about the donation. "Winston will show you out." Winston was waiting in the kitchen to escort me outside, just as he had escorted me inside.

As he walked me outside the apartment doors, he patted me softly on the back like some father would his son. During the patting, he said, in a very quiet and informal tone, "enjoy the read, young man, I suspect you are going to learn quite a lot in those," he pointed to the diaries in my satchel as if he knew what I was about to read. I guess that is to be expected, given he was her butler for what it seemed like a long time.

"Thanks, Winston, I am sure I will," I said as I started to turn away from him when we got outside.

He gave me a small wink with his left eye.

During my walk away from Sophia's apartment building, I wondered what secrets her diary would reveal to me about her. When I found myself standing on Park Avenue looking south, I also wondered how much of a hand did people like Jacky and Sophia have to play in the building of modern day America.

I would soon find out.

CHAPTER 2
Silver Spoon

On an unseasonably cold and wet Saturday morning, I read the following words from Sophia's September 17, 1929, diary entry as I sat at the Minetta Tavern bar drinking coffee:

> *September 17, 1929*
> *Their feet were always dirty and calloused. So I always felt so bad for them. I wondered if I was basically benefitting from their oppression. I wondered if I was a good Christian.*

The Tavern is on a tree lined MacDougal Street in Greenwich Village, and has a black and white tiled floor, long mahogany bar, high ceilings made of tiles, and small round dim lights. My hands were damp and cold from the weather outside.

Sophia had told me during a phone call that she was born on September 16, 1910. During the call, we discussed her donation to MOMA. So she was 19 at the time she wrote the words above. She told me she and was a freshman at Sophie B. Newcomb College, a tony woman's school in uptown New Orleans, at the time. I think she was talking about the black servants at Oak

Alley, an old plantation just outside of New Orleans. According to my research on her family, her parents died in a car accident on October 15, 1915, when she was 15. I read on:

> *I wonder if I am a good Christian because I was told to help those who are weaker than me. Jesus tells me that every day, especially when I go to church on Sundays.*
>
> *And yet I saw growing up that my family had built its cotton and sugar empire on the backs of these poor souls. I used to see them come into the country home's wooden floored kitchen, which had some splinters dug up from all of the years of use, with their bare and calloused feet. I always wondered to myself, why doesn't mamma get them shoes?*

Sophia spoke of New Orleans as "home," and the family plantation was the "country home," I later found out. She told me that her family used to go to Christ Church on St. Charles, which is a stunning white brick gothic looking cathedral.

> *I remember asking mother about this one morning. I think I was ten. I remember looking through the kitchen windows and seeing the fresh sun shining through dew on the wise old oak trees in front of the country home. Mother was having her regular morning coffee on the long wooden kitchen table, and was wearing her white linen morning gown.*
>
> *"Mother," I said as I sat down at the table waiting for Dido, one of our female help, to bring me my breakfast.*
>
> *"Yes, dear," mother said as she looked up from reading her La Nouvelle Mode, a French fashion*

magazine. Mother was so tall and pretty. I wanted to grow up like her one day. She had the deepest blue-colored eyes you could ever see. They reminded me of those turquoise rocks that some of the Indian folk sell back home in the French quarter. And her hair was so blond it looked like she spent all of her days in the sun. But her skin was white, like the color of the stars on a dark night in the middle of a New Orleans cemetery. All you can see is the reflection of the sun off the moon and those white gulf stars shining above.

"Why do we have Dido, Venus, and these other colored folk here? I mean, they aren't from around these parts, and so why don't we send them back home to wherever they from?" *I remember sitting there as Dido brought me some eggs that she had cooked up on the grill.*

"Oh, darling," *mother said.* "We are helping these poor people. They need us. They need us to watch over them, honey." *Dido and Venus stood there at the ready to take our orders. They said nothing. My mother went on:* "if it weren't for our family, honey, these poor folk would be stuck back in Africa, where we got them from, starving, fending for themselves in the jungles. Don't you see, darling?"

Momma looked at me with her deep turquoise eyes.

"I guess so," *I shrugged as I heard the morning birds chirping outside, and the help outside getting to work chopping wood.* "I just feel bad that they don't have shoes, that their feet are so dirty, and that they are so calloused," *I told momma,* "while I eat with this here silver spoon."

Dirty Quiet Money

I interrupted my reading of Sophia's diary to look up at all of the booze on the shelves of the Tavern — whiskey, vodka, gin. I thought about whether she now felt guilty about having the money she has, and living the way she does. I sipped more of my black coffee, and then put my head back down to read:

> *But, God almighty, I still feel dirty for having taken help. I know my family has all of this money. And I feel like they keep it quiet from the Lord when we go to Church back home, and even keep the money quiet when we travel.*

Tony, a bartender at the Tavern, broke my concentration.

"Eh, yo, Hank, whatcha readin' dere, da fucking Dead Sea scrolls?"

A native from Palermo, Sicily, Tony leaned in front of me with his broken looking nose to get my attention. I understand from the street that he got the custom nose job doing some underground fighting to make some extra cash on the side.

"Nah, Tony. I got this diary from a lady who lives uptown," I held up a page to his face for him to look at. "It's old. I am reading about her views of slavery when she was a little one growing up in Louisiana."

I am confident Tony won a lot of his fights. He stood about five foot eight and weighed about 180 pounds or so. He was a regular brick shit house that looked tough to knock over, and maybe even tougher to mentally beat. I think he fought as a never give up until you kill me light heavyweight, just like that bull, Jake LaMotta.

"A regular fucking historian, are ya?" Tony said with a smirk as he slapped me on the shoulder. Just as Jacky wore a black tie and white shirt that night in Paris, Tony wore a white shirt and black tie today in New York City. His sleeves were rolled up. He had small gypsy like tattoos on his arms — a small fish on his wrist, a tattoo of a girl's name on the fingers of his right fist, a mermaid up by his elbow. He usually had a long and wild beard that covered up his small belly.

"Well, I'm just trying to learn about her and her experiences back in the past, Tony, so I can get a better picture of her now."

"Yea, yea, I get it, Hank. You know, uh, a lot of my people come to this city here and tink they can just forget where they came from you know, uh, but I tink dat just gets dem kind of crazy, you know, because dey ain't . . . uh . . . ."

"Grounded?" I asked Tony.

"Yea, dat's right," Tony agreed. "Grounded. It's like dey forget who dey was, you know?"

"I got it, Tony, and I totally agree with you," and then took a last sip of my coffee. It was about 10:30 in the morning now and I still was pretty much one of the only people in the tavern.

"Want some more Hank?" Tony pulled out the carafe of coffee.

"Yes," I nodded, "thanks Tony."

After Hank poured the coffee, he asked:

"Eh, got any music requests I can play before the crowds come?"

"Nah, but thanks anyway."

Tony went over to the jukebox, put in some coins, and then put on, "Everybody Loves Somebody," by Dean Martin.

"Let me know if you need anything else, alright pal?" Tony said.

"Got it. Thanks," I said as Tony went over to the end of the bar to finish his reading of the *Daily News* sports section.

Before I went back to reading Sophia's diary, I lit up a Chesterfield cigarette. I wanted to learn more about Sophia and Jacky. I felt like smoking the same cigarettes as they used to would help me get more into their shoes. I skipped forward in Sophia's diary.

October 19, 1929

I remember how ashamed I was of my family during one of our trips to Paris. I think I was ten or eleven at the time.

We were at a very nice party in the 16th Quarter of the city. We were in this white walled apartment with humongous ceilings, windows, and which smelled of sweet jasmine. My father was speaking to another man as they smoked cigars, and I remember the other man asking my father what he did.

I'll never forget what he said: "We run sort of a fashion house." I could not believe my ears. What hogwash! I knew my parents inherited the family business, and it was all based on African labor. So, I mean, how could they say it was a fashion house when it was all cotton and sugar cane? The clothes came after, elsewhere.

I feel badly feeling this way. Father was an elegant and loving man. His skin was pale and almost sickly looking, but I think that was just his English background. Momma had similar white skin, but it was from her German family. Father, like momma, was tall and regal — with a big bush of flowing grey hair, green eyes, and always in his elegant black suit, black tie, and white shirt. Momma was tall — but daddy was taller than her, which is hard to believe!

When people met daddy, they were so intimidated by him. He had so much land here in Louisiana, and also in Virginia, but he was really warm and cozy once you get to know him. He was nice to Venus and the others, but he knew how to be strict when he needed to be. He'd beat them when he needed to. I guess it's just hard for me to remember him as this big fluffy man when really he couldn't be that way all the time. I think he was ashamed of it. I mean, the way he talked to the man in Paris showed me that.

I heard some people come through the door. I turned around and saw Ezra Pound, the poet, come in with some friends. It turns out that a lot of folks like this, such as Hemingway and E.E. Cummings, used to come to Minetta. I guess I was in good company to be in a place like this. I heard so much about these writers, especially their exploits during the 1920s and 1930s, and so I was inspired to learn more about Sophia's life during that time. I skipped further into her diary to learn about her life during that roaring period in our nation's history. To get my self in the groove, I asked Tony for a song request:

"Eh, mind putting on some Ellington?"

"Yeah, sure, I got some 'Jungle Nights in Harlem.'"

"Good. Good stuff." As I sat there listening to the screeching sounds of Ellington's song, I turned to the part of Sophia's diary when she was a freshman at Newcomb.

> *April 1, 1930*
>
> *The party last night was so much fun. My friend Tommy had people over at his parent's place. They live on St. Charles Avenue. As I walked from my parent's house to his, I could smell the lovely Louisiana jasmines that lined the sidewalk. It is springtime in New Orleans and nothing could be sweeter. The air has a tint of cool in it, the people wear white linen or seersucker to parties, and there is rebirth in the air.*
>
> *Ruby Comiskey, a good friend of mine from college, accompanied me to Tom's party. We dressed up because we knew all of the top people from the city were going to be there — lawyers, doctors,*

Dirty Quiet Money

> *cotton farmers, plantation owners. You name it — they were going to be there.*

As I got ready to read what happened next, Tony asked: "Hey, Hank, how about some bourbon on the rocks?"

"A splash please," I said to him with a small smile.

"Coming right up," Tony said.

The Tavern was now full of people. You had your old and young couples going out for their Saturday morning brunch, students from New York University waking up and coming in for some grub, and then you had the locals like me who came in to drink, read the paper, and watch the rest. Tony put the bourbon in front of me.

"Thanks," I said.

"You got it, kid," Tony said.

I went back to Sophia's entry:

> *Ruby had the classic flapper haircut of the day. She put a little stuff in it to keep it stiff. She has the most amazing green eyes, especially with her dark Irish hair and light skin.*
>
> *She could afford the best of fashion. I think the Comiskey Family came from Ireland, and they made a lot of money when they got big into politics in New Orleans and Chicago. I often come over to have dinner at their mansion — with its chandeliers, large wooden staircases, and servants all over the place.*
>
> *My outfit last night was like hers, but it wasn't as fancy. I also didn't get my haircut short like her. I think it is too much of a fad. I still keep my hair down to my shoulders, and I wore a linen shawl over my head last night to keep my hair in place.*

Silver Spoon

I wore a pair of brown colored t-bar shoes with my outfit, which was also a crème colored theme.

Ruby and I walked down the tree-lined street of St. Charles. It can be cool on even the hottest of days because of the large drooping trees. The street car passed us by as we took little swigs of the gin from the stainless steel flask that she lifted from her father's dresser.

When we arrived to Tom's house, there were about 30 or so people outside drinking gin and tonics, laughing, and listening to the Negro band that was on the side yard. I remember all of the boys looking our way. I didn't know if they were looking at me, or Ruby, or both of us.

Ruby was quite the attention getter with the boys. She was tall and wore this smashing red dress last night — it was down to her knees and made of small beads. She had these just sparkling pearls around her neck, a white hat with a feather on it, and red lipstick. On her feet were these just lovely spectator heels that had red toes and heels which matched her dress.

I think the main leader of the band, a man named Louis Armstrong, was getting quite popular, even with whites in New Orleans. If I remember right, his band was playing one of his famous songs, "West End Blues."

All of the boys watched and appeared to talk about us as Ruby and I walked arm in arm up the old white stairs of the mansion onto the porch. When we got there, Tommy greeted us:

"Well, hello, ladies," he said with an up to something that we didn't know about yet smile. I know

he was back for the weekend from Dartmouth, where he was studying to go into law, like his father.

"Well hello Mr. Tommy," Ruby said to Tommy as he eagerly stood there in his seersucker suit and white bucks like she knew what he wanted and maybe would give it to him.

Tommy leaned over to kiss both of our hands as his Germanic blue eyes gazed at our breasts.

"Please, come inside and make yourselves comfortable," Tommy held his left hand out to direct us into his family's massive mansion with beautiful fresh flowers everywhere the eye could see.

We walked through what seemed like an endless sea of people from uptown New Orleans wearing their spring garb. As Ruby and I held hands and walked through the crowd, we were greeted by all of our friends back from Harvard, Yale, Princeton, and Dartmouth:

"Sophia! Good to see you!" Buckley, a freshman at Yale, said as he kissed me on both cheeks.

"Sophia! It is so lovely to see you. How is Newcomb?" Carlisle, a freshman at Harvard, said to as he kissed me on both cheeks.

"Oh, Sophia, it has been too long!" Blair, a blond freshman at Princeton, said as I walked through the toy-like collection of people with a pat on my shoulder and an air kiss on each cheek.

As Blair's face came close to mine, I thought to myself: if I had another of these snots kiss me on the cheek, I was going to throw up. And yet I wondered if I wanted to throw up at the other part of myself who wanted to socialize with these types of people.

> *Ruby and I continued through the crowd until we got to the backyard of the mansion. People were drinking gin and dancing the Charleston to Armstrong's music. A few people I grew up with appeared to be kissing or getting into it behind the palm tress or wherever else they could hide behind.*
>
> *I stood there watching this spectacle, and I couldn't help but wonder if any of these people really cared about me. I know I have known most of them for my whole life. But I still questioned whether if any of them would save me from hungry dogs if it meant sacrificing their lifestyle.*
>
> *I don't think so. Their uptown homes, galas, and Mardi Gras parades were too important to them.*
>
> *This is something I don't want to admit to because of all these people surrounded me with a safe bubble of glamour — wealth, pedigree, and prestige — growing up.*
>
> *But part of me felt like the safety was an illusion.*

I thought about how Sophia's secluded New Orleans upbringing must have blinded her to the harsh realities of life that others less privileged have to deal with — paying rent, horrible bosses. I soon learned that her life growing up was not all privilege and perfection.

> ***October 15, 1930***
>
> *I sit here on my cold bed and wonder: maybe God wanted to punish me? I felt my breath go away when I asked this of myself.*
>
> *My parents died five years ago today in a car accident on St. Charles. My father was 57 and*

my mother was 45. I remember getting the news from our butler, Charlie. He called my school in the morning and had the principal take me out of my history class.

When the principal handed me the phone, I remember saying to Charlie: "Charlie, why you calling me like this at school? Is something wrong?"

There was dead silence on the phone for a few seconds. That's when I knew something was wrong.

"I be sorry to be habbin to tell you this, Miss Sophia," Charlie said with his old negro raspy voice, which was the type of voice you get when you smoke too many cigarettes, drink too much booze, and sing too much blues.

"What is it, Charlie? What is it?" I asked him anxiously.

He was silent for a moment, and then said:

"Your momma and poppa. They waz in an akzident dis morning, Miss Sophia. Dey gone, now, Miss Sophia, dey done gone," Charlie said as he started to cry.

"Gone" sounded so permanent to me, and I just didn't know how permanent death was at the time. Now I know. There isn't going to be another October 15, 1925 in the future. This is the last and only one. That permanence is what made my breath go away today. It was what made my breath go away that day over the phone. I just stood there at school silent with the phone next to my ear.

"Miss Sophia?" Charlie asked over the phone after I was quiet for a few seconds.

"Oh my God, Charlie, oh my God," I remember saying to him when I started to realize what had happened.

> *I remember his comforting words to this day. He was like a surrogate father or even an older brother to me.*
>
> *"God sittin' right next to you today, Miss Sophia, iz hiz way o speakin to us, Miss Sophia," Charlie said.*
>
> *His voice felt like a warm, soft, wool blanket on a cold winter night. It brought not only warmth, but also the comfort that it will be there to greet you in the morning when you wake up.*
>
> *Maybe God is that way.*
>
> *I remember hanging up the phone and crying. I have been crying since that morning. I will be crying for the rest of my life about what happened. I won't show it. I won't let people see it. That is how I was raised. I was taught to keep that deep dark dirty secret, my frailty, from the glamorous eyes around me. But, on the inside, I am dark and combat the feelings of hopelessness every day all the while I keep the sunny proper Uptown New Orleans lady look on the outside.*

I realized after reading this entry that Sophia was a deep and thoughtful person. She may have had this glamorous demeanor to her. But she had an underside that was all so very real. In the end, she was just as insecure about whether tomorrow will follow today as less glamorous people like me.

"Hey, oh, Hank, how iz da fucking book report going, eh?" Tony interrupted my musings about Sophia with his wide Brooklyn smile. His scarred hands rested on the mahogany bar in front of me. His smile said something like, "listen kid, I've been roughed up plenty, but not all parts of life are bruised and confused, which is why I haven't stopped smiling."

"It's going well, Hank," I said. "Thanks for asking.'"

Dirty Quiet Money

"Yeah, yeah, yeah," he said. "Just don't get too faw into yeh head, see, before you forget about awl of deez brawds out here, you know?" He pointed over to a table of what looked like Danish women speaking with thick accents.

"Thanks, Hank," I said with an appreciative smile.

"Eh, what are friends fowr? To sit around and hold their dicks? Want a little fresher on that drink there?"

"Please, Tony."

Tony poured a little more bourbon into my glass. I then knew that this guy had a lot of class. I had to get on writing an article for Monday's edition and so I didn't have much more time to look at Sophia's diary. But I wanted to read about where she was in her head when she graduated from Newcomb. So I flipped forward through another few pages.

June 7, 1933

Today is my graduation day from college. I am twenty-two.

The weather is warm and humid. The sun shines. Things on the outside are so pretty and bright. I have my life in front of me. I got a job downtown working for a family friend. My grandparents are coming to my graduation. They have been so lovely since the accident, and have really looked after me. So I will have loved ones there.

Part of me wonders where my life is going. I wonder if I will be ever to find a love that really cares about me. I wonder if my unsettled feelings about losing my parents will ever go away.

When I close eyes, I have faith that I will find that love. I have faith that my feelings of fear will go away — or at least lessen — as I get older. But I seem to have these bright feelings only when my eyes are closed, not open. That darkness behind my eyes is comforting to me. And so something inside me says I may find exactly that love I am looking for not in the light and airy, but in the dark and scary.

I finished my bourbon, closed the book, and went to the brightly lit office to start Monday's assignment for the paper. That was the obedient light Chicago boy. The rebellious dark New York boy inside me wanted to go get Jacky's diary entries from Sophia so I could sit in the dimly lit Tavern to start reading them. And so I felt like I understood what Sophia was saying: sometimes we can find our true paths in what might otherwise seem to be a dark place. That dark place for her was behind her eyes. The dark place for me was the Tavern. In both, I think we found ourselves.

CHAPTER 3
Dirty Face

At around 9:00 p.m. on Monday night, I arrived at Sophia's Park Avenue apartment. Winston answered the door after I got off onto her floor.

"Good evening, Hank," Winston said with his characteristic smile.

"Good evening, Winston," I said in an attempt to be as equally formal.

"Please do come inside," Winston's white-gloved hand then led me inside.

When I went into the living room, I saw Sophia sitting and sipping a cup of tea, smoking a cigarette from her holder, and reading that day's *New York Times* through her monocle.

"Oh Hank," she said as she looked at me through her monocle, "how lovely to see you. I was just reading your paper."

She got up to greet me as I walked over. We briefly hugged one another, and I sat down in front of her.

"Would you like to join me in some tea?" She said with slightly pink lipstick on her lips.

"Yes, please."

"I'll fetch some more right away," Winston said.

"Thank you, dear," Sophia endearingly said. She turned towards me with a somewhat serious tone, "how did you enjoy the diaries I gave you?" Her eyes were focused on my satchel. I could tell she was both interested in knowing what I thought about the diaries, and to know whether I remembered to bring them.

"I loved them," I opened my satchel and handed over her first diary.

She looked it over to ensure it was in the same shape that she had given it to me.

"I hope you know how important these items are to me, so I hate to be such a square librarian," she turned her head upward to blow some smoke towards the ceiling.

"Please, Sophia, it's really no problem. I understand how important these things are for you."

"Your tea, sir," Winston came to put the tea on the coffee table.

"Thank you," I said.

"Thank you, darling," Sophia said.

"It is my pleasure," he responded in his Oxford educated accent.

I took a sip of the tea and then Sophia started in with the questions.

"So what did you think?" She inhaled a large puff of smoke and then blew it out.

"Amazing," I said with a boy who gets just what he wanted on Christmas morning smile.

"You don't say," she intriguingly leaned forward.

"You have a lot of faces that you keep private."

"There is more to me than meets the eye?"

"You could say that," I nodded. "I mean, um, well, it's just that people like pigeonholing you know."

"Yes," she nodded. "They like to do a taxonomy of others as though they were doing a study in Africa," she moved her right hand with a large diamond pinky ring on it to sip some tea.

"And yet there can be a lot more complexity to a person than you initially might think," I said.

"Come right out and say it, Hank, why don't you?" She put down her tea.

"Well," I said coyly, "I think most people who meet you would think that you are a privileged woman who has had life fed to her on a silver spoon."

"But?" She asked with a smile.

"You haven't had it as easy as one would think. Most people don't lose both parents when they are 15. Even when your parents were alive, you questioned your status — am I doing the right thing? Am I a good Christian? Am I being fair to these people?"

She nodded.

"What I mean to say is that you did not take things for granted. You aren't fixated on your bellybutton to the exclusion of the world around you."

"I tried not to."

"You succeeded," I agreed with her, "even before your parents died."

She took out another cigarette and lit it up.

"It's easy to take things for granted, just like the next breath you take, until you find out, at some point, that the next breath won't be there," she said reflectively.

"Right," I nodded, "but it is hard to keep that in mind on a daily basis."

"That's why I try to practice gratefulness whenever I can. It is so easy to take things for granted, especially in a wealthy country like ours," she said.

She paused to take a long drag.

"I think that's why I had such a kindred relationship with Jacky," she said with a reflective tone as she patted what I think were his diaries resting on her lap.

"I can't wait to dig into those," I eyed the diaries.

"Here are his first entries about growing up in Marseille," her manicured hand took the diary off her lap and handed it over to me.

"Thank you, Sophia." I handed her back the diary entries she had previously given me. I opened the cover to peek at Jacky's first entry:

February 7, 1939

It now 1939, but I still remembering when I sixteen years old, I stand on edge of my roof looking onto La Canebiere. As I standing, I thinks to myself: momma doing it again.

I not like when she with those strange men, even if she making the good money.

Maybe God punish me for something? Or maybe I never supposed to be born? I standing there looking down onto street. I feel like the living accident when I sixteen.

Sometimes, I feel this way now.

I looked back up to Sophia with my mouth open and in disbelief.

"I know it may be wrong to compare pain, but I think you will see from reading his entries there that my childhood was not as painful," she said softly.

She paused to take a drag.

"I suggest we meet again next week after you have read that one, and then I will give you the next two, one which is about my time in London with my former husband, and the other about Jacky's love life in Marseille."

I took a long sip of the tea that was remaining in my cup.

"Thank you again, Sophia," I said as I got up and to give her a hug.

"It has been my pleasure," she said. "You are keeping my memories alive and fresh by reading what I am giving you," she said with sweet eyes. "Have a splendid evening, Hank."

"You do the same," I said with gratitude back to her.

After bidding a goodnight to Winston, I took the subway back to the Tavern. I arrived around 10:00 p.m. Things were just getting started. Cigar smoke filled the air. Some of the male patrons in the back were smoking their favorite Cubans, and were frolicking with their scantily clad women.

"Who is back there?" I asked Tony as I sat down.

"Some Chicago Outfit guys, I think," Tony said with a shrug in his shoulders. "I really don't know. Even if I did, I probably shouldn't tell any way," he said with a wide smile as a he served me a bourbon on the rocks.

"I get it, Tony," I nodded. It seemed like a lot of underworld guys liked hanging around the spot. It was their Capitol Hill.

"How iz the reading going Hank?" Tony asked.

"Good. I am actually about to start reading about this guy named Jacky from Marseille. He used to be connected with a lot of those types," I pointed towards the back of the room where all of the men were lounging with their women, "in France. I have a feeling he was super connected in the United States, too."

Tony stopped drying the cocktail glasses when he heard Jacky's name.

"I know that Jacky," he said with surprise. I guess Tony was surprised that a straight-laced Midwest guy like me was reading about a no laces guy like Jacky.

"How do you know of him?" I asked sipping more of my bourbon.

"De guy is a fucking legend. He waz, uh, de one who connected dese families here and over dere in France and Italy together. I tink he was de one who brought dat stuff in from Turkey tru France, but Tony here just don't know the details."

He resumed drying the cocktail glasses.

"Even if I did," he started to say.

"You wouldn't tell me," I said.

"So you get where I am coming from on this guy. He ain't on de junior varsity team, kid. And yet I don't tink he iz, ah, as well known as the other cats that run around these parts."

"I know I've never heard of him before," I said as I sipped some more bourbon.

"Well, you soon will, kid, so enjoy the read," Tony said as he walked to the other side of the bar.

I sat there staring at the wrinkled cover of Jacky's old dusty diary. The straight-laced part of me hesitated to open it. I suppose I was scared to read what was on the inside. Maybe I was going to read things that I shouldn't be reading?

But the other part of me wanted to press on. I desperately wanted to read about Sophia and Jacky. I wanted to understand how such unlikely soul mates came to be. And how could I pass up reading about a man who took down those Nazis that night?

After the minute soliloquy with myself, I took another sip of the bourbon and felt sufficiently numb to start reading.

> *January 7, 1940*
>
> *I remembering getting home from school in afternoon one time when I the young boy. Momma make the bouillabaisse for me. Old piece of bread next to bowl.*
>
> *"Eat, dear, eat," she says when I sitting down at shitty old table.*
>
> *Momma putting on this fashion clothing at night, but it always death looking — black dress, black mascara, black smelling perfume, black*

high heels, black stockings, black pearls, black leather gloves.

I wondering why she dressing like that at night, why she come home so late from her cleaning lady job. She never dress like that before papa die from the cancer. I finding out a few months before. I hearing some men in local brasserie.

They says she was star whore in Marseille.

Night before I went to rooftop, my mother come home late. She doing that all month. I not know when it going to stop. I couldn't say nothing. She not know I knew. I never say nothing to her.

But I not handle it anymore.

I go to rooftop to ending my sleepless nights, throwing up, crying. My feet kissing the roof top edge. I closing my eyes. I about to put myself into darkness forever.

All of this sudden, I remembering feeling a breeze from ocean. I opening my eyes and look down. I seeing three men. They was exiting nice cars real slow.

I always wonder who these men was. They always looking like they dress in best Italian suits. They always drove fancy cars. Always had pretty women with them.

"My God boy, get down!" A woman down on the street says to me.

I remember look down at her.

One of the rich men must seen me, too.

He wave me down with right hand.

"Hey, boy, come down here with us, come down here with us."

The other men waving me down, too.

One of other man says: "yea, boy, you not regret it. Get off the ledge. Come join us," he smile and hold out cash in hand.

The first man smile. He have the white gold teeth. They shining like his pinky ring.

I surprised. I point to my chest. I make sure he talk to me. I never feel like anybody care about me. So why it start today, I ask to myself.

But the man nod to say: "yes," so that I knows he talking to me, and only me. Maybe my luck change. Maybe this time my mother stopped being the whore. Maybe it my chance to save her.

So I makes my way down the five flights of stairs to the street. I walk across to Rolls Royce where men was standing. I learn later that this men was Paul Carbone, Francois Spirito, Vincent Antonini. They was the main players in the Corsican Mafia in Marseille.

"What you doing up there, boy?" Vincent saying in anger. He the one who first spot me. All of them were wearing the black fedoras.

"Nothing," I shrug.

"Bullshit," Vincent pull me closer with hand around my tank top.

I scared. I hearing Paul, Francois, and Vincent ran things in Marseille. Kids in school say these men feed their enemies to fish.

I too scared to tell why I up there.

"I getting things for momma," I says.

"Who your momma?" Vincent asked me with the wild animal eyes.

"Marie," I says.

Vincent then looking at me with the sad eyes. He letting go of me.

Small tear in the man's right eye.

"Ok, boy, ok, I get it," he saying.

"Get what?" Paul ask Vincent.

"She work for Alain," Vincent saying.

I later find out Alain was main club owner in the Marseille. He take care of the whores for Paul and Francois. My mother one of these women.

Vincent then ask:

"What your name boy?"

"Jacky."

"Do a small thing for us today, Jacky boy?"

I shrugging my shoulders. I not really care. I about to be splatter on ground. Anything better than being splatter on ground.

"Sure," I nod.

"That a boy," 50 year old Vincent saying as he patting my face in grandfather way.

The thing they asking me was simple. I get the package of the fish from boat that come off the dock, then taking package to Paul's shop. It's called La Belle Poisson. Is on La Canebiere street. This thing they asking me to do seem innocent.

When I getting older, I find out that I not delivering fish — it heroine, the new opium. I know cause I have local kids do the same. We paying the kids little king money. We tell them their kneecaps be cut if they ever looking inside or taking the fish.

That package is my passport into Union Corse. This the secret mafia family that is in Corsica and Marseille. We not as popular as Sicilians. But that because we more secret. We liking it this way.

We have the organization. There is the boss; underboss; a consigliore, lawyer who is part of

> *legit law business; and a capo who leading a crew of the soldiers.*
>
> *By the time I forty, I not a simple errand boy no more. I acting as connection between my family and Simon Pierre Sabiani. He the counselor to the Marseille mayor. I the point guy about late payments and the things that bringing too much heat on mayor.*
>
> *We keep family business out of public eyes. Others in my business don't doing things this way. They always want to be showing others what they having. But I always like the cattle in my farm, but the small belt buckle on my pants. I guess this some American cowboy saying. But I liking it for me. I the Marseille fucking cowboy!*

I looked up from reading Jacky's entries. I thought about the pain I would be in if I knew that my mother was doing that to make ends meet. I think I read somewhere that Louis Armstrong's mother did tricks to pay the bills when he was younger. He escaped the pain into his music.

Jacky escaped his pain into the underworld. In a way, that world saved Jacky from himself. My strict parents always told me to stay away from people in that world. But Jacky's entries got me thinking. Maybe, for some like Jacky, those people can act as a safety net. I took another sip of my bourbon and went back to reading.

> ***January 17, 1940***
>
> *I loving taking care of Agnes when I younger. She was Vincent's 24-years old wife. I take her out when Vincent out of town. Her beauty scaring me of what my hands and cock wanting to do. She not normal beauty you see on Paris or Marseille streets.*

She much more.

She like Annabelle, this actress who in 1938 movie Suez. Like her, Agnes having the same blond brown hair, soft brown eyes, fair skin, smile that bring the sun to room when she walking in. She the light you see off bow of ship on black night.

I picking her up at boss's apartment next to Marseille wharf. The apartment full of the glamour — crystal chandeliers, long tables that look like they from the Revolution, old paintings of Versailles, views of wharf, ancient pieces.

Apartment have this stairway curving to second floor. This where they having servant's quarters, extra bedrooms, big bedroom. This where she keep her Chanel gowns, Italian shoes, fur coats, silk scarves, jewelry.

"Salut, Jacky," she greet me with her sunshine smile. She give me kiss on the cheeks when I pick her up one night.

"Salut, Agnes," I say with the guarded happiness. I knew she boss's wife. I never want the feelings for her. I know that be a trap I not escape.

"Where we going tonight, dear," she ask me in English accent. She educated at Cambridge after school in Paris. I love speak with her in fake English accent cause this making me feel smart.

"Le Petit Chat," I telling her. Le Petit Chat is the small bistro in old port looking at the boats.

"Oh Jacky, I love that little gem," she says. I stare at her pink colored lips and my dick getting hard. I getting excited like fat boy in the candy store.

She always dress the classy way — that night she wear a orange dress, brown espadrilles, Cartier tank watch, bracelets, linen blue scarf on top of linen jacket.

We walking down cobble stone street towards waters. Small cool wind brush up against our faces.

"Jacky," she put her arm with mine, "why you don't have love in your life?"

She looking over at me with eyes making my heart get pumping up and down fast.

I not look back at her. I not wanting to tell her about mother. My wall stopping me. Wall also stopping me from telling her I scared. So I do what anybody do.

I lying to her.

"I not finding the one yet, Agnes," I saying as I turn to look at her. I smelling whiff of her grapefruit perfume. She looking forward and ignoring me.

"I hate when you lie, Jacky," she say with the sadness.

I ashamed that I can't tell her truth. I am the big coward. I smuggle things out of country or slit throats. But I not have the courage to tell her what I feel. I felt horrible because I knew Agnes cared.

She care like a woman who been my wife in another life if it not for Vincent. Twists of fate like that, no? Lives take big turns in the seconds cause we meet stranger that cause us to making turns in seconds.

"I know you protect yourself. So I not mad," she saying as she looking down onto street.

I looking at her.

"Thank you," I touching her back.

She look at me with the sad soul in her eyes.

We have the friendship. But Vincent was my boss. He like the father to me. That is the way I like it. I wishing she not meeting Vincent — I wishing she meeting me first.

But I never wanting the marriage. I never wanting a woman to worry about. I not want to see her get hurt. I not able to handle this. So I just taking care of Agnes when she need me to, and then fucking the other women I meeting.

I sleeping with them, buy them the dinner, say how I loving their perfume, and kissing them on cheeks. But I never get close. I not want to feel. All I want is the good times.

So I never get attached.

This help with my work.

Story about Jean-Paul showing why.

"Jean-Paul," I tap him on shoulder one night. We standing in Marseille nightclub that he running for the family. Everybody like him. He had gray hair, tan, smile on face. He our connection to the Italian families and the other families around France. But he also do side deals in Marseille for his own pocket — and not pay the family.

"Yes," he pulling out his cigar and turn away from the pretty pussies who was dancing.

"I needing to ask you something," I says.

"What?"

"Little bird tells me you doing business on family dime?"

His eyebrows jumping up. He knowing I knew.

"What bird telling you this?" He says through stained worn teeth.

"It don't matter," I says. I feeling badly for saying what I was saying. We standing there looking like brothers wearing the matching London made tuxedos.

He looking towards the showgirls, lit up cigar, then look back at me with the fear in his eyes.

"I take the little peck with my beak. That's all."

He look back at showgirls like what he saying was nothing. He having the family with children. He now know I knowing he have the mistress. This against the family rules. A wife has reason not to tell. Mistress has reason to tell. Jean-Pierre was the big problem.

"Yea, you are right, Jean," I saying as we watching the showgirls. "It just a peck," I pat him on shoulder.

In following month, I feeding police a report about hashish from Morocco on night of February 7, 1930 at four in morning. I tell Jean-Pierre to go port to wait for shipment, board ship to test product, pay the captain.

Ship was called Petit Poulet. It coming in on time and Jean did as he told. There is the few things Jean not know. I tell the captain to leave on dingy before ship docking. Ton of hash on ship was shit and worth nothing. But the stash would get Jean enough time in the can, about two to three years, for him to understand that he crossing the line that he never cross again.

Or he be dead.

After this, Vincent have the more confidence in me. In summer of 1931, he making me the capo. I was forty-one at time. I now have the power to command the soldiers. I not believe this shit! I gone from little dirty face boy with no money and momma who hooked to capo.

I wish momma were alive to see it. She die when I twenty-three. She die from the broken heart.

I don't think she wanting to live anymore. This why she drinking, smoking, and not swimming in the ocean like before. By summer of 1931 I have much money for myself. I know she been proud.

There is no question about this.

And there no question about something else.

No matter my title, I still a dirty face to the lawyers, bankers, politicians who taking our money to fatten their pockets. These princes of the bourgeois was protected by the system they keeping up with they arms. We nothing but street thugs to them. In public, they speaking against us. In private, many of them needing our money, drugs, women.

Ah! I would say to one of them. I might be dirty face, but I am the connected dirty face. At the end of your trials, commissions, investigations, I still am getting away with murdering you. Maybe it not my finger that squeeze the trigger. I maybe even locked up when I order the hit. But I still getting away with it.

You know this.

Fear not the only reason you respect me. You love me. I give you what this secret dark self in you needs to survive in the scrubbed perfect version of life that you clinging to with nails and teeth. I am real. I am dirty. I not perfect. And for this few minutes in your bullshit lives, my dark world makes you feeling alive.

You know this, too.

I felt goose pimples on my body. I always knew there was an underworld. But the underworld I had been exposed to was chaotic, lawless, and without hierarchy. I always thought of the players in this shady world to be impetuous street thugs.

Jacky's entry showed me otherwise.

His organization spread its tentacles throughout the world like a corporate titan would. This is what I found so fascinating about Jacky and his family. That is what I also found so terrifying about them, too.

"Hey, Hank, you want to have one for the road?" Tony asked me as I sat there in wonderment. The Tavern was empty except for Tony and the cleaning crew.

"No thanks, Hank, I think I have had my fill tonight. What do I owe you?"

"I'll add it to your tab," Tony said as she smiled a crooked yet warm smile.

"Much obliged, Tony."

I left the Tavern around 12:45 a.m. and made my way home.

CHAPTER 4
Like Attracts Like

"I told you there was no comparison between our pain, Hank," Sophia said to me as I sat down in front of her. After my shift at the paper was over, I went back to her apartment the next afternoon.

I needed to see more.

I wanted to see more.

I was learning about a world I never had seen before. But I was also learning about myself. No, I have never had a long-term romantic relationship. Yes, I have seen a bunch of surreal ads about perfect couples and their children in toothpaste commercials. The mother stays home and the father goes to work while she sits around with her friends in Tupperware parties. But I felt like Jacky and Sophia had a love that was real and human. It was imperfect because they did not occupy the traditional roles that had been set up. It was also very perfect because they made up their own roles. They invented their reality.

Sophia tried to light a cigarette. Her hand shook slightly. She tried to hide it. But the high-end perfume, the money, the butler, the apartment on the Upper East Side, and the cocktails couldn't help her mask her feelings. She so wanted that mask.

She wanted to feel safe in all of those fancy ornaments of civility. But, deep down, she didn't feel secure. I don't think she has felt secure since before her parents died. So I took out my lighter and lit her cigarette. I wanted her to know that I understood.

"Thank you, Hank, you are a gem," she said as she took a long drag.

"My pleasure," I smiled.

"I have always tried to control my emotions. I was always told growing up never to let people see the way you feel, or else they will take advantage of you."

"Yes, but think about this, Sophia: once you let the cat out of the bag, what leverage do they have over you if they already know it? I mean, you let the stuff out, put it on the table, and then what are they going to do?"

I was talking to her as much as I was talking to myself.

Sophia looked at me.

"I just don't fancy showing strangers my emotions. So I am sorry if I seem frazzled," she took another drag.

"Sophia," I rubbed her arm ever so slightly. "It is alright. I think showing your emotions to someone means you are trying to connect with them on a human level. We are told not to do that, especially in this country with its rugged individualism. But I think being vulnerable with someone is a way of showing that we all have pain. Of course, I have the same feelings as you — I don't like being open either," I smiled towards her.

"Thank you, Hank," she smiled subtly as I took my hand off her arm. "So how did you like what you read about Jacky?"

I paused for a moment to look outside her illustrious window. I needed to think about all that I read. I also thought about how, unlike many of my classmates from Chicago, I wasn't a banker in New York, a lawyer in Chicago, or a politician in Washington D.C. Instead, I was sitting in front of an elegant woman learning about love. But I think it is more than a love story. It is also a story about the nature of power that I couldn't learn in the halls of a bank like Goldman Sachs or law firm like Cravath, Swaine, and Moore. I turned back towards Sophia.

"He was an amazing man," I shook my head in disbelief. "To overcome what he did with his mother and to get where he got to in the organization, I tip my hat to him."

"Why do you say that?" She asked in a testing tone while she sipped an afternoon gin and tonic.

"If I was him, I would have cut the chord a long time ago," I acted like I was slitting my throat.

I paused.

"Do you mind if I join you in an afternoon cocktail?"

"Sure, Hank. What would you like?"

"I'll have the same as you."

"Of course. Winston?"

Winston slowly walked into the room.

"Could you please mix him a gin and tonic like mine for Hank?"

"It will be my pleasure," Winston looked over at me with a grin.

"Thank you, dear," Sophia said.

"Thank you," I said to Winston.

"My pleasure, Hank," Winston said as he went into the kitchen.

I looked back at Sophia.

"Did Jacky tell you what happened with his mother when you first met him?"

Sophia shook her head no.

"I didn't know any of this about him until much later. He was ashamed of it all. I also think he put those memories into the cellar of his subconscious."

"I could see that," I nodded. "I know from studying psychology at Chicago that children often keep things in their subconscious when they get older. They might have been abused when they were younger by, say, a friend of their parents. But they may have no problem being around that family friend when they get older because the incident is shoved so far down into their subconscious. But the pain comes out in other ways. A friend of mine once said: 'hurt people, hurt people.' I think she is right."

"That's right, Hank," Sophia said and nodded as if she were speaking from first hand experience. She dropped some cigarette into the crystal ashtray on the fancy glass coffee table that was between her couch and my chair.

Winston came out with the gin and tonic. He placed it on the table.

"Thank you," I said to him.

"Enjoy," he smiled at me and then walked out of the living room.

"Cheers, Sophia," I raised my glass to her.

"Cheers," she said back to me.

We took large sips of our drinks.

"I imagine one of the reasons why you didn't touch upon the subject of Jacky's mother earlier is that you never had met anyone before whose mother had to do such things to survive."

She took another sip of her gin and tonic.

"There aren't many Jacky types in uptown New Orleans," she grinned.

I took a large gulp of my drink.

"Jacky is your opposite?"

She looked outside her large windows into the burnt orange afternoon New York sun. I could tell my questions had triggered certain feelings in her that she had not felt for some time. She sipped her cocktail and we sat without saying anything for what seemed like minutes.

She broke the silence.

"Jacky is one of the best men I have ever met in my life. And yet I never had met anyone who did more terrible things than he did to survive."

I noticed she kept using "is" like Jacky was still around. I guess it was a form of denial. It reminded me of a friend of mine who kept referring to his recently deceased wife as his wife — even though she was dead. Sophia took out her cigarettes.

"Care for one, Hank?"

"Yes, please." I lit both of our cigarettes.

As we sat taking drags, I thought out loud:

"Maybe you never met anybody like him because none of those friends of yours at the St. Charles party had to scratch, claw, and bite to get anywhere."

"They were already there," she smiled a knowing smile. "Many of them didn't have the capacity to appreciate what they had been given, or to question their place in the world. Maybe the silver spoons in their mouths ensured them that they did not need to struggle internally with themselves — ever."

We took some more drags.

"Growth oftentimes comes from struggle," I said. "Look at the mountains in Hawaii. The earth was not that way originally. It took many years of chaos to create such beauty."

"The same is true with Jacky," she said softly.

"It sounds like it," I said. We puffed on our cigarettes. As she blew the smoke out of her mouth, I boldly asked: "I gather you didn't have Otis with Jacky?"

"How did you know about Otis?" She asked with raised eyebrows.

"I reviewed some articles about you in the *Times* before we met. The paper writes about you whenever your charity donates money — which is often. One of the articles mentioned that you had a son named Otis."

"I am impressed." She took a long sip of her cocktail. "I had Otis when I was with Richard, my former husband," she said after a pause.

"And Jacky also had some sort of romantic relationship before he was with you?"

"Yes," she took another sip of her drink. "The funny thing is that we both went out with people that were from similar backgrounds to our own."

I sipped my drink and then thought out loud:

"Wasn't it Plato that once said 'like attracts like'?" This is my Chicago nerd coming out — quoting Plato to a woman like Sophia, for God's sake.

"I don't know who said that, but a recent psychologist said something about opposites attracting," she said.

"I think the psychologist's name is Winch . . . Robert F. Winch," I said. I guess my geek nature was good for something — naming names.

"Yes, that's him," Sophia agreed. He seems to be right. I mean, look at Jacky and me. We couldn't be from more different backgrounds, darling. And yet we click like the number two follows the number one."

As we sat quietly in the smoke infested room, I thought: perhaps Jacky and Sophia were more alike than she thought. Maybe she was too focused on their superficial differences — their ages, classes, his criminal record, her top grades in school. I didn't know it yet, and this was just a stab in the dark, but I wondered if this made her overlook what is arguably the most important similarity between them: their kindred hearts. That can make the rest of the differences relatively inconsequential.

I then asked her:

"You know about his romances before you?"

"They are right in here, young man," she patted the diaries resting on her hap.

"I know I have to give you these before I get those," I said. I opened up my satchel and handed her the diaries I had just finished. "Thank you," I said to her as I handed the diaries over.

"You are welcome, Hank," she smiled and then handed over the new diary entries. "I think you'll get a better idea of my romantic life, and that of Jacky's, before we met by reading through those."

I started flipping through the diaries. Sophia continued:

"Maybe the philosopher you mentioned did say like attracts like, but it seems that opposites really do attract," she motioned with her eye towards the diaries.

"I guess I'll find out," I patted the diaries.

"Yes, you will," she smiled.

It was about 8:00 in the evening by the time we finished our parlay.

"I'll bid you good evening. I am eager to get into these later tonight," I patted my satchel with the diaries in it.

"As is to be expected," she patted me on the hand after putting out her cigarette.

I leaned over to kiss her on her cheek. She did the same to me. When I left her apartment, a cool June breeze came up across my face. There was a brisk humidity to the air, as though New York was torn between letting go of the spring, and moving forward into the twilight nights of the summer. I wondered if Sophia was also torn between finding security with a man like Richard, and love with a man like Jacky. I took the subway down to the Tavern.

"Hey, look who the fucking cat dragged in," Tony said to me in his thick accent as I walked into the Tavern.

"Hey, Tony," I said to the stout bartender. "Looks like it was a rough night in here, eh?"

The place was environmentally unfriendly. The regulars were there puffing cigar smoke into the air. The smoke mixed in with the old gin, whiskey, and bourbon that was left on the glasses to make a hybrid perfume only the Tavern could make. The clean air was piggybacking on the dirty Tavern air, rather than the other way around.

"Yea, yea, dese fucking guys been here since de late afternoon, and, by now, you know, dey like full of the piss. Even dem

Like Attracts Like

broads are out of it," he pointed in the back through the thick smoked air.

I looked back towards the rear room. The regular guys were all lying back with their gals passed out on their laps looking like they were getting suntans. All of them were, as usual, dressed to the nines in custom made suits, and the women were wearing elegant dresses by Chanel, Valentino, and other designers who were in the press at the time. Their expensive garments look stained.

But they didn't care.

They could afford to buy a $100.00 suit a week.

"So what you drink tonight, Hank?"

"A black coffee. I need to get some work done before I hit the hay."

"Ain't you goin to have a little splash of something in dea?"

"Nah, Tony, thanks anyway. Maybe another night." I smiled graciously.

"Awright, awright," he put his arms up like he was surrendering in a robbery. "I give up. I'll get you a kawfee," he said sounding let down. I knew that the Tavern had never been robbed. I think that's because most people wouldn't want to rob the people in the back. I also knew that Tony always kept a shotgun behind the bar and a .45 pistol under the register.

As he poured the coffee into the mug, he looked at me:

"Howz them diaries goin?"

"Good, Tony," I nodded. "I am learning so much."

He topped off my coffee.

"Yea, you know, dey say you learn from othas who fuck up, you know, or by fucking up yourself," he said wisely. "So I guess it's better to learn from other stupid fucks. You ain't going to learn from otha dumb fucks in here cauz there ain't many dumb fucks that come in here," he said using his index finger to point down to the bar.

"Got it," I nodded my head in agreement and sipped my chicory blend coffee.

"Let me know if you need anyting else. I got to go back and take care of dem fucking invalids back there," he pointed to the back.

As he did, I heard "heya, Tony, where y'at," a guy with what sounded like a thick New Orleans accent yelled out. "We need to get some of dem bittas over here for my darlin, ye hear?" Tony told me that the regulars included people from Los Angeles, Las Vegas, Chicago, Cleveland, and many from New Orleans.

Tony took off to the back and I took out the first diary from my satchel. It was Sophia's. I was curious to see what her life was like before Jacky. I took a sip of my coffee, which was the blend that the New Orleans visitors liked. The wrinkled leather cover of the diary was so aged it could have creaked when I opened it. I turned to the first page.

> *July 16, 1933*
>
> *I just met the most amazing man while I was visiting the Boston Club with my grandparents. His name is Richard. He is an angel sent from God!*
>
> *Where I met him matters. Founded in something like 1841, the club is one of the oldest and most selective in the country. I was with my grandparents in the grand ballroom having lunch. I heard this man with an English accent speaking to some other people at the table next to us. He sounded like the type of person who wanted to go to, and had the connections to go to, a club like this. That is the type of man I wanted to be with.*
>
> *"Oh, John, old chap, how have you been?" I heard the man behind me say in his thick English accent to another man at the table. I looked back. All of the men were dressed in seersucker suits and bowties.*

Like Attracts Like

"Richard! I haven't seen you since Oxford. How have you been, old boy?" I heard another man say with a Mississippi accent.

My parents used to tell me that it was not polite to stare. But I couldn't help myself. I turned around to look at the table of men. I then saw this stunning man with the English accent — he had blue eyes, blond hair, and fair skin.

He was just like the boys that I grew up with: well mannered, well groomed, and, with an Oxford pedigree, had the right credentials to get into any gentleman's club. I wasn't sure of his age. But I knew that I liked him right away. He turned around to look at me when I was looking at him. He winked at me.

Like a little girl, I blushed and turned around to look away. I looked back because I couldn't help myself. He was staring right at me. That's when I knew he liked me.

I was dressed in my finest summer dress. I had a ribbon in my hair, and I was subtly splashed with my finest English perfume. People always dressed up to go the club, especially if you were a woman. My grandparents were also in their Sunday's best — my grandfather with his seersucker and bowtie, and my grandmother wearing a white linen dress. We had just come from our St. Charles church, and were planning on having our regular Sunday brunch.

I nodded towards him, and he nodded towards me.

After a minute or so, the fancy looking Englishman was standing next to me and introducing *himself to my grandparents. I got goose bumps all along my arms.*

"Good afternoon, my good neighbors. My name is Richard Stimson, III. I was sitting next to you. I couldn't but help to want to introduce myself to such a fine group of people, especially after having heard the good word of the Lord on this beautiful day."

"Oh, you are a member of Christ Church?" My grandfather asked in his thick New Orleans accent.

"I am, sir, indeed I am," Richard answered with his English accent.

"Well, it is a fine pleasure to meet your acquaintance," my grandfather stood up to shake Richard's hand. "My name is William Gordon. This is my wife, Betty," my grandmother got out of her seat to shake Richard's hand, too. "And this is my granddaughter, Sophia," my grandfather looked over to me.

I got up to shake Richard's hand. He kissed mine instead of shaking it. This was a very aggressive move, especially in the Boston Club.

Richard stood about six foot four, and was very elegantly dressed. He did not appear to be married, even though he was in his thirties, which was very odd. And yet I liked the fact that this man had broken convention.

I was twenty-two and just out of college. But I knew this would be my chance. He would be the love of my life. He had to be.

"Any member of the Church is a fine person for my family to know," my grandfather said to Richard in the eye.

"Why thank you, Sir," Richard said as he almost bowed his head in respect.

I had a feeling meeting this man would change the rest of my life.

December 20, 1933

It has been a few months since meeting Richard in New Orleans. Things have been moving along so very smoothly. He sends me train tickets to New York several times a month, and he also comes down to New Orleans to see me.

This time Richard got an express train for me to New York with big news.

"Oh my love, I have such wonderful news for you," he told me over the phone from London as I sat in the parlor of my grandparents' New Orleans home on State Street. As I sat looking up at the 25-foot high ceilings with ancient engravings, I wondered: a new job, a raise?

"I want to meet you in New York to tell you in person. Are you free to take the train up for the holidays? I have business there," he said over the phone.

"Sure, honey," I remember telling him. "Just send me the tickets for the train and I'll meet you where?"

"The Carlyle on December 24th at 7:00 in the evening," he told me with conviction. "I've reserved a room there for you."

I wondered what the news would be.

I knew it had to be important for me to spend Christmas eve with him, instead of with my family in New Orleans.

I guess I would soon find out.

December 25, 1933

I arrived in New York at 10:00 a.m. yesterday and I was tired. I took a taxi to The Carlyle. I checked in and went to take a nap. He had left a chocolate on my bed for me with a note: "Darling, I so look forward to seeing you tonight. Your love, Richard."

After I got up from my nap, I took a brief tour of the city and then came back to get ready for the evening. I got my manicure, pedicure, and other grooming done downstairs at the hotel. I put on the Chanel dress that he got for me from Paris during one of his trips, plus the lingerie that he sent along with it. I wanted this to be a special night.

When I got into the cocktail room, I saw Richard sitting next to the bar in his tuxedo — white jacket, black tie, his family crest signet ring on his left pinky.

"Oh hello darling," I kissed him on each cheek.

"Hello love," he said warmly. "Shall we have a cocktail?"

"'That would be lovely."

After a few martinis, I was tipsy. And so when I went to grab my next drink, I didn't see the thing that was at the bottom of the glass until I was about to chomp on it.

It was a platinum engagement ring from Tiffany's! I could not believe it!

"My love," he grabbed my left with his, "will you be my wife?" He then pulled the ring out of the martini glass and put it on my ring finger.

He knew I would say yes because I let him put the ring on.

I put my right hand over my heart and opened my mouth with a partial smile.

"Oh Richard, honey, I cannot believe it." I gazed at the ring on my finger. And then I exploded: "Of course, yes, yes, yes!"

I said this so loud that people around us started staring. Then they started applauding and standing up once they saw me gazing at my ring.

We smiled and kissed.

It was one of the happiest days in my life.

February 18, 1934

Richard and I had our wedding yesterday. It was at the Carlyle. The reception was out of a Hollywood movie. Champagne flowed everywhere, men were dressed in their tuxedos, and women wore their most glamorous gowns. Men smoked their finest cigars, and the women smoked their cigarettes with holders.

There was a large ice swan with champagne dripping down from it in the middle of the reception. Circling around the swan was a slew of food — fresh salmon, fine French cheeses, fresh fruit, and the best Russian caviar that money could buy.

Richard's parents were able to get Benny Goodman's band to play the event. I couldn't believe this one. I knew how popular Goodman was at the time. It must have cost Richard's parents a fortune. It meant a lot to me — Richard knew that Goodman was one of my favorite artists.

We got tipsy at the reception and then we caravanned to St. Thomas on Fifth Avenue.

I could barely stand up!

The dress I was wearing was so tight! I think it was by Chanel, but Richard had me try on so many, I really can't remember which designer it was.

Everyone from New Orleans and English high society was at the wedding. I think Richard's whole class from Eton, the elite English school Richard went to, was in attendance, too.

Other than getting proposed to, and perhaps whenever I have children with Richard, it was one of the best days of my life.

March 1, 1934

This is my first day in Paris. Richard was transferred here to work with his textile company's Parisian branch. We bought a lovely chic apartment in the 16th quarter of Paris. All of the city's most wealthy patrons live here.

Part of me misses the simple things of New Orleans — taking the streetcar on a warm day in the spring, seeing the parades during the holidays, and seeing the little children eat their flavored ice during the summer.

Of course, my family emphasized the more complex things of living during my upbringing — the clothing that people wore, how they ate their food, and the types of parties they went to.

But I have always been a simple girl underneath all of the fancy packaging. This is something that I sometimes deny to myself. This denial is getting harder for me to do, as I am finding with Richard.

"Oh, love, isn't this place just to die for?" Richard asked me when we got inside the apartment.

I admit that the place was very plush — stained wood floors, 20 foot ceilings, bright white walls, and a modern yet old world way about it. I mean, I don't think he could have picked a better place in the city.

"Yes, darling, it is to die for," I insincerely admitted to him.

I could have been just as happy in a one-room shack with him. But I didn't want to disappoint.

Maybe it's because I kept telling myself how good we were together. And yet perhaps that was just on paper. Maybe, just maybe, he would have preferred dying over living in the humble way I would have preferred living.

The same doubts that haunted me as a Newcomb girl going to the plush parties in uptown New Orleans were revisiting me here in Paris. There still was no truce in the civil war between the part of me that wanted the false sense of security that came with the sterilized uptown bubble, and the part of me that needed the uncertainty of real love — where you know that every kiss is one less you will have.

It bothered me that I had not yet resolved this civil war.

But I had faith that, someday, I would.

March 25, 1934

I am missing my period. I know it. I just know it. Richard and I have been going out a lot in Paris to high society business parties, where you have to watch every move you make. I wonder if my missed period is because of stress or because of a baby. Time will quickly tell!

March 27, 1934

I just went to the doctor and he told me what I hoped — I am pregnant!!! The next few months are going to be busy — I need to get ready!

November 25, 1934

I had my first child three days ago — his name is Otis. The boy is stunning. I can't believe I had him. If someone told me growing up in New Orleans that I would be living in Paris when I had my first child, I would have told them that they were nuts!

Here he is — in the flesh. I feel so fortunate. So many things could have gone wrong. But they didn't. Thank God he is healthy. It's a gift from mother and father above.

Now it is my turn to earn my keep. I don't want to feel like I was given a gift without appreciating it. I felt like I needed to redeem myself for growing up the way I did — with the help, the schooling, and the love.

"How about more cawfee," Tony broke my concentration.

"Sure, thank you," I said with an appreciative smile.

After Tony filled my cup half way, I took a few sips and flipped a few years forward in Sophia's diary to 1938. I was curious to see how her relationship fared with Richard.

December 15, 1938

Richard has kept up his antics.

He keeps going out late with his co-workers and not coming home until real early in the morning. I really don't know what to do about it. I am getting so tired. On the one hand, he tells me "I love

Like Attracts Like

you." On the other hand, he keeps treating me like hired help.

I hope that God will not make me endure this much longer. I hope that this man changes into something that is bearable. I know I took my vow. But I know that this man who I bid my life to in front of God's eyes is now going out and seeing other women.

I often smell perfume on his neck when he comes home from going out. He doesn't even try and cover it up. Perhaps he doesn't care about it. He feels entitled to do whatever he wants whenever he wants it. That is the way he was raised. He is a user.

I just don't know what to believe anymore.

I always thought we were made from the same ethical cloth because we were from the same backgrounds.

But maybe this was naïve of me to believe?

He couldn't be farther from the way he looks.

Sometimes, maybe the devil is camouflaged in church going clothing?

Unlike other women who would be told to grin and bare it, I will do something about it. It's one thing for him to bring me into his womanizing, but it is another thing to raise a child in the infidelities, too.

What kind of man is Otis going to be if he thinks that men can do whatever they want to women because there are no consequences?

I felt so inspired by Sophia's entries. She looks very upper crust. But underneath this fine crust is a hard-boiled woman who endured a lot of pain at a young age. She was no stranger to adversity. And I think this under the crust part of Sophia

Dirty Quiet Money

wouldn't let others trifle with her. This inner Sophia came out to protect her from Richard. This is the part that knew about machine guns, muscle, and covert ways of getting information, as I found out that first day.

"Heya, Hank, we are shutin' the joint down for tonight," Tony interrupted my thoughts. "How about a night cap?"

"Sure," I nodded. "How about an Oban on the rocks?"

"Coming right up, kid," he said.

I wondered what I would find in Jacky's diaries. I gathered from reading Sophia's diaries that Richard looked good but was rotten underneath. I wondered if I would find the opposite with Jacky. I opened up his diaries to the first entry.

> *February 18, 1939*
>
> *I have the butcher hands but the eyes that likes the books.*
>
> *Sometimes, I not feel like the man.*
>
> *I like the art more than the sports.*
>
> *I love speaking to the women more times than fucking the women.*
>
> *I don't like the violence and know her darkness.*
>
> *But I out kill any man on this earth.*
>
> *This why I been alone. Women wanting the regular man. He talk about sports when not working, he thinks war is pretty. He is normal and I am not normal. This why women love and hate me. They like that they not figure me out, but they don't like that they not figure me out.*
>
> *What men want most from women, which is the pussy, is at most times what I want least. I know the price for the nice purring pussy. I sell it all of the time.*

These words give a glimpse of Jacky's complexity and feelings of aloneness.

"Here you go, kid," Tony said as he placed the Oban on the bar in front of me, along with a bowl of nuts.

"Thanks, T."

"You got it. Let me know if you need a Shirley temple to wash that down," he smiled and then gave me a smack on the shoulder.

"Sure thing," I said with a smirk in appreciation of his humor. He went back to tending to things behind the bar.

I took a long sip of the scotch. It warmed my body. I snacked on a few nuts and continued with my read:

> *This way keeping me alone for years.*
> *I feel the shame and disgust in me.*
> *I not able to saving my mother.*
> *I kill so many man that I forgetting how much.*
> *I remember one man I had killed. His name Christophe. He was mule for family. He smuggle North Africa goods — hashish, cash, weapons.*
>
> *"Christophe," I says to the tower of dark night Nigerian. We standing in middle of water-flood basement of family nightclub. "Be the good mule. Don't start thinking what's best for you. See?"*
>
> *We stood in the long bad silence. His dark night skin shine in lights from cracks in wood floors above. He giving me a serious walking on a tightrope glare. He take drag off his cigarette and smash it with foot in shitty muddy waters under our shoes. Basement is quiet except for dripping water from cracks, jazz music from above, large rats making the squeaks at our feet.*
>
> *"Yes, boss," he breaking the wicked silence.*

> "Good," I says as I putting my right hand on shoulder. I leaving it there so he feel dead body as it sink in concrete if he fucking up.
>
> I finding out year later this fuck is not listening to me.
>
> Christopher in charge of hashish shipment from Morocco. It was a ton. He supposed to split up shipment into parts and send those parts to our friends in Rome, Amsterdam, Stockholm.
>
> A week after shipment, we getting complaints from the network that there not enough product. One of this complaints was from Emilio. I knowing him from Marseille.
>
> "Ciao Jacky," Emilio says hello to me with two kisses when we sit for espresso in old port.
>
> "Ciao, Emilio," I says to Italian mentor who born in Ventimiglia, Italy. This home of every fake shit — Chanel, Rolex, Cartier.
>
> Emilio looking phony. He wearing the real flashy necklaces that rest on his belly hanging over belt buckle. He never leaving the home without high-priced pussy on his arms.
>
> But he the real man. During the Christmas, he give wads of the money to children's hospital. When times getting hot for me, he in my shovel crew.

I stopped reading right there. I looked up at the bar in the Tavern. Shovel crew? I thought to myself. What's that?

"Hey, Tony," I leaned over the bar to get his attention.

"Yea, what's up?"

"I have a real quick question for you."

"Want to know the meaning of life?"

"Well, not that, at least for now." I looked around to make sure nobody was listening. "I wanted to ask about a phrase that I never heard before," I said.

"Yea, which one is that: go fuck yourself?" He smiled.

"I kind of have an idea of what that one means. The one I wanted to know about is: shovel crew."

Tony looked at me sideways.

"Where you hear dat?"

"I read it here," I pointed down to what I was reading.

Tony looked around to make sure nobody was listening, too. He asked me to come closer with his index finger. I leaned over the bar, and he leaned towards me.

"Yea, so dem guys usually use that to mean somebody you can call in the middle of the fucking night and who would be ready to come over to your house with a fucking shovel to dig a fucking ditch for yas where ya needed it, get me junior?"

"I get it," I nodded as I looked at him.

Tony leaned back and I leaned back, too.

"I see," I said to Tony. "Thank you."

"Yea, any more questions professa?"

"I got it covered, thank you."

I went back to my reading:

> *"The shipment is light," Emilio says.*
> *"How light?" I asking.*
> *"Light enough," he say back.*
> *"I take care of this," I saying to him.*
> *"I know it not your fault. Tutto bene, Jacky, ciao."*
> *"Ciao, ciao," I says back.*
> *We kissing on each cheek, finishing our espressos, get up from small table across street from port.*

> *Christophe is doing the skimming. I know this. But I not know how much. And then I get message from Faas, he our man lover connect in Amsterdam. His shipment short. Annika, our small blond in Stockholm, send same message: her shipment not enough.*
>
> *It not matter how much Christophe stealing. He not know what hit him anyway.*
>
> *After Christophe kissing children and wife goodbyes in morning, he eating at Atlas Café every day.*
>
> *That is where I order the hit.*
>
> *Alex is French looking black cowboy who not take many showers. He do the hit. He smell of old eggs, but he have chemical smarts. Boy had the Sorbonne chemistry doctorate. We have him cook up poisons that hard to trace during the autopsy.*
>
> *The one he make for Christophe called the black widow.*
>
> *We give the money to owners of Atlas Café when it open. So the owner happy to have cook put some black widow into Christophe's coffee.*
>
> *"Smack!" Alex clap his hands together later when telling us the noise that Christophe's head make when it hitting the table. "I was in ze kitchen, and, when I hear ziz sound, I take a peek outside ze kitchen door. Everyone in the café stare at ze dark body lying zere," Alex telling me in his shitty Senegal accent with big little boy smile.*

I stopped reading. I felt a sudden fear. I thought about Christophe's family, this dead mule, and how they would survive without him. I thought about what type of man it takes to order the death of another over money — and perhaps not that much of it. And yet I knew there was another side to Jacky. Sophia told me about it. I could feel it — in some ways — lurking underneath the stormy waters of Jacky's murderous ways. So I kept reading.

> *There is another side to black widow side of me. It is the butterfly.*
> *This side of me bring love to the flowers.*
> *Like Emilio, every holiday, I go to children's hospital. I giving the clothing and the money. These kids is like me.*
> *I guess this why I protect our women at clubs. I think of my mother when I seeing them.*
> *Many women want to love me.*
> *But I not letting them.*
> *I not deserve it. I better off alone. I safer. It better than being with someone who leave me some day.*

I realized how lonely this tough man, this gangster man, this murdering man, this menacing man, had been. It was hard for me to believe. I always thought people like him didn't care.

But Jacky was different.

"Yea, uze ready for another there, Hank?" Tony asked after I finished my scotch.

"Sure, thank you," I nodded.

"It was looking like you was in a daze there, looking into space?" Tony said smiling.

"Yea, I was just thinking about how book covers don't always match the inside."

"Shit, I've known that for years. I mean, you know, uh, many of dem fellas that come into this space here have families, and some, but ain't all, is good family men," he looked around to make sure nobody was listening.

Dirty Quiet Money

"But you wouldn't know lookin' at how dey do der business — dropping bodies there," he plopped an ice cube in my glass, "dropping bodies there," he dropped another one inside the glass, "and den cutting them up real nice," he dropped a final lop of ice into my cup.

He looked up at me with a wicked smile.

"Gotcha," I said nervously to him.

"I knew you would, kiddo," Tony said with a wink and then went back to his drying.

I took a sip of my scotch and read.

> *March 1, 1939*
>
> *When I have the 39 years, I meet the beautiful woman. Her name is Marion.*
>
> *I sitting in Café De Flore in the Saint Germain de Pres with Antonio, Jean-Luc, Pierre.*
>
> *This pretty painting of woman walking into café — the fair skin, the green eyes, the dark brown hair, she standing strong, wearing all black, the fancy jewelry, the money looking it was doing the drip like the water from her wrists and neck. Corsican, Sicilian, I not know.*
>
> *Two tough monkey body guards with her.*
>
> *She sit down two tables away and cross her legs. They have the dark tan. She took out Le Figaro newspaper, took out a pack of Gauloises, one of her men light up her cigarette. I staring at her red lips squeezing end of cigarette. I imagine her inner milk thighs squeezing me.*
>
> *She looking over at me. I winking lucky wink at her.*
>
> *I thinks to myself she a bitch because she ignoring me.*
>
> *At first.*

But I keep looking. She lay it on me heavy with her green eyes — made me feel like I walking the barefoot on mountains of green grass spring day in country.

Doll likes me.

"Excuse, mes amis," *I tell my friends and walk to her.*

Her tough monkeys getting in my way.

"No, it alright," *her smoky voice saying.*

"Merci," *I walk past her human trees.*

She put her hand out. I kiss it.

She smiling. Maybe nobody ever kiss her hand like this. I tell myself this so I not feel scared bout being with woman from money like her and me being so not from money like her.

"Name is Jacky," *I says to her after my lips leaving her hand.*

"Marion," *her soft pink lips saying to me.*

"I join you for the coffee?"

"Please sit," *she pointing to chair in front of her.*

She like Agnes — same style, same grace, same warm smile. Or maybe I putting these things on to Marion just from this meeting.

"Where you from, Marion?" *I asking after I sitting down.*

"Marseille," *she saying.*

"You say Marseille?" *I ask.*

"Did I stutter?" *She says — I like this.*

"Me too, I from Marseille."

"So why you here?"

"Business," *I say.* "You?"

"Shopping," *she point to Louis Vuitton bags at feet.*

"Busy day?"

"Every day busy," she say funny.

"Monsieur," the waiter saying to us, "I get you something, yes?"

"Un café," I say, "Marion?"

"I have the same," she said.

"Two please," I telling the waiter.

"Of course, sir."

I remember look back at Marion. I not know that wink I gave her changing my life.

March 3, 1939

Marion and me is together for eight months. She want me to moving in with her.

It feel it too soon. I scared this the only time I feel this way about the woman.

I remembering Vincent, he Agnes's husband, he tell me: "love is like a shark. If it not move forward, it die. It need oxygen of the movement to feel like it living. If it sit, with fins not moving, not eating anything, not seeing anything, not living, then shark dies."

March 10, 1939

"So you do it?" Marion say about me moving in her place. I remembering it is about January 1931. We sitting outside café by port. It is sunny day. I feel good about my life — for once.

I touch her hand. Make her feel safe. "I not see how I could not do it. I mean," I saying to her, "you special. But I feel like . . ."

She not let me finish: "you walking away from emotions because you can't control emotion," she looking into my eyes.

"You could say this," I agreeing with her.

She moving her hand over and start caress my hand on table.

"I glad you putting your guns on table with me, Jacky."

She stop to look over at port across the street, took a smoke on her cigarette, then turn back to me as she crush cigarette on ashtray.

"I know you sleep with the one eye open, and the one eye close."

She light up another cigarette.

"Or sitting with one hand on table and other under the table with pistol ready. Right?"

I lit up my cigarette and I listen to this seagulls across street.

"You right about me," *I saying.* "But before you judging, you not know my road, the people on my road, rules of my road."

"An excuse! You know this. Look at Vincent. He play the game. But his doors is open to the love. You make seem like you need be the way you are. It keep you nice and safe in your little world where you control everything until you die."

"Yea, and so?" *I say nervous. I wondering if my heart been living in cave the whole life. Marion make me see like I not see before.*

"I know little world of yours is not at peace. Living means taking the risks. You know this, and I know this," *she say with her hand on my forearm and then pulling it off.*

"Another coffee?" *The bald big waiter asking us.*

"No thank you," *I saying to him,* "but maybe she liking one?"

"I have the whiskey," Marion says, "with the rocks."

> *She stare at me.*
> *There is violence in the silence between us.*
> *"If you keep your heart in that little world of yours, Jacky, without open it up to life, you will die alone. And I not meaning that you be sitting in your house one day, or gardening in the back under sun, that your family will come home to find you."*

I needed another drink. Jacky and Marion's talk stressed me out. I could only imagine how Jacky must have felt at the time.

"Tony, can you hit me with one more before I go?" I asked as I sat there with my finger in the diary entries so as to not lose my space.

"You got it, Hank," Tony came by and poured some more into my glass.

"Thanks."

"You got it, pal."

I heard some of the regulars in the back yell out to Tony to get his attention.

"Hey, Tony, my Cadillac is outside. Can you get someone to move it for me?"

"Sure," Tony said back to the well-dressed man. "I got to go, Hank."

"I understand," I said back and went back to reading Jacky's diary:

> *"What I mean is," Marion saying to me, "nobody going to find your body there next to the bullet you shooting yourself with."*
> *"Your whiskey, mademoiselle," the waiter comes by to drop off these drink.*
> *"I'll have one, too." I says to the waiter.*
> *"Of course, monsieur, coming right up."*

She take the long swig of her whiskey. We is sitting in the silence for minutes. The waiter then brining my drink, too.

"Thank you," *I says to the waiter and take a big gulp of the potion calming my nerves inside.*

"Your body be found only cause the smell is bother the neighbors. They have to call police. And so it is police — your paid off help — that find you there. The people you been running from or paying off your whole life is the ones finding you lying face down — not the people who loving you, cause you got nobody."

"Of course," *she continues this,* "you died the way you wanted — not open up to any woman, never open your heart to love, never show the sun your shame about your mother, about yourself, and the rest of your fears."

"At least I successful not showing all of that to public people," *I say in my joking voice. This anger her — she not laughing. She looking down at her glass with hopeless looks. I took another big gulp of he whiskey.*

"Listen to me," *I putting my hand on hers,* "I move in with you because I take the leap, okay? I know what you is saying. I tired of being scared of my heart. I not scared about other things. But this one thing I never look in the eyes."

She just staring at her whiskey.

"I ready to look fear in the eyes with you."

She looking up at me with the hope and the smiling.

She moving across the table and we kissing.

On the inside of me, there was this little voice. It asking: Is this woman the way she look

> *on outside? Is her heart honest with you? She love the same things about life, family, time? She likes the shopping, do you like . . .*
>
> *I not want to hear this voice. I want to close my eyes and forget his old bitter man voice. I wanting so bad to feel safe. I wanting to feel like nothing is going to hurt me when I with her. I wanting to feel like she never going to hurting me.*
>
> *But this doubting man is still in my heart, and I wondering if he going to be right?*

It was about 1:00 in the morning. My eyes were growing tired. I needed to wake up in the morning and hit the newspaper hard. I was behind on some stories. I planned on continuing my reading the next evening.

"Hey, Tony, can I get the check?" I asked.

"What check?" Tony said wryly.

"What do you mean what check? I mean the check for tonight."

"I don't know what you tawkling about," he said playfully. "It's on the house tonight, Hank." He looked at me earnestly like he appreciated the work I was doing. It's as if he knew what I was reading, had read it before, and was happy that I was traversing the same land that he did. I felt like I was reading something a lot of people in the Tavern had perhaps read. Maybe I was merely one more on top of the heap of people that had read these diaries of an underworld legend.

"Thank you, Tony. I'll see you tomorrow night."

"You betcha," Tony said.

CHAPTER 5
Appearances Are Appearances

October 28, 1935
Richard is a God dammed scoundrel!
I smelled another woman's perfume on him again today.
I have deceived myself. I put the clothes over the person. That is the way I was brought up, the way most of us are brought up, and yet I feel now that it has come back to haunt me.

Sophia's words greeted me when I sat down to start reading her diary at the Tavern.

"The fucking cat keeps dragging the same shit in every night, don't he?" Tony said as he held his hand out to shake mine.

"I guess I am the same shit?" I said as I shook his hand.

"Well, pal, you sure ain't the fucking cat, is you?"

"Last time I checked, I wasn't a piece of shit either."

"Heya, that makes two of us, don't it?" He took his hand out of mine. "What you have tonight there Mr. Hank? How about a Gin martini?"

"That sounds good, Tony. I used to love having those with a girlfriend of mine back in Chicago."

Reading Jacky's diary entries about Marion made me think of Brit. She was an Irish woman who was from a small town not far from San Francisco.

She had the most touching smile, sandy blond hair, and was taller than me by a few inches. She had a piercing gaze that could see right through you, even when you didn't want her to see right through you. Like Marion with Jacky, Brit would look at me and know that I had my walls up.

To keep those walls up, I studied, kept my life in the books, and didn't bother myself with that messy thing we call "emotion." Jacky, on the other hand, turned to a life of crime — and not of the mind — to keep his emotions out of his system.

But Brit wouldn't let me hide. She made me feel my wall by taking down hers. It's not that I wasn't ready — I was basically incapable of doing what she did, even if I wanted to do it.

That all changed when I got out of school and I realized I had lost her — forever.

She went ahead to marry and had children. Brit and I no longer had any contact with one another after that. This hit me hard. I knew that a woman like her doesn't come by often, and I still haven't come across one like her since.

Brit, like Sophia, had her own issues with worshipping the pedigree, the fraternity membership, and all of the benefits that come with that. And yet I knew that she was good underneath all that status worshipping.

"Whatcha thinking about there Hank?" Tony put the gin martini in front me.

"Just an old love of mine from college."

"Must have been a good love for you to think about it that long?" He said as he wiped a glass clean with his construction torn hands that had seen their days in sun, rain, and snow.

Appearances Are Appearances

"She was a good love," I said to Tony. "And yet I didn't realize it at the time just how good she was. I had a big blind spot and she was right inside of it."

"Yea, yea, some motherfuckas tink dey have to travel around the fucking world to find a broad, or even to find demselves, ya see," he wagged his index finger in front of my face. "But all dat shit is oftentimes right in front of ya face, but you aint' ready to even see it that way."

I sipped my martini and then thought out loud:

"I think Proust once said something like 'The real voyage in discovery consists in not seeking new landscapes, but in having new eyes.'" I then realized I was sounding pretentious when I didn't mean to be, kind of like when a drunken man accidentally misses the toilet when he is taking a piss, and only realizes it when there is that sound of his liquid hitting the ground. It's quite embarrassing, not that I have ever done that.

Tony stopped wiping the glasses dry.

"Who the fuck is that?" He looked at me oddly.

"Who?" I looked around to see who he was talking about.

"Proust," he said to me with a curious tone.

"Oh, him," I took another sip of my drink, "he was a writer," I said sort of quietly, kind of like how the guy quietly leaves the bathroom after cleaning up his piss off the ground.

Tony started wiping the glasses again.

"Yea, well, he might say the same shit I say a with a little more, what's the word, elo-fucking-quence?"

He looked at me like I was a snob. He knew I wasn't. But he liked playing that game anyway.

"But, hey, great minds think alike, right?" He smiled and patted me on the shoulder with his right brutish hand.

"Right," I nodded. "So, going back to Brit, that's what happened with her. I was a young man cut off from my emotions. She showed me them."

"Eh, fucking a, at least someone introduced you to them. Some of these folks dat come in here don't even have dat going for dem, cauz their head it so up in the clouds — money dis, cars dat, fur coats here, and whatevah — dat dey ain't really living."

A group of finely dressed men came in with their extravagant mink coat wearing dates.

"Heya, fellas," Tony said to them.

"Heya, Tony," they greeted each other as though they had known each other since the first grade. Tony turned his attention back to me.

"Right, Tony," I said, going back to his comment about Brit. "Sometimes you got to feel hurt in your heart and soul to feel alive, I suppose."

"You betcha your bottom fucking dollar, pal, dat dat's right," he banged the bar with his palm. "Any night you want me to smack yas around so that uze can feel alive, I'd be happy to do it for a few bucks," he patted me on the shoulder again. "I got to go and serve dem back dea," he pointed to the back.

"Gotcha, Tony."

I sat there at the candle lit bar with my gin martini. I was the only guy at the bar reading someone else's diaries like some weirdo voyeur. I took a few sips of my cocktail before I went back to Sophia's diary. As I did, I thought back to what this Supreme Court justice, I think it was Justice Jackson, once wrote after he changed his mind about a legal ruling: "The matter does not appear to appear to me now as it appears to have appeared to me then."

It was a long-winded way of saying that things are not always as they appear to seem. I think one of the reasons why this is so is that we come to every situation with our own bent of mind, our own prejudices, and our own set of brainwashing that we all have undergone growing up.

Our young brains record our experiences of love and try to recreate them when we get older — even if they are unhealthy experiences — because they make us feel at home. They are the prototype we have of love.

We are aware of some of this brainwashing, whereas other parts of it are unconscious rules we have learned over time. I think Sophia had some of this going on with her choice of Richard, and I am pretty sure I would see the same thing with Jacky.

After taking another sip of my cocktail, I opened up Sophia's diary:

> *October 29, 1935*
>
> *Oh lord, I just can't believe it anymore.*
>
> *One of my girlfriends at Otis's school today said that she saw Richard with our nanny out at a café. They were laughing with one another. He was feeding ice cream and other things to her. They kissed a bit and he hugged her, my friend told me.*
>
> *If someone would have told me Richard would have ended up like this when I met him, I thought they would have been crazy. I mean, I met the man that one Sunday and thought he was such a peach. For God's sake, he was going to the same church as my family! How much safer could I have gotten than him?*
>
> *Maybe this is just one more dalliance by him? Maybe he is just under a lot of pressure at work and needed to let some steam out. I need to know if this was just one thing that he got into, or if it's going to be something I am going to have to be dealing with on an ongoing basis. I need to know.*
>
> *November 18, 1935*
>
> *I went to hire a private investigator today. His name is Sammy. He is one of the best in the city.*

I was so nervous going to his office, which is in a windy little cobble stone street.

But when I met him, he eased my anxiety.

I opened the door to the receptionist room, and the light from the outside shined inside the dark room — which was more fitting for a vampire than it was for a businessman. But I understood more about why he kept his place like that when I met the man.

"Sammy is waiting for you," the sportily dressed receptionist said to me when I walked inside the room.

The receptionist room had stone floors that looked like they were from when the city was originally founded. His office was in the 4th Quarter of Paris — otherwise known as Le Marais. The ceilings were high — I think they were about thirty feet high, or something close to that.

The receptionist led me into another room and opened a medieval wood door — dark and sturdy. Inside the room, sitting at a large black desk, was Sammy.

He was on the phone. I heard him say:

"Excuse moi, Frank. J'ai un client qui arrive. Je te parles a tout l'heure," he said to his client. I studied some French at Newcomb, and this basically means "Excuse me, Frank, I have a client, I'll talk to you later, ciao."

He put out his cigarette on the crystal ashtray as he hung up the phone.

He got up out of his chair and came over to me. He was not what I expected him to be like.

For one thing, I could tell he was wearing Charvet from head to toe — a midnight blue suit, white shirt, midnight blue tie, white handkerchief, and I think J.M. Weston black boots. Richard loved wearing those boots.

"Bonjour," he said to me with his white teeth shining from what appeared to be his dark Algerian skin, "you must be Sophia."

He also wore a black rose on his lapel. He looked super connected. The man, in short, was very elegant — and dangerous.

"Yes," I said to him.

"It is my pleasure to meet you," he then took my hand and kissed it. "Please have a seat," he pointed to one of the black leather chairs in front of his desk. "Would you like to have a whiskey? You seem nervous."

I was tempted. But a drink would have made me more nervous.

"No thank you, Sammy," I said coyly, "but I appreciate the offer."

"You speak awfully good English," I pointed out.

"I studied English at the University of Toulouse, madam. Plus, I have many American clients," he smiled proudly.

"Cigarette?" he took out one of his Gauloises and held it out for me to take. "Yes, thank you," he lit my cigarette and then lit up his own.

"So how can I help you?" He said through the smoke brewing in the room as he sat in his office chair.

"Well, I am kind of ashamed to be here, but I want you to find something out about my husband."

"If he is a woman?" he said and I smiled. His humor broke the tension.

"If he was a woman, I don't think he would be doing the things I think he has been doing," I responded.

"Women do the same evil, too," he said. "You suspect him of what?"

I asked him to move closer over the desk by waving my hand.

Sammy leaned closer.

"Cheating," I said with as quiet as a voice as I could muster.

He leaned back in his chair and smoked his cigarette.

"May I say something, Sophia?"

"Of course, Sammy. That's why I am here. What is it?"

"You are a brave woman."

"Why do you say that?" I asked him.

"Women around these parts don't usually look into their men doing such dirty things. Women usually look the other way."

I leaned carefully forward in my chair and stared into his dark beady eyes.

"Not me," I shook my head and leaned back.

He smiled a smile like a proud father would to his daughter. Sammy was about 63 years old.

And yet I could relate to him. He had these caring eyes. They were sweet. I know he was one of the most prominent — if not the most prominent — private investigators in all of France.

I thought to myself: perhaps it is his humanity that made him so successful with his clients.

But then there was his thoroughness. According to what some of my friends have told me, he was a member of Deuxième Bureau de l'État-major *general, or Second Bureau of the General Staff in English. This was France's version of England's Secret Intelligence Service. All of his staff had experience working in the Second Bureau, too.*

"All right, madam, I respect your wishes," he said with the cigarette dangling from the corner of his mouth. "Please give me his full name. I will do the rest."'

I took my pen out, wrote out Richard's full name, and handed it to Sammy over the desk.

He looked at it and then glared at me.

"Then, of course, there is the matter of the money," he said.

"Yes, of course," I handed him more than he expected in an envelope.

"I have your answer in a month," Sammy said with a small grin as he looked at the money.

"Only a month?" I was so surprised that they could find out so much about a secretive man like Richard in only a month.

"A month," he said to me, "or you get your money back," he said like he knew something I didn't.

"Merci, Sammy."

"It is my pleasure, madam."

I exited the lair that was Sammy's office into the bright Parisian sunlight. I felt warmed by the thought that he would find out for me something that would give me closure to my wounds — whatever that closure was going to be.

I readied myself for the news.

December 26, 1935
I went to Sammy's office earlier this evening.

Sammy's secretary, Esther, was there. She seemed to have a curious way about her. She was short and stout, like a fire hydrant. She had a pug dog nose. She wasn't exactly pretty, but she wasn't ugly, either. She reminded me of twilight. She wasn't nighttime, but she wasn't daytime.

And yet there was something about her that made me want to be around her.

That was her style and the pride with which she held herself out to others. I remember someone telling me how she used to make all of her clothes.

By hand.

I think Sammy got her shoes for her — they looked like they were hand made in England by John Lobb. I don't think she could have afforded the shoes on her salary.

"I take care of the people that take care of me," he said during our first meeting with this mischievous-looking grin on his face like he spoiled Esther.

I could see why. I was sitting there for some time waiting for Sammy to get off a call with someone in New York, from what Esther told me. All the time I was sitting there she was typing up his notes, machine like, and taking care of the day's work.

She sat there with her red lipstick, hair up in a bun, and smoking one cigarette after another. I admired her fortitude.

I read the day's edition of Le Figaro, and smoked my own cigarette, when I heard Esther in the background: "he will see you now, madam." She went to open Sammy's office door. I got up and walked inside. I closed the door slowly and quietly behind me.

Sammy got up off of his chair to come and kiss me on both cheeks.

He was so warm to be around. I appreciated that about him.

"Please, take the seat," he pointed to one of the leather seats in front of his desk.

"Thank you, Sammy," I nervously sat down. My hands were shaking as I went to light one of my cigarettes. I was so nervous to hear what he had to say, kind of like how you might go to the doctor's office wondering if you have cancer.

He put his left hand on my shoulder and rubbed it.

It was a comforting rub. It soothed me.

"Things will be alright, Sophia. Please trust me. I know things seem tough for you right now, but this will all work for your benefit in the end."

He moved his hand off my shoulder and went to sit behind his desk.

He took out a file. It had photos and written reports in it.

He slowly lit up a cigarette. The room was dark, except for the light on his desk, and the light from his cigarette.

I could see the shadow of his black rose in the distance, and I could make out a scar on the right side of his mouth. The other half of his face was dark.

"This is your husband's file," Sammy started putting out his cigarette.

I could see his right eye in the light from his desk, but his left eye was mired in darkness.

"It is worse than you thought," he said as looked at the file.

He paused as he shuffled through the documents.

"But this is better for you in the long run," he looked up at me with his one eye in the light.

He formed a smile on his face without showing any teeth, how a mischievous teenager might smile when he has caught his parents doing something they shouldn't do, and knows that he has leverage to negotiate with — to stay up later, or eat more candy, or maybe even skip school the next day.

I went into my purse to get another cigarette and to fetch my lighter. My hand was shaking.

Sammy reached across his desk to light my cigarette.

"Thank you," I said to him.

"He has been with many others."

He paused.

"Not just the nanny."

He paused again.

"Wives of heads of state and of major bank presidents in Paris," he said to me as he looked at some papers that I could not see.

"How do you know?" I blew smoke slowly out of my mouth.

"I have the photos right here," he said like a poker player going through his arsenal of cards.

"Do you want to see for your own eyes?" I remember him leaning forward in a way that said to me, in an implicit way, you don't want to see for your own eyes.

"No," I shook my head back and forth. I could not stomach the feeling I was having. I felt like I was going to throw up, like I had been a victim of food poisoning.

I couldn't hold it in.

"May I use your restroom?"

"Of course," Sammy took me to the dark door next to his desk. I went inside the bathroom, which was dimly lit with candles. I went to the toilet and threw up several times — for what felt like ten minutes or so.

Sammy knocked on the door: "Sophia, Sophia, can I help you?" He tried to open the door. But I locked it. "Please just grunt to let me know you are alright, or I'll break this down," he said in a stern tone that let me know he was serious.

I grunted a zoo animal grunt.

"Alright, I'll be right here outside the door."

I sat there on the black tiled floor of this bathroom hugging the toilet. It was my stability in the eye of a storm that I had never been through in my life. I never had experienced such a betrayal before by someone that I thought was in my family. I sat there looking into the toilet of vomit remembering back to when I first met Richard, in New Orleans, with my grandparents.

It was such an enchanting day.

And I felt like I did all of the right things — everything was right with him.

On paper.

Part of the reason I threw up is that I felt disoriented — I didn't know what was up or down anymore. I also threw up because I never felt so much pain before — I suppose I always cut these things off from my mind — and heart.

But this one stuck me — and stuck me hard. Rather than crying, which I was always told not to do because it showed weakness, the only thing that my body could do to let it out was to throw up.

I flushed the toilet, got up off the ground, and opened the door.

Sammy was leaning against the wall smoking a cigarette.

"Feel better?" He asked with concern.

"Yes, thank you," I said as he softly took my arm and walked me over to the chair in front of his desk and helped me sit down.

"Can I get you a glass of water? I have some fresh mint that I use for my tea that I could sprinkle in the water to freshen your mouth up, if you like."

"That would be lovely," I said ashamed.

"Please, Sophia," he walked by me to get some water from Esther and put his hand on my shoulder again. "This is very difficult for you, I know this is totally against your nature — what he has done. So please don't be ashamed or feel like you need to hide from me. I'm here to help you. And, as you will see shortly, that is what I will do."

He walked outside the door. I felt reassured.

I felt even more reassured when he came back into the office and told me his plan.

It was so devious that it bordered on a piece of art. I left his office that night with a small smile on my face.

December 30, 1935

"Hello, love," Richard said to me when he met me at Café Procope, in the 6th Quarter earlier tonight. It was one of our favorite cafes in the city. We had our regular table in the back corner. He leaned over to kiss me on the cheek.

"Hello, love," I said back to him in a cold and yet calm tone. He looked at me with some worry

as he kissed me on both cheeks. He could tell something was wrong.

We both sat down and ordered our regular drinks. We usually started with martinis.

But when he sat down, he saw there was an envelope on his chair with his name on it. I had never looked in the envelope.

"What's this?" He asked.

"Your late Christmas present," I said with a bear about to eat her prey grin.

I could tell the folder had an effect on him. He opened it up and his hands started shaking. He looked up at me like a trapped dog in a cage with smoke around him and with nowhere to look or turn.

His forehead started to sweat.

"Where did you get this stuff?" He asked.

"A friend," I said with my eyes focused clearly on his so that he knew I knew.

"And what are going to do with it?"

"It depends on how you respond to my demands. I have a list here of all of the major newspaper editors in the county, and in England, with their home phone numbers."

I handed the list to Richard. Sammy had given it to me.

"This list has more than editors," he looked up at me. "It has the prime minster's home phone number on here, plus those of the members of his cabinet!"

He paused uncertainly.

"Where did you get this information?" He asked me angrily.

"A friend," I said with a contented smile. "But that is of no importance to you. What is important

is what you are prepared to do for me so that the envelope in front of you doesn't reach its tentacles throughout this country, and to the rest of Europe."

"They will have my head for this!" He put his face in his hands.

"They will have more than that," I said as I took a sip of my drink after the waiter came and placed it on the table.

Richard took his face out of his hands.

"What is it that you want?" He asked me with desperate eyes.

"A divorce," I said.

"But how will you make do without my income? And, anyway, you weren't raised to get a divorce. That is not the lady that I married," he looked away in disgust.

"You are not the man who I thought I married."

I remember pausing to gather my thoughts — and my courage. I continued.

"You will also give me enough to take care of my needs until the day I die, and so that Otis is properly provided for."

"I don't have that type of money right now, goddam it!" He pounded his fist on the table. "And even if I did, why do you think I would give it to you?"

"You will make do. You will make yearly payments in this amount into this Swiss bank account," I then handed him the sheet of paper that Sammy gave to me.

"From what money, I ask you?" He said.

"From these accounts," I then handed him a balance report from the various accounts that

Sammy had found in Switzerland that were under Richard's name, or that of his family's name.

I still don't know how Sammy got the information. It amazed me when he gave me the sheets.

"How did you get these accounts?" Richard asked me with a snarl in his lips. "Who the hell gave you this information?" He demanded.

"From a friend."

"Only a dirty son of a bitch could get this illegal information," Richard said in disgust. "Who is he?"

"Wouldn't you like to know. I'll keep that information close to my breast, just as you have kept what you have been doing all of these years close to yours."

"And," I continued, "I don't think you are upset about him being a dirty son of a bitch. I think you are upset because he is a dirtier son of a bitch than you could have imagined."

I remember Richard's drink stood there on the table. Beads of water dripped down its sides. He had not touched it since we sat down.

He paused to look around to see if anybody was listening. We were pretty much alone in the ornate café, except for the waiter, who was in the kitchen.

"Very well," he nodded. "You have your divorce."

He slammed his napkin down on the table after he wiped the sweat off his brow.

"And you have your goddam money. Let's be done with this."

I took another sip of my cocktail. I felt so proud of myself. I felt like my parents were watching over me and were smiling for me standing up for myself.

I felt like they were proud I had become not only a woman — but a force not to be reckoned with.

Richard interrupted my self-satisfied moment.

"I mean, if I don't do as you ask, my life will be ruined," he said as he looked down at the folder. A spoiled brat whose toys are taken away from him and who realizes that he has been living in a bubble all of these years, artificially protected by his family money and connections. He couldn't get his toy back this time. And he knew it.

"You'll be more than ruined, darling," I said with a smile as I shoved the knife deeper into his stomach.

On than note, I got up from the table and, for my finale, went over to kiss him on the head. After I did, I said my goodbye: "I expect the money to be in the account on the agreed upon dates. And I am sure you know to never be late," I caressed his head as I slit his throat — with my words and my smile.

As I walked out the café that night, I could see Richard's lifeless body figuratively sitting there on the chair with his cold lifeless face on the folder. The knife that I just stuck in his back stood there as a testament to my hidden power that he forced me to release.

July 4, 1936

After the high of getting what I wanted out of Richard late last year, I now find myself feeling depressed and hopeless.

If Richard had all of this privilege going for him, and all of the benefits of being born into the class he was born into, and could still be the human being he was, perhaps the reverse is true of class — maybe it tends to rotten the fresh apple?

As I sit here writing in my diary next to the ocean in Nice, Otis is playing in the sand. The waves are ebbing and flowing slowly onto the shore. Fisherman are out in the ocean looking for their daily bread, couples are next to me necking, women are lying topless all over the place. I stop and think about what I just wrote with my hand. And then I come to a realization.

For every Richard, there must be another who doesn't have what he had, what he grew up with, and the tools that were at his disposal, but who is his opposite. I remember learning about yin-yang, one of the principles of Chinese philosophy, while at Newcomb.

Polar opposites are interconnected in the world. Richard's ways would have no meaning if there didn't exist an opposite.

My fears and feelings of hopelessness meld with the ocean. I feel calm and assured there maybe is someone out there in the world who would have the same heart as I, but it might be camouflaged underneath several layers of dirt.

As I sit here now writing, I don't know this to be true. But I believe it to be. I believe there is another half of me out there, and I may not find it in the most expected of places.

No.

Maybe I'll stumble upon him, like I would stumble my toe on the beach on a stone and then discover that the stone was not a stone at all — but a beautiful shell that I wash off, take home to my living room, and put above the fireplace to make me remember the day when I felt something hurt, but how out of that hurt something beautiful was born.

That is what having a child is like — you go through the pain of carrying the baby, having it take your energy, and then you have the excruciating pain of childbirth. And yet, out of all that, there is the creation of a contented and connected life that I would not have had if it weren't for him. Otis is a gift to me.

And yet that gift came from pain.

I looked up at Tony. He was smirking at me like he was up to something.

"What?" I said to Tony.

"Nuttin, Hank," he shrugged, "but you been sittin' der for like fucking hours and you ain't seen none of dese dames walk in?"

"I guess not," I shrugged.

"Hank," Tony leaned over the bar to put his hand on my shoulder, perhaps how Sammy did with Sophia in his office, "sometimes you gotz to look up around yaz and smell dem fucking flowaz, you know?"

"Yea, I guess sometimes I get too caught up in my work, Tony."

"Yea, well, it's good to be into yaz work dea," he pointed to the diaries, "but don't be forgettin' to live here and now, too, ya see?" He pointed towards the beautiful women down towards the other end of the bar.

"I need to let go," I said as I looked over at the women down the way. "And I will in my own time," I said as looked back towards Tony.

"And maybe you just need the right broad to get you to let go — you know, like a fucking, uh, what's dem tings called," he snapped his fingers, "a roller coaster, you know, like at Coney

Island. I mean, uh, what I'm trying to say Hank," he looked around to make sure nobody was listening and then continued, "iz that some broads take you by the hand, and pull you some way, where uz don't know where uz going, and you might be like a scared little boy who just wants to go home to mommy, because you know mommy and what that's about."

"But when uze get goin, you know, with the broad, and that fucking ride you know that she is, den you come to dis point where you forget about that scared little boy inside dea and just fucking put yaz hands up becauz you ain't got that fear no more," he looked at me. "No, brotha, that fear is gone and you in that moment, you know, where you hold that broad's hand and don't want to let go, cauze you know dis going to be the fucking ride of your life! But you wouldn't have gone on de fucking ting, you know, if she hadn't taken you by the hand and pulled you, ya see?"

I looked at Tony after he said this to me and realized: he was a lot smarter than he looked. I think he looked around to make sure nobody was listening because he *wanted* people to think he was stupid. He *wanted* people to underestimate him. I think that gave him comfort because, that way, people wouldn't have any expectation of him. They would just think he was a dumb former boxer who happens to work behind the bar. But underneath his stupid demeanor was someone that I found was just as smart as, or even smarter than, many I have met who want to places like Chicago, Princeton, Harvard, or Yale.

"You are right, Tony. Sometimes we all need a nudge in life, and maybe a lady like the one you are mentioning can be just the ticket to the ride that I need to take."

I smiled at him.

"Awright, awright, enough of this mental jerking off or whateva de fuck you cawl what we doin hea, I got to get back to work, you know." Tony nervously walked away to the other side of the bar to tend to the customers.

After he did, I took a long sip of my cocktail to prepare myself for my jump into Jacky's diary entries. I opened the front cover and started to read.

August 8, 1933

Me and Marion I go to Cassis today. This the fishing village next to Marseille — it has the white houses, the clear ocean waters where you seeing the fishes, the soft sand so you sleep at night with the woman if you liking, the calm breeze like the old grandma tell you all is going to be okay.

It was pretty day — it start this way. We drive down in my Bugatti Royale with the pretty long coast next to this ocean, the cool air traveling and washing through my hair. Marion wearing the black scarf around the hair to keep her pretty styling in the place. She rubs my neck as I driving. We have the smiles like we is just make the love but we not make the love — we just having the happiness to go to Cassis.

We getting to ocean, getting out of car, making our picnic by the waters. I bringing the pate, bread, olives, tomatoes, wine.

"Oh Jacky, I so happy to be with you," she telling me as we sitting and watching these little children playing in waters. She drinking the red Bordeaux I bringing. I sipping the wine too.

"Me, too," I telling her.

Things going rocky that night when we getting to place I renting.

We sitting in the bed, I do the caress on her bronze body, but I feeling like she not there. I feeling this way for much time with her. She is like someone who says they listening, but then they always asking you to repeat what you say.

This worse than person not be there at all; if they not there, they don't make you feel like you not mattering to them.

We lay naked in bed, I touching her belly with backs of my fingers in the soft way, I needing to say something to her.

"I always the one giving." I keeping the caress going. "You close off from me when I open to you."

She turning her green eyes on me.

"What you mean?"

"You never doing the nice caress to me. I always the one doing this. Or make the plans or giving you the pleasure you when we fucking. I am on the one way street, no?"

She look up at this ceiling fan that move the cool air off ocean to making the room feel fresh.

"I feel like I here, but I not here," she saying to me.

"Why?" I asking.

"Maybe I am scared."

"Of what?" I asking.

"Of have the feeling," she says to me.

"Why?" I asking.

She staring again at ceiling without the answer for a moment.

"Because I never feel all the way. I always stop the swimming too far into the ocean waters, and too deep," she says.

"Because you like the swimming where you feeling the sunshine?" I turning on my back in bed to look at fan with her.

"It making me feel safe. Maybe I scared of what I find about myself if I swimming in the deeper waters, where I not see this part of me that I know so well?"

I start to touching her on side again.

"I understanding this. For my whole life, I swim in deep ocean waters, where the light not going, only ancient fish! I am in the museum without the light try to find my favorite painting, you see?"

I stopping to think to myself.

"But only swimming in the deep waters is trapping me. You helping me swimming in lighter parts of waters. I wanting to swim with you there, Marion."

She looking at me with the sad eyes. I looking back at her.

"And for this I loving you," I says to her.

All was quiet. Just the sound of the fan above and crickets outside you hearing in country.

"But you not never swimming in my deep waters. Is you too scared to losing the control by going where you not go before?"

"It not you, Jacky," she break the silence. "This is my problem. It something I need working on."

I look to ceiling fan — again.

"This my shit," she says.

"But maybe the other man making you happy? I maybe the wrong man for you?"

She say nothing.

"This the first time in my life I been in the love. This is the big step for me."

"I know," she nodded.

"You telling me before that you have the other loves. But maybe you never allow yourself to having the great love?"

Appearances Are Appearances

"Maybe, Jacky, maybe," she not sure of herself.

"I cut my emotions off," she says, "after my sister try the suicide so many times. And so I hiding my needs from my parents, from myself, so that I not be the other problem for my family like my sister, you understand Jacky?"

"To be the good daughter?" I asking.

"Yes, but this stop me from feeling the things that other women is feeling. It like I stopping when I putting the wall up against my heart."

"Maybe this wall keep the lies you telling yourself alive?" I says.

Marion saying nothing.

"I have the friend," I said, "her name is Francis. She cut my hair down by port. She telling me once about her niece. She touched in the bad way by her father. He now in the jail. But niece don't want the help. She not accepting what her father is done to her. She wanting to live a lie that her father is best friend. To keeping this lie alive, she doing the drugs, doing the traveling, go from the man to the man," I says.

"Why don't she get help?" Marion asks.

"Francis thinking if she getting help and getting better, she don't have the excuse to act the way she doing. No more the excuse to give to herself."

"She'd have to be responsible?" Marion ask.

"Yes," I says.

"Why you telling me this story?" Marion ask.

"Cause you having the image of yourself. Maybe this image is right. But maybe it the lie?"

I caress her more. I not try to make the attack. I just try to explain what I feeling in her soul.

She look up to the fan. She say nothing. I went on.

"Maybe you thinking you is the caring, sensitive, giving woman. But maybe you is really the uncaring, not sensitive, selfish woman?"

She say nothing again.

"But you not know if you just swim in the same waters, understand? That cause there is need to question — that only happen when you get out of these waters you knowing so much."

"Let's not talk about this anymore," *she say to me as she move on her side to looking away from my eyes.*

I stop the talking. But go to sleep with the big worry on my mind.

August 3, 1933

We waking up today to the shining sun running its legs through bedroom window. It was open and I could hear birds singing.

The naked body of Marion is next to me.

I slowly touching her side and playing with her hair.

She opening her eyes.

"Good morning, love," *she says with the sweet smile.*

"Hello, love," *I says to her with the crack of the smile on my face.*

"What you like to do today?" *She wrap her arm around my body.*

"We doing the picnic at the beach, yes?"

"Yes!" *She nodded starting the nice kiss my arm.*

We staying in bed until we make some coffee in country kitchen — bricks, island, big oven, high ceiling, wood floors.

Marion starting to making the food.

A super day!

We getting to beach around 1:00. We stop in little secret part by the rocks where we dip without the noise and in peace.

I taking my clothes off, walk toward water, then feeling the big thump against my back!

I falling into the ocean.

It was Marion who tackles me onto fucking ocean floor!

I loving this part about this woman.

She giggle with me very much in the water.

We swam into the ocean, we kissing, make the love, eat on the sand naked.

This was a best time for me.

September 8, 1933

Our problems in Cassis coming again. I inviting Marion to dinner last night with Vincent and the family. She said she come. She not come.

She saying to me yesterday she feel like going out with friends tonight. She says she also forgetting this family dinner.

The night was important to me — but she not care. Everything is the joke to her. She that butterfly who go from one flower to another but never really caring cause the butterfly is always busy flying to next flower.

Today we sitting outside in café by the port in the late afternoon. The sun going down. The sky was the dark blue with the bright stars. There is the sound of the wine glasses around us.

"I can always meet them another time. I don't see what big deal is," she telling me.

I forgiving her — again.

"Alright, alright. Another night," I says.

September 10, 1933

The final straw is happening.

Marion and I went to club in Marseille. She wear the tight black dress, no stockings, no bra, the black heels she getting in Italy. Her hair put up back, and she having this red lipstick I loving. She so pretty.

I wearing my tuxedo. I own it the several years.

"Oh, Jacky, there is George!" She saying with the excitement when we entering the club.

"Who George?" I asking.

"The guy I almost marry. You not remember when I say his name before?"

I nod the yes. She telling me she break off marriage with this man cause she wants to be free. She jealous that he went on to marry the very pretty rich Jewish woman from Cannes.

Marion a moth to light when she seeing this man.

"Oh, let's go say hello!" She tugging on my shirt.

"I not wanting to interrupt them," I says.

"We won't — trust me. He wants me to come over — I just know this."

We walking over to George, a tall man, greying dark hair, olive skin, lean build, a tuxedo on, the dark brown eyes.

George by himself. Marion telling me he go out by himself and leaving his wife at the home.

Marion feeling all over the body of this George. She rubbing his shoulders, rub her hand on the back of head, touch his hand, keeping her hand on his shoulder after we sitting down.

This is fine if I live the way she doing — nothing serious, everything light.

But I not like this. Having someone I can have the trust separate the living second from the dead one in my life.

We leave the club.

"Why you not hold my hand?" She asking me.

"This not working. You need the butterfly man like you," I saying to her.

She getting mad with me.

"Just because I am not as serious as you don't mean I need to change. Life not so serious."

"I think the problem is that we not same spirits," I says.

"But I want keep the trying," she saying.

"This too much work. It like lifting the bricks on the hot day with no water to putting on my mouth, and no people to laughing with. That cause I alone — you wanting me to come to you — but you not coming to me."

She not say nothing.

"So what you want?" She asking me.

"It more about what I need. I need the woman who swims in my waters, I will swim in hers."

She looking at me with the tears in her eyes. She knowing that we just not good lovers — she never bring the wall down.

> *Maybe in future she not moving out of her shell? I remember thinking. Or maybe she meet right man who wanting her to staying in this shell?*
>
> *I not know.*
>
> *I know that I could not be with the woman like her.*
>
> **October 22, 1933**
>
> *I happy and sad. My life is open to woman who ready to be open with me. But I sad because Marion almost ready. She first person I been in love with, but she not ready to be in love.*
>
> *There is the other reason I sad. Marion like Agnes — classy dress, from same place in Marseille, and the same type of the family growing up. And so it look like we having the same heart.*
>
> *But we not have the same heart.*
>
> *And so I wondering to myself if what's inside the box that make the present when you opening it to looking what it is, or is the thought of the present, the outside of it, enough to make the happiness?*
>
> *Maybe there is woman who is having the package that is cold and mean — but is the warm and loving on inside?*
>
> *I think she the bitch, but in the end I love this bitch cause she no bitch?*

I couldn't but help and think of how two people could be more different on paper than Sophia and Jacky.

"What the fuck! You gonna sleep hera?" I heard Tony say in the background as his Brooklyn accent took me out of my head.

"Shit, Tony, what time is it now?"

"Fucking Christmas time. What does it matter? We shutting dis place down, partner, so I sayz you stawt getting yur shit together so yuz don't end up sleeping in da fucking closet!"

"Got it. What do I owe you guys?"

I got the bill and there was only one drink on it — even though I had three.

"Tony," I pointed to the bill, "you guys forgot . . ."

"We didn't forget nuttin," he said with a smirk.

"I got it. I'll get you guys back next time," I said as I put some money down on the table.

"Alight, partner," Tony said to me. "See uze next time."

"Goodnight," I said back to him.

I left the Tavern onto MacDougal Street. I wanted to see what Sophia would give me next. I planned on going to see her the next day after work.

CHAPTER 6
University Of Treachery

"Jacky could be an angel when he wanted, when he liked you, when you were on his good side, when you were on that bright side of him," Sophia reached over the coffee table to ash her cigarette. I browsed at Jacky's entry below as she did:

> *January 1, 1934*
> *This the first night in the shit hole. Cell is small — this the fucking size of the small asshole on the crooked mayor fuck, I thinks to myself. Four men here. This place full of the piss, the shit, the rats. We pushing cloth into cracks of walls. This keep out fucking rats.*
>
> *In the summer I hearing this cell getting like oven. Half of he peoples locked here not convicted. They locked up anyways. This is why the fat man in my cell saying this shithole has highest suicide rate in the Europe.*
>
> *My five years here is going to be the slow torture.*

It was about seven and the rush hour traffic noise from Park Avenue below came through the window. Sophia was tired. She lived in a luxurious place and seemed to live a luxurious life. She leaned back in the couch after putting out her cigarette ash. She went to grab another from the box next to the couch.

"What a day, Hank, what a day," she sighed as she sipped her martini.

"What are your days like?" I said as I looked up from the diary. I reached over to grab my lighter before she could reach hers.

"Thank you, Hank," she breathed in a large puff of smoke after I lit her up and released the newly minted smoke into the classy living room.

"I usually wake up around 6:00 in the morning, go for my walk in the park, come back and Winston has breakfast at the ready. I usually get done with that around 7 and then get ready for the day. Right when I get to the office, one of my assistants, Iris or Hope, brings my itinerary for the day — meetings, lunches, drinks, dinners, plane flights to Paris, plane flights to Washington D.C., plane flights to Los Angeles, and so on. They usually book around 4 to 5 meetings for me a day."

"What do you during these meetings?" I lit up my own cigarette. "I mean, who are you meeting and why?" I let a large puff of smoke out. As I did, I realized her seemingly leisurely and luxurious way of living was just a mirage.

"Before we get into my working days, which will either bore you to death or make you tired just listening, you'll need a drink, darling. Shall I have Winston make you one?"

I nodded yes.

"Thank you," I said as I did.

"Winston, Winston," she said softly.

Winston came into the room wearing his trademark tuxedo.

"What can I get for you madam?"

"Oh, would you be a dear and make Hank one of your splendid, and I do mean splendid," she stopped to take another sip of hers to make her point, "martinis."

"Of course, madam."

"Hank," Winston looked over at me, "would you like a vodka martini, or perhaps you would like to try one of my gin martinis, which I think you would like very much."

"I'll stay away from the gin, but thanks anyway, Winston. I have had my wars with that spirit. I think Fitzgerald did too before me. So I had better stick with vodka."

"Very well."

Sophia looked back over at me, not missing a beat, and continued:

"Hank, as the head of Veritas, my non-profit, my days are busy with meetings."

"If I remember my Latin correctly," I rubbed my chin, "Veritas means truth?"

"Bulls eye," she raised her martini to me in a cheers motion.

"So what does Veritas exactly do?" I sort of knew what her non-profit did after I did my research on Sophia before meeting her the first time. But I didn't know the details.

"It provides funding to arts and educational institutions in the United States and developing countries so they can buy books, make class rooms, and pay teachers."

"Here is your martini, sir," Winston placed the martini on the table.

"Thank you, Winston," I said with appreciation.

"My pleasure, sir," he said with a smirk that betrayed his serious exterior.

"Do you work in Africa at all?" I asked Sophia as I sipped my drink.

"Yes," she sipped hers. "We do some work in Nigeria, in addition to some other countries in North Africa. I often travel there to meet with various government representatives to ensure foundation money is going to the right places — and not lining politician pockets."

She looked at me wickedly.

"I understand," I nodded. "It's a long trip."

"A good opportunity to catch up on my reading," she smiled. "I recently re-read *The Great Gatsby* during one of my trips over there."

"And what about the states? Where do you go in the states?"

"Where don't I go, darling? California, Arkansas, Louisiana, Mississippi, Florida, Illinois, and other states that I am sure you have heard of but never been."

"Whew," I shook my head and sipped my drink. "That is a heck of a lot of traveling."

"That's not even taking into account my meetings in Gotham," she smiled and put out her cigarette. "I have several meetings with mayor Wagner about funding for the city, in addition to meetings with several mayors from Newark, Philadelphia, and Boston, plus their school boards. And then you have people who donate to the foundation."

"You have donors?" I asked. "It's not all of your money?" This is where my "sort of know" about Vertias becomes "I have no clue."

"Part of it is family money," she said as I lit another cigarette for her. "Thank you, dear," she said as she puffed. "The other part is other people's money — various corporations, like General Electric and Ford, put money into the foundation. I have to account to their executives for where and how their money is being spent."

"Their return on investment?" I sipped my drink.

"Yes," she nodded. "How many more students are graduating from the schools we support? How many are not only graduating, but also moving on to higher education? And how many of those are actually becoming productive and working members of society?"

She paused to sip her cocktail.

As I sat there looking at this elegantly dressed woman, I told myself something that I would never doubt — Sophia was no dummy. She was shrewd, but she didn't let you know it right away.

She was the type of woman — and type of person — you rarely meet in life. She had these street smarts about her that put her head and shoulders above so many others. And yet she also had this book smarts to her that put her above those that had the street smarts without the book smarts. She was a double threat. But she was also so very pretty, so I think I feel comfortable saying that she was a triple threat! Sophia interrupted my thoughts as I sat there looking at her:

"Numerous metrics measure these things, but I don't want to bore you more than I have," she smiled.

"You are not boring me at all," I sipped my tasty cocktail. "I was very interested to hear what you do with your days. It gives me a better understanding of who you are, and of what role Jacky had in the making of who you are now."

"I think that is fair to say, Hank," she puffed her cigarette. "I wouldn't be having these meetings, and I wouldn't be speaking to you right now, if it weren't for that rascal."

She paused to let her comment sink in a little bit, and continued.

"I am all the more appreciative because I know what Jacky had to do to get where he got."

She looked outside the window towards the buildings across the street. As she did, she said:

"You'll see what he had to endure when you read his entries I put on the table there," she nodded over to Jacky's diary I had peeked at.

She looked back at me and explained:

"Jacky spent five years in Le Sante Prison, which is an old prison in the middle of Paris. I think it was built in something like 1867. Someone told me it has housed poets like Paul Verlaine and Guillaume Apollinaire. I believe it also held Paul Gorguloff, the man who assassinated Paul Doumer, the French prime minister, in 1931 or 1932. In those entries you are about to read, Jacky writes about his time there, what he learned, and how it made him go where he went when he got out."

"What did he get locked up for?" I asked.

"The Marseille police made up some counterfeiting charges against Jacky so that they could try and squeeze him to squeal on Vincent."

"Who is Vincent?"

"Vincent Antonini," she said with a serious tone. "He was the main head of the family down in Marseille."

"I see," I blew my smoke high up towards her stunningly ornate ceilings, "and where did Jacky go after being in prison?"

"To the top," she pointed to the ceiling with her index finger.

"Why?"

"Because they knew they could trust him," she finished her drink. "But that trust came at great cost to Jacky. Even though he continued writing in his diaries and dreaming of becoming a novelist some day, he still lost a big part of himself in that place."

She looked gravely at me. I felt like I understood that look. It meant the writing couldn't act as the damn around Jacky's soul in there. I finished the last sip of my martini and leaned over to put out my cigarette,

"I had better be going. It is getting late."

"I need to get my beauty sleep, too, Hank. You aren't the only one who wants to look good for lady fate when she shows her face!" She patted me on my knee and started to get up.

I started to get up, too.

"I will look forward to our next meeting. In the meantime, enjoy your read," she pointed towards the diaries.

"Thank you. I am sure I will."

We hugged one another and I exited the apartment building into the electric New York City evening — cars honking, people

Dirty Quiet Money

whistling for taxis, men laughing with women on their arms, little children walking with their parents pointing at window dressings.

Some of Sophia's money was likely dirty. What I didn't know was just how dirty that money was. But it was obviously being put to good use.

I took the subway downtown towards my lair — the Tavern. When I got out, bullets of rain came down on my head as I walked. I was drenched when I arrived. I think this was meant to be. I was about to read what it felt like to be drenched with the smell of urine, feces, and vermin in a Paris prison.

"Just a minute, ladies," Tony said when I came into the Tavern. Surrounding him were several blond and brunette southern belle lookers who were probably models moonlighting as escorts for some of the men who had yet to arrive. They were kept women and were laughing at Tony's jokes. He was a ruff fellow, but he had a way with women when he opened up through that tough exterior.

"How uze doin?" He came out from behind the bar to take my raincoat and ratty old Borsalino fedora. "Uze soaked, partner," he said as he took my garments.

"Yea, it reminds me of Chicago weather. One minute it is sunny, and then the next, what do you know, it's raining!"

"Yea, yea, well you have lived long enough here to know that. This ain't the Midwest anymore, Dorothy. What can I get uze, Hank?"

I often smiled when Tony spoke to me. He pronounced "you" like "use." He was not an endearing looking fellow — but he sure could be endearing when he liked you, I suppose kind of like Jacky.

"An Oban on a scotch rock, please." I sat down at the bar and put the diaries on it. They were slightly wet, but I had kept them safe in my satchel, which looked like something a Southern lawyer would have under his arm running from house to house during the dusty summer.

"Coming right up, kiddo," he said with pleasure.

The women that Tony was talking to looked over at me. I would have talked to them had one come over to talk to me. But my insecurity stopped me from going over to them. Or maybe it is my Chicago upbringing. We were always taught to have someone introduce you to a lady, especially with so many gangsters in the city for so long. You never knew if the woman you wanted to talk to was someone else's lady. Talking to her without permission could get you killed in certain parts of the city. So I just kept to my reading and opened the first page of Jacky's diary, just below from where I had read before.

"Here you go," Tony left the scotch on the bar.

"Cheers," I raised my glass to him.

"Anytime," he smiled and went back over to the women at the bar.

January 2, 1934

There is many human fucking rats who is hiding behind these walls we need to be killing — rip the head off let the blood drip out.

Our people wearing the boots that is too big so they smuggle the weapons in the toe area.

Guards never catching our sneaky monkeys. They only search regular area — crotch, underarm, leg.

Guards lazy — they overworked, underpaid.

January 3, 1934

I haven't say nothing since I got here.

The fat man in my cell says something to me today: "That crack need something to keep them fucking rats out," he pointing to wall crack where rats come into cell like is their little hotel for the fucking.

"I got something," I says to fat man.

I ripping my sock and put it in crack.

"Thank you," he saying to me. "Name is Maurice," he holding out his uncooked Polish sausage fingers to shake.

"Jacky," I says.

Thinning gray hair is covering the sides of his pig head. He bald on top. His belly hang over pants. His belt was stretch to point of the breaking on last hole.

He smell like he not wash. They only take the bath one time a month. My ass must have smell like the fresh flower they wanting to smell all day, I thinks?

"What you in for?" Maurice asking me.

"The counterfeiting," I say.

"And you?" I asking.

"Shoplifting," he stopping, "from the candy stores," he smiles. "No," he laugh a happy full to his belly fat man laugh, "I lift the green candy from a big fucking bank. And this candy not make you fat — just rich, eh?"

He smile the big shit eat smile of the happy fat Buddha.

"What happen?" I ask.

"A fucking rat getting us pinched!" he looking mad at me.

"How so?" I ask.

"We the crew who break into bank Société Générale in Nice," fat man says.

"Your crew?" I surprised. I respecting the art of the good bank robbery. I wonder how people doing this — and not getting put in the can.

He nod proud.

"How you do it?" I ask.

"We sliming our way through shit in the sewers and digging this tunnel under vault wall. For this we needing the many tools — tanks for torches, jacks, lamps. We transporting our tools with us in sewer on little shit rubber boats."

"You full of shit?" I says.

"I still am," he says with the smile.

I lucky to have funny smart fat man around like this.

"Fine. You full of shit. Cover in it. What you do when you get into vault?"

"We locked the mother fucker!" Maurice say.

"So the fucks outside can't come inside?"

"Yes," he nod proud.

He laughing so loud so the walls is do the laugh with him.

"We inside for so long, we leaving our own shit all over the place. Oh, we having the fun, too. We finding porno photos inside of the many big time Nice politicians, lawyers, bankers. We taking those out and posting on the vault walls. We taking names down of these peoples and put on list so we have the big stick to hit the bastards if they coming after us!"

"I love it, I love it," I clapping my hands with the joy at the beauty of how they fuck the bank without her know she being fucked — until she already been fucked!

I then stand and stare at fat man. I not believe he pull this shit off.

He sitting there happy like he eat much food on new years day and need, how they say in the English, the nap?

I know why.

Papers say the fat man and his men hitting 10% of deposit boxes, but bank don't know exactly what stolen cause they not know what inside the boxes. Must have been things customers try to keeping the secret. Some papers say they is stole 30,000,00 to 100,000,000 fucking francs!

Maurice had years to do in this shithole. But he having stash of money somewhere ... maybe in Morocco? He going to dip into the money when he get out. This man was made for the life. He could do the jerking off of his pig penis and he not worry cause he have the money to do the jerking off — or paying the women to jerking him off.

And he know it.

"How you know if stolen money is the real money?" *The man on bunk bed asking Maurice in the sudden moment.*

"What you mean?" *Maurice asking back.*

"What you mean what I mean? This question is the simple one. How you know? You check the money?"

"No," *Maurice saying worried.*

"Then you not know," *the man on bunk saying.*

"What's it to you, you fuck? How you know if money is the real money?" *Maurice asking with the angry voice.*

The man jumping out of the bed and standing in front of us. We sitting on ground in front of bunk bed.

The man from bed stand tall, had the curly brown hair like on the man penis, the brown button eyes, crow's nose, hands of the child. They not seen a hard day's work.

"I should know cause I'm in for making more of the fake money than you ever seen," the man said cocky. *"I am Adolf, Adolf Burger,"* he holding out his hand to shake.

I held out mine cause I was happy. I always love the artist who make the bullshit money. Maurice see me be nice and he holding out hand for the shaking, too.

"So? What make you the expert?" Maurice asking Adolf as they shaking the hands.

Adolf very skinny — he looking like he have nothing to eat after weeks in desert — but I think he like it this way. He not seem to be the person that like eating much. Maurice look at Adolf with the surprise.

"Where you from, Adolf?" I ask.

He looked to me with intense look.

"Slovakia, but I living in 16th Quarter of Paris for past few years,"

"Why there?" I ask.

This screaming fucking rats trying to bust down the paper we putting in cracks.

"I loving the women there," he making the dirty old man grin as he closing his eyes to remembering.

"You had many?" Fat Maurice ask as he rub the polish sausage hands together like he getting ready to eat.

"One every night of week. I taking rests and pacing myself."

"They must liking you," I say.

"They liking me — and my money, too." He grinned this pig.

"How you make it?" Maurice ask Adolf with the interest.

"Printed it," Adolf saying with the smile.

I touching Adolf on shoulder with my hand.

"Where?" I asking him. I smile the smile you make when a friend says you have pretty woman who loves you but not telling you who it is.

"I make the money in my shitty basement!" He smile a self satisfy smile for many seconds. "When I run out, I printing more. My broads go around the country buying different things with the fake money I make — the mink coats, the cars, the shoes. Then they returning the things to get the real money. The tit and ass of the pretty woman was the perfect laundry!"

"A pussy laundry?" Maurice joking.

"You could say, yes," Adolf answering and nodded. "And I sure that money you steal from bank was the real money," Adolf say to Maurice to calm him.

"How know?" Maurice ask.

"That money was old family money and was sitting there since before the great war. There no way it has my funny money in it or some other funny money in it."

Maurice grunting the cave man at dinner that eats something he likes very much grunt.

"How much of the fake money you think you making in your life?" I asking Adolf. He was the celebrity to me!

"Let me see," Adolf start the counting his fingers. "About 10 million francs."

"In your life?" Maurice the fat fuck asking.

"A month," Adolf says serious.

"A month! A month! A month!" Maurice's slippery swampy sweaty body get up off ground with quickness. Adolf making more in year from *his pussy laundry than Maurice did crawl through the mud and shit to the bank of Nice!*

This battle of ego was a good pass of the time for me.

"Calm yourself, calm yourself," I putting my hand on the fat shoulder of Maurice. *I wanted Adolf to finish his story.*

Maurice sitting down slowly.

"Let me asking you, Adolf," *I touching his leg to get attention.* "Exactly how you make the money?"

He looking at me. "I have heard the good words about you. I know what I saying to you not go past these walls. But a girl must having her secrets of the beauty."

"I understand," *I saying.* "But you can show me the ankle or the lower leg without show me the pussy itself, no?"

"Let me see, um," *he sat in thought for the second,* "I use the car paint for ink; I sketch watermark by hand and make the mold to use on machine; I use the old newspaper from mills in the south. This paper looking like the official government money paper."

"A real fucking Picasso!" *I says with little boy excitement.*

"This why the ladies calling me Pablo," *he laughing.*

"How long you been making the bullshit money?" *I ask.*

"10 years," *he say serious.*

Maurice and me. We looking at one another cause we know how much money this meaning: something like 1.2 billion francs!!!

"If you ever need anything," *Adolf say to me as he resting his hand on right arm,* "you let me *know and I giving it to you."* He wink his right eye towards me, this just as good as handshake. *"I know about your family, Jacky."*

He looking outside bars to see if anybody listening.

"I knowing how your family does the business — very professional. You are, how they say, the species endangered — that is what you are."

"The same," I putting my hand on his. *"Call us if you needing anything,"* and I winking back at him.

January 15, 1937

I losing my power to write. There is no point. The winter is horrible cold. We have nothing to keep us warm. We have this bullshit paper thin wool bed sheets we can wiping the ass with and it breaking.

But my spirit coming back. I write to forget the cold. And this morning the guards bringing in new fun for us. These two new prisoners. They look like the African apes. The guards bringing them into gate as Maurice telling me about what he going to do when he getting out.

One ape shoving off guard's hand. The ape thinking he is a celebrity in Hollywood and should have the red carpet. This how the ape man act.

The other ape man just laugh crazy. This other look at me and Maurice sitting on the floor and saying to us: "you getting married, or is this the one night stand, you fags?"

Smart ass jungle apes! I thinks to myself. I loving this shit!

The guards throwing the shorter ape next to me. The other ape man walking the calm church walk into our shit hole to sit on bottom bunk bed. The guards slam cell door.

"No fucking respect," the ape say to me with his Parisian accent. He slowly understand he not at Hollywood premier. He an asshole! But he a funny asshole!

"Where you from?" I ask this man.

"China. You, you fuck?" He smile. I like his humor. A fresh air of breath.

"Marseille," I holding out my hand. "Jacky," I look into his eyes.

He surprise to hear my name.

"Oh yea, yes, yea, I've heard of you," he says as he hold out his hand, "Julian, Julian Reles, but people calling me Monsieur Twist."

"I call you Mister, just to make shorter, this okay?"

The 23 year old nodding yes.

"And where you really from, Mister?"

"Paris," he say, "Montmarte."

"I see," I say.

"I was told to listen to you before I come in here," he say to me.

"Why?" I asking.

"Cause you keeping your mouth shut," he says serious.

This making sense to me. I not say nothing about the family all this time. I having my chances for shorter sentence. But I would have jumped off roof in Marseille if it not for the family. This why I do my time like the man. I not live with myself if

I ratting. I need the pain today. This the sacrifice for the tomorrow.

"Come to think," I says to Mister, "I hearing about you, too."

"That so?" He touching my shoulder with his hand. Mister shorter than me, have the kinky hair, the strong ape hands with scissor fingernails, I thinks he Algerian or Tunisian or Moroccan?

"Yes," I nodding.

"Like what?" He asking.

"You love cleaning with the ice pick," I say.

He smiling a I just won award smile.

"This is true," he taking the dirt off of his pants.

"One hit of yours becoming famous in the South," I say like he the musician who play the good music for the ears to hearing. "You inviting the target over to your momma's house, pick him in the back yard, have dinner with momma, cut up man in the basement before dropping in the river."

"Yes," he said with proud papa smile, "this is true."

"Know how to make the pick out of spoon or fork?" I ask.

"Just say the word," Mister putting his hand on mine like Adolf doing with his hands before.

"Thank you, Mister," I giving him this good guy pat.

"What about me?" The other monkey say.

The other funny monkey was jealous.

"Bruno Scalise," but people calling me Brunt. He standing up and holding out his hand to shake. Brunt the same age as Mister but taller. Had what seem like the glass right eye. He have the brown

slick hair parted in middle, had this pale skin that not see the sun. The pimples is on his skin.

"A pleasure," his fucking banana fingers covering mine.

"Where you from?" I ask.

"The same as Mister. We partners."

When he saying that, I have the feeling they was planted here as the tool for me to using for the bad things.

"I not Mister, I don't use dinosaur tricks like a pick," he look over to Mister. They the two competitors in a who-can-kill-best beauty pageant. "I like use the knife. You turning it once it get inside. Then see the person's eyes light up with the pain."

"Like cherry on top of profiterole or the ice cream," Mister make the sick smile to me.

"But I can cook the poisons from the simple household things. I could even do the cooking in here with the right things," he looking over at Mister.

They smile this two new people been married on vacation smile.

January 28, 1937

When I waking up early this morning, I hear a noise. Someone rubbing up against bars. I don't know. The noise waking me.

I got up and walk over to bar. I step on the piece of paper.

It not left there by the accident.

I open the paper and in the messy writing it saying: "Damien." I knew what this mean. We needing to kill this man. He must be the rat with the big fucking mouth. We need to kill him before he did.

February 16, 1937

"Who is he?" I asking Brunt.

"You mean they not tell you?" He look at me with this eyes so curious.

"No," I stop to thinking. "But I remembering we have this man in Paris high up mayor's office. I think his name was, um," and then it hitting me when I snapping my fingers, "Damien!"

Brunt looking at me with smile and then says about this man Damien:

"He walking on our side of tracks, but he not know the golden rule."

"And what that?" I asked like I not know.

"Never bite hand that feeds you." He smack me had on the back.

"Right, Brunt," I looking outside the cell to make sure nobody listening. I turn back to him. "You know he on our payroll for years?"

"No idea," he says.

"Damien working under this Prime Minister Poincare. I mean that he does the every little thing: schedule meetings and all this other bullshit."

I looking again outside cell make sure not the anybody listening.

"He gambling at our spots. He owed us the money. He loving our girls. He not able to keep his hands off them. He owes us for touching our girls the many times. So we make deal with him. He pay us off by doing favors. Each favor make less what he owing. He knew the dark side. He played in it. But he act like he didn't, this motherfucker."

Brunt look at me with surprise in his eyes. Mister hearing our conversation. He look at me *with mouth open wide. A little boy see the waterfall for first time?*

It was a waterfall — in a special way.

Many people taught that the peoples working in government think of the people first. As I getting the age I see this mostly not true. For many days, government workers is in back pocket of this person or that business. If you not right person, you sit like fat duck in front of the pistol with nowhere to go.

*My family always have many of these governments peoples in our back pockets — cause we **can't** lose.*

Mister finally speaking up: "what Damien do for you?"

"I can't telling you everything. I tell you that he get Prime minister to protect our construction contracts."

"So you paying him to be in your back pocket?" Mister asking me.

I looked at Mister.

"There more to it than just paying. There is art to this game. It can't be in the obvious way," I say.

As fat Maurice keeping a look out, he start to be the professor of the corruption for the tough monkey boys from Paris. He says in the direction of the boys: "if woman has many coins in purse, and cash, she going to notice when you taking it all. But lift some coins and make the replacements with the small stone and she not going to notice — until she checking her purse when she getting at the home."

Adolf on second bunk reading Le Journal. He start the laughing. "The hell with that," he saying and then waving his hand over in don't go wasting my fucking time way at Maurice. "I just make them fucking coins!"

He went back to the reading. Maurice look with disgust at Adolf. I like watch these men do the marry couple arguments. It taking my mind off this fucking cold. Mister touch my shoulder to get my attention.

"Why you want to get rid of Damien?" He asking.

"He has the rat mouth," I says.

"Maurice?" I asking him to making sure nobody coming.

Maurice nodding that all is good.

"There is the investigation into Paris corruption. Damien is star witness. He not a good boy. He give up names — top people in family."

"His mouth will get him off easy, but not get off in right way like when the cock is too sore from the fucking," Maurice saying with dirty old man grin as he stare outside the cell.

"Is to be expected," I says. "They buy the Damien cow so you get his milk."

In this sudden moment, Maurice started singing the Marseillaise, "allons enfants de la Patrie, le jour de glorie est arrive! Contre nous de la tyrannie."

This mean guards is coming.

We started whistle the song. We make the nice boy's choir?

The guard stopping to listen.

We not do the plan that night.

March 28, 1937
Today we talk about the hit on Damien.

The problem is Damien usually in the population general. They guarding the little fuck. They know he a target.

"So how we get him?" Mister asking with the impatience.

Brunt says: "this is simple, stupid. The man work out with others during work out time."

"I thought of this," Mister slapping Brunt back on shoulder. "They going search us before we come into that yard. Everyone is felt up and down. Nobody has nothing on them."

There a reason why they was the good muscle.
Brunt stopping.
He snapping his fingers.

"I have the fucking answer," just like he make the invention that save the lives of the children with the flies on the face.

"What?" Mister asking.

"Jacky, you have guards on the take?" Brunt asking.

"Yes," I nodding. I knew where he going, but I like to see him go there for by himself.

"We get one of the guards," Brunt slapping Mister on his chest, "to be in on it."

"What we need?" Maurice asking.

We standing in circle at center of dingy, dark, rat shit cell. Not the pretty place to do the thinking. But they saying the necessary is the mother of the, um, invention?

"We need something that go deep into his body," Mister says like the doctor who plan the operation.

"Why?" Maurice ask.

"We want to kill the fucker, not tickle him," Mister say.

*"The pricking with the pin won't kill him,"
Brunt saying too like he say something new.*

"That's nice," fat Maurice says, "but don't got no knives."

"This no problem," Mister saying. "All we need is two forks. We can make into shank."

"Where you get two forks?" Adolf asked.

"From my guard," I says.

The men is surprised at me and what I say.

April 15, 1937

I leave note on floor for Jonas. He the guard that dropping off note. I writing "two forks" on the note with pencil. There also a date on note. Jonas walking by and picking up the note this morning. He look over at me and smile big.

Jonas on payroll since he start working here. We pick him to apply so we have man on inside. He had the law problems — the drugs, taking, selling. Our Jew lawyer help. Jonas go straight so he could work for us in this castle of shit.

He knowing exactly what I needing. Two forks in our cell on date so we bringing them to courtyard and do the kill.

May 23, 1937

Two forks is here last night. Mister taking them early. Bent all fingers on the forks. Making one shank from this two forks.

Mister has the talent, I thinks to myself.

May 31, 1937

"We did it," Mister says when he get back into cell today.

"How it go?" I asking.

"Smooth. Brunt and me walk into courtyard. Jonah's guy not search us. Shanks in our boots," Mister whispered into my ear as he kept looking outside with nervous eyes.

Brunt lean over to my ear as Mister moving away to make room.

"Right," Brunt saying. *"We walking through security and heading to middle of courtyard where the rat fuck do the working out."*

"We act like we was going to lift weights," Mister go on, *"like we was stretching. But Brunt just taking shank out boot, you know? He hold the shank in palm, with point up to his wrist. That way, nobody seeing it."*

"We see Damien do the bench press over by wall," Brunt said.

"We start walking over and Brunt telling guy next to Damien to beat it," Mister says.

"I looking down at the rat as I standing above him. His eyes scared. He never expect this," Brunt saying.

I understanding why. Damien growing up in the privilege. He never pay his own rent. His family taking care of that. He went to right schools. He had right wife. He was father — this make him, how they say, trusting, trustworthy?

"I went up to his side, right where lungs is," Brunt says.

"Then," Brunt say, *"I took my shank and . . ."*

I stop the monkeys.

"I know what you done. But I not like this violence. This killing is part of business — but is a part I wish we not having, see?"

I did not feel the sorry for this Damien fuck — but I still not like the killing.

June 6, 1937
In here, everything/everyone has the price. The system outside make it look like there the good guys and the bad guys. But some of good guys got bad eyes and some of bad guys got good eyes. Maybe inside is the more true life than the outside.

June 28, 1937
Boys start to bringing powder from Afghanistan in boats to Marseille. They shoot in arms with the crap needles. I try some last night — one of the best feelings in my life. All of worries gone — I not remember my past, not knowing my present, not have worry about future. Everything the way it should be I thinks when I taking the shit. And that is why I am going to keep doing it — I get to forget. Forgetting is better than the remembering.

July 1, 1938
A year since I start the shooting. I can't stop. I have so many marks — hard to find clean vein now. I start shooting my feet. The only open land I have left!

October 29, 1938
Prosecutor for the organize crime make me another offer to talk. Calling me into his office — school degrees and pictures with prime minister on walls. I saying nothing to him. I just stare at the wall like the crazy man.

University Of Treachery

December 15, 1938

One more week here. I should be happy, no? But I not happy. I feeling like this my home. We shoot up every day. We have laughs, we sit, we talk, we have our exercise. I not look over my shoulder. We own this shit hole. And now I must leave it?

I am look forward to the ocean breeze on my face. This one thing I miss about outside — and smile on the child. The rest of world outside is the bullshit.

January 1, 1939

This morning I getting out. A Sunday. God's day, family day. They give my clothes back, my watch, my ring, everything I coming in here with — but not my clean arms! I never have them backs again. I very happy about this. This white powder we cook is my new best friend.

I walking out into Paris sun.

Black Citroen sedan parking and waiting. I heard about this car when I on the inside. It like long swan. But this swan is black.

"Salut, Jacky, name is Ariel," this tall 26 years old boy come out of driver seat to welcoming me. "Welcome back," he kiss me on cheeks.

Not the ones on my ass.

"I hoping for someone prettier than you," I says to old boy with the looks of the model from the Vogue magazine, the dick getting the sucked by the women at night, the face of the Greek god, the body of the same — is chisel, no, with the muscles so tight. I betting he helping me get the nice pussy if I go with him at Paris in the night.

> *He laughing a son laugh.*
>
> *"Thank you," I saying with sincere, "for picking me up."*
>
> *He opening the back door of car. I getting in. He getting back into driver seat. Next to him was large black man with the black patch on left eye. I not believe how big his hands was. As I sitting there, I thinking about how big his cock must be. I bet is like the big carrot! Wow. I wishing I have the cock like this — I have the, how they say, e-n-v-y?*
>
> *"Name is Nico, Monsieur Jacky," the black say from his bottom of the sea dark black skin. "It a pleasure meeting you," Nico says with Trinidad accent. New muscle in the family, I thought, weighing 125 kilos!*

As I sat there in the Tavern, with all of the cigar smoke going around me, I had no idea how much 125 kilos was. So I figured I might ask Tony.

"Heya, Tony, how much is 125 kilos in pounds?" I asked through the smoke.

"How the fuck should I know?"

Luckily, an old Englishman who was sitting next to me drinking a scotch chimed in: "mate, it's about 275 pounds."

"Thanks," I nodded in the Englishman's direction and then went back to reading Jacky's diary.

> *"Where you taking me?" I asking Nico.*
> *"Your new home."*
> *"Where is this?"*
> *"The Marais," he turned around and smile.*
> *I heard of it but I never been. It was big Jewish quarter in Paris. Working class, Jewish, my style. But I wondering: why not back to Marseille?*

"And Marseille?" I asking confused.

"They make you boss of Paris," Ariel say as he driving the car fast with the black gloves on his hands through the small as asshole streets of Paris, with the bikes, women, pasty shops, French police with the small mustaches, museums, old stone apartments — I loving Paris.

"But what about Marseille?" I ask like I not hear what Ariel saying. I happy at what he say about boss. This good. But I not happy what he say about not go back to Marseille. This not good.

"Things taken care of in Marseille, Monsieur Jacky," Nico says with deep swamp sound voice. "They need you in Paris."

This not make me feel better, but I keep quiet cause I know it the orders from the south.

"Please, boys, just please calling me Jacky," I says.

They nodding yes as we driving with the fast speed in winter streets. We coming to small apartment in Marais. It in the middle of quarter, close to local butcher shop, on street with the stones of the cobbles.

Boys help me up stairs. This a simple apartment — but they put the best furniture, cognac, bedding, cigars in it. They know I like all of this. There is custom kitchen. They knowing I love the cooking. I think of myself making dinners there for the pretty pussy.

As boys put my things in living room, I asking: "what is my front?"

They start laughing — like the little fucking schoolgirls.

Oh shit, I getting nervous!

> "It's nothing, Jacky," the mean and shy Nico says to me.
>
> "It is actually something," Ariel, the lady man, got closer to me.
>
> They start smiling together at me.
>
> "What the fuck is my front?" I ask with the worry.
>
> "You going to be a shitty janitor at the rich kid school in ritzy 16th quarter of Paris, Jacky," Ariel finally says with the fuck you smile as he patting me on the back.
>
> "What the fuck?"
>
> I could not believe this bullshit.
>
> A fucking janitor for the snotty childrens?

I could only imagine Jacky's reaction. I smiled when I thought of this man being a janitor at a high-end kids school.

"What's up with the smirk, professor? Get laid?" Tony asked.

"No quite, Tony. I'm just reading about a fish who is going to have to spend the next few years of his life out of water," I smiled to myself as I closed this part of Jacky's diary. It was about 11:00 in the evening.

CHAPTER 7
Big Bang Theory

As I have gotten to know Sophia better, I have found her less about labeling people based on their clothes, education, and background. But I thought otherwise when I read her words below in the middle of the Tavern the following night:

> *January 9, 1939*
> *"Mamma, mamma, there is Jacky," Otis tugged my blouse in excitement as I dropped him off at school this morning. I remember seeing this Jacky man sitting on some type of rickety wooden chair next to the door of his janitor's closet. He was sipping an espresso coffee. Yes, Otis tells me Jacky plays with all of the children. Yes, Otis tells me that all of the children adore Jacky. But I can tell he is a brute and a thug — nothing more, nothing less! This makes me think of Charles Baudelaire. He once said something like: "the greatest trick the devil ever played was convincing the world that he did not exist."*

> *I cannot believe this thuggish man is playing with innocent children. He is the Devil incarnate. I can tell just by looking at him. Dirty hands, crass looks, needle marks up and down his arms, tattoos on his forearms that peek through his rolled up sleeves, and primitive eye sockets — they droop down over his eyes. He looks as though he just came from the jungle. I have no doubt that this man was in prison — for a long time. He didn't get out of there without some trouncing and playing in the gutter. But he has pulled the wool over the children's eyes. I don't know how such a piece of trash got a job at Otis's school. Maybe be bought someone off?*
>
> *And so who could blame me for not wanting Otis to play with this heathen? He is dirty in more ways that I can say — a filthy person through and through. I don't know how Otis could look up to this man. When this Jacky man looked in my direction with his beady black eyes this morning, I clutched my Hermes purse in fear of what he was planning.*

Maybe I was wrong. Maybe my image of Sophia was not the real her.

At the same time, I can't fault her. I imagine that Jacky **was** dirty looking. He **was** from a dirty background. Sophia was not wrong about him — in some ways. But perhaps, just perhaps, this man potentially had a better heart than anyone she had met — including Richard the churchgoer.

"You day dreaming again dere Hank?" Tony waved his hand in front of my eyes to get my attention. "House of the Rising Sun," this new hit song by the Animals, was playing in the background. It was one of my favorites.

"No," I said with surprise, "just getting into the diaries here."

People were packed into the Tavern. I was an island onto myself. I sat in the middle of the morass of married advertising executives who came in with their girlfriends, hippy looking musicians who maybe just got off a gig, and some guys who looked like they just got off the shift working on the subway.

One of the reasons I loved this place so much was that it was a true New York spot — people from all walks of life would come in at night. I found comfort and anonymity in the loudness — just as I had found the same in Gotham. Nobody noticed me because they were so into whatever or whomever they were doing that night.

"Yea, yea, yea," Tony said with the brush of his hand, "dem diaries is nice and all, but check out those dames over there." He pointed down the bar towards this group of gorgeous women in their 20s and 30s. They were all gathered around wearing long dresses, heels, hair down to their backs, and soft make up — shades of pink lipstick, red lipstick, and even one with some clear shiny stuff that was getting traction in fashion.

"Wow. Those are some pretty gals, Tony," I said how a boy scout would say about some girl scouts.

"Yea, I know that, that's why I waz waking you up. Why iz you always looking in dem diaries and not checking what's going on around here," and then he started pointing around the bar. "You scared of livin?"

He looked at me intently.

"I don't know," I shrugged, "I don't think so," I shrugged again. "I feel like I learn more from what I am reading than what I can learn from others."

"Oh yea, you think so, huh?"

"Well, I suppose so," I said unsure of myself.

"Try this one on for size there junior," Tony was 30 years older than me. "What if I told you that the guy you iz reading about in dem diaries didn't learn nutting from no books, and

Dirty Quiet Money

dat everything that man knew was learned right out dea," he pointed outside the large window facing the street.

"You know about Jacky?" I asked Tony.

"I ain't going to tell you no more. All I gotz to say is check out what iz going on around you and not only in dem books. Dey only going to take you so far, junior."

I remember Tony pausing to look into my eyes to let me know that he knew more than I thought he knew.

"Now, I tink you need to going to have a drink before you keep on going in dem diaries dea," he pointed his chunky finger toward what I was reading. "I tink you need a martini, cauz, uh, you know, a cawfee is ain't going to cut it for ya."

"Whatever you recommend," I put my hands up like I gave up.

"Good, partner," he said. He went over in front of all the wine bottles that were stocked on the top of the glass shelves and started making my martini.

As he made my drink, I wondered how he knew what I was reading about. I thought about all the knowledge that wasn't in books, written down, and there for the reading. I felt like this other part of the mind — the darker more mysterious part, and yet the one that is more in tune with others and their secret little worlds — was downplayed in our society. Maybe it's because you can't teach it, reduce it, reuse it, standardize it, and put it into some nice little box with a ribbon of your choosing on the top.

"Here ya go," Tony teed up a nice martini on the bar for me.

"Thanks, T."

"You good, kid. You good. You just got to ferment a little, like a nice fucking bottle of wine, eh?" He slapped a grandfather after giving you a nice little Christmas present that made you happy slap on the shoulder.

I smiled. I took a sip of the booze. It calmed me.

I was curious to see what Jacky thought of his life at the school, and about his first sighting of Sophia. I opened up Jacky's diary. I turned to around the same date range.

Big Bang Theory

January 3, 1939

This my third day at this fancy school — there is no fleas, cockroaches, murderers, dirty cops, rats, shank like I have in the prison. No, instead I got the children.

What money these little ones having! They got peoples making them the breakfast in the mornings. Same cooks making them the lunch. I seeing in mornings. Family drivers dropping off, picking up when the night coming.

I know this.

I have get here in morning around 9:00. I light my cigarette in closet they giving to me. This closet is face the parking places for the cars. I keeping door open so I can hearing this pretty birds singing the blues songs for my ears to hearing. I smell the fresh cut grass. These some of the things I liking outside of Le Sante.

I sipping coffee and puffing my cigarette. Waves of the children is coming to the school in the big black cars. These cars is dropping the little children in front of my eyes. None pay me the attention. I just sit and like watching them.

I not care if they seeing holes in my arms. I not care what they thinks of me. This place is not the real life. I do my time, just like I do before. This some story that I reads in the book that has the fairies. But I love be around the children.

"Excuse me, monsieur, what your name?" A little boy fives year old asking me as he tugging my sleeve.

"Jacky," I says to little boy. He standing next to my knee. I sitting on little shit chair. He the very cute little one. His hair is blond and having

the curls. They coming out of his head like is the fat belly of Maurice coming over belt to seeing what happening outside. His eyes was the Mediterranean blue, his skin the Nordic or Viking peoples color that would coming to Marseille when I was boy. He wearing blue school uniform with school hat.

"What your name?" I ask little boy.

"Otis," his smile could be lighting up dark night without a big moon or many stars.

I holding out my palm so he could slap.

He slapping my hand. He giggling and jumping up and down. I love how he gets so much joy from this simple thing.

This one of things I liking about this place. Children not know the wicked. They making me feel young. They is a joy of the living.

"How old is you, Otis?"

He start the counting of his fingers, holding it up his hand when he finishing — five years old.

"Five," I says to him with smile. "This a good age," I patted his little shoulder, "I remembering your age," I says as I put out my cigarette on working shelf full of the wires, saw, hammer. I keeping little chocolates in closet. I always like chocolates. I snack on one a day. I taking one out.

"Take this." I hold up my finger to my mouth and say shhhh! "You not telling other peoples that I giving you the treats for the fat boys, okay?" I held out my right pinky to him, and says to him with smile, "put your pinky with mine, this is called the pinky swear."

He smiling as our pinkies touch.

"So no telling?" I asking.

He nod and then say "thank you" while he shine his smile toward me.

"You is welcome," I says back. "Do the good grades in school today, little boy."

I patting him on the head.

January 7, 1939

I get into school this morning and this little Otis waiting for me.

"Hello, little one," I says as he standing outside. "I see you bringing the friend," I smiling at the boys. The other boy having the freckles, big red hair, the white Irish skin.

"And what your name, boy?" I asking.

"Ewan," the boy saying with Scottish accent. We shake the hands. He smiling as he looking over at Otis like they meeting the movie star.

"You don't say nothing about our little secret?" I asking Otis. He was very smart boy. He put out his pinky finger. He understands.

"Good," I smiling as I opening the door to the shitty closet. It before the school hour. So I spending time with these little boys until it s time for the school.

"You can come in, but only for the little." I pat them on their backs. "You have to get to your studies so you make the good grades!"

After the boys inside my closet, I keep door open so the cool air come inside. They leaning against wall, and I leaning against work-bench.

"What those marks?" Otis point to my arm.

"You mean these?" I point to them.

"Yes," Otis say with small smile and his head going up and down.

"I falling down and these is marks from when I getting hurt." I need to lie. I not feeling happy about myself. They looking up to me. They can't know the truth about me.

"Wow," Ewan say with surprise. "You falling a lot. Holes all over your arms," he pointing to holes. "Wasn't there no way you could stop from falling?"

The question a good question.

I think about how to answer it.

"Sometimes you going to fall, sometimes you can't stop the falling. So you get the ouches from the falling. But the ouches and scars is making you strong later."

The boys looking at one another. I thinks to myself: maybe they don't know what I mean?

"You know what a sword is?"

They both nodding yes.

"You know that a sword needs to taking the form in the heat before it can become a sword? The heat bruise it, scar it, ouches the metal before it become to be what it is now, you see?"

"So you a sword now Monsieur Jacky?" Ewan asked with the big smile.

"I am sword in making," I make big laugh to myself.

"You have children like us?" Otis asked me.

"No," I says. "But I wish I did," I pinching Otis's cheek.

"Where you from?" Ewan asking me.

"Marseille. Know where this is?"

They shaking heads no.

"In the south, close to ocean. Been to the ocean?'"

Ewan shook no, but Otis nodding the yes.

"One of most pretty things in this world," I saying to Ewan. "It has the fish, it had the whales, it has the waves, it has the birds, it has the wind, it has waters that make you feel fresh."

"I want to go!" Ewan says. "Maybe you take me?"

"Yes, yes, yes, yes," Otis say as he jump up and down. "I want to going too!"

"Maybe your parents taking you one day.'"

"I not see them," Ewan say, "only in morning and late at the night. They is not home during weekends. I spending the time with maid, not them," Ewan looking down to ground with the sad face.

"I see momma a lot," Otis says. "Momma says I can't sleep over until I having the dinner first."

Boy not know how good he having it! I wondering about his mother. I wanting to meet her.

"Almost the school time," I looking up at clock in closet. "Let's have the fun before you run." I thinks to myself I always wanting to be the big poet or the writer — but this not my, how they say in the English, d-e-s-t-i-n-y?

They smiling.

"Okay," they saying.

"This a game where I acting like something, maybe tiger, monkey, lion, okay? And then you guessing what I am." I pulling out the chocolates and put them on table. Boys have eyes that light up, that is why they fun to play with.

"You understand?" I asking.

They nod the yes.

"Alright. This the first one." I moving my arms on my side. I moving my head back and forth like the pigeon or the turkey walking on the street.

I do same sounds as pigeon or turkey and then I stopping.

"What am I?" I ask the boys.

"Turkey," Otis saying.

"Pigeon," Ewan saying.

Shit! They both could be right!

"You very smart little monkeys! I give you both the chocolates for this one."

I handing the chocolates to the boys. Their giggles was the bubbles and suds on top of ocean in Marseille. They making me very happy.

"Let's do again," I wanting to play again seeing if I can win this, Ewan says.

"Yes," Otis says with the little rascal smile.

"Yes, yes," Ewan clapping his hands.

"This the last one," I says.

I make a fish look with the lips. I open my eyes like the big fish. I moving around room as fish in water with arms.

"A fish! A fish! A fish!" The boys saying.

I snapping my fingers like they getting me again.

"You got me!" I say to them.

I give them the chocolates.

"Now you go to class to do the study, study, study. Don't work in the place like me when you getting older?'"

"But we want be like you!" Otis say as he eat the chocolate.

Ewan eat his chocolate and rub chocolate hands on his shirt. He like the food and not caring about the dirt on the clothes. He my type of boy!

"You boys good," I say with big smile on my face. "Be smarter than teacher!"

I holding pinky out to Otis. He whispering into the ear of Ewan.

They holding out pinky fingers and we doing our pinky shake.

We all giggle little school girl giggles I hear when I see them in groups walking together into school here.

"Now get to class, you little hustlers!"

I think to myself I go from shit prison to bourgeois school. Maybe, if there is God, there is plan for me.

January 9, 1939

I waking up in this morning. I take my coffee and cigarette in school closet. The boys not there. I guessing they late.

I sitting in my spot of the regular. I smoke my cigarette, drink my coffee. And then it happening. I see Otis leaving his black car with his mother.

Coffee shaking in my hand, teeth chattering in my mouth, shivering on my body. I not feel this way unless I doing the dangerous things. I closing my eyes and putting down the coffee. I needing to calming my fears inside.

She look like Greta — Grata — Greta Garbo, from this movie Anna Karenina — but Otis mother much better. She got the Nordic blue wolf eyes like Otis, never seen nothing blonder than her hair down her back.

This the top classy pussy I seeing in my life — she wearing the long black dress down to lower legs, beret tipped to side of her head, black stockings, what look like black heels that the hands making, black gloves.

She not like other mothers who come here. She wearing the poker black sunglasses that hiding her eyes. No other mother wearing these. I guessing sunglasses not good for them because they think covering eyes too, how they say, s-h-a-d-y?

Her beauty is a wave that splash against my chest to make me feel the new again. It her beauty on outside — and what she hiding on inside — that make me feel this. I could telling she hiding this inside beauty from outside eyes — like mine looking at her today.

She not wearing the make-up on her face. Other women wearing much make-up to cover up that they not happy? Maybe they want other peoples thinking that they do anything to follow rules, like the good Germans do?

Not this fucking woman.

I thinks to myself — may she able to be herself in public this way — with the dark glasses cover the pain I see in her inside — behind the black sunglass.

Maybe she save her secret self inside for the someone special on the outside. Or maybe she having the deep sadness so she want to hide behind these glasses.

I not know.

I have this feeling this woman is like me. No, she got no marks on her arms. No, not having my edges. Yes, she has got secret sadness that we get from living, loving, losing. I could see with my eyes that she blaming herself for some thing like I blaming myself for the many things.

But I feeling she not losing herself in needle like I losing myself in it. No. She hiding inside the cave — and this cave is herself. Maybe she keeping it in so no pain seeing the day, or it reminding her that she, like me, don't have the real love.

She see me looking at her. When she getting back into car, she look over to me before she close door. What she thinking? Maybe she just the rich bitch with the no feeling? Or maybe she is the way I feeling she is — like me, the lover with no love?

Whatever she like — it the first time I feeling my heart in the many years.

I closed Jacky's diary. I finished the cocktail that Tony poured me. Reading these entries made me ready for another drink.

"Hey, Tony, how about one more?" I pointed to my empty glass.

"Sure, coming right up kid," he said.

As he started to make my drink, I thought back to what I learned about nuclear fission in my physics class at Chicago. This is when you take a nucleus — the center of an atom — apart so that you make energy from it. The split makes the energy. The other way of making energy is fusion. This is when you take two separate nuclei — the centers of two atoms — and join or fuse them together to make one heavier nucleus.

It seemed like Jacky and Sophia came from the same nucleus. Maybe they had the same heart even though they had different backgrounds. I theorized, like some pipe smoking professor, that the energy Jacky felt from Sophia was that original split, when they were broken apart, sometime long ago, perhaps even in a past life. Perhaps that is why, when they met later on, they created energy.

"You tinking up der again," Tony said as he put the cocktail on the bar in front of me and made a knock on wood type of knock on my forehead.

Dirty Quiet Money

"You caught me red handed," I put my hands up. I sipped the drink. "I guess I can't help it. The more I read these diaries, the more I think about love."

Tony just looked at me. I started reading Sophia's diary from around the same time period I had been reading Jacky's diary entries. I wanted to see what she felt about herself behind those black sunglasses.

> ### *January 16, 1939*
> *I dropped off Otis this morning at his school. The air was crisp. I wore a thicker pair of stockings. They were one of my favorites — with small holes along the side so that you can see some of my skin.*
>
> *The stockings got me thinking. I used to dress up more before Richard. Since him, I have not been trying. I don't feel like trying. I felt bad about myself after him. Maybe I didn't please him enough? Maybe I didn't pay enough attention to him? Maybe I wasn't imaginative enough? I don't know.*
>
> *The stockings are a remnant of the way I used to be — chic, and yet simple; sexy, and yet understated; classic, and yet with an edge; formal, and yet with a bohemian spirit. I also wore my favorite shoes today — a pair of black alligator heels — along with a form fitting black dress that one of my favorite tailors in Rome made for me.*
>
> *I did this all for myself. I haven't been with any man since Richard. It's not that I haven't had my chances — men seem to flock over me as pigeons would to crumbs on the table. But I was never interested. They all seem to think the same way (want sex), want the same things (money, power), and have the same needs (to be looked at as being*

powerful by the other men). I had enough of that with Richard. I didn't need more.

There was a woman once. I had a crush on her. Her name was Ginger, an actress who was a rising star in Hollywood. An ex-pat friend of mine named Gertrude Stein who lived on the West Bank introduced me to Ginger.

Gertrude was a writer from Pennsylvania. She moved here in 1903, or thereabouts, with Alice, her companion, who also acted as Gertrude's secretary. I remember meeting Gertrude and Alice one day at Café De Flore. Their independence was so sexy to me. They left the United States and didn't look back. Her and Alice looked so happy with one another. I longed to have this in my life.

"Sophia, I have the perfect woman for you," Gertrude said to me with her short gray-cropped hair showing her life's pains and excitements. I had told Gertrude what had happened with Richard — it was not long after — and I think she also thought maybe a woman would be a better fit.

"I couldn't, darling," I remember saying to Gertrude as I nervously smoked my cigarette, unsure if I even knew what I was saying. It's like when a girlfriend of mine tells me that they don't like a guy when, in fact, they do, but they are afraid to let the guy know it out of fear — that the guy won't like them back, that the guy will eventually lose interest, or that the guy will walk out the door one day. This fear paralyzes many — it paralyzed me that day.

Gertrude wouldn't put up with it.

"You are going to meet her if you like it or not," she patted an elder to her student pat on my shoulder. Gertrude had a lot more experience than I did

with women matters. I turned and smiled at her. She was taking me under her wing. I loved her for it.

"*Alright, alright,*" *I surrendered.*

"*We will meet her here tomorrow afternoon,*" *she leaned over towards me to make sure I would show up.*

"*I'll be here,*" *I promised.*

The next day, I dressed up for the first time since splitting with Richard. I went all out. I wore my: garter belt he got hand made for me in Italy; best fedora — a rich burgundy color that I used to tilt over one of my eyes; black pencil skirt — form fitting, but not too tight so that someone could see my garter; a tight black silk blouse; and English spectator heels.

I was so excited!!!

When I got to the café, Gertrude and Alice were sitting inside drinking their cocktails in the cloudy smoky artsy café. Sitting right next to them was one of the prettiest women I had ever seen.

It was Ginger.

I sat down next to her and she introduced herself.

I wanted to fall out of my seat.

"*Hello there, my name is Ginger,*" *she said with a slight Missouri accent. She held out her hand and I shook it as I looked into her eyes — large blue ones that were almost too big for her head. Their size made me want to stare into them even more.*

"*Pleasure to meet you, Ginger, my name is Sophia,*" *I remember nervously saying to her. I think my hand was shaking before it met hers.*

Her shiny long red hair flowed ever so naturally down to the middle of her back. She looked shorter than me. Her breasts were about the cup of my hand, and were peeking through her tight dress. She wore a light honeysuckle perfume that smelled like some of the uptown streets in New Orleans during the summer when I was growing up — quiet except for the sounds of children playing, bees buzzing, and the slight flow of wind off of the river through the honeysuckle trees.

This woman made me feel at home.

This was the only time that Ginger and I met. We sat together for what seemed only like a minute — but which was actually a couple of hours. At the end, I remember Ginger having to leave for an appointment, and Gertrude telling me, after Ginger left the café, "she likes you, Sophia, she likes you," as Gertrude rested her hand on my shoulder.

"How do you know?" I nervously asked.

"When you went to the bathroom earlier in the night, she told us that she really liked you," Gertrude said with a smile.

I didn't believe it. How could such a pretty woman like me? Didn't she see that I wasn't up to snuff? Didn't she see that I was damaged? That I couldn't even keep a man? How could I keep a woman?

"I liked her too. But I have to be leaving for New Orleans soon for a few months, so I guess it will have to wait until I get back," I said to Gertrude and Alice.

It was a lie.

Gertrude slapped her knee in frustration. "That's too bad. What timing! If it's meant to be, you will see each other later on in life!"

I nodded sheepishly. I avoided the café for the next few months. I didn't want to be discovered.

That was the only time I had even been close to interested in someone else — but I was too much of a coward to try.

I regret it to this day.

I used that regret to motivate me to dress up — just a bit — earlier this morning. As the car drove up the driveway to Otis's school, I looked through the window and saw the Jacky janitor thug drinking his morning espresso and smoking. But this time he wasn't alone. Ewan, Otis's friend, was playing patty-cake with Jacky as his cigarette lounged between his lips. When I got out of the back seat, Otis took his bag and ran over to Jacky and Ewan.

"Otis, Otis!" I yelled to stop him.

I was secretly elated. I had never seen Otis this excited since Richard was around — before his true self came to light, and before Otis knew what was happening. Children are smarter than we think.

"Let me play too, let me play too!" Otis yelled as he ran over.

"I'll be right back," I said to the driver, Francis, a five foot five or so petit man from Lyon that had been working for Richard for years, and who I inherited in the deal with Richard.

"Of course, madam," Francis said.

I rushed over to where the boys were.

"I'm sorry, I'm so sorry," I said to Jacky. "I know they don't pay you for this."

He looked up at me. I felt like clutching my purse again. But I didn't this time. There was something gentle and yet mysterious in that closet thug that I didn't see the first time.

Big Bang Theory

"They not have to pay me," he smiled and revealed his gold teeth.

He continued playing with the boys for a moment.

"Coffee?" He took his cigarette out of his mouth and put it out.

I was so surprised. I thought he was going to be rude and crass. We were so different. He was obviously not from my background, and he seemed about twenty hard years older than me. When I first met him, I thought he would curse my existence — out of anger and jealously. And so I hesitated for a moment before responding to his offer for a coffee.

"Yes, thank you," I said with a smile of appreciation on my face.

The kids kept playing as Jacky went inside his dingy closet to make an espresso on his make shift burner. As I stood there watching him play with the kids while the coffee brewed, I thought: Was I wrong about this man? Was there something on the inside that he didn't show to the outside world? Was he someone he did not appear to be?

Part of me knew the answers to my questions. He was sitting there playing with the children like a child himself. I knew he was the farthest thing from a child with his needle marks, atrophied muscles, grey hair, and tattoos. So I had a feeling this man kept up a public front. I just didn't know how much of a front it was.

Jacky looked over at me as he played with the kids with a grim stare. His eyes were hazel colored — a mix between brown, green, and yellow.

They focused intently on me as a panther would his prey right before he pounces. These were hunter eyes — not the nervous always looking over your shoulder eyes of Richard. I felt like I was the only thing in his world at that moment in time.

But his stare didn't scare me. Maybe it should have. It soothed me instead. It brought me outside of my head, from the inside, hiding from the world with my own problems, my own fears, and my own insecurities. I was there and was present with him. His eyes made me feel this. It's like the stare said to me: be careful, I am dangerous, be present or I will sense your fear. That is exactly what I did — I was present.

"Your coffee," he said to me.

I didn't even hear him.

"Your coffee," he held out the small cup of espresso in front of me.

"Oh, oh, thank you," I said, "I'm sorry, I wasn't paying attention," I smiled nervously towards him — I thought about his eyes the whole time.

I think he could tell I wasn't paying attention.

"You want the sugar?" He asked softly.

"No thank you," I moved my hand toward Otis to caress his head as he played. I sipped some of the espresso. It was very good.

"Italian beans?" I asked.

"The only one I using," he lit another cigarette and started playing with the children again. He dropped some ash from his cigarette, and turned towards me, "Jacky," he said as he held out his scarred right hand for me to shake.

"Sophia," I shook his coarse and hard hand. I felt wrinkles and crevices in it — a valley that

had been beat up and cut by years of rain, flooding, and draught or, maybe in his case, waging war against the world.

We stood there having our coffees for five to ten minutes. I felt like we didn't need to speak. I felt calm with the silence. It was natural. It sounds odd. But I felt like I knew this man even though I just met him. There was something about him that was very familiar to me. I didn't feel this calm kinship with Richard, even though his background was closer on paper to mine.

And yet I felt afraid, just like I did when I was with Ginger. I closed myself to what Jacky could maybe offer to me other than good coffee. The fear made me do it.

"Thank you for the coffee, but I must be getting on now as I have appointments."

This was another lie.

I could sense Jacky knew it was a lie, too.

After he struck up another cigarette and slowly placed it in his mouth, he said, with doubting eyes and a knowing smirk, "when you stopping by my high class café again, we serving the fresh croissants."

Now I felt like I knew why the kids loved this man. He seemed like a youngster at heart, but had been worn down all of these years to become aged wine. Plus, maybe they liked him because they sensed he had a whole different world inside they didn't know. But he didn't let them know it in one fell swoop. He did it through little smirks, hand gestures, and glances that, collectively, implicitly gave you a collage of his hidden wisdom.

This has been one of the most interesting days I have had in my life for a long time.

January 17, 1939

This morning was my second morning meeting Jacky. We spoke with such ease — I couldn't believe it! It felt so natural.

"You wanting another coffee?" Jacky said to me as he and Otis did a high five.

"Please, yes, that would be nice." Ewan, Otis's friend, was already there hanging with Jacky. I think Ewan's car is one of the earliest ones to arrive at school for some reason. And so the boys started playing. It was another lovely crisp winter day. The tree branches swayed in the breeze as the wind came in off the river. The air was cool and damp, but refreshing after the long hot summer.

Jacky went in to his closet to start making the coffee with his cigarette dangling from his mouth. I followed him inside and, as he made the black morning potion, I started looking around. His cigarette now sat on the edge of the counter where he did a lot of his woodwork for the school. I also saw his stash of cigarette cartons underneath the work counter in a bag. A few things took me by surprise.

He smoked Chesterfields. I thought it was quite sophisticated for a blue-collar French guy like him. Next to his stash was a tuxedo and a black Borsalino fedora. I had to look twice — I couldn't believe my eyes. It didn't look like any cheap tuxedo either — it looked custom made. I could tell from the look of the fabric. But then I thought to myself:

he was probably holding these things for one of the parents at the school.

"This for you," Jacky held out the coffee.

"Thank you."

We walked outside to stand in front of the closet door entrance.

"May I have one?" *I couldn't believe I asked for one of his cigarettes. I usually wouldn't be so forward, but I felt like I could with him.*

He lifted a cigarette from the box and held it out. I was taller than Jacky and so he had to angle up his arm to me from below. He stood about five foot seven and I was about five foot nine. Our different sizes — and ages — endeared him to me for some reason.

I put the cigarette in my mouth and he pulled out a Zippo lighter to light me up. I had seen these lighters starting to get some traction in France, even though they were American.

"Thank you," *I said as he lit my cigarette and then went to light his own.*

"Is my pleasure," *he smiled a blighted smile. It was a hidden gem to see — I had a feeling his life tarnished his spirit, and yet it still shined through via this faint smile of his.*

"I won," *I heard Otis say in the background to Ewan.*

"No, I won!" *I heard Ewan say back to Otis.*

"Okay, okay," *Otis said.* "You got me this time!"

Jacky turned to me to show me a good wolf guarding his flock of sheep grin.

"Your husband," *Jacky started to say but then took a drag off his cigarette,* "is proud of Otis?" *He took a sip of his coffee as he looked at the boys.*

I was speechless. I didn't know if I could open up to this man. I regretted that I didn't with Ginger. I didn't want to make the same mistake again.

"I am actually divorced," I took a nervous hit off my cigarette.

Jacky's hazel eyes turned their gaze upon me, and I turned to look at him with my blue ones, unsure if he was judging me or not.

"I sure you have the reasons." He put out his cigarette as if he were putting a period on the statement — crushing the cigarette a few times in the ashtray on the wooden chair that was outside even after it was clearly out. He lit another.

"I did," I nodded. "May I have another?"

He held out another cigarette for me as we stood there next to the door of his janitor closet with our espresso cups. The boys played in front of us. He lit me up — and when I say that I mean more than just my cigarette.

"Thank you," I cracked a guarded smile.

He nodded.

I took a puff and we watched as more children started arriving at school. I confided slightly to him.

"There were many reasons — but there was one that I could not just look over," I looked at him through the corner of my eye as I blew my smoke out upwards.

"I thinking I can guess which reason this for you," he looked at me knowingly.

"And?" I sipped my coffee.

"He not having the loyalty," a sharpshooter who hits his target on his first attempt.

I nodded to him. He put his espresso cup on his chair, next to the ashtray.

"I tipping my hat for you," he tipped his imaginary hat my direction.

"Why?" I asked with secret self-hatred.

"Look around," he waved his hand towards the mothers arriving with children. *"You thinking they would have done it too like you? You think they giving up the pretty security for the ugly truth?"*

I didn't want to listen. The insecure part of me tried to stop me from listening. But I knew better. I felt like Jacky was helping the pretty part of me came out. He was helping the good side win in that civil war within me.

"No," I said as I slightly looked to the ground. *"They would rather live the lie,"* I looked in his direction, surprised at his insightfulness.

He patted me on the shoulder.

"The lie for most peoples has more pretty than the truth. The lie has the glamour dress, perfume from Paris, expensive lipstick. But she have nothing under these things when you scratch with your fingers the outside away. This outside is the false oasis of our minds, no?"

I looked at him. I had never met a man who spoke to me like this. I couldn't believe it was coming from him. He could tell he had an interested audience.

"It takes courage to make a split like you did, especially in your high class waters," he said looking towards the driveway. *"In our time, where the wicked men winning women with money — not with this four-letter word we calling the love."*

He looked passionately at me.

"Thank you for saying this to me."

> "This not necessary," he said as he took my coffee cup and his to put them inside his little closet. "You must be thanking yourself."
>
> I heard the bell ring for school.
>
> "I had better be going."
>
> "You have the appointments?" He smiled sarcastically.
>
> "Every day," I said back to him in a touché way. "In all sincerity," I put my hand softly on his shoulder, "thank you for today."
>
> "This my pleasure. Maybe we have the other days to talking."
>
> "That would be nice," I nodded.

My martini was almost gone. I wanted another. I liked reading the diaries with a little bit of a buzz. Maybe the booze helped me see another side of things that I wasn't able to see.

"Heya, Tony," I said over to his direction. "I am getting a little dry here," I pointed to my empty glass.

"Hey, look at de college boy tying one on! Maybe I'll take a picture of dis day for later?" He smiled a smart-ass smile. "You got it, son," he said after a slight pause. "I got one coming right up for you."

"Thanks, T."

"You got it," he said with a smirk.

I closed Sophia's diary and opened up Jacky's. I wanted to see what he thought of her. Tony came over with the second martini as I was opening up Jacky's diary.

"I made this one with gin," he smiled, "cauz, uh, I tink dem herbs inside dera going to make you nice and loopy," he smiled devilishly.

I nodded and raised my glass to him.

"Cheers, Tony."

"Hey, enjoy it, junior," he said back to me.

I sipped the drink and started reading in Jacky's diary.

January 19, 1939

I never think I get to know woman like this Sophia. She classy. I not feel this way. I feel no class, I small minded man, I the simple man. I surprised she like be with the man like me. Maybe cause I know a world she is don't know? Maybe I know things she never knowing but wants to knowing?

This morning I have seen her third time. I smoke my cigarette, drink my coffee. I need my morning friends to welcome me. Every night I hitting the family clubs in this city. I leaving school late so nobody seeing me wearing my night working clothes. I live the two lives. That is the way the family want me to living. This is not easy. I hide in open. I hiding when I in front of this women. But I like to knowing her more.

But I can't. She can't knowing me.

"I see you know how to spending your days, Jacky, sitting in same spot, same time, doing same thing," she saying to me with smile this morning. Otis come running to me. I playing with Ewan. Sophia hanging her coat for the rain on hanger inside my closet. It small raining when Sophia and Otis come. A dark and sad day outside with the clouds. But I feel happiness inside when they coming to my universe.

"Habit — she my girlfriend," I says to Sophia. "I love her. I know what going to happen one day to next, from one month to next, you see?" I looking out to driveway where all the cars coming to bringing the children for the school.

"I appreciate that," she saying. "You know I just teasing," she put her classy clean hand on my dirty shoulder.

"I know," I saying to her. "I am old tree. I dropping the little pieces of branches. But the main part of me sticking around for the long time. You want the coffee?"

"Please," she saying in shy way. I starting the flame on the burner.

"Cigarette?" She holding out the Chesterfield box — this my favorite. I look at her with surprise eyes. She smoke the same as me. She is liking me. They say when a person copying you it is best of the compliments, I thinks.

"Thank you," I lighting our cigarettes.

The boys playing. Coffee starting to boil. I pouring her some. She liking the coffee black. This surprising me.

"Thank you," she says with lady smile. I put coffee in her hands.

I sit on wooden chair and she stand watch the boys playing. Cool wet air use her fingers to touching our faces as this breeze coming off the river.

"Is good to be free," I say watching the children playing the tag.

"What you mean?" She drink her coffee with the nervous feelings.

"Really want to know?" I looking at her pretty eyes.

"Yes," she nod to me, "I do."

"I was in Sante — five years."

She look at me for many moments and thinking. I could tell.

"What they charge you with?" She finally ask as she puff.

"Making the fake money," I says.

"Where they say you doing this?" She asking me.

"Marseille."

She looked at kids playing before she saying something again.

"What it like in there?" She asking me.

"It like a sewer with rats that talking and all the drugs you wanting," I looked over at her.

She looks at me like I crazy.

"But really it good if habit is your girlfriend. We waking up at same time every day, eating lunch at same time, go to sleeping at the same time. Most calm and rest I have in long time. My cellmates is good company, and we shoot . . ." I stop before telling her.

"Shoot what?" She looking at me with the curious eyes. She touch my shoulder and wanting me to go on, "please, Jacky, you can telling me. I tell you about my family. This hard for me."

I feel good with this woman. On outside, she different than me. I scared she looking to judge. But I feel like she not asking to judge me. She asking me cause she wanting to open me up. She wanting me to do same with her.

"The shit into my body with needles, needles, needles — as many as I can find to sticking in the arms," I looking at her as I slapping my arms with the hands.

She look at me with pain on her face.

I looking away with the shame towards the children.

"It's alright, Jacky," she soft touched my shoulder again. "I have feeling in my heart you had your reasons," she saying to me.

"Yes. Every day the same. You taking it and everything is fine. The needles is my best friends when I inside," I light up another cigarette, "then there is the mates with me in the this shit cell. They like the brothers to me, understand? They and the needles is all I needing in there."

"Who your cellmates?" She asking.

"Counterfeiter, bank robber, two hit men," I look up at her.

"All star cast. Just missing the dog for your mascot," she put her sunny pretty smile my way.

"They all star outcasts," I said when I realize how these, how you say, savants would have been businessmen of top style but had directing their energies toward the black market crafts.

"They did the shit too?" She asking.

"Yes," I nodding to her.

"Still have the urge to hurt yourself more?" She point holes on my arms with worry eyes.

"Sometimes," I saying not knowing — I guess I in between.

I scared. I not have feelings for a long time and I know this woman never care about guy like me. I feeling the danger of getting the hurt by her. I wanting to smash that feeling of this pain — I not want to feel nothing for nobody.

"Jacky, I knowing heart break. You know from what I telling you about my husband. Some of these feelings coming back when you telling me you want to shoot that stuff in your arm." This time *she making sure to look in my eyes. "I am here to talk to if you need an ear."*

She looking back to the little ones. I guessing she care. But I not want to show her I knew. I feeling more scared than I had feel in my life — a woman who might care, but who I could lose in next second — a hit, an accident, a tumor, she don't love me no more?

She talking over my thinking.

"Seriously," she looking back towards me and putting her hand on my shoulder.

"Thank you," I nodding my head in gratefulness from my heart — this woman good.

"You say the sweet things other day," Sophia saying, "it meaning much to me. My way of saying thank you is to telling you what I just tell you. This hard for me. I not like showing people my emotions. I not like relying on the other people. I like stick to myself. But you is the fresh air I not feel in long time." She stopping to look at Otis and Ewan. "I wanting to let you know this."

She giving me her coffee.

"I have to get go now," she say in the scared run from yourself way, "I see you soon, Jacky," she rubbing my shoulder.

"Yes, soon," I say back not believing her.

She taking the kids and walking them to the class. I sitting in my empty closet. I wonder when she realize she making this biggest mistake of her life in getting to know me — dark, dirty, dangerous closet man. My bottom of the ocean world will ruin her, I thinks to myself. Or maybe this the shitty dark demon self talking.

Dirty Quiet Money

I could not help but wonder that most people, at some level, feel the same things about themselves that Jacky was feeling — not worthy, not up to snuff, not up to par. I often feel that way about myself. Maybe that's why I don't ever talk to the women in the Tavern. Maybe, like Jacky, I am scared that once I find love, I won't know what to do with it out of fear that I will lose it, at any moment. This thought terrified me. It scared Jacky, too, even though his soul was already scarred, bruised, and wrinkled. So I was learning a lot from Jacky.

"How about one more for the road?" Tony said to me from the background.

"I won't be on the road too long if I have another one," I said back to him.

"That's the point," he slapped me on the shoulder — one construction worker celebrating with another after finishing part of a tough house.

Tony went to make my drink. I closed Jacky's diaries and moved back to Sophia's. Tony came by with my gin martini after a minute or so after concocting my roadie.

"Thank you," I said to him.

"You got it. Now get back to your reading dere," he pointed to the diaries, "so I can go back to the dames," he pointed down towards the end of the bar.

I took a sip of the drink and opened up Sophia's diary.

> *February 20, 1939*
>
> *Today was a lovely winter day. The crispness in the air let you know that spring was just behind the dead of winter — short days, cold weather, and rushing from house to house to evade the cold.*
>
> *I saw Jacky again this morning.*
>
> *I am surprising myself. I feel like I need to see him. It has become a nice routine for me. If someone had told me back in New Orleans that I would be*

having coffee and cigarettes with a former convict at my son's school, I would have told them to stop smoking opium!

But maybe they would not have been so nuts.

"Good morning, Jacky," I said to him as I arrived with my custom-made wool coat shrouded over my shoulder. Otis was with me. He rushed off to the playground.

Jacky was sitting there on his wooden chair, smoking his Chesterfield, and drinking his coffee. He looked tired, like he had late nights somewhere, but I don't know where. His hours weren't long at the school. Maybe he had a woman on the side? Perhaps he wasn't showing all of himself to me? I had a feeling there was more to this man than met the eye.

"The espressos and the cigarettes — the woman's best friends?" He said as he got up off his chair to go inside his little closet to start making my espresso. I put my coat up on the closet coat hanger. I walked out to stand by the door and look at the children being rustled into the school doors by the drivers, butlers, and mothers.

"Here," he handed the coffee to me. A cigarette was neatly placed on the small plate with a cut of lemon. I smiled coyly at him. "Thank you," I sipped his luscious coffee and picked up the cigarette.

He lit my cigarette before he sparked up another for himself. I started puffing slowly and intently.

I imagined myself kissing him.

"You not have the man since your husband?" He asked in his broken syntax grammar as he blew out the smoke.

I was happy he was curious about my life. I was also scared. I didn't know if he would judge me if I told him about Ginger. I paused in fear. I took some more drags off the cigarette.

"You don't need to telling me," he stood next to me watching what I was watching.

"No," I looked over to him. "I want to tell you — I need to tell. There was only one. Her name was Ginger," I said quietly.

"Good taste in names, no?" He smirked. "Nice on the eyes, too, I bet this woman was, yes?" A smart aleck smile followed.

He made me feel funny — not self-conscious — about her. It was so not consistent with my upbringing. My life so far made me feel like I wasn't living up to what my parents wanted me to be like, first because I got divorced and, second, I was in love, albeit temporarily, with a woman. But Jacky enabled made me to feel comfortable about myself. I opened up to him about what happened — and what didn't happen — with Ginger. I smashed the cigarette nervously on the ground with my boot.

"Keeping in touch with her?" He asked.

"No," I said with regret.

"Why not?" He slightly brushed my shoulder with his hand like he was disappointed. "A quality woman, no?"

"How would you know?" I looked over at him.

He looked up at me defiantly as he slowly extracted the cigarette from his mouth.

*"How you **don't** know?" He gave me a I won the case, the race, and with grace smile.*

"Well," I paused, "I guess you have a point," I looked away from him. I wanted to act like I was

upset with him for challenging me. Yet, deep down, I loved that he did. So many men in my life are yes men — they say yes to everything I say, want, just because they want to please. They put me on a pedestal I don't want to be on.

Jacky took me off that pedestal. I loved being off it. It made me feel like a woman. It made me feel human — not some object for the arm.

He cut my thoughts short.

"Sometimes, Sophia, you needing to putting yourself outside. Yes, it is scary," he smashed his cigarette into the ground, "but it make you feel more alive, no? Living in little bubble seem safe. You stay away from the things out of control. But these helping you becoming the woman you meant to be, understanding me?"

"Another?" He held out his cigarette box.

"No thank you," I waved my hand. I didn't know how to respond. I didn't expect any of it. I didn't know how to respond even if I was expecting it.

He called me on my stuff.

He lit up his cigarette and we sat there silent for a moment.

"You are a smart cookie, Jacky," I turned to him and said in a sincere tone. "I don't know if anybody has told you that before, but I wanted to tell you."

He turned to me.

"Why you saying this?"

"Saying what?"

"Why tell me I am the smart cookie?"

"Because you have told me things that nobody has ever told me before. You know me very well even though you don't really know me at all. Part of that

is because you are the smart cookie I just said you were. Part of it also is that maybe you and I are more alike on the inside than we are on the outside."

He looked up at me.

"Maybe we the two peas in the pod, car, on horse, of course?" He smiled with his stained teeth. I had to ignore the teeth and focus on him, his comments, his warmth.

"You could say that," I smiled shyly. I wanted to let him know that I liked him, but I didn't want to let him know how much.

A woman has to have her secrets.

Soon it was time for me to go. I had to meet a lawyer to discuss money payments from Richard.

"This time, I really do have a meeting to head to," I put my left hand on his shoulder."

"Meeting in your head?"

"In real life," I smiled.

"Have the good meeting," he held out his hand for me to shake.

I looked around to make sure nobody was watching. I worried what Otis's friends' parents might think seeing me talk to an underworld guy like Jacky. He saw me do it and I could tell it hurt him. I then realized what I had done. I had reverted backwards to what my New Orleans uptown brainwashing told me to do — always keep up appearances, you never know who is going to see you! I didn't know what to say or do to make him feel better other than leaning over to kiss him goodbye on both cheeks.

That's exactly what I did — very softly.

He looked at me — touched, surprised, hopeful. I could tell he thought there might be something more to our relationship than morning coffee and cigarettes. That scared me. I knew the fire was starting in him, a fire that I ignited and I felt the need to put it out a little bit.

"I'll see you when I see you," I said in a Devil may care tone. He was a snow flake that could be here, not here, and I wouldn't know the difference.

There was pain in his eyes after I said this — I could tell. He didn't know if we had a real connection, or if I would just fly away one day without saying goodbye, like I didn't care.

It hurt him. But I didn't know how else to act. I was scared to feel this way. The only way I know how to act was to light the fire and yet also want to put it out. Bottom line was that I was doing all of these gymnastics because of one simple fact: I was falling in love with him.

At first, I felt like she would probably want to hurt him so that he would stay away from her. And yet, as I read on, I saw that another part of her wanted him in her arms.

I understand these conflicted feelings. But Jacky did not understand them at all. He thought maybe she didn't like him, and even wanted to hurt him. Perhaps the worse part of it was that Jacky took it all personally. He felt like it was **him** she was rejecting, and not **herself** for loving a man that she was scared to love.

"O-fucking-k, Chicago boy," Tony jarred me out of my thoughts.

I looked. Tony was tapping his watch. I had been so engaged with the diary that I lost track of time. It was closing time at the bar. I was the last person there — other than Tony.

"Sorry, T," I shook my head back and forth, "I guess I lost track of time."

"Yeah, yeah, yeah, that's what I said to this broad last night that I was on the dime with," he smiled raffishly.

"Let me settle up," I did a signing something motion with my right hand.

"Do it later, Mr. Chicago, I got a hot date," he squirted some cologne on his neck. It was the type of cologne you could smell from down the street on a long Chicago block even when the wind is blowing, the snow is flowing, and the fires in the trash cans on the street are glowing.

I smiled at Tony. He smiled back at me in the mirror as he tightened his tie.

"Thanks, Tony."

"You got it, kiddo," he said as he continued changing out of his work outfit into what looked like his date outfit.

I smiled at him through the mirror as I got my things into my sack.

I was done reading the entries that Sophia had given me. I was eager to go and see her tomorrow afternoon to get more diaries about what happened during the war, and afterwards.

I couldn't wait.

CHAPTER 8
Sex, Drugs, & Jazz

February 23, 1939
I watching this needle hit my skin last night. I only feel the relief, the safety, the warmth.
This needle is like the fire next to a cold winter beach with no sun at night and stars looking down on you. You alone but you not feel alone cause you having the needle and starlight is hugging you. I feel happy like I did before momma dies.
I getting feelings for Sophia. This making me want to get away and not feeling nothing — in my needle, my vein, no more pain. Thanks to God I do the needle again! I feel safe like I feels safe in Le Sante.

After I glanced over Jacky's diary entry above, which Sophia had just given to me in her Park Avenue apartment full of cigarette smoke the next evening, I realized something: Jacky had gone back on the stuff to run — from himself, from Sophia, from freedom. He didn't like being out — other than playing with the children or being next to the ocean. But the rest of it he could do without.

Paris, while beautiful, didn't fit him well. And yet I had a feeling he would have dealt with it all — working at the school, living in Paris, and being away from the inside — if Sophia's pushing and pulling didn't make him feel like he needed to escape.

Escape he did.

"Cat got your tongue?" Sophia said to me as she sat, chicly dressed, on her couch.

"No," I reached for my cigarettes in my satchel.

When I arrived earlier, Winston told me Sophia just got home from a long trip down to Louisiana. He told me she had meetings down there with Governor McKeithen about the use of the foundation's funds for educational initiatives around the state. Winston hinted to keep my visit short because Sophia was tired.

Sophia's feistiness hid her fatigue.

"Here," she held out her cigarette box. "Please take one of mine," her smile showed her sky white teeth through her light pink lipstick. She was wearing an elegant sleeveless black polka dot Valentino dress.

"Thank you," I took one.

She held out her lighter. That surprised me. I was usually the one that lit her cigarettes. I was brought up that way. And I guess that is why I liked being around her. She was not your regular run of the mill gal. She did things other women didn't do, and would never have the courage to do. She inspired me.

"So what did you think?" She nodded to the diaries I had just brought back and took a sip of her nightly martini.

"Addictive," I smiled.

"I forgot my manners, please forgive me," she put down her martini, "Something to drink?"

"I'll have what you are having."

"Winston, Winston," she directed her attention into the kitchen, "be a love and make Hank one of your smashing martinis."

"It'll be right up," I heard from inside the kitchen.

She looked back at me.

"So why were they addictive?" I could see she usually wore simple petit white gloves with her lean fitting dress — she had her gloves on the top of the coffee table. She was off duty, but she was not off.

"Your friction with Jacky enchanted me," I said looking at Jacky's diaries I had just given back to Sophia. They were flirting with her white gloves as though Jacky was inching up to her any way he could. "You were both from such different backgrounds and yet your hearts both seemed to tremble with the same fears. It is like they . . ."

"Beat together?" She asked with a rhetorical tone as she looked outside the window towards the illustrious Park Avenue apartments across the street. She looked back and gave me what I think was the same type of smile that made Jacky feel so good with her, but which also made him so sad when she pulled back. In a way, that smile made him go back to the smack.

"Yes," I nodded. "But I also think that you didn't want your hearts to beat together. You were so scared about what that meant."

I took a long drag.

"I mean, from Jacky's view, you were from this highfalutin background and family. He saw you as being from the other side of the tracks," I took another drag. "He felt insecure around you because he didn't know if he could compare to others in your life — Richard, your father, and so on. He was David and your background was the Goliath."

Sophia listened as she sipped her martini and calmly puffed her cigarette — I took the silence as implied consent to continue.

"The same probably went for you. You saw him as this nefarious character who could not be trusted. That is what you were brought up to think — bad guys wear black hats, do bad things, and will hurt you if you get next to them. Plus, you probably didn't think he had any money, and you were used to being around money growing up. I don't mean that you consciously thought all of this, now," I looked at her to make sure she understood I wasn't judging her. "It's just that it is hard to break those habits as you — as we — get older . . . unless you consciously work on breaking them everyday."

I took an even longer drag off my cigarette — a long distance runner taking some water close to the finish line — and kept thinking out loud. She looked at me with her ocean calm blue eyes. I felt like she enjoyed what I was saying — maybe it was like the student showing the teacher what he learned so far.

"But Jacky seemed more cavalier about it all. He had less to lose. He just got out of prison, had never really had any relationships, and then all of a sudden he meets a woman like you. I think that is when things changed for him."

Sophia started looking outside the window as she listened to me. She looked back at me with a slight nod so as to proceed while she slowly sipped her drink — oil for her brain, maybe as she processed what I was saying.

"You were sensitive because Richard burned you. Part of you hated yourself because you felt like it was your fault. Needless to say, perhaps," I shrugged my shoulders and took another swig of my booze, "but it's hard to let someone love you — or to love someone — when you hate yourself. And yet you knew that Jacky was a rare bird. You wouldn't get an opportunity to meet a man like him — perhaps ever. This inner conflict, I think, caused you to push him away, and then pull him in."

There was a short pause between us when the only sound we could hear was the traffic on Park Avenue. She broke the silence after she had another two more sips of her cocktail.

"You are very perceptive, Hank," she said with a surprised pleased customer smile that these insights would come from a young Midwest man like me.

"Sir, your drink," Winston came with my martini and handed it over.

"Much obliged," I smiled towards him.

"Enjoying yourself?" He asked almost like he had heard it all before from her.

"Yes," I said smiling back at him.

"Good," he patted me on the shoulder. His touch said: "stay here, chap, and you will get a doctorate in a field called things you never knew, and that you never thought you'd know," he smiled warmly.

"You are a love," Sophia said to him and blew him a parade kiss.

I looked back at her. She started opening up to me, perhaps because she knew that she could trust me, or maybe because she thought I was smart enough to understand her complexity. Or maybe it was a little bit of both.

"I wasn't ready for him, Hank. I wasn't ready for a guy like him at the time. And yet I needed just what he had to offer."

"Meaning?" I sipped my drink.

"Let me see how to explain it," she paused to look outside the bay window. "Ever been swimming with friends when you were younger?"

"Yes," I nodded and sipped more.

"Everybody is in the ocean, pool, or lake, and then there is often one hold out. That one person who thinks the water is going to be too cold, too deep, or too dirty. They sit there in their bathing suit wondering if they should jump in or not."

I paused to think and then remembered:

"Come to think of it, I took a trip one time with friends from college to Michigan. We were all in the lake. There was this one girl who was in her bathing suit. Part of her wanted to jump, but the other part worried: Is the water too cold? Isn't a lifeguard around?"

Sophia blew her cigarette smoke up to the ceiling.

"I bet y'all nudged her to jump in. You knew she needed to jump in because she would regret it if she didn't and went back into the house, while her friends were out there having fun."

"Yes," I puffed my cigarette, "she eventually jumped in. She screamed because the water was so cold, but it was also exciting to her — I remember her smiling and getting into a water fight with me. If I remember right, this gal was a real control freak, didn't like doing things that were out of her control, or else she got anxiety."

Sophia took a big sip of her martini and asked:

"So she was relieved to jump in once she did. But she initially didn't want to, right darling?"

"She didn't get what she wanted, but she got what she needed," I said.

"Precisely," she softly slapped her knee in agreement. "Jacky was that lake to me. I didn't want to like him. I didn't even want to be around him in the start. But I eventually found that I *needed* him. He gave me strength I had never felt before."

"Care for another?" I held out my box of cigarettes.

"Please," she said softly.

I handed her a cigarette and held out my lighter. The room was full of our smoke and smelled of martinis.

"Thank you," she puffed and looked up to the ceiling to ruminate.

I sipped more of my martini. I was pretty tipsy and loose at this point.

"I think you hid your need for Jacky pretty well, Sophia, from what I read so far," I said as a doctor would his patient.

"You are right, Hank."

She paused.

"Not something I am proud of," she held the cigarette in the corner of her mouth and looked down at the ashtray on the coffee table.

"I didn't mean to judge, you know, I was just . . ."

"Giving me your observations. I appreciate it. You are absolutely right," she nodded in agreement. "I am ashamed about how my fears conquered me in the start with him."

"Why are you ashamed about it now?" I asked.

"Because of the effect it had on him. He didn't deserve it — he was kind and open to me."

"So he was hurt by your warm and then cold and then warm act?" I asked like I didn't know.

"More than you know now," she looked at me gravely and then handed me the new diary entries. "You'll see in these what he did to take the pain away."

I took the diaries. That's when I quickly read peek at Jacky's entry above from February 23, 1939. I got a glimpse into the effect she had on this man. I wondered how far Jacky went to take his pains away and what she did to stop him. I could only imagine as I sat there.

"Take good care of those, dear," she touched my hand with hers. "Some of my most sorrowful days, but they are the ones that made me feel most alive. It was when I was sad that I realized, later on, what it meant to be happy. And what it meant to be happy was to be with him."

She put out her cigarette in the ashtray.

"I should be turning in for the evening. I had a long trip to Louisiana, and have another one tomorrow in New Jersey, where I am meeting with the governor," she got up off the couch and took her gloves.

"Please leave any messages you have with Winston. He will get them to me."

We gave one another a kiss on each check and a warm hug.

"Thank you," I said as we did.

"My pleasure. You are helping me relive some of the best and worst times of my life. I thank you for that," she gave me a grandmother to grandson pat on the cheek.

I left Sophia's illustrious digs on Park Avenue for my haunt at the Tavern. The night was chilly. It was the start of fall in New York. Some Octobers are warm, but this one was brisk. The cool wind wrapped itself like a wet blanket around my face as I walked down Park Avenue.

It was about eight in the evening on a Friday night, and the subway was full of: longhaired youngsters wearing ripped jeans, leather vests, and bandanas around their heads. They were probably going out in the Village to hear music and/or listen to poetry. There were also preppy dressed couples from Westchester and other places outside the city who wanted to hit the town for dinner, and college kids wearing their Princeton and other school sweaters who wanted to come to the big city for the weekend.

Instead of following the stream of strangers to walk the streets of the West Village, I headed to my bat cave at the Tavern. Part of me didn't care that I wasn't like the rest of the folks on the train. This is the part of me that wanted to be different like Jacky and Sophia. The other part of me did care. That other part of me felt like I wasn't doing what I should be doing with my life at my age — settling down, having a family, and so on. Reading about Jacky and Sophia made that other part of myself — the ashamed afraid part — feel slightly more comfortable.

But I still didn't totally feel comfortable with that other part of myself.

And yet I know that Jacky wouldn't have gotten to where he got to if he just followed the crowd. The same is true of Sophia. Their diaries started making me feel more comfortable about myself. In reading them, I wasn't only learning more about these two amazing people — I was also learning how to love myself.

When I got to the Tavern, the usual cast was there.

"What'll have, pal," Tony asked as I sat down. On my right was a stunning blond couple from The Netherlands, and on my left were what looked like pretty sisters — one blond, the other brunette — in their 20s catching up on their lives.

"How about a scotch?"

"Iz you asking me, or iz you telling me?"

"Oh, yea, well, asking," I said unsure of myself.

Tony patted me on the shoulder.

"Hey, loosen the fuck up, what you got, fucking hemorrhoids?"

He lovingly smiled at me.

"Sorry, Tony," I am just eager to get reading, and I pointed to the diaries.

"Yea, yea," he said with a poo-poo tone. "Them diaries aren't going to go anywhere, you know," and then he leaned over, "but them dames next to you ain't going to be there foreva," he said.

I looked at him like the conflicted woman looked at the lake in Michigan — part of me wanted to talk to the women, but the other part of me was scared to.

"It's alright, Tony," I said to him, "I have a bunch of work do to here," the excuse I always give myself.

"Alright, alright," he put his hands up, "but don't say I don't try, kid."

Tony had a point. I was too much to myself. I was afraid of my emotions. I wouldn't be able to measure up to the old money men like Richard. So I just kept away. And yet I knew I needed that companionship. Maybe I would go there when I was ready.

"Here you go, pal, your Oban," Tony laid the scotch in front of me. Tonight, on his right pinky, he wore a fancy gold ring with a diamond on it. It shined when he left the drink on the bar. I haven't asked him what the ring means — yet.

"Thanks, T," I said.

"You got it," he smiled to me, "let old Tony know if you need anyting else."

"Sure thing."

I took a sip of the scotch. The martini at Sophia's had worn off by this time. And so the scotch helped ease the anxiety of sitting next to these two beautiful sisters and not talking to them. I had two sets of diaries in front of me — one from Jacky, and the other from Sophia. I opened up Jacky's because of the February 23, 1939, entry I read in Sophia's apartment.

February 25, 1939

Never been the man who fucking all of the women that I can fucking. I love the women, love to watch the body of the woman, love smelling them, love eating the pussy. But I not fuck them all. I putting my eyes on the feast of pussy I have, not on the next pretty pussy that coming — or maybe is not coming.

This changing last night.

I leaving the school. I wear my tuxedo. I have the clubs to visit. The first in Montmarte. I not know it, but it was my last for night. I not plan this. It just happening this way.

The club was Chat Noir. It full of the beautiful women. Some women was with women. This the new thing in Paris. The women who fucking the women. It about 11:30 when I getting to club, which is the cave — have to go down the stairs to get there, candles is your only lights. People doing as they like — women jerking the cocks quiet under the table, fucking in bathroom, in the dark corners, but you not seeing what is going on because it so dark and everybody dress the nice dress.

Mickey was the security this night. I always likes when he did. He keep the things calm because he look at the people behind his black sunglasses — they not act up when he around. His dark size and look cool the people down.

"Ciao, Jacky," Mickey says when I walking in. He kiss me on cheeks. Mickey speaking the Italian and act more Italian than an Irishman in the France. He the hard man to putting into the hole of the pigeon, no?

Sex, Drugs, & Jazz

"Ciao," I saying back to him. Mickey about half my age. I giving him my hat, overcoat, scarf.

We standing in club's long way for the entry. It small, narrow tunnel that lit only by the candles. After you passing through this tunnel, the main room of club putting her arms around you: 600 square meters, 15-meter ceilings, 8 art deco lights on the pretty ceiling. Small tables spread like the bread crumbs like all over this main room. Center of room cleared so people could do the dancing, kissing, touching, petting in the darkness of the morning. We having one of best chefs on staff — short, lean, man named the Benoit Pepin. He make best fucking dishes in Paris.

I looking inside big room. My local jazz band favorite called The Desperados is playing the music. They is the mix of white and Negro jazz players from Paris and Africa. Most have the prison in history. The family get them gigs so they make money without going back to the prison — we loving their music so much we not want to miss. The Desperados mostly play the new tunes from States. When I get in that last night, they playing "Stormy Weather," by this man I love Duke Ellington.

What am I seeing in front of my wanting to fuck eyes? Three of most expensive pussy in city — they sitting drinking, laughing, in red velvet private booth against walls. These booths have the small drapes that people can use to make their dirt go away from people's eyes in the club when they wanting.

I looking at these pretty pricey pussies. They looking back at me and raising their glasses to me. I been out of Le Sante and many people is happy

I was out. They all drinking the champagne. The long haired red head waved me to come over. I pointing to my chest. You wanting me?

The red head nodding the yes.

I looking back to Mickey. He standing behind me in entrance.

"Some not so secret lovers tonight," he smiled, walking over to me, pat me on back.

Mickey know I shy. Being on inside for so long, outside was the stranger to me. A child who forgetting how to riding the pussy bicycle?

"It a work night," I says to Mickey, and . . .

"Jacky, I know how long you been inside. You need to go there," he pointing to women and looking back at my eyes through his glasses of blackness.

But it not the professional to be with them, I says to myself.

Mickey not care.

"Man got his needs," he smile. "Now go over there. I make the plans in case you not make it to other clubs," he give me one more good guy pat on the back.

Mickey the very powerful man when you feeling his heavy long paw of the bear on your back.

"If you saying so," I give him the smile like the father would give his son after the son telling his father to do the new things.

I walk to three women. The dance floor full — Parisian politicians and business people. Wives dancing with lady lovers, husbands dancing with boy lovers, other couples dancing. I part this sea of peoples in the fog of smoke.

I get to booth. The red head standing up.

"Elodie." She giving me soft kiss on cheeks. Her neck smelling like the lavender. She tall and wearing the very tight black dress with no back. It wrapped around her neck and show her freckle shoulders. The dress go down past knees. She not wearing any stockings. I wonder if she not wearing the panties. I think of her wet pussy. I want to kissing it.

"These my friends," Elodie putting her piano player long fingers on my back — I look down and see she wear black snakeskin heels that making her very tall. Her red hair was thick and go down to her ass. Black pearl necklace, black pearl earrings, bright red lipstick making me want to kiss her mouth after I kissing the pussy. Her fingernails in bright red.

"This is Josette," she show me to this Negro angel sitting next to her. Josette standing up, give me the two kisses. She smell of the honeysuckle. Her dress is black lace gown that go to just below bottom of her pussy and ass. Josette wear snakeskin heels — natural snakeskin color. Long white pearl necklace, white pearl earrings, same red lipstick that Elodie wore. Bright pink nail polish on her long black fingers. I wanting her hands on my back as I cum in her pretty insides.

"Very nice," I says with the big smile.

"And this is Ditte," Josette presenting me to Danish goddess. Long blond hair that go below ass, this black cocktail dress that wrap around shoulder and touch her tits. Her dress short like the others. I love looking at this woman's milk color thighs. She wearing the black snake skin heels that

I wanting her to walking on me with and then licking my ass, is good!

Ditte kiss my cheeks. Smell like the fresh orange in this club of the cigar smoke and the booze.

"Don't be shy, come sit with us," Ditte say to me with the warm red lips that I wanting around my cock. She wrap her arm into mine to say we don't take the no for the answer.

"Why not?" I says.

This is when the fucking night starting.

"Dom Perignon," Ditte say to waiter.

I sit in middle of girls. Elodie and Josette is on the right, Ditte on left. Red drapes of booth was open. I look over to Mickey and shrugging. I don't know what night having for me. Girls smiling at me, I smiling nervously at the girls, with the worry I not good enough for this pretty pussy, me the dirty face janitor from the Marseille.

In the sudden, I feel Elodie hand sit on my thigh. I also feel hand on my other thigh. Their hands staying there for rest of night — until I going bathroom with Ditte.

Waiter coming back with the champagne and this Russian caviar — is the best. We drinking champagne and eat the caviar. By one in morning, this place is ripping with people. Smoke in air. I loving the women and their hands.

Desperado band starting to playing "Blue Moon," Ditte lean over to me, she whispering: "come to the toilet with me." She squeezing my knee. Her blue eyes saying everything — she wanting to do the heroin snow or the coke. I like both. I not say no to this shit! Jacky is no fool!

I nod the yes.

She looking over to other girls. They all nodding yes. They having this planned. Ditte taking my hand to walk to dark corner away from the entrance. Under her arm is black pouch purse. I know she not have the perfume in there. We walking down the stone stairs to the bathroom by the candle lights. She opening the wood door to bathroom. Door have the peep hole in the middle so peoples inside can seeing who on outside wanted to get inside.

"After you," she say with the smile.

I walking into bathroom with the stone walls.

Ditte locking door. She putting her black bag on sink. It is a rock with bottom cut under and the water coming from above through this little metal pipe.

She looking at me — "you want it?"

I wanting both — the smack and her pussy. I nodding yes. I have not done the needle since Le Sante, but I need her.

She pull out long needle, spoon, lighter, coke — 30 grams of it. I like to fuck on the coke. Ditte make my hit on sink — coke in spoon, cook it, into needle.

"For you," she my priest holding spoon for me to take the communion, like the good catholic boy? I take off jacket, roll up sleeve, wrapping my arm with the rubber tube so veins pop this night. After landing strip on my arm is ready, I look as needle go into vein, I feel good in my brain.

I taking rubber tube off my arm and I rest against stone wall like it my bed. Ditte make her landing strip on foot — she too expensive pussy for marks on the arm.

After she take hit, she look at me. We hugging. I kiss her neck, chest, ears. She grabbing my cock as I pushing her against bathroom wall.

This last for what seem like the hour — but it only minutes or so after I look at my watch when we leaving and sitting back down with girls in the nice booth.

"You like?" Elodie asking. She kissing my cheek and put hand on my lap.

"I love," I saying.

"We going to do same then we go to your place, yes?" Elodie touching my face soft with her hand.

"Yes," I say back.

Elodie and Josette getting out of booth. They taking Ditte's black bag, go to bathroom. Ditte kissing me and touching my cock under table. I touching her wet pussy with my fingers under skirt with the wetness going onto her thighs am so high I could die — I sigh with the pleasure and pleased.

When they coming back, Josette taking my hand: "let's go."

We leaving club. Mickey saying something when we walking outside. I not remember what he say but he grabbing my arm and show us to car that was waiting for us outside. Ariel was in driver's seat. I not need to give the directions.

When we getting to my apartment, we falling into bed. This all I remembering.

February 28, 1939

I have the nail marks all over my body.

I waking up with the naked women. I naked also. Not remember what happening after I getting home last night. I very late for work this morning.

Cock is sore. Never been like this before. Only other time was with Marion on the weekend trip. This time I more sore cause I feel cock is going to rip open!

I remembering sweating and getting the nails on back. Coke help me stay longer with girls — they half my age.

March 7, 1939

Same last night as last week — Le Chat Noir, shot up, got up, fuck all the night. Tomorrow night be the same thing — I am loving this shit.

March 10, 1939

Last night is another fucking pussy storm — I don't know if I can stop the pussy and coke and smack. I feel loved and peaceful.

March 14, 1939

Holes in my arms start to show. Not many right now — two, three, four. They like when it start to rain slow in morning. There is the calm feeling. I sit in middle of quiet rain. Wonder if there going to be more rain. I look at these little holes. I think of the morning rain. I wonder how long this last? It like being back in Le Sante — but with the prettiest fucking partners I can get with the money, but I not pay nothing!

March 16, 1939

Another night. Another storm. Storms getting stronger. Thanks the God.

March 21, 1939
I missing yesterday at the work. I not care. I love not caring about nothing. It make me free like Marion — she not care.

March 24, 1939
Devil is jealous — shooting up, ass fucking, drinking, sleeping, eating, sleeping, eating, pussy fucking, shooting, mouth fucking. I not want to never come down from these pussy coke smack mountains.

March 25, 1939
Needle marks is good friends that coming to seeing me one by the one. That is what the marks is like. I looking at them in mirror. They prettier than my ugly face, old body, stupid mind, bad luck.

March 27, 1939
This morning, I getting to school late, but nobody notice. I go into closet, closing the door, drink my coffee, do my work.
I thinks Sophia knock few times on door. I not sure. No way this woman care about man like me. She not like my kind. So I stay in closet. I not want nobody to see my arms — know about my nights.
It been the few weeks with girls. I missing Sophia but I knowing she not miss me. She better without me. She need the richer, taller, sporty man. She not needing some old man full of the smoke, shit, sin.

Tony yelled at some of the patrons in the middle of the Tavern to move to their seats. I sat there at the bar wondering what it would feel like to be with three stunning women. I have fantasized about doing something like Jacky did. I am sure most men do. I guess maybe not my father. My parents were always very straight and narrow Midwesterners. But I do think most men in the city of Gotham would have given their weight in gold to have nights like Jacky.

"Top you off?" Tony asked about my drink.

"Much obliged," I nodded to him.

He poured more Oban into my glass, which by now was about a quarter full.

"Thanks," I smiled.

"Yea, yea, whatever, just give me the summary of what you readin' there later on partner," he pointed to the diaries on the bar. "Is there some good stuff in them fucking books or what?"

He smiled a wise guy smile like he knew something I didn't.

I looked at him and wondered why.

He walked away to serve the other folks at the end of the bar. I wanted to see what Sophia was thinking during the same time period. I opened her diary.

March 27, 1939

I went by Jacky's closet this morning. I knocked. Nobody answered. I've been doing this over the past few days. I don't do it every day. I don't want him to know it's me. I do it one day, don't do it for a few days, and then I do it again.

I miss him so much that I feel like crying every night.

I feel stupid for feeling like this.

I feel like I am not strong. I need to be strong. Especially for Otis.

But I can't help the way I feel. I wish I could. I wish I could cut out my heart from my body. I wouldn't be sad. I wouldn't miss this man who is the devil incarnate.

I don't want to like him. I don't want to love him. I don't, I don't, and I don't. The more I say this to myself, the more pain I feel. The more I try to untangle the wire, the tighter it becomes around me.

This scares me.

Part of me regrets not showing him I care before. I feel like I need to show him the way I feel now. I'll hate myself more in the future if I don't, just like I did after Ginger.

Tomorrow I'll not only knock, but will let him know it's me. I need to let him know it's me.

March 28, 1939

I knocked on Jacky's door this morning.

"Jacky, it's Sophia," I said after I knocked. "Please open up. I haven't seen you for a few weeks now."

He opened up the door. It was dark inside. His eyes were tired, worn, and overworked. He was wearing a wrinkled and sweat soiled tuxedo shirt and pants. One of his sleeves was rolled up. He wasn't wearing any socks. I could see fresh new needle marks on his arm. He looked like he just got up from the cot. His hair was messy.

"It nice to see you," he said in a calm and quiet voice with the slightly ajar door covering his face.

"Are you alright?" I asked with reserved concern. I didn't want to show him too much.

"Yes," he said.

He was lying.

In the back of his little closet I could see an espresso cup and old cigarettes. They looked like they had been chain smoked without really being fully smoked. I could also see a fedora in the corner, these custom style English shoes that Richard used to wear, a pair of cufflinks, a blind-fold, and what looked like a tourniquet.

Dark outside, tail end of winter, and Jacky didn't have the light on in his closet. A sad and dim candle was lit above the cot. The soft candlelight illuminated part of my face, while the rest of it remained in the darkness. His closet was a devil's den like the opium retreats I saw growing up in New Orleans.

"I'd invite you for the coffee, but I been very tired," he said as he leaned against the door.

"It's fine," I said in the best way I could while at the same time hiding my feelings. "We can do it another time."

He smiled a broken smile.

I felt like crying.

But I didn't. That little voice inside me told me to keep those feelings quiet and out of the sight — especially from the eyes of men like Richard who could hurt me.

"I see you later," he said slowly as he closed the door shut.

I went home and cried for about an hour. And then it stopped. It stopped because I thought this was just a passing phase, and that Jacky and I would soon be back to old times soon.

April 6, 1939

Maybe I am wrong.

It has been a week or so since I knocked on Jacky's door, and he still has been keeping it closed. Every morning his door is closed — not just one day, or another day, or open and closed. I mean every single day.

I needed to knock again this morning.

"Jacky, please open," I said after knocking softly.

The door slowly opened. It was a bright day outside. He put his hand up to keep the sun out of his eyes.

"You pretty in sunlight," he said in a brainwashed tone that made me think he was physically present but was mentally somewhere else — somewhere I had never been, didn't want to go, and never wanted to.

He was even more haggard than before. The little needle bed bug looking marks now plastered his arm. There was a constellation of them. I opened myself up more this time. More, perhaps, than I ever have opened up to any man — even Richard.

"Jacky," I said as I looked at his arms, "I'm worried about you."

This is the first time I really let him know I cared.

"Sophia," he smiled exposing ancient mariner pirate teeth, "I been working very much. No time to sleep."

He was lying again to me. I know because when I am not feeling well, when I feel sick to my stomach, I lie to other people and tell them I am fine. I don't want to have to rely on anybody. I see myself in Jacky. I see my lying ways so well in this crude and unwashed on the outside — but sophisticated and shrewd on the inside — man.

"Are you sure?"

"Just as I sure that your hair is the blond color and my skin is dark," humor to camouflage his pain. I wondered if he could stand up without

leaning against the door. I felt like he would have fallen over if it weren't for the door.

I looked around to see if anybody was looking. It was an old habit that I was brought up on: being overly concerned with what other people think. This worried about what other people think way of living is why I married Richard.

But I found with him that appearances are often appearances.

Dammit — I thought to myself when I found myself looking around. I should know better. Why do I care so much about what these people think? They don't care about me.

Before I knew it, Jacky's door was closed. I stood there looking at it as a dog who had been locked out of her home. I felt so lonely standing there. But I was also angry at myself. My heart said one thing, but my mind said another. My heart said: tell him you love him. My mind said: never tell him how you feel because you will be hurt.

I just stood there in emotional purgatory. I wasn't moving forward, and I wasn't moving backward, for about a minute.

April 13, 1939

I can't stand my I don't care — or won't show that I care — attitude anymore. When I got up this morning, I told myself I would go to that door, knock on it, and would stop this madness.

At first, I knocked softly on it.
Nothing happened.
I knocked again.
Nothing happened again.

So I then pounded at hard as I could.

"Jacky, open up!" I felt like I was talking to myself. I felt like I was asking him to open up as much I was telling myself to do the same: "Sophia, open up!" The door was me. The way he probably felt in front of me, or with me, or speaking to me, or even loving me. For Jacky, loving me was the same as loving that door that won't open up.

And then I realized, in that split second, as we realize most things in life in split seconds, why this man had started down this path of self destruction: he felt that I didn't care, that he didn't matter, and that I cared as much about him as I did about the next coffee and cigarette — all replaceable.

After my several minute barrage of pounding my fists on the door, he opened up. He looked like he had spent the night naked in a bed bug farm. He weighed about 3/4 of what he weighed before. His out of shape and sleep deprived eyebrows drooped over his eyes.

"Sophia . . . something is wrong?" The morning light went into his dark beady eyes.

I didn't ask this time. I didn't hesitate. I pushed him to the side. I storm trooped into his lair and slammed the door behind me. It was pitch dark except for the candle that was lit and the sunlight that snuck in underneath the door.

"Jacky, darling," I rested my hand softly on his shoulder, "please stop." My eyes were full of a trail of tears that had never come up from the bottom depths of my heart to see the light of day.

Until the now that is now.

"Why?" He looked into my eyes. "I love feeling being back in my Sante."

I suppose we all get those chances in life to make a change, to make a different turn in our lives, from the right to the left, or the left to the right, or, in this case, from a closed door to an open one.

The trail of tears in my eyes grew.

I put my hand on his stubbly cheek and caressed it.

I then softly said to him, in a loving whisper, "because I care about you."

I was doing it again. I was holding back. I was hiding. I was hiding just like I did before. And I wouldn't do it again.

I paused, gathered myself, and then jumped in head first:

"Because I love you, because I love you, Jacky, that's why." I broke down and started crying on his shoulder. I gave him the strongest hug I could give Otis.

He stood stiff for a moment. I was so scared. I got so scared as I stood there hugging him. I told myself to stand steady. That is what I did.

The most refreshing light I have ever felt is the light coming from the sky after days, months, of rain. When the rain doesn't seem like it is going to stop, the light comes and blankets your face with its warmth.

I felt that warmth when his arms started slowly wrapping themselves on my back, in the stubble of his face against mine, in the tears that started dripping off his face, and in his very faint and yet sincere voice when he said:

"I love you too."

We stood there holding each other and crying for a moment that will, for me, last an eternity.

It will exist in the leaves I see on a fall day, in the breeze that comes in off the ocean during the morning dew, and in the droplets of rain that comfort my face after a scorching day of heat.

We broke our embrace. I put my hands on his face, as tears ran down my face, and asked his eyes: "Promise you will stop."

He looked at me for a moment.

"If you open to me," he said with tears going down his face. "Then I not feel like I, how to say, I is nothing to you, understand?"

What I had felt in front of the door was right. This was an opportunity of a lifetime. I wouldn't come across another man like him. If I didn't take this gift, this present, and use it as fuel to grow a better skin, without the sadness and lack of faith that I had with Richard, I would die a slow death on the inside.

"I swear on Otis I will," I said to him.

"Then I stopping, but I sick when I stopping."

"I'll take care of you," I quickly responded. "Whatever it takes to get you off that," I pointed to his arms.

We left that moment realizing that the war we had been waging, every so slightly, ever so subliminally, was now over.

There was peace between us.

That's why, when I got home, I didn't cry.

I laughed out loud to myself — joyously.

Tears were coming down my face as I finished reading Sophia's diary. I felt odd feeling this way. Like her, I was brought up not to show people my emotions, especially in a place like the Tavern, which was full of tough guys, mad guys, rich guys, but not crying nerds. Maybe I had made a mistake tearing up like this in the middle of the sometimes Cro-Magnon Tavern.

"Take these," Tony held out a napkin to dry my tears.

"Thank you," I dabbed my face.

"Good stuff?" He asked.

"Some of the best I have ever read," I finished drying my tears and looked around to make sure nobody was looking.

"It's alright, pal," Tony said in a comforting tone. "That stuff you is reading there don't happen that often, trust me," he said like he knew what was in the diaries kind of tone. "And when you read stuff like dat there, it's like, what they call dat thing, dat comet?"

"Haley's?" I asked.

He snapped his fingers.

"Yeah, that's it! Fucking Haley's whateva," he smiled and gave me a pat on my shoulder. "Want one more for the road," he looked at my drink.

"Thanks, but I got to get going."

It was about 11:00 p.m.

"Check?" I asked.

"Take care of it later. Get home. Get some sleep."

"Thanks, Tony."

CHAPTER 9
Wake Up Call

September 1, 1939

I waking up early in this fucking morning when I hearing the loud gun shot. I thinking is the family of some fuck I kill who finding me wanting to killing me then giving me to dogs for the eating.

But it not the fucking gun shot!

It the fucking book I been reading falling off shelf and hits the cold wood floor! This motherfucking book. It wakes me at the 8:00 in morning or something like this. Sophia get me into the reading and writing more — I getting better. She always talk about the different books during mornings. This book that falls to floor was called Grapes of the Wrath by man who is called John Steinbeck.

I trying to go back to sleep — but not able to. No sleep since I trying to kick white shit and coke I been doing like the cocktails. I on my back all the night long make the stare into ceiling, sweating, with much worry.

> *In sudden moments, or I should say moment, I think, I hearing knocks on front door. Yes, I needs to get more snore, but I putting on the Levi's jeans and t-shirt to open door. It my neighbor from below with this scary glow — old lady Georgette who 89 years old with the shy eyes, the thin gray hair, thick bottoms of bottles glasses.*
>
> *"Monsieur Jacky! Monsieur Jacky!" She says with the fear voice as she grabbing my t-shirt.*
>
> *"Yes, yes, what it is Madame Georgette? What it is? What it is?" I says to her.*
>
> *"The Germans! The Germans! They just attacking Poland! Oh my God, they attacking Poland! Oh my God, oh my God!"*
>
> *She cries in my chest.*
> *I hold her.*
> *She is old but she no fool.*
> *She knowing what I know when she says this to me.*
> *France is next.*

"What the fuck!" Tony smacked me on the shoulder and took me out of my concentration as I read Jacky's 1939 entry above in the Tavern around 9:30 the next evening. I got so into the entry I didn't notice Tony in front of me. "I mean, what the fuck!" He smacked me again.

"What? What, Tony?" I asked.

"The fucking Yankees, Mr. Chicago! They goin all the way this year! I'm fucking telling you, son, they goin all the way," Tony said with his wife just bore a baby boy excitement.

"I wouldn't know too much about going all the way," I said very dryly. "I mean, being from Chicago and all, the Cubs are what we like to call 'The Lovable Losers.' They never win. But

Dirty Quiet Money

they are sure fun to watch, kind of like a fling with a gal that you love to look at but know things aren't going to go anywhere with," I said this with a smirk as I gave him a loving junior pat on his back.

"I know why I liked you kid, I know why I liked you," he waved his thick bruiser finger at me as he giggled. I giggled with him. "Now, befaw you start jumping in dem fucking waters," he pointed to the diaries, "what you having?"

"How about a Budweiser?"

"I like it! Start simple, then go to third base, kind of like one of your dates, eh?" He said as went to get the beer.

When he came back, he put the bottle in front of me.

"Yes, but I usually just get the walk," I said as I took a long sip. "Thanks, Tony," I raised the beer bottle to him."

"Anytime, Hank," he nodded, "let me know if you need anyting else, I gotz to tend to dem folks," he pointed down towards the plumber and electrician looking men at the end of the bar. A lot of union guys were regulars at the Tavern, too. You had these guys with crusty hands sitting next to guys with manicured hands. A yin and yang of New York, you could say, right in one place. I guess these guys liked the food — and the women.

I took a long sip of the cold beer and looked back into Jacky's diary.

> *September 4, 1939*
>
> *I drinking the coffee and smoking the cigarettes with Sophia this morning. It been weeks. This to me is the spring day after the long winter. I missing her.*
>
> *"You still knowing how to make one of those?" She asking me as she walk up holding the hands of Otis. He come running to give me the slap on the hand. I standing outside sipping my coffee in front of this closet that is my morning home and feeling very much not alone.*

After quitting off the needle, I been keeping the door open and standing or sitting on outside. I guess to myself, this better than be on inside in the dark with the needle and the spoon not far away from my hungry hands.

"Yes," I say with the smile. "You want the sugar?" I ask her as I walking into closet.

"I takes it however you do," she say as she put her soft hands with their the pink nails on my hard hands and dirty nails under the September sun with the clouds high above and Paris buildings around us.

There is some things, I think to myself, different about her today. She wearing make-up. Not like some painter would put the colors on the house — but just little colors that can making the woman come alive as snow does for the mountain tops. The mountain tops was for her the cheekbones, jaw, long legs, skinny eyebrows, black fur around shoulders, little fedora, long blond hair coming out and rest on the fur, tight black wool pants, black boots that going up to her ankle, black blouse that showing off her bare white chest. I wanting to say all of this cause I like touching my cock sometimes when I thinks of her looking like this.

A caterpillar who becomes the butterfly she was, yes?

Whatever causing this, I wanting to seeing more of it.

I start to brewing the coffee. She standing outside to watching Otis play. She taking out Chesterfields to light. She not know I looking at her — but my eye not lie. I had the one eye on coffee, one eye on American swan with the black streaks, ah yes!

The butterfly loving to have the good bumblebee for the protection, this true, no? There was little bumblebee in her spirit now. I now thinks, as I many times do, that maybe she lost this bee after Richard — maybe now she finding it again.

"Slow in old age?" *She smile at me as she blow out smoke.*

"This coffee I makes is slow — I not slow," *I saying back.*

"I hope you aren't slow," *she smile the big smile as she look down at my cock.*

I finished making the coffee and I taking the coffee to her.

"Thanks, Jacky," *her mouth says while her blue eyes say all they need to saying to me. She putting her hand on my arm. She never this way before. Something in her mind and heart changed — a corner she turning, as I hearing the Americans saying, between now and before when she was in darkness with herself.*

I winking at her with same eye that looking on her when I making the coffee.

She winking back at me.

We sitting smelling the cool fall air almost sip the coffee with us.

But there something deadly swimming under these nice September winds coming off river. This what Georgette telling me other morning about Germans fucking Poland in asshole.

"Know what happening in Poland?" *I asking Sophia.*

She look at me with fear that I could tell was already painted on her her blue eyes.

"A nightmare," she nod serious at me. She looking away to watching Otis playing.

"This just start," I looks at children with her.
She hearing me.
But she not looking over.

She only wanting to watch the children play. Someone who want to study the butterflies, whales, stars to run from the evil that the human do to the human.

I understanding this.

I have this feeling that something needing to be done. This cancer going to spreading in the Olympic speed to the finish line of our deaths in mind, body, spirit.

"Our government — they having it under control," she saying with the eyes of hope to me. "The French and English declaring the war on Germany yesterday. This stopping the German madness." She says with wishful dreams and then looking back at children playing.

I light the new cigarette.

"Ever fight the bully?" I asking and looking at children.

She not saying nothing.

"Have you?" I tapping her shoulder to getting the attention.

"No," she saying after the silence.

"Well," I taking this long smoke off of the cigarette and let it out, "my experience speaking to me in the ear and she saying to fight the Germans without clean, fancy, tea gloves on hands."

"Meaning?" She looking over to blow some smoke upwards.

I make sure nobody listening. I not want anybody at school hearing me what I saying.

"There is kid when I the young boy. He popular when I in the school. I not popular. He knowing everybody in neighborhood cause they liking his money. He was from the very rich family, but I not sure. Everybody seem to like him cause he had a lot of everybody over at this house for the parties — I not everybody. I was loner boy who likes other lone wolves and not the sheep at the parties of the everybody."

I take hit off cigarette to do the thinking.

"And? And? Go on," she taking another cigarette out of this fancy purse with the scarf tie on handle.

"One day comes this boy not forgetting for rest of his life. He walks next to me and tapping me on shoulder with finger for whole time on street, and he saying 'What you going to do about it? What you going to do about it? You got no friends — I the one who has the friends.'"

"He blond and taller than me. I not want to do nothing stupid."

"But?" Sophia looking over at me.

"If I letting him do this to me, he do worse later, others thinking they could do same things to me."

Sophia listens.

"So this one time when we was in the school, I seeing him putting his books in locker above him. Other people is around. Right when he not looking, when he putting his books in locker, I shoving his head into locker and smash locker door onto his

face until he dripping with his shitty royal blood. I yelling with the pleasure and release and revenge and focus when I doing this."

Sophia look at me like I the crazy man.

"A teacher must stopping me," I say to her.

"Jacky — that no way to act!" Sophia saying to me.

I looking back at her — she not knowing what she talking about.

*"This **exactly** way to act. He never fucking with me ever again in his life. The whole school knew not to fucking with me like he done."*

Sophia keeps herself company to think as she smoke.

"I get it," she smashing her cigarette with the foot. "You making an example out of him," she saying with my type of grin.

"Yes." I says with the love as I slowly rubbing her back. "This what we need to do to Germans, but this not happening right now."

"Why you say this?" She ask me.

"We thinking we have too much to lose," I pointing to pretty buildings in Paris.

"You think we giving up to save the Louvre?" She asking.

"You said what I thinking — yes, exactly!" I says.

"I hope this not happen," she put her hand on my shoulder with the worry.

I finished my beer and felt like something stronger. I liked being a little boozed up when I read Jacky's entries. I don't know exactly why. Maybe it's because the booze acted like a truth serum. Instead of seeing the world through the eyes of a nerdy

Dirty Quiet Money

and introverted college educated boy from the Midwest, I saw the world through Jacky's black market tinted eyes.

"Hey, Tony, scotch please?"

Tony was at the end of the bar talking to some pretty gals who had just come into the Tavern.

"Coming right up, kid," he gave me a playful salute.

It was now about 10:00 in the evening. I wanted to finish these entries before I went back to Sophia's tomorrow to get more. So I skipped a few months to the month when the Nazis marched into Paris. I wanted to see what effect, if any, this had on Sophia and Jacky.

"Here is your drink, pal," Tony left the scotch on the bar.

"Thank you, mister," I said back with a smile.

"You good looking, kid, but them dames down there is much better looking, if you catch my drift," he winked at me. "So if you don't need nothing else, I'll make my way down back there."

"You got it," I raised my glass to give him.

I took a few sips of the Oban and let the scotch take its effect. I turned the pages in Jacky's diary to June 14, 1940.

June 14, 1940

Just as I thinking to myself. When the Germans going into Poland, I knew they coming to Paris one day. This day is here.

A traveling organized circus of death. The Nazis come to Paris this morning on Champs-Elysees. Horses, tanks, trucks, music bands coming behind Hitler. Men my papa's age was crying at the sight of this Hitler fuck and his German cancer.

The Nazis celebrate with the laughs. I looking around to see the mobs of the peoples hugging and crying out of the fear for the future of Paris.

I have the bad feeling this going be start of long street fight.

June 18, 1940

I have the breath of fresh air today. It coming from this man with name of Charles de Gaulle. He some tank officer in army. I drink the coffee in my local spot. The owner, he an old Jewish man named Stan, telling me to come to the basement. He set up radio. He close the door and turns radio on. I know Stan's son. He a boy named Guillaume. He working in the government of Paris.

Over the radio I hearing: "This the BBC. We have message from the De Gaulle from England."

I writing down speech from De Gaulle as best as I can remembering cause it so exciting. It was first day of spring for my ears and my heart. He says something like this:

"Is the last word said? Has all the hope gone? Is the defeat final? No. Believe me, I telling you that nothing lost for the France. This war not only in our sad country. This war is world war. I invite all French soldiers who in Britain or wherever, with their arms or nothing, to get in touch with me. Whatever happening, the flame of French resistance must not die and will not dying."

"The flame of French resistance must not die and will not dying." I loved this. I never forget it.

June 23, 1940

"Petain sign the armistice yesterday! They sign it!" Sophia says this to me as she walking to me this morning with the bright smile on face. She let Otis go and play.

I didn't want to say nothing to her while Otis around, so I waiting until he not there.

"You not seem so excited? Why you not happy?" She ask with the worry in her eyes.

"Let me make you the coffee and I explaining," I saying to her.

She standing outside my janitor closet and takes spot to smoke the cigarette. I love her as I make her coffee.

"Jacky, put some sugar in mine?" She saying through the cigarette smoke. "I need a boost," she smiles to me.

"May, of course," I says to her.

I am happy to know again this woman because she calming me. I feel safe with her. I feel her spirit. She feels like home. I not know why. She is from such a different place in the world than me. I think she feel the same way. Since we cry together that day in my shit closet, she opening up like flower in garden. The way she dressing, the way she looking at me, so many other things have allow me to see the woman I always knowing she was — but that she forget how to be.

I give her hot espresso and little lemon for her to suck.

"You a doll, Jacky," she says as she holding out hand to taking the coffee.

She sip and taking out cigarette.

"Care for one?" She holding out the cigarette box to me.

"Thanks," I taking one.

As she puffed, she huffed with the stress.

"What?" I asking.

"Why you not believe in this peace?" She turning to looking at me.

"You listening to De Gaulle's speech?" I ask.
"Who?"
"Forget about it," I taking the long sip of espresso.

Like this beating I gave to the bully of boy when I younger, my views of the Petain deal with Germans not be popular with people in this school. I sure most like the deal cause it protects their fancy living — butlers, drivers, maids, mistresses. I look around to make sure nobody listening.

"I telling you why," I says to Sophia with whisper. "Nazis going to be like the parasites. They going to rob this country. Petain's Vichy is puppet for Nazis. Vichy is going to do Nazi dirty deeds — then washing the laundry after it done so no shit marks left to show the world, see? Frenchmen going to be turning Frenchmen into the Nazis, you understand? We going to see the worst in the man."

I looking over to Sophia, and she nodding to me: "please go on," and then she sipping her coffee.

"Look at the Vichy bullshit saying," I says to her. "It is 'Work, Family, Fatherland,' and not 'Liberty, Equality, Brotherhood.' Vichy is not care about the freedom — they about smashing our culture, our freedom, for the Nazis. Vichy have not the interest in the free spirit. For them, it enough that we not fight."

I smoking my cigarette.

"We going to pay the big price for taking it in ass from Nazis — price is our spirits, our souls, taken by these fucks," I looking at Sophia with eyes you use at the cemetery when looking at the family after one dies and you left with rest.

Sophia sipping her coffee. She thinking about what I saying, and she just waiting, like black cat, for right time to jump.

"Petain not going to water the French revolution garden. He going to try and changing into a new France — no Jews, Communists, Freemasons, or anybody that don't fit into Nazi model."

"I hope you wrong, Jacky. I have the feeling you might not be. But I hope that what Vichy did was to save this country — and this city. I hope that Otis will grow up here without seeing what this country seeing during the first war. I just hope. That's all."

She pause for many seconds.

"Another part of me, I must admit, feeling like you do — that we must resist. But we must first having the idea of the resistance," *she put out her cigarette on the floor and then look up at me.* "Every great leader not liked by many, but loved by more. And it because of an idea that challenge the normal — and that make the people feel not at peace with the way they thinking. These leaders, these misunderstood, holding up mirror to the others. These others didn't like what they seeing."

I thinking to myself when Sophia speaking: this why I love her.

She moving to pull out another cigarette, and I lit it. I very happy to see the real Sophia, the inner Sophia, the private Sophia — the strong her.

"Thanks, Jacky," *she lightly touch her hand on mine after taking the light. I lighting up mine.*

"Jacky, I just hope. I hope resistance idea spreading until fighters in underground become upper ground," *she looked at me with understanding eyes, like she had just read the same page as me in the book eyes.*

My hand on her arm and I saying smiling, "Sophia, I hope, too." I kissed her on cheek, took her glass, went back into the closet to putting the things away.

July 22, 1940

I hearing today that Secretary of State create committee to review the citizenship give to many French peoples since 1927. Guillaume tells me this. He is one of my moles in government. He party at our clubs very much.

He tell me that Raphael Alibert is the man in charge of the committee. He wanting to focus on Jews. Guillaume says he will telling me when he knows. He saying there is other things coming down that will fuck the Jews, too.

I knew this was coming. I telling Sophia, like large wave coming in off the coast in Biarritz. It seem like wave is start to grow as it come closer to shore.

October 3, 1940

Vichy today passing their "good boy" law.

It make the Jews wear gold stars on arms. No more Jews in army, news, industry, government. Vichy say Germany not mother of these laws. This is hard to believe for me. Germany have the same laws for many years now.

I having the whiskies with Guillaume last night. He telling me it all because of Nazis. Vichy wants to kiss ass to Nazis, he telling me.

Dirty Quiet Money

My Oban was about finished. I was ready for one more before I delved into Sophia's diaries. I wanted to see what she thought about what was going on in France at the time, especially since she benefitted from Vichy. She was one of the privileged few whose assets would be safe from the Nazi grip — but only if she supported Petain.

"Hey, Tony," I said with a sort of kid like yell as I heard myself in the bar, "can you hit me with another?" I held up the empty glass for him see.

"Do I use 'fuck' in every other sentence?" He smirked. "Coming the right fuck up, pal."

Tony placed the drink in front of me like a fine waiter would in a four star restaurant in one of Chicago's Gold Coast restaurants.

"Fresh off the grill," he smiled.

"I like your grill," I smiled back.

"Enjoy, Hank."

I raised my glass to him. "Cheers," I said, and then gave him a big smile.

I took a few sips of his drink. It was easier for me to get Jacky, but a little harder for me to get Sophia. Maybe it's because I wasn't from her background. While I certainly didn't have Jacky's bare knuckle upbringing, I guess I associated with him more than her. But I would find myself learning otherwise as I kept reading her entries, learning more about her, and growing to love her.

> ### October 16, 1940
> *Woke up this morning to have coffee, get ready to go with Otis to school, and welcome in the clear and crisp fall day in Paris. I have been dressing up more lately. I feel so good about doing it. I don't know where this thing with Jacky is going. But I love the way he looks after me. I admit it: I fantasize about him sometimes. Laying naked*

in bed with him, smoking our cigarettes with the windows open and letting the cool air fall over my breasts, making them all so hard while he caresses and kisses them.

When I put on my stockings, my heels, my hat, my scarf, I think about him. I think about other men I see walking on the street. Jacky has awoken in me something that has been sleeping for some time — the will to feel alive, and to open myself to the uncertainties in life.

I got to school this morning and told Jacky what I read in Le Journal: that of the 15,000 people whose nationality was revoked, some 40% were Jewish.

"I knowing this," Jacky said calmly as he slapped Otis's hands. Jacky and I both looked in a meeting of the minds type of way at one another. Otis smiled like it was another day in the park.

"So you know? I thought you didn't like reading the papers?"

"I don't read this bullshit in the papers," he said quietly to me as he kept slapping Otis's hands. "They full of the bad news — people love the suffering of others," he said with a small cynical smirk.

"But I not need to reading the papers to get my information," he continued. "I have my sources."

I didn't understand what he meant by that. He was a mere janitor from the slums of Marseille. But I didn't pry any further.

"Otis, go play with your friends," I gave Otis a slight nudge.

*"But mommy," he looked up at me with his small blue eyes, "Jacky **is** my friend," and then he smiled a smart-ass smile. This kid had my smarts, all right, I thought to myself.*

"Yes, honey, I know he is your friend," I smiled, "but I meant to go play with your **other** friends," emphasizing **other** so he knew I understood him and didn't underestimate him.

"Well, alright," he said and gave Jacky one more slap. "See you tomorrow, Jacky?"

"Yes, little one," Jacky said with an appreciative smile.

Otis ran to play.

"So what you think about this?" Jacky asked. "Wait, let me make you the coffee so you can oil the machine in your head," he smiled as he took the Chesterfield out of his mouth and put it out on the floor.

"Thank you," I gave him my full-length black fur coat. He went to hang it in the closet and then, after a few minutes, came back out with his lovely trademarked black Italian coffee.

I took a sip. It made me feel like I was back in Louisiana, sitting with my mother in her kitchen at the plantation, for some reason. I guess it's because I felt safe with Jacky, just as how we all feel safe with some people.

"The best way I can explain it is by telling you the way I felt about Jim Crow," I said after I sipped some more coffee.

"Jim Crow, he is a former lover?"

I giggled.

"Why you laughing?" He sipped some more coffee and took a drag off his cigarette.

"Jim Crow isn't a person, silly. Jim Crow is a set of laws that were passed in the late 1800s in the United States. They are similar to the laws recently passed by Vichy. But Crow was against black people — not Jews."

"Ah!" He raised one of his hands up. "I am an ass to not know this!"

"Don't say that," I put my hand on his arm. "Your 20/20 vision of some things but blind spots in others is endearing," I remember telling him. "It makes you unique!"

We exchanged smiles.

"I grew up with Jim Crow living in Louisiana. My family had a plantation in western Louisiana. We always had slaves around during chores for the family."

Jacky just sat there listening like I did to him when he told me about Petain.

"I always felt like they were family. I wasn't black, but I loved them like I was black. Their color didn't matter to me. I don't think it mattered much to my mother — she was kind to them. But I always felt guilty about them under Crow — separate bathrooms, barred from holding certain positions, and being horribly enslaved by a lot of people. I mean, my mother was kind, but some of our neighbors were not so kind — they would whip these people, torture them even, to instill fear into their minds and hearts."

"So you see this Vichy type of bullshit before? You have the experience with this?"

"You could say that," I handed a cigarette to Jacky and then took one for myself, lighting them both up.

As I did, I thought to myself: I like how Jacky and I trade rolls — sometimes him lighting me up, and at other times me lighting him up. Sometimes I learn from him, sometimes he learns from me. We weren't stuck in this form that people thought we should play. I thought this man I stumbled upon was rare for that — not wanting to just accept his role like a machine.

"But you not scared about Vichy because you not Jewish?" Jacky asked as he puffed.

"It doesn't matter. I still care."

"Yes," he said as he put his coffee down, "but you willing to risk the way you living with Otis, where you send him to the family school, for the Jewish peoples?"

"Meaning?" I looked at him upset.

"Vichy good for you. You live the way you been living before. Your life is not change much, no? But if you put up fight, rock big nice boat you riding, then your life change."

"That is what I am worried about," I looked at him with worried eyes. "I want to do the right thing, what my heart and soul says I should do, but I also am worried about Otis, and what would happen if people knew the way I felt?"

"Why they need to know?" He asked like he knew how to hide things — I could tell by his smirk.

"How could they not find out?"

"I help you," he put his hand on my arm.

"How?" I looked at him with appreciation as I imagined a prospector would a piece of rock he discovers in a quarry of mud, thinking there is gold in in, but who wants to hide it from the other prospectors when he goes back to camp so as to not give off the treasure he had just discovered.

"I need to go, but we talking soon," he said secretively.

He kissed me on the cheek, I got my coat, and I left his little closet area wondering what I was getting myself into.

October 19, 1940

It has been a week or so since I saw Jacky. His door has been closed. I don't even think he has been coming to work. I hope he isn't back on the horrible white stuff he was putting into his veins before. He promised me he wouldn't!

October 31, 1940

I finally saw him today. I was so happy after I did.

I slowly knocked on his door, which was slightly open.

"Come in. I make you the coffee," he said as he let me inside the closet, closing the door behind me.

I couldn't believe my eyes. He was in one of the most stunning tuxedos I had ever seen. It had to be hand made it fit him so well. His janitor's uniform rested softly on his wooden chair as he started to take off his black dress socks.

"Please close door, Sophia," he said to me as his socks came off, exposing his needle marked feet. "It not closed all the way."

"Of course," I slowly closed the door. "Long night?" I asked him sarcastically."

He looked back at me as he stood, barefooted, making the coffee on his little stovetop.

"Very," he smiled and then went back to making coffee.

I looked over underneath his table where I previously saw his cigarettes and other items. Peaking through some of his janitor clothes and a copy of the Steinbeck book I got him was a wad of cash and what looked like a .45 caliber pistol. I should know — a lot of the men in Louisiana carried them.

He turned back towards me and handed me the coffee. He folded his fancy looking socks and put them in his stash as he smoked his Chesterfield from the corner of his mouth.

I quietly sipped my coffee. I could smell what I thought was this Italian cologne, I think it was called Acqua Di Parma, that I had seen in some of the most elegant shops in Paris. I sat there processing the information as Jacky pulled off his tuxedo jacket. Underneath, he was wearing a gun holster. He took that off, took off his elegant dress shirt — it looked like it was from Savile Row, where Richard used to get his shirts — and started to put on his janitor uniform.

"Cat gets your tongue?" He smiled mischievously.

"What's going on?" I asked in a confused tone.

"I getting ready for the work," he smiled again.

"Come on, you know what I mean," I sipped my coffee.

"What?"

"You go missing for days, pop up wearing a suit you can't afford, carrying a pistol, wearing cologne you can't afford, and, on top of it, stashing a wad of cash over there under the Steinbeck I got you."

"I won at the craps, yes?" He took his cigarette out of his mouth and put it into his little North African looking gypsy ashtray.

I looked at him with my own beastly eyes.

"Alright, alright," he said as he put his arms above his shoulders like he was being arrested all the while grinning, knowing he would get off on a technicality anyway.

He put his hands down and pulled out another cigarette.

"Well, lay it on me? I mean, should I sit down for this?"

"No, Sophia, I not the transvestite," he chuckled.

"Thanks for the update, Jacky," I sipped my coffee calmly and played along. I don't know why, but I felt calm, even though I felt like he was going to tell me something that maybe would change our lives together forever. Something inside me said I was ready to go on a journey, and that same voice told me there was no better person to take the journey with than Jacky.

"I not who looking to be," he puffed his smoke.

He stood up, opened the door to look around, and then closed it — as a burglar closing the door in a home where people were sleeping would.

He took the cigarette out of his mouth and then hit me with it: "I run the Paris nightclubs for the very powerful Marseilles family."

"What type of family?" I asked with a curious tone. "The royal Rothschilds?" I said sarcastically.

"In the many ways, we as powerful," he said to me with a tone that I didn't question what just came out of his lips.

And yet I had been brought up to think institutional power, whether it is the government, the monarchy, or old blue blood families like the Rothschilds, were the ones that had power.

So part of me didn't believe him.

"How so?" I drank my coffee in a having some type of intellectual conversation about philosophy, art, or fashion type of way — slow, no pressure, detached, and in an ivory tower.

"Sometimes these types of peoples — rich peoples, powerful peoples, politician peoples — call us to do things for them, and sometimes we call them to do the things for us. They scratch our backs, we scratch theirs, is all I trying to say."

"What types of favors are we talking about?"

"They needing to find the person in Rome, we can find person in Rome. They needing some information on what's happening in Moscow, we have connections there to get the information. They need someone bumped off in New York, we do the bumping."

"Bumped off?" I asked naively.

He looked at me with predator eyes.

"They killed."

I nervously sipped my coffee now.

"In exchange, we get the favors back," he said.

"Like?"

"We have the products come in from all world to France, and then take to rest of the Europe. Sometimes, police need to make the small arrest to make it look like they doing their jobs. But we will tell them what off the limits."

"And if they don't?"

"They suffer," he looked at me. "But we suffer, too. So is bad for everybody."

Jacky went to sit down so he could put on his janitor pants.

"You wanting to turn the other way, or I put on dirty man show for you?"

I hated to admit it, but I found him charming.

"I'll watch, depending on the charge," I said.

"Sometimes the best things in life, they is for free, no?" He said.

I sipped my coffee as he took off his tuxedo pants and put on his janitor pants.

"So how big is this family of yours? I mean, where are they? In France?"

"Where they not? This better question cause we have the peoples all around the world. Don't think of us as in France only. Better way to think about us is this big fucking spider web around this world we living."

He pulled up his janitor pants and tightened his belt as he kept the cigarette coolly in his mouth. He got up off the bench and was now standing facing me — so close I wanted to kiss him.

"And the clothes, the money, all this stuff?"

"You not believe how much I make in a year," he looked at me through the heavy cigarette smoke.

"Try me."

"You sure?"

"Yes."

"You guess?"

"100,000.00 francs?" I asked.

"Money for the small infants," he answered.

"1,000,000.00?" I asked.

"Bigger infant," he said.

"10,000,000.00?" I asked.

"The young man," he said.

I looked at him like he was nuts. I guess I was so naïve about the workings of this underworld that

I never knew. I was Columbus and Jacky was the new world that I accidentally discovered.

"Alright, I give up." I put my coffee down.

"13,000,000.00 — and this is no tax to take off."

I looked at him with my mouth open.

"Better close that," he pointed to my mouth, "or you get the flies inside."

"All that money from running nightclubs?" *I asked naively.*

"I more than nightclub runner," he said. "I run many things. I have my hands in the different pots. I know many people in the place you think of as the power, like the government, but also on the street, where you not think the power is living. You is surprised how much power in the streets."

I was speechless.

He lit another cigarette and lit one for me, too.

"Remember when you asking me how I could helping you?"

"Yes," *I nodded*, "I asked you a few weeks ago."

"This right," *he nodded*. "Well," *he put his hand softly on my right shoulder*, "I give you the small picture — my connections, my moneys, my muscle, my wicked mind, my love."

He softly caressed my face with his right hand.

I never felt so taken care of in my life. He hadn't even done anything for me, other than make me coffee and get me smoking Chesterfields. But I had a feeling, deep down in my heart, that this was a man who would be standing there next to me in the muck during the night when there is no moon, no stars, and no light to keep things bright.

"Thank you, Jacky," *I smiled shyly as I put my hand on his.*

"Alright, we can do the séance later, yes?" He took his hand down and smiled. "Before we go, I have the small joke for you."

"Give it to me, Jacky," I hit him on the shoulder like some tough guy would another. I was a tomboy at heart when I was younger, going out late at night and hanging with the boys, so I know how to be around guys.

"What is the difference between the Mafia and the government?"

He looked at me with his sparkling eyes.

"I have no idea," I shrugged my shoulders.

"Only one is organized."

He looked at me deadly in the eyes — a bank robber to another — and then he leaned over to kiss me on my cheek as we left the janitor's closet.

Have I been making friends for the past few weeks with my guardian angel camouflaged in Lucifer's clothing? Or was he just that — Lucifer? If I went by backgrounds, and purely used my head, the conclusion would be clear. But where did that get me with Richard?

November 18, 1940

I have been going to several Vichy party meetings lately. The mothers in Otis's school have gotten me into it. They go to the meetings with their husbands. Many of them are the biggest industrialists in France. Of course, the German officers send their little ones to Otis's school. Officer wives often come with drivers to drop the kids off, just like the other mothers do. But you know they are different. They often have their fancy Nazi flags waving from their Mercedes limos.

I go with Bruna, the mother of one of Otis's friends, to the parties. She is around my age and is from a prominent Berlin family. All of them are in the Nazi party.

Her husband has been working in a Mercedes office in Paris for some time now. He is one of the attaches between the company and the party throughout Europe.

So he is a big shot.

Bruna is a brunette woman, and is petit. She has short hair, kind of like you might see on a movie star, and has delicate features. Her bones are small, and she often wears cutting edge designs from Berlin — what she liked to call Berlin Chic.

"Oh Sophia," she would say to me after bringing her son into school in the mornings as she smoked her cigarette with a holder, "aren't those German soldiers just so sexy in their outfits?" She'd then laugh and then touch me on the arm like I knew what she was talking about, and as though we were on the same team.

I didn't actually like her much. But it was good for me to keep up appearances.

If anybody knew the way I really felt about what was going on, I would be in danger — and so would Otis.

"I especially like when they wear those tight pants," I responded to her with veiled contempt in my sincere sounding voice.

Bruna and I would go to various Nazi party meetings and cocktail parties at the Hotel Meurice, located on the rue de Rivoli. Many members of Vichy would be at these parties, which were full of the crème of the crème of the French government. Even Petain would sometimes be there

I would even donate money to the party whenever they had fundraisers, especially for their Youth Party, which was meant to get young German boys indoctrinated into Nazi ideology. I held my nose when I gave the money, but it was good camouflage.

I knew I had other intentions.

They didn't.

But nobody would know how I truly felt about the Nazis if you saw the way I was living, and who I surrounded myself with — other than Jacky, who I kept as a quiet companion.

"Hello, Frau Gordon," one German officer, I think his name was Goebbels, said to me one night at the hotel. I received the same type of attention from other German officers at these types of events. Although black tie, the events were full of German officers in their uniforms.

I could have thrown up going to these things. But it was good for me to see what they were like.

I think it was Sun Tzu, the Chinese philosopher of war I read about at Newcomb, who once said: "If you know the enemy and know yourself, you need not fear the result of a hundred battles."

I wanted to know the enemy as much as I could.

My way of doing that was to attend these meetings, and to make friends with as many of the mothers at the school that I could. I had a feeling that these "friendships" would give me an opportunity to learn more about them than they knew about us — and when I say "us," I mean Jacky, me, and the silent majority of others who feel we are heading towards the wrong page in history.

I intended to keep that from happening — and I think the rest of "us" did too.

December 17, 1940

Today was the first time that I took part in something that I have always wanted to take part in deep down — rebellion.

"There is new paper coming out," Jacky told me with his broken syntax over coffee this morning in his little closet.

"What is it?" I asked over the cloud of cigarette smoke.

"They call this paper 'Resistance.' Some of the local intellectual peoples write it. They led by a Russian named Boris . . . Boris Vilde his name."

"And how do you know this?" I blew my smoke out towards the ceiling.

"He coming to club the other night and he telling me about what they doing. I think their first printing was on the 15. They want us help them hand out pamphlet to certain peoples who come to clubs."

"Like all of those nice Nazi officers? They would use it as their toilet paper." I smiled towards Jacky.

"Maybe — but even for that it too good for them," he smiled back.

"So are you going to help?" I asked.

"What you think?" He asked me back.

"Yes?" I said cautiously.

"Of course. But we need careful about this. Here is copy for you," Jacky handed me a small copy of the pamphlet.

"How can I help?" I asked him after thinking for a moment. I thought to myself: I don't think I have ever really done anything subversive in my life, other than more or less blackmailing Richard, but I don't know if that counts.

"By keep your looks as the good Aryan mother who loves Vichy, see what I say?"

"So I can get information from them?" I asked rhetorically.

"And so you can check the Berlin fashions on officers' wives. God knows I seen what the officer mistresses' wearing," he joked and offered me another smoke, I took one with a nervously shaking hand wondering what the hell I am doing here. He lit both me and him up with a scarred and really calm hand that was certain of its purpose — and its immense capability.

We sat there in his little closet smoking — two chimneys in a pod. I smiled in his direction. I loved how he could be so sarcastic and full of humor in the most serious of times. I would have felt so scared if it weren't for him being there next to me. Not that I haven't seen danger before — or been through hardship, like when I had to deal with Richard's antics. But I think Jacky had seen a whole other level of the school of dark knocks that I hadn't seen — yet.

"I am coming to understand you more and more Jacky, almost where I feel like I know you," I said after a small pause in our talk.

He looked over at me with a smile. *"How you gotten to know me better?"*

"When I was going to school in New Orleans," I said as I puffed my cigarette in some Vienna coffee

house type of way, "I really loved philosophy. One of the philosophers I used to love to read was Sun Tzu. He wrote a book called the Art of War."

Jacky sat there sipping his coffee. I felt good that he had a lot to teach me — but I also realized that I had things to teach him, too.

"One of the things he says in the book is something like: 'Appear weak when you are strong, and strong when you are weak.'"

He stood there for a second smoking his cigarette calmly — some Greek philosopher pondering some profound thought.

"This the art of the deception," he smiled, "the Cheetah who hide into brush before he pounce on the prey, no?"

I nodded in agreement.

"That's why my family work with the Allies." He put out his cigarette and looked over at me.

"What?" I put my coffee down and looked at him with my mouth slightly open as I thought to myself: a man like him, with the types of connections a man like him has, and his crime family, working with the U.S. government? This shocked my conscience.

"We getting their weapons shipped to us — machine guns, grenades, pistols, machines of the kill. My family — we was well armed before. But now we is small army, eh?" He broke a proud gold toothed smirk open and wore it for a few seconds for me to see.

"It seems you have had De Gaulle's idea of resistance bloom inside," I said.

As he blew out his cigarette smoke, he looked towards me: "it always been there. I been resisting since I little boy. For my life, I resist police, government, law, convention. I never been under them. Being on the outside means you not on inside."

He puffed some more and sipped his coffee.

"But this don't mean I can't reach the inside," he smiled and showed his tarred teeth towards me. "We in touch with De Gaulle."

A man like this has been in touch with a man like that? I asked myself.

"De Gaulle the one who got the English and Americans to sending us weapons over the Channel," Jacky said in a very clam and matter of fact way.

I stared at Jacky for a moment. I couldn't believe this was the same man who, not long ago, I was wondering which day was going to be his last. I saw him go from one hole in his arm, to two, to three, and then an ant farm of holes.

But now I see an underground general, a black prince, a dark light. And maybe the wake up call wasn't only my tears. It was my belief that he cared — about me, about Otis, about himself, and for his country.

*I know from dealing with Richard that you can't truly love someone else if you don't love yourself. Richard didn't care about me because he didn't really care about himself — he only cared about what his self **looked** like to others, but not actually how it **was** when nobody was looking. In those alone moments, when nobody was looking, he was a sad soul, a miserable selfish creature, who would be completely selfish if it didn't **look** bad.*

Jacky didn't care about what others thought. He seemed to care only about what he thought. Sometimes what he thought took into account the

thoughts of a select people that he loved — and who loved him.
It felt like I was becoming one of those people.

I closed Sophia's diaries. I was amazed at the traction that these two people had made in their relationship from that day of crying in the closet to now. They were like a yo-yo. They got close in the start, and then distant, but then reconnected on a deeper level. I knew this because Jacky told her things that I am sure nobody knew outside his family. That's why she could say, with the clarity of thought and knowledge that I can say two follows one, "It felt like I was becoming one of those people."

"Okay, okay, dem fucking diaries must be good, but fuck, Hank, you been sittin here for what, like, uh, hours now, and you ain't seen none of these dames walking around here, who waz, uh, circling around like stars, or whateva, on a clear night in Coney Island," Tony stood in front of me sort of schooling me like a cool uncle would when you are afraid to ask the girl you like in school out for a dance or a ride at the ferris wheel.

I just smiled.

"One of these days, kid, one of these days, you going to open up, see, and when you do, you going to thank uncle Tony here," he pointed at his chest, "for making those smart little fucking eyes see what I seez, see?" He smiled slightly back towards me.

"I get it, Tony. I mean, reading these things are actually helping me with my own issues, come to think of it."

"I bet they iz, kid, but you gotz to practice what you read, can't just be tinking what happen in dat," he pointed to the diary, "is going to happen now unless *you* make it happen."

"Got it," I nodded.

"Awright, kid, iz time to close."

The Tavern was empty except for Tony, me, and a local 40 something year old Sicilian guy named Dean. He made sure nobody messed with Tony — or the cash — in closing hours.

This made sense. Dean was an imposing figure — about six foot four, had a bald head, big tree trunk arms, and a long boxer like reach. Plus, he carried two pistols underneath his leather jacket, and always had two black Cadillac sedans waiting outside with a crew of guys. You wouldn't want to mess with them, either.

I looked over my shoulder at Dean, who was standing behind me.

"We'll be here tomorrow night, kid," he smiled with his arms crossed. A gold tooth in his mouth shined hello. "We like kids like you coming in here," he patted me on the back, "cause we need some smarts with all of these knuckle heads coming in from all over the city," he grinned again.

"Thanks, man," a nerdy voice came out of me — typical. I threw the "man" in there to sound cool. I hope I didn't make a fool of myself.

I turned to look at Tony.

"What do I owe the house?"

"On us, kid," Tony said.

I looked back at Dean.

"It's on us, brother," he smacked me an older brother would his younger brother smack on the shoulder. Strong enough to let the younger brother know that the older brother is bigger — but also strong enough to let him know that his older brother's strength is there when he might need it.

"Thanks, guys," I said shyly.

"See you tomorrow night, kid," Tony said.

I put the diaries in the satchel and got up to leave. It was about 12:00 in the morning and I was beat. But it was no feat for me to read as I did tonight. And while I had a full day ahead of me tomorrow, I knew it didn't matter: I was meeting up with Sophia to get the final installments of the diaries. And that would complete my journey.

CHAPTER 10
Action-Reaction

August 21, 1941
They listens to me.
Today, we killing first German.
Our man who do the killing is called Colonel Pierre-Georges Fabien.
He did the killing at the Barbes-Rochechouart station.
The hit makes me think of something.
I hear someone saying sometime, that, for every action, there is the reaction.
This our reaction to the Nazi action. And there be more to come.

After I snuck a look at Jacky's entry above, I looked up at Sophia through the cigarette smoke in her apartment. It was about 7:30 in the evening. She was wearing a form fitting double breast pinstripe suit with a pretty white blouse. It was normally a man's look, but she made it a woman's. She wore a fancy silk blue scarf around her neck. I bet she had a long day of meetings in that get up. I could tell by the fatigue in her eyes. Even so, I could see the faint hint of her smile through the smoke. She was a trooper.

"Do you like what you see?" She said sarcastically as she nodded towards Jacky's diary entry on my lap.

"Yes," I nodded. "I can't wait to read the rest," I smiled at her.

"You'll have your chance, Hank," she said as she puffed her cigarette, "but let's have a drink and talk about the diary entries you just finished?" She smashed her cigarette into the ashtray.

"I'd love to," I nodded.

""Winston? Winston?" She said towards the kitchen.

"Two martinis?" I heard Winston say. His question was more of a statement.

"You took the words out of my mouth," she said to him and turned to me to smile. She uncrossed her long grasshopper legs and then crossed them the other way to get more comfortable. "So what did you think about the entries?"

I didn't know what to say to her. But I didn't need to. She helped me.

"Do you remember when I told you the last time we met that I think you'll see in his entries what he did to take the pain away?"

"Yes," I nodded. "I remember that."

"Did you see that?"

She pulled out her pack of cigarettes.

"Care for one?" She asked.

"Not now, but thank you."

She lit up another smoke and started calmly puffing.

"I couldn't *not* see what he did to take the pain away," I said with a serious tone. "I didn't really want to see it. I cringed when I read about his arms filling up with holes."

"You saw the gulf between us widening?"

I nodded yes.

"And then you saw it close?"

"That's what was so pretty about it," I said. "I feel like you both helped each other deal with your fears in a way that you had never dealt with them before. And so . . ."

"Because I never met a man like him before," she interrupted.

"And he never met a woman like you before," I said warmly.

"Awfully kind of you," she blushed.

" I mean it," I said earnestly.

"I mean it, too," Winston said as he came in with the drinks. "These might be the best martinis I have made in a long time," he grinned.

"Thank you . . . darling," Sophia said as she put her cigarette in the ashtray.

"A pleasure," he said back. "Will you be needing anything else?"

"Not right now," she turned to look at him and patted his arm, "but thank you."

Sophia and I sipped our drinks. I think her martini was gin. She fancied gin, but I couldn't handle it. It usually made me say things that I regretted the next morning.

She put her drink down.

"I thank God every day of my life that I opened up to him that day in the closet," she picked up her cigarette off the ashtray.

I waited for her to continue.

"That's not just because I saved his life," she said with a wicked smile. "I mean, I wouldn't mind saving someone's life on, say, the subway, you know, but I felt I just *couldn't* not save Jacky."

She paused to gather her thoughts.

"He was too special to me. Have you ever had someone like that in your life?"

"I don't think I have," I nervously sipped my drink.

"Well, you will. You just have to be open for it," she paused to think. "Sometimes it also takes the right type of person to make you feel open," she puffed her cigarette. "Plus," she put her drink down, "I saw him soar, Hank. And I mean soar."

"How so?"

"He wasn't the man who I thought he was. He was much more. You know, when I got to know him better, I really liked spending time with him. I never suspected he had this other life. And then, when I got to see under the hood, if you'll allow me the poetic license," she smiled my way.

"I love poetry," I smiled back and raised my glass to her.

"Once I saw what was under his hood, I was even more enchanted than I originally was with him. I guess you could say he gave me a new way of seeing the world. I mean, let me see," she stopped to search the files in her mind.

"Almost like he gave you new eyes?" I finished Sophia's thought.

"You could say that, yes," she nodded. "I saw power in a different way after I got to know him better. I mean, I grew up thinking the mayor is powerful, the president is powerful, the senator is powerful, and so on. I thought that these institutional figures were the seat of power."

She sounded like me, I thought to myself.

"And Jacky changed that for you?" I sipped my drink.

She nodded.

"You'll see why, darling, when you read those," she pointed to the new diaries that I had put next to my chair.

"So you not only loved him for who he was, but for what he did to you. I mean, the effect that he had on your life, and your view of things?" I asked.

"Yes," she sipped her martini. "Oh, I didn't want to forget one more thing while we are on the subject," she said.

"And that is?"

"He changed how I understood love," she smiled warmly. "I lost hope after Richard. Sure, I saw my grandparents together when I was growing up in Louisiana. I knew there were other ways. But I didn't think those types of relationships existed anymore. I felt that I was doomed to live alone for the rest of my life," she took a big gulp of her martini.

"Not such a bad thing if the alternative is Richard," I smirked a little kid would to his teacher in first grade after making a smart aleck comment.

"Point well taken, Hank," she raised her glass to me. "I heard you Chicago boys were sharp," she cut her other hand like a knife.

I looked down shyly at my shoes. I wasn't good at taking compliments.

"Be proud of being sharp, Hank," she said, picking up on my insecurity. "Be proud of who you are and what you are about. Eventually, you'll meet someone who appreciates it."

"Thanks, Sophia," I smiled slightly.

"Think of the great men like Copernicus, Einstein, whomever. They have had one thing in common."

"What's that?"

"They were unique."

I smiled. She finished her drink. I was nursing mine. I didn't want to get too liquored up before I read the diaries later at the Tavern.

"It looks like you are taking that drink slow," she smiled and pointed to my half full glass.

"I don't want to get too much in me before I start reading these," I looked down to the diaries.

"No need to explain," I can't handle drinking and reading. "I like to read while drinking coffee or tea. But I heard you like going to the Minetta and having your drinks there?"

I looked at her with surprised eyes.

"I've been going there for some time," she explained, "and Tony is a dear friend of mine. I also know the owners, and a lot of the regular characters who go there," she smiled knowingly.

I felt like some ignorant sheep blindly roaming the mountains of Scotland who finally finds a herder who has an idea of where she has been, where she is, and where she is going.

Action-Reaction

"We'll have other occasions to have drinks," she smiled. "I'm sure we'll have a lot to talk about after you read those," she pointed to the diaries.

"No doubt."

I got up, went to hug her and kiss both her cheeks, and left her apartment for the Tavern. I had three more entries to read. I was biting at the bit to get there as soon as I could. The pouring rain was thick as smoke and made it hard to see. I had to almost blindly feel my way to the subway. When I got into the Tavern, the place was packed, as usual.

But tonight was packed with more human tuna than I had ever seen before.

I soon found out why.

I hung my fedora and coat up. I walked over to the bar. It was almost full except for one seat. It was a lighthouse on a stormy night. I sat down amongst the revelers, and Tony came up.

"What'll you have tonight, son?" He asked with a smile on his face and some sweat on his forehead. The place was humid with all of the body heat, although it was cold outside.

"What's going on tonight? This place is packed!"

There were more black folks in the Tavern than usual. The place is in Greenwich Village. So it wasn't unusual to have some color in the place on other nights, which endeared me to it. While my heart is big for Chicago, I never liked how segregated it was. The Village was like its own little pocket of melting within the larger New York City pot.

Tony looked around as though he wanted to make sure nobody heard him, like he was about to tell me some big secret or something: "yea, so I'm not supposed to be broadcasting this or anything, but you know Louis Armstrong?"

"What? Do I know Louis Armstrong? Am I a Cubs fan?" I said sarcastically.

"He is in the back dere, in de back room, with a big fucking group of people, and I think Lansky is back there with dem, too," Tony looked at me with more serious eyes than he usually does.

"Meyer Lansky?" I asked.

"No, Tommy Lansky," he said with a chuckle, "what other Lansky would I be talking about?"

"But why is he back there?"

"Why? Do you know where Armstrong got his start?" He said "Armstrong" like "Armstrawng."

"Yea, he..."

"Before you answer that, what you drinking tonight kid?"

"My usual Oban," I said looking at the stunning women walking around the bar with their dresses, heels, long hair, short hair, blond hair, black hair, light skin, dark skin, stunning bodies. I felt like I was in some foreign land, but perhaps it was just because I was becoming more open to the people — like pretty women — that were around me. Maybe, I thought to myself, reading the diaries was changing me? Maybe they were helping me to accept myself?

"Here you go, kid," Tony slid the drink in front of me. "Yea, so what we waz saying befaw," he looked around, "oh, yeah, did you know that Armstrong got his start in New Orleans?"

"Of course," I nodded and took a sip of the Oban,

"But you know how he got it? I mean, where he got his breaks to play for dem white folks down there dat couldn't go to no other bar to hear dem black folks playing jazz?"

"Not really," I shrugged my shoulders.

"He got his start in Storyville — dis a small dirty district near de French Quarter. Dis place was full of brothels and broads, and Mr. Armstrong over there," Tony pointed in the back of the restaurant. "He started playin round 1917 in a joint owned by the Mantranga Family at the time. Dis one of the most powerful families in New Orleans — and in dis little country of ours."

I was impressed by Tony's notes-from-the-underground knowledge.

"So why is Armstrong meeting with Lansky? It is because of Vegas?"

"Ding, ding, ding," Tony said like I had won a round in one of his boxing matches. "I tink dey talkin bout the bands and artists that Lansky wants to play there. Armstrong is some kind of music expert or whateva. Plus, I tink he supposed to play some stuff later on tonight here. That's why all of them people fightin' over demselves in here."

"Got it," I nodded.

"So you readin' them diaries again, eh?"

"You know it," I said. "I forgot to ask, but how long have you known Sophia?"

He looked at me with surprise.

"For a long time, kid, she a quality woman, a rare bird."

"How did you meet her?"

"A long time ago, I tink when she first moved back to the States from, where was it from, France I tink?"

"Yup, France," I said.

"Okay, I thought I was going nuts or something for a second," Tony smiled as he dried a beer glass.

"And you, how you meet her, kid?"

I told him how I met her doing the story on the MOMA donation, and how I started asking questions when I saw the photo of her and Jacky.

"So dem diaries there is their diaries, right?" He asked.

"Yes," I nodded.

"Yea, well you take good care of dem things, kid. You ain't going to find stuff like that just laying around the street, ya know," he smiled.

"No question. This stuff is a shot in the arm."

"A strong shot, eh?" He slapped me on the arm. I didn't know if he was referring to Jacky's smack use or a literal smack in the arm — or both. This was my inner nerd overanalyzing again. The annoying mosquito you can't get rid of on a hot summer day when you have sweat pouring down your arms, sitting on the porch, trying to keep cool by drinking ice cold lemonade and listening to the Cub game on the radio.

"Yes," I said like the nerd that I am, "a strong shot indeed."

"Sir, sir, can we get the check please?" A proper Upper East Side couple was sitting at the end of the bar, and the man was using his right hand to make a writing motion as though he was signing a check.

"I got to go, kid, but you enjoy your read tonight, and we'll catch up later about what you learned."

Tony took off. I sat there looking at the diaries. I was about to open them when I thought of what Jacky said about action and reaction in his diary entry.

I heard that before.

I think it was in a University of Chicago physics class. We learned about Newton. It was his third law. It said something like all forces exist in pairs, or, if I am getting this right, to every action there is always an equal and opposite reaction. I don't know where Jacky picked this up, but I am guessing that he got it from Sophia. She brought him a lot of book smarts. He brought her a lot of streets smarts. They seemed to meet somewhere in the middle between these two extremes.

I took another sip of my scotch, and opened to Jacky's diary entries before the August 21, 1941 entry I read at Sophia's.

June 22, 1941

Germany invading this Russia bear today. I hope this waking up big fucking bear from the sleep. Maybe this the big mistake Germany making in the war? They not taking Russians serious.

Action-Reaction

July 4, 1941

"I telling you so," I say to Sophia over the morning coffee and cigarettes. "But is worse than I thinking."

"How it worse? How this worse?" Sophia asking me.

She looking over at me and asking as I start to make her the coffee. She wear the elegant tan linen skirt down to her knees, these brown Espadrilles on her feet I like to kissing, white linen blouse, pretty red colored necklace beads. She wearing her hair up with the Chinese chopstick made of the pearl or bone or something white and pretty I thinks to myself — is just like her. I needing to touching my cock when I thinks about her.

I lighting up the cigarette. I sitting smoking. I listen to the making of the coffee.

"So how it worse?" Sophia asking as she taking out her cigarette and lighting it up. We inside my shitty dirty closet with doors closed. After Germans coming we start the talking in closet so nobody hear what we saying.

"Well," I let a puff of smoke out and wiped the coffee bean pieces on my dirty janitor shirt with Jacky on patch.

I stop to think to myself in my head.

"They been grabbing up Jews. I expecting them to doing this," I says to her as she stand classy against door while I sitting in my old wood chair. "But they also grab up others they think as worse than the dirt under your fingernails — the immigrants, the Freemasons, the Communists."

"Right," she nodding to me. "I remember you say they go after Jews," she says looking up at ceiling, smoking, remembering on our talks.

"Why you think they taking more peoples than the Jews?" I ask. "I mean, knowing the Jews was in for it. They been in for it in the other countries for long time now. But why they taking the others peoples? What you think?"

Sophia looked down towards me and she thinking for the moments with the cigarette smoke coming from her mouth with the coffee in it. She taking the cigarette from the red lips I loving so much on mine.

"I read about this," she saying to me, "I loving these political philosophies while I at Newcomb," she put Chesterfield into ashtray. "I going to the library few days ago and I looking up the thinkers who talking into Nazi ears."

The coffee start the whistling. I going into closet to taking off stove, putting some into espresso cups, giving Sophia one.

"Love this stuff. I feel homesick without it," she taking the espresso cup from my hands, she look at me, she smile the big smile. "Thank you," she say as she doing the big stir of the coffee with spoon.

I drinking my coffee.

"There is man named Maurras," Sophia says slowly, "Charles Maurras. This man the father of the Anti-France. He thinking that France having too many foreign peoples."

"Even before this war?" I asking.

"Yes," Sophia nodded. "Boris tell me that this man Maurras whisper into Vichy ears. This why Vichy been making outsiders disappear.

Maurras thinking peoples in four states must be killed or kicked out of his pretty true pure France: Protestants, Jews, Freemasons, foreigners — but he also thinking Gypsies, homosexuals, left-wing must be getting out too."

I think to myself as she speak. This one of reasons why I loving this woman. Yes, I getting the dirty information of the black market without her — who sleeping with who, who buying what from us, how we can using the informtion to getting what we wanting from the governments. That cause I know the things before these shitty newspapers.

But Sophia know how to explain things so I see how one thing go with the next in history of the world which I not knowing like her from her level — I know the dirty level, she knowing the top clean level of the philosophy. When we together it like how one pool ball get hit, hit the next, hit the one at end of table — we making the team of the balls. She not have my connections. That not matter cause she making new connections for me in my mind between what happening now and what happening before this.

This why I cannot help my feelings for this woman.

July 18, 1941

"Jacky — it over 13,000! 13,000 Jews! And children? They don't care about no children. They not care at all," Sophia saying to me this morning with the tears in her eyes. She not crying though. She not like to show the emotion. She standing inside my shitty closet against my door, sip her coffee, blow this cigarette smoke so it find home

next to ceiling. I know she want to cry. But I know she not cry — not now.

I not tell Sophia, but I crying to myself when I find out. Few days ago, the head of Vichy in Paris, this man name Rene Bousque, grab the 13,000 Jewish families, many children, for shipping to Drancy. Guillaume telling me that, from there, these people transport to concentration camps in Germany and Poland. Guillaume telling me these peoples is getting killed in the camps.

I hoping he wrong.

But hope and faith make me tired cause it do nothing without the action.

It time for the fucking action.

August 8, 1941

Boris coming to club late tonight.

I needing to meet with him. His Communist party has take no position in this war. That until Russia getting the anal fuck by the Germans, no? Now Boris not so the smiling hope boy. Now they see that it nice to wanting peace. We all wanting the fucking peace Boris. You young boy. You stupid boy who living in the clouds.

That cause sometime the war coming to your door in the morning and do the knocking. You in bed having the coffee after fucking the pretty woman. The knocking happen again. But you not want to answering the door cause now you eating the pussy. War keeps knocking. You knowing you must be getting the door and fucking up the war on the outside on the street. Or else the war going to come through the door and kill you in the bed with your woman. Blood is everywhere in house. Is better for the blood to be spilling outside of house and not on the nice fucking sheets, no?

Boris have the blond hair, blue eyes, the serious look — he knew what he need, and do anything to getting it.

I sit in my office smoking the Cuban cigar. I not much like bright in my office when I having the meetings, so I lighting candle and turn off the lights. Not romantic candlelight — I not like the man. I doing this natural light to calm my nerves. I always having Mickey or other muscle around when I having the meetings in office. But this meeting personal. It is something that I feel much passion about, it not about the money. It about what I feeling in my heart, which is something I feeling with Sophia.

"Nice see your face, Boris," I say as I putting down the cigar.

"The same, Jacky," he shaking my hand and put his hand on my elbow — I thinks to show his happiness for me meet with him.

"Something to drink?" I ask Boris — he wear the old man look stripe tie with the slick hair.

"No thank you, Jacky," he smile. "Water please."

It about 11:00 in the night.

I pour myself whiskey and soda, and pour him the seltzer water.

"Take the seat," I say to him.

"Thank you," he say with nervous in his voice, not know why I call him to place like this. Maybe he scared that I going to cut him up and put him in the concrete when we making the buildings in Marseille?

I giving him the water, I going behind my desk, take the seat, picking up the place where I leaving off — smoke my cigar and do the planning — not about the way to making more money, bringing in more girls, bringing more men into family. No. Only thought is how to kill most Germans without getting caught in Nazi the fish net. How? How? How?

"So why you want to meet?" Boris asking after he taking the big gulps with the fear from the water.

"You like to eat the meat?" I ask him with devil hide behind my smile.

"Yes," he says, "why?"

"What you have to doing before you eating the meat?"

"Cook it?"

"Before that?" I smoking my cigar. We hear this nightclub music of 'Dolores,' this is a song by Dorsey and Sinatra, coming through my office door or maybe it through the floor.

He just sitting there in light of the candle, with cigar smoke cover above, office full of pretty artwork, alligator body that one of boys bring back from safari, I thinks it in Africa. Boris sitting on leather chair that soft, but not so soft that he forgetting who he in front of, and where he was.

"Cut it up?" He trying to catching the fly in sky but he not know how or why.

"Before this?" I take the long puff and blow it in the face of Boris.

He sit looking up at pretty wood panels of office above him. His eyes follow then looking at ceiling fan go in the big circles, like I doing before with Marion. He look like his mind travel through all of the civilize bullshit rules that make him forget we living like we did when we living in the caves. But now we have the nice clothes and phones and

Action-Reaction

cars even though we still killing each other like we doing before. Now we doing it better with the machines. And we still need to kill the animals to eat the animals.

This not changed.

Oh, butcher do our dirty works. But I thinks by look on the face of Boris, cause he now looking at me with more certainty, that he understand that you having to get your hands bloody in life sometimes. This go against the church on how to be the good people or the good citizens. But the church do the many bad things and killing the many people anyway. So that is much bullshit, I thinks.

"You kill it," he finally say to me with the show of his teeth the canine teeth we have to biting into the meat.

I nod to him.

"I not eat them, but I love to feed them to the fucking dogs, or maybe even feed them to themselves, cause we slice them up, make meat of out of them, get the product onto the trucks in Germany for the front lines," I stare at the eyes of Boris with the small smile that Lucifer is jealous of, I thinks to myself.

"Them?" Boris asked me.

"Who you think?" I asking him.

He pointing outside to middle of the club. SS officers was there to hear the Desperado band and buy our women. Music is forbid for them — music played by Jews, blacks, but these is people who Nazis is jealous of.

I nod without saying a word to Boris.

He looking at me with mouth open. Maybe he feeling this electric feeling I feel when I do the things not normal for me to be doing — like talk to a woman like Sophia. I feel like stranger to my old routine, to myself, when I do this. Some say when you do new, you renew. I thinks they is right.

"You serious Jacky?" He asking me with the fear in this voice.

I stare at him.

"Where did your fucking protests against them in November of 40 get you?" I asking him the boy who think he is the man and the leader but who is just the boy who don't understand the dark forest of the world.

He looking down at his feet.

"Peaceful protest — this the luxury, Boris. It is for the people who listen to the protest. Some people," I pointing to my head with my finger like it the pistol, "they need gun to head."

"I understand," he nod to me. "So how we starting?"

"With this Gestapo fuck who at Barbes-Rochechouart stop every morning at 9:00. He taking this line to Gestapo headquarters," I giving Boris a photo that we taking of the man. "We start by killing him," I points to the photo.

Boris not know what to say.

"They hitting us back, and hitting us back hard, you know?" He says with fear in his voice.

I leaning over my desk.

"This ***exactly*** what we want."

I smile.

"What? Why?" He ask with the surprise.

I leaning back in chair. I lay back like I in Saint Tropez. He look like the scared school boy in the exam he not know the answers to. I smoke my cigar with the leisure and with the pretty women next to me, with the ocean in front of my eyes, and no care. He wanting to bite his nails cause he have so much stress in his body.

"The more we killing them, the more they killing us. This wake the French people up that Nazis and their Vichy bitches is not our friends, don't you see?"

I leaning forward back toward Boris out of St. Tropez and back into Marseille slums I grow up in.

"Peoples soon understanding these Nazi fucks is maggots we must kill, kill, kill or else they eat our body, our soul, our country, don't you see boy?"

He start the slow nodding of his head.

"So you can getting someone in your party to do the hit?" I ask.

He nod yes.

"Who? I don't want nobody fucking this up." I say.

"Man named Colonel Pierre-Georges Fabien," he looking around my office to make him feel that he not dealing with little boy who not know what he doing. "He telling me before he want do the same things as you do, Jacky, and he fighting in Spain. So he kill before," he look back at me. He look like he feel more comfortable with the train track we about to be getting on.

"He sound like the good man," I putting my ash into tray and getting up out of the seat. Boris getting up off his seat. "We not talking after this night, but I sending you the messenger boy when we ready. Nothing in writing. All words of our mouths. Understand?"

> *I putting my right hand on his shoulder.*
> *He nodding he understands.*
> *"Good," I slapping his face soft.*

A crowd of people walked behind me at the Tavern. I looked up from my diary readings to see Lansky and Armstrong walking next to one another to the door. I wasn't interested in joining the crowd around them. I wanted to see what else happened after Jacky's meeting with Boris, other than the hit on the German officer. I suppose I live a lot of my life like that. The life of the mind was better than the life of flesh, the life of fame, or whatever it is called that these people were doing. So I looked forward in Jacky's diary entries to October 20, 1941.

> ***October 20, 1941***
> *The plan is working.*
> *Today Hitler the midget mustached shitty artist is killing the 100 hostages he holding. This his answer to our hit on the Gestapo fuck in the Vichy zone.*
> *Resistance is getting stronger.*
> *"I want in on it, too, Jacky," one of our best girls, her name Stardust, says to me one night. She sitting in same seat Boris was sitting in my office with the smoke and smell of the good pretty nice women in the air cause they all dancing with the customers close by. Stardust got the sweet smelling legs that taking up most of land on her body. Her tits is small like the lemons, but she have the tight ass, short skirts, thigh highs, skin like the baby.*
> *A Danish baby — Stardust is one of our Danish girls.*
> *But our customers think she Dutch.*

"Give me the Dutch, Jacky, and make it quick, cause I got this itch that not quit until she scratching it," the fat banker with sweaty hands telling me one time when he come during the summer weekends. His wife is gone with kids to southern beaches. He loving when Stardust walking on his face and hands with her heels. She never touch him. He love being the dominated man.

"I want to do some good, this my chance," Stardust saying to me with these big Sardinia water blue eyes. She looking at my cock as she sitting in same seat Boris sitting in my office. She biting her lip. But it not my cock she really wanting. She knowing that other girls giving me the good information from their customers, and Stardust want to do the same.

"Alright, Stardust. You try with this one," I show her the picture of this piece of shit SS officer Gustav Franz Wagner. "I want you to know his travels. Make the house call, yes? Look at his papers after you giving him the little pill to making him sleep, see?" I sliding the little pill over the table. It funny how most powerful things in life is sometimes the smallest — the pussy with the pill can be better than the big bad machine guns.

Guillaume telling me that Wagner become very powerful family in the Nazi party cause he step on the many people his way up the ladder which the Nazis loving. They giving him the good money and more responsibility. Men like him loving the house calls so they not have to travel in the public eye for the vice. Our house calls giving us the information on the Nazi officers and their families so we can *pushing them against the wall to get things or else we making the information public.*

I have the feelings that Stardust going to have to working for this one cause Wagner is sick man. This exactly what happening.

"He is dirty son of bitch," she says to me morning after.

"How?" I asked with a dirty smile.

"He stuck it in there," she pointing to her pussy. Many politician and businessman pay to go there. I not understand why she complain.

"Where you expect him to stick it? In between your toes?"

*"It not **that** he stuck it there, it **what** he sticking in there Jacky," she say as she make a pistol with her finger as she look at me. "And then he take out and sucking his pistol, force it my mouth, yell to me to suck, while he stick me with his little pecker."*

"This not surprise me," I shrug my shoulders like she tell me it raining or snowing outside in winter. "These men loving power over the beautiful things like you," I soft touching her shoulder in good friend soothing way.

"Thanks, Jacky," she say to me.

She smile.

"Get addresses? Information? That is the very important thing."

"Yes. And, yes," she nodding to me, "he is marry and has the children. I see the pictures of them all. Very old pure German family, I saw. I have the feeling they not much like him whoring with me," she smile a good girl smile.

I kissing her with my love on her cheek.

> *"Write info here and we putting it his file."*
> *I give her a card to fill.*
>
> *I thinking to myself when she give me the address, here some of best women in Paris. They wanting to use their pricey pussies as the secret weapons for the Resistance not to make the more money, but to get the information from the Nazis.*
>
> *Like the many politicians and businessmen, I knew these Nazi men was two-timers — they have the German wives back in stolen mansions, send children to school like Otis, but getting the girls that cost much money.*
>
> *This is going to be the deadly problem for them.*

I closed Jacky's diary. My drink was getting low. But I knew I needed to take it slow. I didn't want to go. So I went with the flow of the evening, and started smelling the most beautiful perfume I had smelled in a long time.

I looked over my right shoulder. This young woman sat one stool away from me. She was reading a book. She smelled naturally fresh. She looked over at me and I stared back into my diaries. I got caught cheating a look at her answer — which was her beauty — and I didn't want her to know.

Her answer was in her smell, hazel eyes, swimmer body that was softened by her thick brown hair that went down to the middle of her back, natural colored clothes (long brown peasant looking dress, brown clogs, lavender shirt, worn and frayed Levi's jean jacket, orange scarf wrapped around her neck), and in the smile she gave me through her lightly colored pink lips.

It was a light smile.

It was the lightness of the sun rising in the crisp fall morning and barely kissing the tops of the rows of Illinois wheat flowing in the wind. It was that type of smile. I should know.

Dirty Quiet Money

My parents would take me to the country all of the time growing up in Chicago. I used to go by myself, too, just to clear my head. I couldn't handle the city too much, and being in the country, or on the prairie, soothed me. It was a simple life, but sometimes things got so complicated in the city that you longed for that simple life, where things weren't more about gadgets like this or that, but more about people like this or that. I'm no Neanderthal. And yet I also think sometimes the city makes you nuts with all the action — at least it does for me. So getting my hands dirty in the country, camping in the forest up in Wisconsin, helped calm me.

The way she read her book and drank her tea soothed me for some reason. She was in the middle of the chaos and debauchery of New York, but wasn't overwhelmed by it. She was from somewhere wild and untamed, like Montana, Colorado, or California. Maybe that's why she wasn't overwhelmed by New York's nervous energy — maybe she left the city, and let the city leave her, when she needed to. Like I did. But maybe she went to the ocean by herself, like I did when I went to the country by myself, instead of going with the crowds to Woodstock or wherever else the crowds go.

I loved this woman.

I loved her energy.

The energy was like me, but it was not of me. But I was too scared to even think of love, or loving anybody other than my reading, writing, and life of the mind.

That was my safe world.

Love to me was a scary world full of rough waters, cliffs, and heartache. At least that is all I wrote and read about in the papers. That's what sold.

Love didn't sell. Nobody wanted to read about love.

Especially nothing like Jacky and Sophia's story. I kept to my safe world for the evening. I took another sip of my reading potion, and opened Sophia's diaries. I wanted to see her view of the other side of the coin that was her relationship with Jacky.

November 20, 1941

We were in Jacky's little closet this morning. But it didn't seem so little after getting to know him like I have. The closet was the tip of the largest — and filthiest — iceberg I have ever seen. He weaved his dirty little secret global cobweb from this place — one of the cleanest upper crust schools in all of France.

My mouth opened — and stayed open — when he told me.

"He put his pistol where?" I asked Jacky when he told me about some German officer putting his pistol where I only thought men wanted to put a piece of themselves, not their piece.

"You hear what I say," Jacky started to make the coffee.

The air was cool outside and the door was closed. I was wearing a fur throw around my shoulders, one of my favorite black furs, and was also sporting this lovely hat that Richard got for me in Chicago — a nice little black fedora that I wore titled over my right eye.

It was winter — or close to it — in Paris, and so I have been dressing up — for myself, and for Jacky.

Black gothic Victorian stockings that also gave him a glimpse of what was underneath through the embroidery. A lean black skirt that hugged my body in all the right places, and a lovely black jacket with a tie around the waste that was hand made for me in Vienna. Hand made Italian black boots up to my calves.

Jacky made me want to dress up for him more than I have ever wanted to dress up for another man, or another woman.

I know he isn't a good man. A husband who goes to Church every Sunday and takes good care of his family is a good man. And yet I am learning that being good is relative. Good church going people in Vichy are doing horribly bad things. Bad people who still live in medieval times like Jacky are doing heroic things.

I mean, when they say "the Mafia," people think "the" refers to some organization with parts that all work in the same direction or purpose, just like parts of "the bike" make it go forward.

But I knew from speaking with Jacky that there were many families with different ways of doing business. The original one was from Sicily. They have serious rules for admission, a ten-step list, such as not cheating on your wife because it only gives the mistress leverage.

Just as not all families do business the same way, not all with power wield it the same way. Auguste J. Ricord, a powerful black marketeering man Jacky told me about, is collaborating with the Nazis.

But not Jacky.

"Sophia," he told me one time, "I making more money if I playing for them, but our team make me feel the better feelings," I remember him pausing to take his cigarette out of the corner of his mouth to ash it and put it back, "and a lot better looking, too."

He winked at me.

Boy could he make me feel swell.

The way I tell it to myself is that Jacky had the choice of being some other way like this Auguste Ricord character but decided against it. The rest of it, his career choice, his way of life, and so on, doesn't make him good. But it is what he does with the power that he has accumulated that makes him good — for now. At least this is what I tell myself.

"Aren't you worried that one of these officers will see what you are up to with these women you are sending to meet them?" I asked Jacky as I lit up my trusted Chesterfield.

He turned to look at me as I rested my back against the closed closet door. I rubbed my legs together as I took the cigarette from my red lips. He looked at me with serious eyes, I did the same with him, but also with the playful movement of my legs, which I know he liked because I would always catch him looking at them, like now.

His eye peeked down to see what I was doing down there.

He smiled a pleased customer smile, and I smiled a pleased shop owner smile of whatever I started selling in my shop.

With his tuxedo tucked away in the background, he said in so a matter of fact way to me: "why worry when I have the information that ruin this man's life forever?" He chuckled and then went back to making his coffee.

Jacky turned me on more and more as the days went on. His daring and boldness are things I thought I had when I left Richard. And I did have them. But these character traits have been dormant since then. They have been ready to pounce, on *something, or on someone, but they haven't had the opportunity.*

Maybe I would be with Jacky in a way I never thought I would want to be with him. Maybe it's because I never thought I would need a man like I how I feel like I need him.

This all led me to one thought that I only write here because it is only to me and nobody else: I promised myself I would live to have this man's child. I can't believe I just wrote that! I can't believe I am thinking it! Otis, I always told myself, was the last one. Yes, I thought about adopting. Yes, I thought doing that. No, I never would be with another man, and bear another child.

That's until I met Jacky.

February 24, 1942

"There is the fucking rat in their crew," Jacky said to me this morning through the thick cloud of cigarette smoke in his closet.

"How do you know?"

"How Germans knowing about where they printing the Resistance paper? You know they killing Boris and others yesterday?"

"I know," I said as I slowly sipped my black coffee. I looked into the coffee grinds swimming around inside the blackness. To cover up my sadness and to forget about the dark Nazi clouds brewing, I thought about Jacky's sperm swimming up stream and having his child. I looked up at him with that secret goal in my heart and soul. My secret fantasy was one of the few things that gave me hope.

But he couldn't know — for now.

"What is it?" He asked me when I looked at him.

"I was just thinking."

"What you thinking?" He asked.

"The future," I smiled coyly.

"What about it?" He sipped his coffee.

There are those times in life when you say one thing but want to say another that is on your mind. But that thing on your mind is oftentimes something that you don't want to see the light of day. So you pick up a diversion for a thought, something that is the opposite of what you are thinking about, to sabotage the original thought. I was thinking about having a child with him. My sabotage thought was to think of his death — or mine.

"If they have someone on the inside, how do we know they don't know about us?" I asked him with worry in my voice.

Jacky put down his coffee and wiped his mouth.

"Croissant?" He held out a basket of freshly backed croissants.

"Thank you," I took one and dipped it into my coffee.

He calmly sat there and took a bite of the croissant. He chewed it slowly. A cow chewing his wheat couldn't chew any slower.

"I not know this," he said peacefully.

He took another bite of his croissant. He did the cow chew for the next minute.

"But I soon finding out."

He took another bite.

"This informant will soon be put on the ice," he looked at me with the same intensity in his eyes

that I used to look at him with when I was thinking of how beautiful our child would be.

But his eyes had the look of mayhem, quiet mayhem, in them. Mine were full of peace and serenity. I suppose the intensity in both eyes is the same — they are the eyes of having a goal, and working towards that goal, like an athlete does.

"Aren't you worried about being found out?" I asked in a maybe you are in the same boat as I am tone.

He looked at me. The rookie.

"They not know my name, not what I looking like," he smiled. "This why I never letting people taking my photo. I am the ghost."

"So what do they call you if not your name?"

A freshman question, I thought to myself.

"Blacky," he smirked.

"How did they dream that one up?"

"The Allies not know how I get the black market information that I giving them," he looked at me with proud eyes, the type of eyes that used to not be so proud, wherever they came from, but which now owned that pride. "One British officer start using this name, and it sticking. I don't meet with them direct," he said in an educational type of tone, "only by messenger."

My prize was a child with Jacky, but his prize was getting this informant. I suppose getting the informant was what they call a "condition precedent" in the law, as I understand from being around Tulane law students at Newcomb College when I was younger. This is something that needs to be done before another thing can be done — a

> *lawyer needs to be admitted to the bar in a state before he can practice law.*
>
> *The informant problem needed tending to before we could think of longer term plans, or else we wouldn't survive to have those plans.*

I closed Sophia's diary. I looked over to where the lovely young woman sitting next to me was. She was gone. Once again, my mind controlled my heart.

It was my life story. I was getting tired of it.

I knew that I needed to tend to my heart before I could make the leap and try to connect with a woman, just as Sophia and Jacky needed to deal with their informant before Sophia could think of having a child. I wasn't quite ready to go into the affairs of the heart. Maybe I did need to meet a woman would help me, just as maybe I could help her, as Sophia once told me. It was just about closing time at the tavern.

"Good reading tonight there pal?" Tony asked me as he dried a glass with a white rag from behind the bar.

"Excellent stuff," I raised my glass to him and finished off the last drop that was in there.

"A little fresher for the road?" He asked with a grin.

"Why not?" I said as I bent down to start putting the diaries into my satchel.

I found a dried out rose on the ground. It looked like it had been in someone's book for a long time. I picked it up and inspected it. I wasn't in Egypt, or anywhere resembling a dig, but I inspected it, smelled it, and held it up to the light as though I were. It smelled like the woman who was reading at the bar. It had that fresh smell to it.

I remember once going to Rockaway beach in Queens, and walking on the sand only to find a dozen or so roses scattered close to the water. I didn't know if that was a sign, other than

God or whatever it is out there showing me something beautiful for the day, for me to remember along with my dog, Rusty, kissing me on the face when I was younger.

But I took this rose at the tavern as a sign. It was a sign to me that maybe I needed to be more open more like Sophia started doing with Jacky. Maybe I needed to be more like her — and him, too.

"Here you go, kid," Tony put a splash into my empty glass.

"Thanks, Tony." I sipped. "Ever get inspired by a woman?"

"Sure, plenty."

"What do you think it's like? I mean, how would you describe it?"

Tony stood there for a moment drying a glass.

"It's like dat little splash I put in your drink dea, kid. It gives you a little more to fuel your fire inside. Sometimes you ain't got access to this fuel on your own. That fuel stored somewhere in a file in a dark closet with dem cob webs on it that you never open befaw cauz it got a big lock on it. But the right woman can give you the key to dat lock."

"Never knew you were such a scholar, Tony," I said with an appreciative smile.

"Learning sometimes happens over there," he pointed to where NYU had most of its campus, "but sometimes it happens right the fuck here," he pointed to the ground in the bar.

"You got that right, Tony." I raised my glass to him.

"You one of my best students, kid."

The street PHD and his white sheep student — me — exchanged proud smiles at the relationship we were building.

I finished my drink and settled my tab.

"I'm off for the evening, Tony."

"See you tomorrow, kid."

"You got it, Tony."

After I left the Tavern and started walking towards my apartment, all I could think about was how I was learning about a whole different side to business, politics, philosophy, love, and relationships through reading the diaries that I wasn't exposed to at Chicago. I could only imagine how much more I was about to learn.

CHAPTER 11
A Woman's Best Friend

"If it bleeds, it leads," a magazine editor gal once told me. She is right. All I pretty much write all day are stories about murder, divorce, car accidents, layoffs, and cousins of those. There are the positive stories here and there, but they don't get the front page as much as they should. I'd love to have a paper in New York called "Good News New York," or something like that, which only features positive stories. But I'd go out of business in a New York minute. So I keep working at the paper while also living this double life at night. As I took the subway down to the Tavern, I read Jacky's entry below.

> *March 1, 1942*
> *"What his name? What is name of this fucking rat!" I says to Guillaume today in basement of his father's store.*
> *"I don't know, I don't know," he say with the feeling of worry voice. "I have it for you tomorrow."*
> *A long time ago, I asks my peoples in Marseille for the good source for the dirty information in this*

shitty Paris government. My family is giving me the piece of paper. Guillaume has his name on it.

When I meet with him, he smoke his Lucky Strike cigarette with nervous breaths. This man was a nervous man. Tall, lean, shifty, crafty — I think this wire of a man running every day. He have the blue eyes of the baby that calming you into think all is good. When this man has the fear, these same eyes make you believe world is coming to the big shitty end with the shit everywhere on the walls, on the faces of the peoples, in the ocean, cause shit is everywhere, this eyes making you thinking! But much of this man's fear of the world coming from his mistrust in himself.

I think to myself that his family is Russian or something like this. Whatever they is, they is Jews. This is way the Nazis thinking — whether you Jew or not, not whether you is smart, with good looks, ambitious, connected. It Jew or not Jew for this fucking Nazis.

But they not knowing Guillaume's family is Jewish. He stealing the state file on his family. He then writing in records that they is Aryan — even the monkey from Africa looking more Aryan! I loving this story when they tells me it down in Marseille.

He playing the fool.

He wanting people to thinking he the fool.

But he no fool — I know this.

And yet he worries. He worry so much he worry me even when I got nothing to worry about. His worry making wrinkles on his face. When he stress, his body is like your tight asshole when someone trying to stick the broom handles into it, non?

"When tomorrow you get me rat's name? The longer we waiting, the more this shit rat getting away," I saying to him as I looking around the dirty basement. One light, one radio, a leaking roof that keeping the sound of the drip of the water coming to our ears.

He turning his wrist over to looking at his watch. I smile when he doing this because he do it even when I didn't ask him nothing. This man timing himself all the time — when he take the piss, when he eat the sandwich, when he take the walk to work, maybe when he do the fucking. I guess it good to know mother clock existing. But if she ruling your life, you the walking dead.

"By noon tomorrow," he say to me.

I moving closer to his face.

"You sure?"

"Yea, yea, yea, Jacky, I get it for you," he says. "Now — how you scratching my back after I scratching yours?" he smiled.

"You pick of any talent you liking at our clubs. I giving you this and drinks on the house until you not in this world no more."

His face moving closer. I not know what he like — the blond, the black, the both? It don't matter to me cause he good man. We got whatever he liking: blonds, browns, reds. We have the good look men at the club for the men who like the good look men, and the good look women for the men who likes the good look women.

"And if you killed?" He asking with the worry in his eyes.

My cigarette sitting on my lips. I letting the ash fall wherever they want to falling like the rocks from the mountains.

"I get you on the books," I say to this biting his fingernails nervous man.

We keeping all of our deals on the books. I not know where we keep it. I thinking it somewhere in Marseille. I only know the man to contact. He putting my deal with Guillaume on this book.

Guillaume know this.

"Alright then, we have a deal!" He had big grinning wrinkles around his mouth. He was the good man. I also knew he like his naughty things, just like we all liking the naughty things. But he not the man who liking too much of the naughty things cause he like doing things behind the closed door and not in the lights of the camera. He not like the other government people. They like to push their fat power in our face when they come to clubs. Guillaume smarter than this.

We shaking the hands.

I squeezing his hand hard and pulling him close to me after we standing.

He not the physical strong man and I knowing he hate the violence.

I not care.

"You better be right," I putting my hand behind his neck like I do with the men who I stab deep in the stomach so I can smell their last breathing moments in this world we living.

He nodding yes to me. His eyes telling me that he understanding the squeeze of my hand

> *on back of his little neck that Mickey snap with the easiness of a run down hill with the wind on your back, non?*

I was anxious to read the rest of Jacky's entries. When I put them inside my satchel and was about to get off the subway, I couldn't believe my eyes when I saw the rose pedal woman from the Tavern.

She was wearing a bright orange dress, like you would see in Spain or in some ocean town, down to her knees that showed off her lovely calves; some low top Converse All Stars; a tight white t-shirt underneath the same Levi's jacket she wore at the Tavern, but this time with a red bandana around her neck that she used like a scarf.

As I left the subway, I took a peek at her. She was reading a book. She caught me again looking at her, and she smirked playfully towards me. I looked away and in front of me. I was getting off track and wanted to get back on it.

But I really didn't want to get back on track. I wanted to stay and talk to her.

Instead, I talked to Tony.

"Fuck me, look who it is, Father Hank Flannigan live from the *Times*," Tony said as I sat down at the bar around 7:00 p.m. "How was the day at the paper, Father?"

"Pretty much the same as it was yesterday, and the day before that," I said dejected.

"Yea, yea, yea," he waved to me, "who knows what is true and what is false anymore pal. I could learn a lot more about what is happening sometimes from the local bodega owner that I can learn from de paper," he said as he needled me.

"A lot of times, I feel the same way, too, Tony," I put my satchel on the bar.

"But you doin good kid," he leaned over and said in an encouraging way. "You cutting your teeth over dea. And, who knows, maybe one day you win the Pulitzer Prize, or whateva, after you keep practicing, see?"

He grinned a he knew something and I didn't type of grin.

"I see," I agreed not knowing why.

"Yea, well, even if you don't, I'm getting first round, pal, so don't say no." He showed me his fist with a smile behind it.

"I'll have a martini then." I missed Sophia and her positive influence on me. Tony was a like a cousin to that good influence. I'll get whatever piece of that family I can.

"High martini roller tonight? I guess your martini drinks with Sophia is rubbing off?" He smacked me in the arm lovingly — but hard.

"You could say that," I appreciated his tough uncle love.

Tony went to make the drink. I looked around. The bar was pretty empty. I saved the rose that I found the last time I was here, and used it as a place marker in the diaries Sophia gave me. The rose made me think of the gal who dropped it, and gave me hope that I would again stumble upon her, or a gal like her, one day. But, this time, I would have the guts to meet my dream rather than ducking it like a bullet. I opened the place in Jacky's diary where I had been reading from on the train, and took the rose out.

March 2, 1942

I getting the name today from Guillaume. It written on the small piece of paper that deliver to school. Written is this name "Jacques." He living in 16th quarter of Paris and he loving our African women. My women is telling me this.

I know the perfect woman who going to killing this Jacques man.

March 3, 1942

"Will you kill him?" I asking Divine as she siting in my office. She from Ghana.

She sat there staring at me with her sand brown eyes. She loved smoking the cigars from Cuba. I letting the girls smoking my cigars as long as they replacing them for me.

Divine is dark chocolate in package of the human. She has the long arms, legs, is lean, fit like women who do the gymnast tricks in Marseille bedrooms. I seeing these women walking in Marseille streets when I a boy working for the family and I wanting to touch my small junior cock when I going home to thinks about them.

She wearing the tight black see through dress, no panties, black boots that the cowboy wearing. She have this tight top that circles around her tits and ties in the back. Her long hair has the big braid in the back that going down to her ass I thinks about eating sometimes.

This the perfect woman for the kill of this man. I know she not having a problem killing the right people when the right time to killing. Mickey tell me this once.

"Yea, Jacky," Mickey says to me one night with some of these rain drops on his face full of the scars. We standing in the alley under black umbrella that protecting us from the rain so we can smoking and talking about the type of things you talking about in a dark rainy alley at night with a man like Mickey and a man like me under black umbrella.

"She a heavy hitter." He saying to me as he lighting up my cigarette and then his. "Word on street is she once take care of pimp that was trying to squeeze her and other girls out of the pay. One night after pimp taking her back to his place

to try and fuck her when she not wanting to fuck him. She putting the pills in the man's champagne that knock the man out — he one of those guys, acting like the classy champagne drinking man and then do the things that not having any class, you know?"

Mickey touching me on chest with back of his hand to see if I listening.

"I know this type of fucking man," I spitting on ground below and smiling the little boy smile.

"So she putting this stuff into champagne, and he not know cause he busy licking this fine pussy she born with."

Mickey take the long devil inhale of his cigarette and looking around the alley to making sure nobody is listening to what we saying.

"When this man waking up," Mickey saying, "he in the fucking lake of blood, and that blood not from her. It from his cut off cock that is smiling at him as it sitting next to right eye of him!" Mickey smiling the mean motherfucker smile as he pointing to his crotch with the cigarette in his mouth.

"It hard for him to take the piss that morning, no?" I smiling back with the cigarette in my mouth, too, and wise eyes that meet with his cause we both speak the same language with our mouths, eyes, spirits.

He smiling back to me. It that smile you smile when you at beach with your friends and you knowing the people not at beach is having the sweating balls and pussies in the city. But you at beach in sun, with cool air keeping your balls or your pussy very nice cool happy on the trip where there is smiles and kissing and touching and loving.

So you looking at your friends, they looking at you, with the same team smile that saying you is on the same fucking team.

"He never mess with any of them again?" *I asked funny cause I knowing the answer.*

"Well, he not around much after that, cause I thinking he bleeding to death that day. But no other guy wanting to fuck with her crew," Mickey says as he smokes the big smoke of his cigarette in alley.

I patting Mickey on his shoulder.

"Ah, and now that she in our fucking crew, I hoping that she not cutting our cocks, eh Mickey!" *I laugh the laugh of the king after a meal has fill his fat belly cause I have the mean crazy bitch on my team.*

Back in my office, I sitting across from Divine. She uncrossing her muscle legs. She crossing them other way to give me the peek of her pretty black cat.

But I just keeping my eye on her eyes cause this the important business that I need doing with her. There no time for her nice pussy. This what I not liking about this business I in — I got to keep the eye on the business sometimes when I wanting to so bad to looking licking touching the nice pussy that is nice to look lick touch.

"How I take him out?" *She moving forward toward me out of the darkness to show her black skin to light above my desk. She dropping some cigar ash onto elephant tusk ashtray on my desk. Then she leaning back into the darkness.*

"With this," *I holding up a needle.*

"I like it. What's in it?"

"Cyanide," *I says.*

> *"Give it to him when he sleeping?" She lean forward again to ash. I know she know the answer to question. That is why I pick Divine.*
>
> *"This not a problem," I says. "He live in the rich area of Paris. He has the women guests like you at the early mornings so that nobody is around to seeing him do the dirty things in the clean house. You in-and-out like the oiled machine that kills motherfuckers like this, yes?"*
>
> *"When?" She asking with no pause. That cause she wanting the blood on her hands. She can't wait to do it to this man and make the notch in her head of another shitty man that she killing.*
>
> *"Tomorrow night," I says. "I don't want him running from ice on your fingers."*
>
> *"It will be done," she says as she put out her cigar.*
>
> *"There be nice Christmas present for his head," I says to her.*
>
> *She smile the pretty smile at me.*
>
> *"I cut it off real nice for you, Jacky," she licking her lips.*

I looked around the Tavern to see if anybody was reading what I was reading. As always, I was in my little bubble. But I didn't want somebody to see this stuff and think I was some oddball for reading it. At least I didn't want them to think I was a dangerous oddball.

"Alright, junior, here is your martini," Tony left the drink in front of me.

"Thanks, Tony," I said with an appreciative smile.

"You know it, pal," he winked at me.

I took a few sips. I was tempted to start smoking a cigarette like Jacky did in his diaries, with it dangling at the end of my

Dirty Quiet Money

mouth. But I didn't want to look like a poser. So I just kept sipping the martini until there was about quarter left in the glass, and then I turned to the next entry in Jacky's diary.

> *March 4, 1942*
>
> *I walking to school this morning from metro. I walking by this dark Divine lady I have the dream of fucking many times.*
>
> *She nods to me.*
>
> *This telling me everything I needing to know. She did the kill. That man take the sleep he never getting up from.*
>
> *May 10, 1942*
>
> *I have the coffee today with Guillaume.*
>
> *He looking happy but there is smell of trouble on his lips.*
>
> *We standing in this wet shit basement under his father's store. I wondering why we always needing to meeting at this place. Why not the nice place with the nice women and the nice drinks? Fuck. It cause we wanting to keep, how the Americans say, the profile that is low? Or is it quiet?*
>
> *Cigarette smoke and the smell of our coffees filling the air. He like to smoke his hash. He filling his cigarette with the hash from Morocco.*
>
> *"A little Jacky?"*
>
> *"Thank you," I putting my hand up. I not do this when I on the business.*
>
> *He smiling the big smile.*
>
> *"More for me," he finish loading up his cigarette.*
>
> *The sound of him roll his papers, a honk or two outside on the street, that sound of the drip from the roof was only sounds in the shit basement.*

"Been liking the toys in the clubs?" I asking him but I knowing the answer.

Drip, drip, drip, drip — the water coming from the roof.

"I loving them all," he smile smoking the cigarette with a nervous hand. I don't read like Sophia. I not able to add the numbers like the man who adding the numbers like he breath the air with the no effort in his body, what his name, the, what is, the accountant?

But I picking up on this man's energy without him saying nothing.

"What going on?" I moving forward over the grandfather old table between us and putting my dirty face and arms under the light above. My suit jacket was off and sleeves was rolled up. I not need to put on front for him.

Drip, drip, drip, the water went.

"What you mean what going on?" He dumping some hash ash from his Lucky Strike onto tin ashtray.

"Got something to say?" I say serious.

He looking up at light, over to water dripping, back at me. He wanting to look at anything but me.

Drip, drip, drip, the water goes onto ground.

"What is it?" I asking.

He take the long drag.

"They know about Sophia," he say with the same focus eyes he must have had when he stealing his family Jewish records. They was professional eyes you must trust. I not care that he smoke the hash. Some people I selling to in Marseille went to the school and becoming top professors at the schools like Oxford or the top business peoples in

Paris. They coming to our clubs to hear the jazz and smoke the hash. We the only clubs that having the jazz. He this type of smart man.

"Know what?" *I leaning back in chair.*

"A few things," *he saying back.*

"I waiting," *I says.*

He was wearing the government man uniform — cheap suit, tie, shoes, shirt. Is the type of clothing that all of these men wearing so they followers of the body that is government they is parts of. But he not having the government man's mind. He thinks with the different mind. He love knowing things nobody else knowing. He like me. We sharing a love of the dirty information about important peoples that nobody knowing.

But us. Ah, we know the dirty fucked up things about these people that is trying to be so clean but they is so dirty.

"They know she helping giving out Resistance to peoples in Paris," *he say.*

"I bet through Jacques," *I says.*

He nod.

"He dead," *I says.*

Guillaume look at me with the deer eyes of surprise when they not see the car coming — until it too late.

"So what else they knowing?"

He leaning over the shitty old table to ash his cigarette. He took long hit that seem like it not stopping.

"The name of her family," *Guillaume finally saying.*

"So?" *I says back.*

"Know what that was?" *He asking.*

"No," I says.

"Bethe," he say.

"Yea? This the German name. So who care if she from the German family?"

"Jacky," this nervous man looking at me for the seconds of time which is dancing with the drips of the water that is coming from above, "she from the Jewish family," he said with the eyes I use when I stab, or that I use when I telling someone I going to stab them, and then stabbing them.

I whisper to myself in the surprise at what he saying.

"Sophia — a Jew?" I says to myself.

"They got her name from the boat records when she coming into France," Guillaume say as he dumping more hash ash out into the tray.

I lighting up the cigarette and leaving it there to play on the lips of my dirty mouth — the smoke is the good friend when times is not good.

"What boat records?" I asking.

"She coming here with her husband before they marry and put the name Bethe on the papers when they asking what mother's family name is — to see who is the Jew or not," he say.

I stopping to speak so I can doing the thinking.

"Since I meeting with her, she using Gordon, her father's family name, no? Her father was the Protestant. Bethe must be name from her mother family?" I says in a streaming of my mind to Guillaume.

"That explaining things," he taking a long puff and this time his eyes is more droopy. But he was still smart sharp — I not knowing how.

Dirty Quiet Money

"I understand all of this now," I says with the calm in my voice to Guillaume with my legs cross over another.

"I'm sorry, Jacky," Guillaume say with the sad eyes.

"It's okay. It just another thing on my list I need to take good care of."

He looked like I had told him I was going to climb the tower Eiffel naked and with the rose in my mouth like the crazy man.

I getting up and shaking his hand.

"This information about Sophia is not include in our deal," I say as we shaking the hands. "We taking care of you, Guillaume. Someone be by your father's store tomorrow with the something to make him happy."

"This info is on me, Jacky," he smile.

"I insisting you take the present," I says.

I getting to club later. I telling Mickey for 25,000 francs be sent to Guillaume's father's place in the basket of croissants and jam next morning by one of our boys dressing up as the pastry delivery.

Time not on my side.

June 10, 1942

"I certain of it," Madeleine says to me today over the coffee in Left Bank. We sitting outside the Café De Flore. "They coming to get her and her son at the school."

She an older woman and working at phone company. Her family is from Marseille. I knew her father very good. He was the man of my neighborhood who having the respect. He one of few men I have respect in my life. I promise him I looking after *her after he died. So I did. She is on family payroll. She listen to German officer phone calls. She also listen to the Gestapo phone calls from their center at the Number 84 Avenue Foch in 16th Arrondissement.*

"When this supposed to happen?" I putting down my coffee on the warm summer night and taking off my jacket. I used to wear the pistol when I was the muscle. I stop being the muscle. The pistol got no class.

"The morning of the 12th," she pick up her coffee and sip it with calm.

The writers, poets, philosophers is sitting all around us. I not really care too much about any of them. All I care about was Nazi officers in the middle of the pigeons. I wanting to make sure the blond wolves not hearing us talking about how we going to take one blond Jew sheep from their noses. What I means is not that we going to pick the blond Jew out of their noses, like we picking the shit out, what I means is we take, how they Americans say, from under their noses?

"You sure?" I look into the Madeleine eyes.

"Yes, it going to happen this Friday. I know how important they is to you, Jacky," she put her hand on mine, which on the table. "So I wanting to letting you know I positive. Gestapo going to be there in morning at the school to pick up her and son."

"Know who the order given to?"

"Rene Bousque," she lean over to tell me with the whisper.

I finish my coffee very slow and thinking it must be true.

I getting up, leaving money on the table, taking my jacket, kissing Madeleine on head.

> *"You a lifesaver, God bless you," I say as I giving the kiss.*
>
> *I had to make the moves — and make moves fast.*

My head was spinning from how fast I drank the martini. Plus, it was later in the night. There was a slew more folks in the bar than there were before. There was more smoke in the air, both cigar and cigarette, not to mention perfume, after shave, and the smell of cash.

I also think reading these entries, and knowing just how close Sophia and Otis were to the Nazi talons, made me nervous. I was a machine gun virgin, I guess you could say. I was more into reading the cartoons when I was growing up, or making up cartoons, than I was in playing war games.

"Dat too strong for ya?" Tony pointed to the empty martini glass in front of me.

"You could say that again."

"Yea, but I won't," he slightly patted me playfully on the shoulder. "How about something softer, like a Shirley Temple?"

He was kidding. I wasn't.

"That sounds perfect!"

"Are you sure kid? I don't want them gals thinking you light in your feet or something, coming in here and drinking a drink like dat," Tony gave me a concerned older frat brother look even though I had never been in a fraternity, so I could only imagine what the look looked like. But I think it was probably pretty damn close to that look.

What would Jacky do? What would Jacky say? I thought to myself.

"Let the kid have what he wants to drink, and the hell with everybody else," is what I imagined Jacky saying.

"The hell with them," I said to Tony.

He was surprised.

That makes two of us.

"Alright, you got it, kid," he said with a smirk that was happy that the little scrawny nerdy kid didn't back down. It's not like I was fighting in a gun battle or something. But I still felt like I was making moves in my life — even though it started with just a Shirley temple!

"Here you go, Shirley," Tony said as he put the drink in front of me.

"Didn't make it too strong, did you?" I smiled.

"Yea, I put some of my special sauce in there," Tony pointed between his legs to his Italian sausage. "Enjoy, junior."

"Thanks," I sipped my drink in a self satisfied way. I didn't care if I didn't look tough enough, rich enough, whatever it is I don't think I have enough of and that they can get elsewhere from another guy.

But I reckon, as they say in Australia, there is always an elsewhere.

That's why I loved reading about Jacky and Sophia. They were making their own elsewhere. They were making it up out of whole cloth, with their own ideas of what elsewhere should be like. They created that elsewhere every time they saw one another knowing that would be one last time they would be able to do it. Mother time doesn't stop for anybody.

Nor did the Nazis.

I wanted to see what happened that day at Otis's school when the Nazis came. But I think it would be better looking at it from the sheep's — Sophia's — eyes, and not from the wolf's — Jacky's — eyes. I opened to that day in Sophia's diary.

June 12, 1942
Oh my Lord, it all happened so suddenly.
I arrived in the morning earlier than I usually did with the driver and Otis.

As usual, the driver parked the car. I got out to walk Otis into the school.

Except this day was different.

It was Otis's birthday.

I remember Jacky telling me yesterday, "go to closet at 8:45 and wait for me with door open just a little bit. I wanting to wish Otis the happy birthday and give him the present," he said in his broken English as he put his hand — what felt like a paw — on my right shoulder to emphasize to be on time.

"We will be right there when you ask," I said to him with appreciative eyes. I was looking forward to seeing Otis feel like he had a father figure in his life that he could respect, and I was looking forward to feeling like I had a best friend in my life and not some substitute — another car, apartment, or trip to somewhere exotic.

They were no substitutes for a good man.

As I walked over to the closet with Otis, I heard Francis, the driver, speed off in the background with the car. I thought it was odd. I even thought of trying to chase the car. But I figured something was wrong with the driver's family or something that morning, and knew I could get a ride home by calling a taxi from inside.

I knocked on Jacky's closet door. Nobody answered. So I opened up and saw that everything was cleaned out. I mean everything! It's like nobody had ever been there before.

"Mamma, where is Jacky's things?" Otis asked me as he tugged my dress.

"I don't know, my dear, I don't know." I remember putting my hand over my mouth. I didn't know what to do. But I knew that Jacky

said to wait. And while everything in me said run, don't trust, don't be open, close your heart, and you messed up by opening it in the first place — I stayed right there. I was tired of running. I was tired of feeling scared. So I just stayed there in that dark janitor's closet with Otis next to me, the door just slightly open, just like Jacky asked, so that we could see outside.

All of a sudden two black cars screeched into the parking lot. The men in the cars slammed their doors as they got out and were speaking German very loudly to one another. I looked closer through the slightly cracked open door and saw that the four or five men were Gestapo officers. One spoke to the principal of the school. The principal pointed the Gestapo officers in our direction.

I asked myself: Did Jacky set me up? Did he turn me in to make reward money? For some more heroin or coke? For some whore? I should have never trusted this underground trash!

The mass murdering Gestapo men in black trench coats started walking in our direction. I didn't know what to do. I just froze and kept my eye looking through the small crack in the door. The men slowly approached.

When they were about half way between their cars and the closet door, about four mothers whose children went to school with Otis came out of the woodwork! The women screamed and yelled at the men. As the women did their fanatic dance, they smacked the Gestapo officers on the head with large envelopes. Then the women let go of the envelopes and started pulling the officers' hair, violently scratching their faces, and spitting in their eyes.

Black and white photos came out of the envelopes. The photos flew all over the parking lot.

What on God's earth did these women have in those envelopes?

These Gestapo men must have been the women's husbands.

Before I knew it, there were two tall men standing in front of the crevice in the closet door. They were wearing black leather trench coats, just like the Gestapo men wore.

I thought Otis and I were dead.

The taller older Irish looking man with the long beard and dark sunglasses opened the door. In one of his hands was a Thompson machine gun, not normally carried by Germans. I thought right then that these men had to be Jacky's men. The Irish man held out his left hand for me to take.

"Jacky sent us. Come with us now," he said to me with a do or die tone.

My choices? If I stayed, me and Otis might be killed by these Gestapo. If I took this man's hand, Jacky's underworld may ruin me and Otis in the end anyway.

I took Otis's hand in mine and grabbed the large Irish man's hand. The two men walked us over to a waiting black Rolls Royce Phantom III with tinted black windows. Inside was a black driver with a black patch on his left eye sporting a black leather trench coat — just like the rest. Like his Irish brother, the black driver looked like he had killed many. I knew this car very well. Richard used to love his Rolls Royce and I think he either had this one, or the Phantom II. But I didn't know these men at all. And yet I was putting my family's life into their hands.

Otis and I scurried into the car as fast as we could. I looked back and saw one of the Gestapo men push what I think was his wife to the ground and start running our way.

"Halt, halt, halt!" He yelled, which means "stop, stop, stop!"

He was too late. His bullets hit the back window of the car as it sped away. But the men inside the car didn't duck. Otis and I did. We were sitting in back right next to the Irishman.

"Bulletproof," the Irishman smiled down at Otis and I. "Jacky wouldn't have it any other way," and then the man just sat silent.

We sped through the streets of Paris so fast that we were on the highway to the coast before I could count to 60.

"Mickey," the Irishman held out his hand for me to shake.

I shook his hand firmly, not like a lady would, but like a woman would.

"And you are Sophia?" He asked as he shook my hand.

"And you are Otis," Mickey smiled through his scar tissue from too many fights at Otis.

Otis was so scared he just sat there and cried. I held him tight to me.

"Jacky . . . Jacky . . . Jacky sent you?" Otis asked with tears running down his face and onto my clothes.

"Yes," Mickey said.

"Where are you taking us, Kansas City?" I asked.

"To Deauville, for now," Mickey said looked forward with no emotion.

"Deauville?" I asked with stress because I didn't have any control over the mess.

"Jacky will fill you in on the rest," Mickey looked over to me and then turned to look straight like a good soldier would.

As we drove through the tree shrouded roads outside Paris towards Deauville, the resort town of gamblers and other vacationers from Paris, I wondered did people know when they were younger how quickly their lives could change, in a matter of minutes, if they never had anything drastic happen to them — a death, an accident, or sickness? I knew all too well from my parents' car accident.

My intuition told me that my life was about to change forever. I guess it already changed the first time I met Jacky. It changed even more when Mickey and the others came to the school. But that change was after the first, and that first was the one that caused the rest, like the butterfly flying who flaps its lovely wings and causes something to change half way around the world.

That butterfly was Jacky.

I sat there with Otis sleeping on my side. I looked outside the tinted car window at all of the people playing and frolicking at the beach as we arrived. I wondered if I would ever be able to do that with Jacky, Otis, and maybe a child of our own. Then again, I wondering if Jacky had some wicked plan up his sleeve?

I wondered, wondered, and wondered some more.

"We here," the driver said with a short but polite voice as we drove up to a large hotel overlooking the beach — but close enough so that you could walk to it with bare feet.

"Where is here?" I asked the driver skeptically.

"The Hotel Barriere." He looked back at me and smiled at sleeping Otis.

"Need help with him?" Mickey asked me.

"No, I got him," I scooped up Otis in my arms. As he rested his pudgy face on my right shoulder, the driver came around and opened the door for me. We got out and exited into the warm sunshine. "What a glorious day," I remember saying out loud.

"It is," Mickey said as he and I looked towards the ocean waves washing up against the sand. "But we must go," Jacky is waiting for you and wants to brief you on everything.

We walked slowly up towards the grand dame hotel. Mickey opened up the stained old world looking wood front doors, which towered over the driveway.

"Thank you," I said to Mickey. He nodded. I looked back and the two other men were standing by the car. Another two similar cars drove up and parked behind the first, one right after the other. They were all filled with intimidating looking men. I turned around and looked up. Men wearing nice linen suits were standing on the rooftop. They said nothing to me. They searched the horizon like eagles would for their prey.

"A pleasure," Mickey said as he closed the door behind me.

The hotel was a throw back to the times of Napoleon. It had a lot of windows, richly textured walls with ornate designs, expensive colorful Persian rugs, and a regal spirit that reminded me of my home in rural Louisiana. Except this place was right by the ocean and wasn't country looking but kingdom looking.

"We many things to talk about," Jacky said as he walked up to me wearing shorts, espadrilles, and a white tank top. They called it a "Marcel" in the South.

"We do," I looked at Jacky with Otis on my shoulder in a distrustful but wanting to trust kind of way. I was on the fence with this man, in a way, but hoping to be more on the side of believing that knew that there was a good reason: I was just shot at by Germans, why he left his position at the school, and why I was in some strange place.

Before I knew it, Jacky came up to my face. He kissed me on both cheeks, or what he could of my right cheek with Otis laying against it, and then offered:

"Please, let's go up to my room, take the seat, have the drink, talk about what just happen, what will happening tomorrow, what will happening later in the time."

He put his hand softly on my back. For some reason, I felt relieved. His touch, to me, said more than any of his words could.

We went upstairs to his room. It was on the top floor of the hotel. We sat on this simple burgundy bison leather couch that was firm and yet soft, old and new looking. A glass coffee table was in front of us. I remember he had some record playing.

I think it was Armstrong's 'Lucky Guy,' one of Jacky's favorites. There was a bottle of Pastis, a licorice tasting liquor drink popular in the south and banned by Vichy, some glasses, and a crystal full of ice on the coffee table. I took it from looking around that this was Jacky's private room. It had his touch to it.

I sat down with Otis on my shoulder. I felt a load come off me even though a load was still on me.

"Care for the drink," Jacky asked as he sat next to me with his cigarette dangling from the corner of his mouth.

"I need one," I nodded and calmly rubbed Otis's back.

Jacky started making the drinks. I just sat there looking at him wondering whether I wanted to punch him or kiss him. I guess love is like that sometimes. Sometimes there is no person in the world you hate more than the person you love. That emotion is so strong you lose control over it when your fear takes over and it gets channeled in the hate direction instead of the love one.

"Coucou," he said as he handed me my drink. This surprised me. He never called me "coucou" before, a term of endearment in France. Somehow, and for some reason, I liked it. No matter, I was still keeping my skeptical mind cap on.

He held his drink up to me.

"To the health of us — for now and forever," he smiled sincerely, like we were celebrating. My arm started sweating at this point from Otis resting on it. I was so stressed out I didn't know how many drinks I would need before I would calm down.

"To our health," I cracked a small smile as a breeze from the ocean came through the window and calmed my nerves — for the moment.

"Mamma, mamma, mamma," Otis said next to me as awoke from his sleep, he opened his eyes, and rubbed them with his hands. "Where we?" He looked around. And then, when he saw Jacky next to us, Otis said loudly: "Jacky!" Otis got up off my shoulder and went over to Jacky before I could say boo!

They hugged for a few seconds. Jacky closed his eyes when he hugged Otis. I wanted to cry, but I didn't want to show Otis. I didn't want to show the little one how scared I was back there — and still here, although I was feeling better.

"I have present for you, you little man," Jacky said to Otis as he lay on Jacky's shoulder.

"Really!" Otis said as he pushed himself away from Jacky's chest.

"Want to see?" Jacky asked.

"Oh boy, oh boy, yes!"

"Now, boys," I said to slow them down and then, before I could, Jacky had taken Otis into another room, which looked like the dining room. I followed them there. I saw Otis taking off the gift-wrapping of a New York City toy fire truck with all the trimmings.

"Oh mother, oh mother," Otis said, "isn't this swell?" He started playing with it as a bee would a flower. "Vroom, vroom, vroom! Calling all cars, calling all cars," Otis said. I put my hand over my mouth to calm my self and stop, again, from crying. I was so emotional.

Jacky looked up at me as he helped Otis play.

"A New York friend ship this in for me," he said and then got up to walk my way. *"He like it,"* he looked at me and gave me a peck on the check. *"We need to have the talk in the next room, okay?"*

What was I supposed to say? Take me home? The Germans would be waiting. Take me to the airport? The Germans would be waiting. Take us back to the school? They were already waiting there.

So I walked with Jacky and gave him the benefit of the doubt. We sat back down on the couch. We could hear Otis playing in the background with the fire truck — "vroom, vroom, calling all cars, we have an accident!"

Jacky slowly caressed my shoulder as I took a sip of my drink. And then he softly said in a concerned voice, "these Germans knowing about you." He put some ash out of his cigarette into the crystal ashtray on the coffee table.

"Can I have one?" I asked without addressing what he just said to me. I learned a lot from this man. One thing I learned is to look cool in not so cool situations. It throws people off and sometimes you can trick yourself into thinking all is well.

I think Aristotle wrote about this once. I read him at Newcomb. He wrote about when we trick ourselves into believing things that are not true, like when we deceive ourselves ever so artfully into thinking we don't love someone when we do. I knew right then that I loved this man more than I had any man in my life.

But instead of telling him, right there and right then that I loved him, I asked him "can I have one?" instead of saying "I love you." Maybe it's because

I still didn't trust him. My doubting self wouldn't put her fists down — yet.

"Of course," he smiled, he didn't pick up on my slight of hand, or so I thought. He handed me a Chesterfield and lit me up. "Been shot at before?" He asked as he lit the cigarette.

I took a long drag.

"No. Have you?" I asked.

*"Yes. When I younger. Been stabbed a few times and other nice things like this," he smiled a touché smile. "I know you scared." He dropped some ash into the tray. "I say to Guillaume, you might know how to read this philosopher and that one, but **I** can read the people. **I** can reading what's inside them by look in the eyes," and then he looked at me.*

I felt like a fool.

"Who is Guillaume?" I asked as I took a long sip of my drink.

"I'm getting to that," he took a sip of his drink.

"And whose room is this?" I asked.

"I'm to get to that."

"You are about to get to a lot of things," I said.

"I hope I do," he said to me and winked.

I felt a shiver. But I didn't let him know. I'm sure it showed anyway.

"Guillaume is my guy on inside. He told me they knows about you and Resistance."

"How?"

"A rat."

"Who?"

"This not important," he put some ash out. "He not around no more." He looked back at me with the same ruthless eyes that I was scared of when

I first met him. Those same eyes now comfort me because I have seen them in a whole different light.

"They know more than this," he said as he took out another cigarette to light it up and let it hang like his long lost fang.

"And what's that? That I'm not really blond?" I said. He turned and smiled.

"This what I loving about you," he caressed my face. Should I say I love him back? What would that mean? Was I ready? Boy did I frustrate myself with my inner doubts. "You have such smart mouth sometimes and I love this," he stopped caressing my face to put some more ice into his drink. I could tell he was getting down to business.

Otis kept playing in the other room — "vroom, vroom, vroom!"

A cool breeze from the English Channel came through the large French glass windows. The Channel's waves crashed softly in the background, too.

People laughed outside as they went to the Casino De Deauville.

I felt a calm sensation in me — like I had heard the worst of it all.

But then he slammed me with the hammer.

"Sophia," he said with his hand on my right knee, "you a Jew," he said like he was telling me I had cancer of the liver and would only have so much longer to live. But he might have as well told me that. I knew what that meant for Otis and I in this climate. I didn't know or understand how that could be true.

"What do you mean I am a Jew? I am Protestant God damn it!"

"Your mother name. It was Bethe, no?" I could have seen some snarky lawyer ask me the same question. But I knew his question came from a good place.

"Right, so? She was German."

"A German Jew," he said with grave eyes.

This is where Aristotle comes back into play. When I was real little, I seem to have a distant memory of my mother's mother going to an Uptown temple on St. Charles. After my parents' accident, I remember my grandparents — on my father's side — talking about how they wanted to raise me as a Protestant. I listened to them talk it over the dinner table one night. I was hiding underneath the table, like I often did, to snoop.

"She'll have an easier life that way," my grandfather said.

"Maybe, but it's all a lie," my grandmother responded. "Why have her live a lie?" She asked.

My grandfather:

"Because it will pave the way for her to live a better life. It will get worse for the Jews one day — just you watch."

That's all I remember. I sort of put the conversation back into my subconscious memory and have kept that out of my conscious memory for all of these years. I have been acting, playing, and loving like I was a true Protestant, as white as the next Anglo gal living uptown or anywhere else.

But it was all one big lie. I loved living the lie so much that I muted that little girl inside who knew better. I muzzled her because I didn't want to hear what she had to say or how she felt. In short, I was in denial.

"Shut up, suck it up, and keep moving on," I'd tell her. "Life is good, so don't go muddying it up!" I was harsh with her, and I was harsh with myself, because by God I wanted Camelot — which was the life I envisioned with Richard: the Church, the castle, the prestige, and the rest of the package. But then I wanted to burn it after I found out who he truly was. That way, I could never be reminded that it existed.

In truth, it never really did exist. It was a projection of all my expectations, of what people told me I should like, needed to be like, and had better be like. My mind led, my body followed, but my heart was still at the starting line with its arms crossed, the cool kid in school who skipped classes, got caught, and who everybody else laughed at. "Now look who is laughing," my heart says to my mind as they are sitting there in bed with Richard wondering how they got me into the mess.

"Sophia, Sophia," Jacky shook my arm. "You okay?"

As he shook me, I realized: that little cigarette dangling from the corner of Jacky's mouth was now my Camelot. I knew there was just as much power behind that cigarette as there was in the Church, the castle, the Oxford degree, and the fine pedigree.

I looked into his eyes. I was a burglar who had been caught. I caught myself but the only reason why is that Jacky caught me.

"In some ways, Jacky," I said to him still looking into his eyes, "I've never been happier in my life," I said.

"Because I wearing the good cologne today?" He smiled, took his cigarette out from his mouth,

and then came close to give me a soft kiss on my lips. I closed my eyes when he did. I wanted to savor that one. "I happy you feeling this way," *he said as he pulled away after the soft comforting kiss.*

"So what happened at Otis's school?" *I asked.*

"We getting to this tomorrow," *he smirked.* "It getting late and I know you have the long day."

It was about nine at night at this point and the sun had long gone down. We got up and went to check on Otis in the room. He was sleeping tight on the floor with the fire truck stuck next to his chest.

I picked Otis up off the floor and we all walked up the stairs to the bedrooms.

"You sleeping there," *Jacky pointed to main bedroom.* "I sleep right next door," *he said with a mischievous smirk as he pointed to the room next to mine.* "Don't worry, I not put a hole in the wall to watch your cream naked body," *he smiled.*

Jacky and I kissed one another on each cheek. He then softly kissed Otis's cheek and left the room. I fell onto the queen-sized bed with Otis, who fell quickly back to sleep, and looked out through the French windows towards the ocean. I grabbed my diary out of my purse and starting writing everything that had gone down today here. I need to process it all — and I always have found the best way before was to journal it. Now I'm finally ready to go to sleep.

June 13, 1942

Knock, knock, knock — I heard on the door yesterday morning. Otis was snoring. My little rogue was sleeping with the fire truck next to his chest. He obviously needed rest. The sun shined through the open blades on the tall French doors. We never bothered to close them the night before.

Knock, knock, knock — I heard on the door again. I tried to lift my head. I was sore. My body was ground meat and yesterday was the grinder. My hair was a mess. And our clothes seemed like they had been thrown around the room, not put away, because we were in such a rush to get to bed.

Finally, the door opened as the sunshine spread its lovely rays on our bed heads with a delightful grace.

"It about 10:00," Jacky said.

He was wearing the same things he was wearing yesterday. I could tell this was the "real" him. He didn't really care about what he was wearing because he knew he wore the tuxedo in his head — not in his body. I think that's why people loved him so much. I know that's why I did.

"I have the coffee and the fresh croissants," Jacky whispered to me.

"I'd love to have them now, but my body is feeling so tired." I lifted my head slightly off the bed and saw that my hair was a mess. "Plus, I need to get ready before we go out in public," I put my head back down in a tired horse way on the hay.

"Don't bother," he said with his grin that I grew to adore having coffee with him those mornings. "I have here for you the scarf from hotel store."

He held out a fabulous Hermes scarf. It was orange, cobalt blue, and gold, and had little horses all over it facing one another.

"Oh, Jacky, you know how to get me out of my shell," I got slowly out of the bed, put on my gown, and walked over to him. I took the scarf

that he was holding out, and went to kiss him on both cheeks. He held me. I held him. And we just stood there holding each other for what seemed like months — even though it was only a minute. I guess we had been holding each other that way at Otis's school every morning. We just never actually did the holding, except that one day in the closet.

We let go of our embrace and he looked at me. He lit up a cigarette.

"I wait outside this door and read my paper."

When he said "the paper," he meant a more mainstream one. When he said "my paper," it was The Chained Duck, a satirical newspaper that made fun of French politics and everything else under the sun.

He slowly closed the door.

I got Otis up, got him dressed in the same clothes he was wearing yesterday, and put on the same outfit I was wearing yesterday, too: a khaki poplin skirt; brown slip on leather driving shoes made by my favorite shoe maker, Dorino Della Valle; a simple white linen blouse; and a Levi's jacket that one of the American women gave me. I had given her a copy of Resistance, and she insisted on giving me her jacket. I have cherished it since.

While the cover doesn't make the book, I have always fancied style as an expression of me. And so I have always treasured a pair of Ray Ban fighter pilot sunglasses that an American ex-pat gave to me when I gave him a copy of the Resistance. They made me feel professional and like I was in uniform. They got me into my bodacious character. I tried to think the way Jacky did when he did his business. But he didn't wear sunglasses. He seemed to see the world through dark tinted lenses already.

I put the scarf around my tussled hair. I smelled, I was achy, and I wasn't put together. But I felt like I was on the cusp of beginning a new life. I never could have imagined this life on the run had someone told me when I was growing up in Louisiana that I would be living it.

"Jacky!" Otis said when we got out of the door. Jacky picked Otis up and they hugged. Jacky looked at me with a warm smile. He rubbed Otis's back. Otis still had the fire truck in his right hand.

"Everything going to be okay, little monsieur," Jacky softly rubbed Otis's back. "We go?"

We walked down the hallway to the elevator. When we exited at the bottom and started walking past the front desk, I heard a chorus line as we walked by:

"Good morning, Monsieur Jacky," a young short sprite blond said from behind the concierge.

"Eh, Monsieur Jacky, so good to see you!" the Negro bellhop said.

"Welcome back, Monsieur Jacky," said the tall brunette woman from behind the check in desk.

Jacky gave them all a lazy air salute with his left hand. It was lazy because his hand wasn't actually straight, and he barely lifted it over his left eyebrow. It was a laid back salute, or one that a guy who wears his cigarette on the corner of his mouth, would give. But it was real. Everyone smiled when he did it.

"You are quite the man around these parts, Monsieur Jacky," I pushed his arm playfully as Otis walked between us holding our hands.

"I trying," he said as he looked over, "to do the help when I can." He then smiled. I knew he had to hurt a lot of people to do the helping. But I guess he didn't see his trade, whether it was women, men, drugs, or gambling, as necessarily always hurting, but sometimes helping, too. I think he thought of it as a sort of public service the government was too proud, or too hypocritical, to provide to the people who could afford it.

We walked along a pathway to the beach.

We arrived at a café right next to the sand.

"Bonjour, Jacky," Carlu, a five foot six Corsican man with taut boxer muscles, said with his raspy smoked too many cigarettes voice. They kissed each other on their cheeks.

"Your regular spot?" Carlu asked Jacky.

Jacky nodded and then slapped some cash into Carlu's hand when he held it out.

We went to sit down at a table right next to the sand, and Otis went to play with his fire truck. Jacky and I sat down.

A five foot eight or so lumberjack looking man came to take our orders. He was burly, with large forearms that looked like they had chopped trees for a living.

"Napoleon!" Jacky said and put his arms up in a I hit the jackpot moment.

"Welcome back, cousin," Napoleon said.

"Napoleon" had to be the man's nickname. He wasn't short and petit like the real Napoleon — but was enormous.

Jacky got up and kissed Napoleon once on each cheek.

"Napoleon is the old friend from Marseille," Jacky said to me.

"I am pleasure to meet you," Napoleon said in his broken English as I got up. We kissed on each cheek.

"Now, what I get you?" Napoleon took out his pen and pad.

"Americano," Jacky said.

"Make that two, please," I said.

"These coffees is coming right up. And the regular, Jacky?"

Jacky nodded.

"What's the regular?" I asked.

"Best croissants in town," Jacky smiled.

I looked at Napoleon as he walked away. He tucked his pad into the back pocket of his Levi's jeans. Just beneath his tucked in shirt was another black bulge. It was a pistol bulge. I'd seen that on the boys growing up in the country. They liked packing wherever they went. I looked over at Carlu's back as he stood by the entrance to the café. He had the same bulge. I started to put the pieces together. These were all Jacky's associates.

And they were packing heat.

"You want to know about these envelopes this women having at Otis school?"

He smiled a proud smile I imagined Otis would give when he outsmarted a teacher and both he and the teacher knew it.

"Do I really want to know what was in those?" I asked out loud.

"We not catch those men fucking the zoo animals in the ass, Sophia, don't you worry about

this," he paused to light his cigarette. "But maybe the zoo animals would have been better than what pictures we having, no?"

Jacky looked at Otis playing. Then, as he turned to look back towards me, he said:

"These pictures is of the more simple things — like the one, the two, the three," he put some ash in the Ricard ashtray.

"And what are the one, the two, the three?" I asked.

He put the cigarette back into the right corner of his mouth, just as I might have put the sunglasses on me to get me into character.

"We always taking the secret photos of these government or rich men that fucking our girls," his cigarette ash dripped onto his white Marcel tank top, and he wiped it off, only for more to drop back down on it, and only for him to keep swiping it off — the fly that never goes away. *"These photos giving us the protection. We know who these men is — the wives, the kids, the grandparents, understand? The pictures stop them from doing the stupid things against us — or else they not have the pretty lives no more. This photos is also give us secret weapon in the emergency like this."*

"How did those women at the school get the photos?" I naively asked.

"Your coffees," Napoleon came back and placed them on the table, "and your treats," he placed a large basket with croissants in the middle of the table with what looked like fresh country strawberry jam.

"Thank you," Jacky said as he leaned forward to take his coffee.

"Anything else?" Napoleon said.

"A sparkling water, please?" I asked.

"Is coming right up," he said.

He turned around and accidentally lifted his shirt when he was putting the notebook away. I got a peek of the .45 caliber pistol. I was right. It was an armed fortress camouflaged in smiles, beach air, sun, white linen and fun.

I started sipping my coffee. It tasted like it was from the same beans Jacky used back in Paris. These guys were all the same beans — but they were roasted differently.

"We having the addresses of these women — they wives of Gestapo officers who coming to school this day," he said as a matter of fact as he dipped the croissant into his coffee. "So this is not the problem," he smiled a triumphant smile as he paused to let it set in. He continued. "We having our children delivery boys bringing the photos that morning on their bicycles, after these husbands going to Gestapo headquarters on way to the school."

I dipped my croissant with strawberry jam on it into the coffee — a French version of a peanut butter and jelly sandwich into Italian coffee.

"So **that's** why the eyes of those women were filled with murder," I said to myself quietly as I looked at my coffee. I meant for Jacky to hear me, but it was more for me to process what just happened. I was giving myself a cold shower. I knew what this meant. It didn't only mean that Jacky saved my life.

It also meant that he put his life on the railroad tracks in front of the speeding Nazi train. These officers will know that those pictures came from

Jacky. He was the only major racket in town that they trusted. I opened my mouth just a little bit, just a crack, from the feeling that I had. I felt like I wanted to throw up. I felt that food come up my throat, that bile, right before you are about to cough it all up, but I kept up appearances. I didn't want Otis to see me this way. Or maybe it was that I didn't want to see myself this way.

So I changed the subject like I always do, but I know this subject wasn't going to be something that I was going to be able to get away from. It would hit me in the face, and I think sooner than I thought.

"And the room? Whose room is that?" I asked Jacky.

"Vroom, vroom, vroom!" I heard Otis say in the background.

Jacky smiled in my direction as he dipped some more croissant pieces into his coffee. His cigarette was parked safely in the ashtray.

"The owner of hotel giving it to me," a cheap wristwatch to Jacky, but there was something more to it than two boys playing nice in the sandlot.

"Why?" I asked.

A small ocean breeze spread over our faces.

I smelled Otis in the background.

I felt so happy that I accidentally stumbled upon a feeling of family.

"I rescuing the owner from the financial problems," Jacky said. "He a good man. On the paper, he with the Vichy peoples, he go to their parties, fuck their women, eat their food, kiss their kids on the heads, but this motherfucker always been with us. He been silent Vichy partner," Jacky chuckled

a good old boy chuckle in a rural Louisiana town where there aren't many phones, not many people, and only you and the good old boy are sitting there, him knowing everybody in town worth knowing, and you sitting there not knowing the half of them.

Jacky and I had some quiet time for a moment with the ebb and flow of the ocean in the background.

And then I forgot.

"But how did you know which officers were coming?"

He seemed to have an answer for everything. He was the smart boy in my elementary school class that I had a crush on but I was too proud, or scared, to admit it.

"We having the woman on payroll at phone company," he said and then chomped into his croissant. Wiping his face after the chomp, "she telling us which men being sent, then we pulling their address cards," he sipped his coffee, a well-trained machine that looks, and acts, at times, like a lazy louse. He put his cigarette back into the corner of his mouth to put the check in the box next to the look of a lazy louse, instead of intense businessman, dutiful churchgoing father, or bohemian artist.

We just sat there enjoying the rest of the day at the beach, playing with Otis, taking walks in the ocean, us walking hand in hand, and all of us smiling like we were in some other land.

And then the sunset came.

And then the sun was gone.

And then the night started coming.

"Dinner?" He turned to me and asked after he had put on his bright red cashmere crewneck

sweater along with a Yankee baseball cap. I already had on my Levi's jacket.

"Since when did you become such a big Yankee fan?" I asked as I looked up to his baseball hat.

"For the long time. You know I been doing the business with the stick up peoples in New York since I the young boy in Marseille," he grinned.

"Stick up people?" I asked.

"Stick it up or lose it," he grinned.

"What?" I asked confused.

"Let's eat," he ignored me. "Otis, you hungry?" He yelled over to the little one.

Otis's vrooming didn't seem to stop all day.

Jacky's question ended it.

"Yay," dinner!" Otis said.

Otis picked up his fire truck and started running in our direction. Jacky picked Otis up and put him in his arms.

"Let's go to hotel. They having best chef in the Normandy," Jacky nodded his head over towards the hotel.

"Lovely," I said as I put on my slip on driver shoes. We went back to our rooms to get ready for dinner.

We headed down to the restaurant together. Jacky had on his trademark black tuxedo. But this one was made of linen. Even his black tie and crisp white shirt were linen, too. He wore black espadrilles with the outfit, which I like to call shabby mellow chic. His tan, brutish, and yet handsome face looked so good against the white of his shirt. I looked at him in the elevator wanting to kiss him. I sported an elegant black form fitting linen dress that went down to my knees, along with black espadrilles that wrapped around my ankle. Someone from the hotel left the dress, and the shoes, on my bed.

"You look smashing, love," I said to him in the elevator.

"You not look so bad yourself," he said to me and winked as he looked me up and down, maybe thinking what I would taste like.

We had a tasty candlelight dinner. While we ate, Otis played with his truck on the floor, Jacky and I looked at each other with endearing eyes, he played with the straw to his drink, I rubbed my legs together, and I tossed my hair here and there. I knew we were sexually frustrated. We had things pent up for months now. I just felt it. Some things you just feel. You don't see them. You know they are there. You are as sure of their presence as you are of your own finger on your nose. Napoleon came by to take our picture. Jacky initially refused — but I insisted. I wanted to remember this for the rest of my life.

"Have the sweet dreams," Jacky said as he kissed Otis on the forehead when we got upstairs after dinner.

"Love you," Otis smiled upward to Jacky.

"Love you," Jacky pinched Otis's cheek and then kissed the hand he used to pinch it."

My heart was racing. My legs trembled. My wetness was unbearable.

Jacky came to kiss me on both cheeks like he always did. I didn't want him to think anything. He looked at me when he did, like he had something else to tell me, but was holding his cards tight to his chest.

"I'll see you in the morning love," I said.

"Or maybe you seeing me in your dreams?" He smiled a horny devil smile.

I pinched his cheek and started to pull him close to kiss him on the lips.

I remember thinking: Wait! What's gotten into me? I am losing control! Showing myself. How dare I do this! What about Otis? What about me? What about being vulnerable? Exposed? Another Richard beckons. Shut-up. I am tired of hiding, being scared, not being, and just acting like I am being. I could be an imposter for me. Take a wax museum form of me, and it would be just as good as I have been acting. I am a not-me who pretends to be me.

No more, my heart says to my mind. I won't let you push me around anymore. The heart, that slacker student in school, the one who took smoke breaks and ditched class and who failed classes, was now in the lead. The heart rejoiced at the revolution in spontaneity.

"What get inside you?" Jacky asked with a surprised but pleased tone after I kissed him.

"Maybe you," I whispered into his ear with my moist lips and then softly slapped his face.

He loved it.

We went to our rooms.

I was naked when I went to bed. Otis was not far from me in his own little bed. I couldn't sleep. I was too excited. So I got up around 1:30 in the morning, put on my jean jacket, and went to Jacky's room.

I slowly opened the door.

I heard him turn in his bed.

"Can I come in?"

There was silence.

"You buy the ticket for the entry?" He said with the playful tone that made me love him so much.

"I have one right here," I took off my Levi's jacket and got into bed with him.

He held open the covers.

He was naked, too.

We slithered, laughed, hugged, tugged, plugged, and loved. And then we slept. And then we woke up after some minutes or so of sleep and did some more sweating, loving, petting, netting as much joy as I felt like we had both felt in years.

"I love you much," Jacky said to me as the sun came up and as he took a drag on his cigarette after our fourth, fifth, or maybe it was our sixth time making love.

He handed me the cigarette.

I took a long drag.

"I love you very much, too, Jacky," I said as I reached over to kiss him.

I gave him the cigarette.

He finished it.

And then he topped me off for the morning.

After Jacky went back to sleep, and as Otis slept softly in his room, I came out here to the balcony overlooking the beach to smoke a cigarette, and to write about what happened yesterday and today —before it passed into the nothingness of time.

June 14, 1942

The other night with Jacky was better than I had ever dreamed.

Maybe it's because I never really dreamed about being this way with this man. I never wanted to like him. I never wanted to love him.

But I ended up doing both.

I guess that's why the real thing is always better than the imagined thing. The imagined thing is planned, contrived, and has bells and whistles on it that were put in place but which don't necessarily win the race in real life.

I got my dream. And what I got was something that I could not dream. I could never have planned or imagined what happened at the school and making love with a former junky.

That's why it all is so pretty to me.

"What's the plan for today?" I asked Jacky as I came into his room.

"I take you and Otis to port for the trip to New York."

He started putting on his shorts.

"Come on, seriously?" I asked.

He kept putting on his shorts and then his tank top.

The sunrise coming over the English Channel kissed the top of the bed, dresser, and his stubbly face with California like sunrays.

After he got his clothes on and as he took a spritz of his cologne, he said to me, in a matter of fact way:

"I am serious."

He looked over to me like it was no joke, not a ploy, not a farce, and everything was real as real could be. It was as real as the splinter in your finger, the bone-chill in your toes, the sweat on your brow during the summer, or the hunger in your stomach.

"What?" I said to him like I still thought he was kidding as I tightened my scarf around my neck.

He walked over to me.

"Sophia," he said to me with both of his hands on my shoulders. He broke a half smile. The other half of the smile was the dark side of the moon. "You never be safe in France — not for the long time," his sharpshooter like eyes looked into mine. Like before, I tried to look over to the sun shining through the window, to the door, or anywhere but in those direct eyes.

He took his right hand and softly pushed my face so that it faced him.

"Please . . . look . . . at me," he said slowly with his right palm on my cheek so that I had no choice but to look into his eyes. "This for you and Otis. I not wanting what happening to the Jewish peoples here to happening to you and him over there," he took his palm and put it back on my shoulder.

"But I want to stay with you," I said with a plea for more desert, for another helping, to stay up later, to have another piece of chocolate.

"You know you cannot staying here," he caressed my face.

I closed my eyes. I knew he was right. My eyes started tearing. Drips and drops came out from them like a fountain in the middle of Rome, except there was nobody around to throw a lucky penny in for good fortune. The tears dripped down onto my shirt, onto my arm, onto my fingers, and then did a high dive onto the ground below.

"Here," he gave me a tissue and I used it to stop the fountain of tears coming down my face.

"I know you understanding why I doing this?" He pled with me — why he wasn't giving me more desert, why there wasn't another helping, why there *wouldn't be another piece of chocolate, for now and maybe forever.*

"Yes," I nodded as I wiped my tears on my face. "But you are coming soon?"

"Soon," he caressed my face. "They needing me," he gave a nod towards them, which could include the guys outside, the guys at the clubs, the Allies, the Resistance, the women who worked at the clubs, and/or the non-Nazi customers that he loved to see. I also think he saw the father he never had in himself at night. And so "they" also included that little Jacky inside. That little Jacky boy who never had any father figure within his family — his natural family at least — to really rely on. All of these parts of "they" relied on the mythical nighttime tuxedoed Jacky.

"The only way I can making sure you not leaving the France looking over your shoulder is by fighting the Nazi fucks there," he pointed back to Paris with his thumb.

I knew what this meant. We leave and live. Jacky stays and dies.

This wasn't certain. He was one of the craftiest people the world had seen. I have seen the best of the best — the Cajuns in southern Louisiana that can seemingly kill an alligator with the tooth from a snake, the good ole Mississippi boys who would tell stories of their families killing Yankees in gun fights during the civil war with half loaded guns and dull knives. And yet the world never saw a killing machine like the Nazis.

That is what worried me so much.

Jacky hugged me closer than I had been hugged since right after my parents died. My grandparents hugged me like that. They hugged me so tight that I almost felt safely cut off from the world in their embrace. I think that is what they wanted. They wanted to close my eyes to the darkness of death with the light of their embrace. It was that type of embrace.

He also softly kissed me on my cheek.

I started to do the same to his.

"Tell him you love him," my heart said.

"No, she might not ever see him again," my mind responded.

"If you don't tell him you love him now, you will regret it for the rest of your life," my heart said.

"Yes, but what if this is the last time she sees him?" My worried mind said.

My heart:

"Wouldn't you rather live and love in that moment, which you will never have again in your life, than to just sit in your safe cocoon of emotionlessness? Oh, it is a nice cocoon, isn't it? You can smile without worrying because you don't love anybody enough to worry. There is nothing to lose. You can wake up and live without fret because there is nobody next to you to worry about, other than Otis. And how do you think you are going to love Otis if this is how you love Jacky?"

"Oh, she'll be fine," my mind says to my heart. "You are overreacting. There will be other men, and Otis is her son, Jacky isn't."

*"Yes," my heart says in a penultimate way, "but you don't **know** if there will be another man like Jacky, do you? And while Jacky isn't her son, he is her son's savior and her savior. Not in a Jesus Christ type of way, but in a bad guy that does something good type of way. A bad guy who you understand*

why he is bad, and yet he has something inside him, something that other guys like him don't have, which makes him: save you instead of profit off of you, love you instead of hate you, open to you and not close off from you."

My mind sat there quietly listening.

*"It's easy after all," my heart continued, "for the good guy to be good because he was born and raised that way. It is hard for the bad guy because every bone in his body says that good is bad, and that bad is good. And, sometimes, that is exactly right. Vichy is supposed to be good, but does bad. Jacky is supposed to be bad, but does good. He walks like a bad man, talks like a bad man, and looks like a bad man — but **can** be a good man. And if he can love, surely she can love, too."*

I voted with my heart.

"Thank you," my heart said to me. My mind stood in the background with crossed angry arms. Its rational western ways were unable to conquer that inner dark primitive voice which made the decision that the mind couldn't touch with its math, science, and measuring sticks.

"I love you," I said for the first time not in response to him, or something he did, but in response to my heart.

"I love you, too, Sophia," he gave me a long kiss on my lips. "My men come to get you. Some of your things from the apartment are on boat. It called Veritas. Is owned by this casino boss I tell you about," he smiled an-everything-was-under-control smile.

But it wasn't. My eyes were still tearing. His lips quivered when he spoke. His hands trembled from the adrenaline that was going through his veins.

Small tears were in his eyes. He kept them from diving off his scarred cheekbones and onto the floor.

I went to get Otis from the bedroom next door.

"Where we going mommy?" He asked me as we took the elevator down with Jacky.

"New York City, love."

"Where the fire truck is from?" He looked up at Jacky.

"Yes," Jacky said as he petted Otis's hair.

We arrived at the bottom floor and exited the elevator.

Jacky received the normal morning hellos on the first floor.

As we walked outside the hotel, the same black wicked looking Rolls Royce that picked me up from Otis's school was there. There was also one parked across the street and another parked down the street. Jacky's men — the Gestapo looking ones who took Otis and I to Deauville, and not to a concentration camp — were sitting calmly inside.

Otis and I started getting inside the back seat of the car.

Jacky stood just outside the door with his tank top, shorts, and half put on espadrilles. He wore his Yankee hat. He leaned over to me through the window after he closed the car door and as I sat in the seat.

"When you getting to New York, my friend Meyer is going to picking you up," Jacky said with his hand on my shoulder. "He is my closest American friend," Jacky said with trusting eyes. Those eyes are rare. My grandfather once said you usually can count the people who have them — your real friends — on one hand.

"Mommy, isn't Jacky coming with us? Jacky, aren't you coming with us? Mommy? Jacky?"

"Yes, I coming." Jacky said in the calmest tone I think I have ever heard him speak. "I coming for you, my little diamond. I have to doing the things here before I coming. My American friends having another present for you and mommy in New York," he winked and nodded at Otis like he was the front bar man, the muscle man, the government official, the girl, the boy, the vagrant, or anyone else Jacky has bought off, convinced, or done business with. He did it all with the same wink and nod. That's all it takes sometimes.

"Yay! Yay!" Otis said as he jumped up and down in his seat.

"Ignorance is bliss" — my mind said.

"Don't be so skeptical," my heart said. "Where there is a will, there is a way."

I looked up at Jacky.

"I adore you. I love you and I will miss you," I put my hand on his whiskered cheek.

He kissed my hand.

"I feeling same inside me as you," he said. "Meyer will let me know when you in New York. They will tell you how to getting in touch with me."

"No telephone calls?" I asked with worry.

"You want Gestapo ears listening how dirty I talking to you?" He smirked. "My fantasies is for you — not them."

I nodded.

"So letters?"

"For now," he kissed my hand again one last time. "Meyer will explaining the things to you."

I nodded like I understood — I did but I didn't want to.

The Rolls started driving off.

I looked through the back window.

Jacky's eyes were full of tears as he blew a kiss to me.

I did the same.

I now knew my life would never be the same. It wouldn't.

I was raised to think that diamonds are a woman's best friend — especially when they are on a ring on her ring finger.

As I sit on the Veritas writing this, watching the sun set on a glorious Atlantic ocean, and with the salty air running through my hair, I now know that a woman's best friend isn't a diamond.

It is a good man.

Marilyn Monroe sang a song in the 1953 film *Gentlemen Prefer Blonds* called, I think, "Diamonds are a Girl's Best Friend." I thought about the song when I finished reading Sophia's entries. I thought about the song because Monroe was celebrated in our culture. Her views had a lot influence on young girls growing up. Heaven knows that the *Times* wrote enough stories about her over the years before she died in August of 1962. I wondered if these young women would ever hear Sophia's view about a **woman's**, as opposed to a **girl's**, best friend.

Part of me doubted it. When I looked around the Tavern, I noticed it was packed with women wearing diamonds around their necks, on their fingers, and on their ears. Sophia wore diamonds — but she didn't overestimate their value. She looked like she did — but her cover didn't quite match what was on the inside — in this respect at least. And so I realized how special a person Sophia was to have met. She was at least a good influence on the young women that she personally came across during her life. I knew she was a good influence on me — and I'm not even a woman!

It was about 11:00 in the evening. I had barely touched my Shirley temple. I settled up my tab with Tony, and made my way back to my apartment. Tomorrow was Friday, and I am supposed to meet with Sophia on Saturday to give her back the diaries. So I had a lot of reading to get done.

CHAPTER 12
Kissing Cousins

My dear God! President Kennedy was killed earlier today, Friday, November 22, 1963. We got the reports in from Dallas. It happened around 12:30 p.m. Reports say a sniper did it. The draft copy of Saturday's edition of *The New York Times* reads:

> President John Fitzgerald Kennedy was shot and killed by an assassin today. He died of a wound in the brain caused by a rifle bullet that was fired at him as he was riding through downtown Dallas in a motorcade. Vice President Lyndon Baines Johnson, who was riding in the third car behind Mr. Kennedy's, was sworn in as the 36th President of the United States 99 minutes after Mr. Kennedy's death. Mr. Johnson is 55 years old; Mr. Kennedy was 46. Shortly after the assassination, Lee H. Oswald, who once defected to the Soviet Union and who has been active in the Fair Play for Cuba Committee, was arrested by the Dallas police.

Who is this Oswald? Did he act alone? Like Sophia, I was always taught growing up in Chicago that the seat of power was in the President — the most powerful man in the world.

Like her, I was taught that institutions matter — the institution of government, the institution of marriage, and the institution of law. Was I taught the wrong things? I feel like my sense of meaning, how I understand the world and its power, is coming down around my ears. I am getting anxiety just thinking about it.

I need to escape. So I left the paper early today. The killing wasn't my story, wasn't my area, and I'd rather not be around while the bridges between the lessons that I have been taught all my life burn into little pieces. If President Kennedy wasn't in power, who was? Forget it, Hank, stick to the diaries my inner voice says. They'll make you feel better. So, as I sat on the train heading downtown, I started reading Sophia's next entry

> *July 27, 1942*
> *"You are Sophia," a five foot tall man with dark beady eyes, a long nose, slick single breasted gray suit, and a grey fedora greeted me yesterday morning after I got off the Veritas with Otis on a dock in Redbook, Brooklyn. The short man held out his hand under the bright New York summer sun to help me off the boat.*
> *I held Otis's hand.*
> *The short man was by himself. Or so I thought. He had a big grin on his face.*
> *"Jacky has told me much about you," he said with a shady older uncle grin. The man was about 42 years old. He suddenly and unexpectedly pulled me to his face to give me a kiss on each cheek the way a pigeon might surprise you with a crap on your shoulder from the tree above. That's supposed to be good luck*

in some circles. I felt like this underworld character was going to be good luck for some reason, too.

"Name is Meyer, doll," he looked at me with his hands on each of my arms, holding me a proud uncle way after you have graduated from college. He shook me slightly, "great to meet you, finally." He then softly patted my face with his right hand. I remember Jacky mentioning Meyer's name before I got on the ship. He seemed like a very powerful and connected man. His last name was Lansky, and I knew that he and Jacky did a lot of business together. But the rest of it was foreign to me.

"And you must be Otis," Meyer said to Otis, who was shyly holding my leg.

Otis just stood there and didn't say a word.

"Well, someone is shy," Meyer looked up at me as he bent down to say hello to Otis. "I have a little treat for you, kid, before I give you the even bigger one." Meyer smiled a I know what I am doing smile.

He pulled out a lollypop and held it out to Otis, who looked up at me for approval.

I nodded to Otis. He took the lollypop in a slow and skeptical cat sort of way.

"And what do you say to Mr. Meyer," I said to Otis, who was now holding the lollypop to his chest along with the fire truck that Jacky had given him.

"Thank you, Mr. Meyer," Otis said smiling.

"You little bubula," Meyer said as he pinched Otis's cheek and then stood up to look at me to say: "welcome to my city."

He then he turned around to offer New York City up to me with his right hand. I felt as though he just offered me a plate full of grapes, chicken, dates, and anything else that my heart desired. Anything seemed possible with Meyer — because I knew he knew Jacky. It was guilt by association. It was power by association, too.

Meyer turned around to look towards me.

"How about we get going? Me and the boys want to show you to your new digs, but they won't be ready for a few days," he smiled the same grin that Jacky would grin to me when he had something up his sleeve. "You going to stay with me for a few days, then you going to move into your new joint."

"What about my things?" I asked.

"They'll be taken to your new pad," Meyer lightly touched my back and directed me up the dock to the five black Cadillac limousines parked on the street. Dangerous looking men were sitting inside the cars — they looked like American versions of the men in the cars outside of Jacky's Deauville hide away. There were also five other black Cadillac coups parked around the corner.

When we got closer to the parked cars, a slew of Italian looking men sitting in the passenger seats got out. They were all finely dressed and manicured. They looked like they didn't miss a day at the barbershop, manicurist, or tailor. They all seemed to be cut from the same mold. All were thick, tough looking, had pudgy fingers, and looked like they couldn't be pushed over in a storm or in an earthquake even if you tried. They were guys you would want on your side when things get tough. In succession, the Cadillac lovers came up to me.

"Welcome to New Yawk, Sophia," the first man kissed me on each cheek, gave me an envelope, and walked back to the car.

*"Heya doll, have a blessed start to ya life here,"
the second man kissed me on each cheek, gave me
another envelope, and walked back to his car.*

"Enjoy Gotham, missy," the third man followed with a kiss, an envelope, and then walked back to his car.

"We give uze a big kiss," the fourth man gave me the fourth kiss and an envelope, and then walked back to his car.

"We is honored to have uze here," the fifth man gave me a final kiss and an envelope. He went back to his car. All of the cars sat idling.

"Quite a reception," I said to Meyer as he stood next to me with a gin grin.

"Fit for a queen," he looked over at me.

"Who were all of those men?" I asked after the fact.

"Representatives from the five New York families."

"There are only five? I thought New York was the biggest city in the states?" I said sarcastically.

Meyer looked at me.

"Seriously though," I made a more somber face, "what are these families?"

Meyer looked at me. You have a lot to learn, kid, I imagined him thinking.

"Yea, doll, they got five families here in New York. Jacky does a lot of business with them." He put his left hand up and then started counting down the families with each finger. His thumb, "this is the Lucchese family," his index finger, "this is the Bonanno family," the middle finger, "this is the Gambino family," his ring finger, "this is the Genovese family," and his pinky finger, "this is the

Colombo family. And there you have it, doll face, one big happy family," he said wryly.

Meyer snapped his fingers over towards his car. A red headed Irish looking man with tree trunk limbs standing what seemed like six foot six came out of Meyer's limo and walked over to me.

"I'll take those off your hands, Ms. Gordon," he said as he held out his hands to take the envelopes stuffed with God only knows what from me.

"Don't worry," Meyer said to me as he opened the door to his limo. "There will be more of that," he nodded over towards the envelopes and smiled.

Otis and I got into the back of Meyer's limo. He came to sit with us and slowly closed the door. The dark tinted windows in the black limo cut off the bright morning light. The car — which really felt like a land boat — started driving.

"What does bubula mean?" I asked Meyer, who was sitting on the other side from Otis.

Meyer looked over at me.

"It's is a Yiddish term of endearment. It is kind of like dear or honey. Jewish Grandmothers usually use it. But I lifted it for my own uses here and there when it fits, like with this kid here," and then he looked at Otis.

I got to my subway stop for the Tavern, closed Sophia's diary, and got off the subway. My head was till reeling from the Kennedy death, and I looked forward to seeing Tony. Maybe he would have some input to give to me as to how this horror fit within my action-reaction understanding of the world. Was this just another example of cause-effect? But how could it be?

"What'll have, kid?" Tony asked when I pulled my chair up the bar.

Kissing Cousins

The shining sun outside wasn't discouraged by the partially drawn shades in the Tavern's stained glass windows. They created a church like effect in the bar. Tony's hands, face, and body were partially in the sun, and partially in the dark. I guess that was fitting for the type of things I was reading about Jacky. I mean, the guy wasn't completely in the light. He was no altar boy. And yet he wasn't completely in the dark, either. He was, I guess you could say, ambidextrous. He could use the light when he needed to, but had the dark there just to throw his enemies off right when they thought they had him figured out.

"How about a good sunny drink?" I asked.

"Gin and tonic?" Tony inquired.

"Too sour." I said.

"Mint julep?" He asked in a stab in the dark way.

"Yes, come to think of it, that sounds grand!" I snapped my fingers.

"Coming right up, kid," Tony said as he went to make the drink. The bar was pretty much empty, except for Dean. He was the towering moneyman who made sure the cash from the place flowed smoothly into the right hands. It was like being in the calm before the storm at that time. I knew the after work crowd would soon be popping into the bar. It was about 4:20 in the afternoon.

As Tony made the drink, I felt like asking him about Lansky. I think I knew who he was, but wanted to know more about him. I also wanted to ask him for his thoughts about the assassination. So I started slow. I went to first base.

"Hey, Tony, can I ask you something?"

"Not what types of briefs I fucking wear, but anyting else iz fair game," he turned around at me to smile and then went back to making the drink.

"Know anything about Meyer Lansky?"

"Yea, you mean the midget circus act?" Tony said.

"Uh, no, I mean . . ."

"I know who you talkin' about, kid. Sure, what you want to know?"

"How did he get into it all? I mean, what made him go where he went in his life?"

"What makes anybody go where they go?"

I just shrugged my shoulders.

"Let me tell you a short story," Tony said as he put the julep in front of me.

"Alright," I said as I moved my satchel out of the way so that Tony could put the drink down in front of me.

"You know who William 'Willie' Sutton is?"

"The bank robber?" I asked as I sipped my julep.

"Right," Tony nodded as he stood there with his big pork chop sized hands on the bar. "Know what he sayz when someone asked him why he robbed de banks?"

"What?" A little kid at the fun park would ask the same question of the clown who is telling the kid a riddle. Tony was no clown and this was no kid riddle. But I guess that's my innocence talking.

"Sutton said: 'Because that's where de money iz.'" Tony then clapped his hands once in enjoyment at the sweet jellybean taste of Sutton's sinful answer. "Ain't that something?" Tony rejoiced at Suttons' blunt honesty.

"It's something, alright," I smiled and drank some more.

"Well, dat same something is what got Lansky into de game, too."

"How so?" I asked.

"Word has it," he looked around, "is dat his family didn't have de oven big enough to cook some stew dat Jews make for de Sabbath on Fridays."

"Beef stew? Or is it called, um, let me see . . . de chloent?"

"Something like dat," Tony shrugged. "So word has it dat his mom would give him a nickel to go to de bakery. But, on his way to dat bakery, he'd pass other Lower East Side kids playing craps."

"On the street? Against the wall?"

"Wherever they could shoot dem dice against, kid," Tony gave me a pragmatic look, "so one day, little Meyer decides to play de craps — but he loses. So his family ain't having dat special stew dat night."

"Must have gotten him into trouble?" I asked sipping my drink.

"Yea, yea, so little Meyer felt like a little prick. Loved his mother very much, felt like he let her down, and himself down. So he vowed to never lose at dat fucking game again. Little kid studied dat game like his life depended on the shit. Learned all of dem tricks and cheats. So, on another Friday Sabbath, little Meyer took his mother's nickel and gambled it again."

"Let me guess," I said, "he lost?"

"No, kid. Little Meyer won. But he never gambled dat Sabbath money again. He waz able to gamble with his own doe. Yea. Little Meyer gambled all over the Lower East Side. Word has it he never lost again. Started keeping a big wad of money. That wad was pretty damn good when ya parents iz fresh off de boat from Russia."

"So how did he start going there instead of there?" I pointed to the dark shade on his shirt for the first there, and then to the light on his shirt for the second there.

"Well, kid," Tony said, "little Meyer didn't like being so little. Felt it was his life's mission to get back at everyone who pushed him around, and who pushed Jews around — like dem local Italian and Irish kids. So he put his mind to tings and founded his own company," Tony said with a smirk.

"Yea, Murder Inc.," I said like I knew what I was talking about.

"Eh, the kid knows something?" Tony softly slapped my cheek.

"Sometimes, when I get lucky."

I played with the straw in my drink.

"One more question?"

Dirty Quiet Money

"I charge by the fucking hour, kid, you know," he pled with me. "What you want to know," he said playfully. "Keep in mind the clock is ticking," he tapped his Hamilton wristwatch. He leaned over towards me, took the straw out of my drink, and started chomping on it. He was chewing the straw like a city cow with a wise guy grin.

"What do you think about what happened today?" I asked.

"You mean when de sun rose at 7:30 in de morning?"

"I mean what happened in Dallas," I said.

"Yea, Tony knows what you meant. So what do you mean what do I think?"

"Do you think Oswald was acting alone?" I asked.

"The shooter." Tony said.

"Yea."

"You mean like he just woke up one morning, had some breakfast, looked at himself in the mirror, and said to himself, 'hey, today, I am going to kill some poor motherfucker. Never done that before. It's never too late to start — until I'm dead. And, hey, what do you know, it might as well be the president of the United States. Why the fuck not?'"

He looked around. Then he looked me straight in the eye.

"You mean like that alone, kid?"

"Yea," I said.

"Let me tell you a little story," he patted me nicely on the arm. "You know who Robert Kenney is, right?"

"Yeah."

"Good."

"Know his father?"

"Joseph Kennedy."

"Right. Good kid, I see why you done good grades in college. And you know how old man Kennedy made his money?"

"Stocks?"

"Try again."

"Bonds."

"Nope — booze."

"Not a financial instrument I know of," I said sarcastically.

"Better than that bullshit."

"I bet."

"So de prohibition stops in 1933. Right when dat ends, Kennedy and James Roosevelt, son of FDR, start themselves Somerset Importers. And, guess what, kid," Tony backhanded my right shoulder, "they had dem exclusive rights or whateva you call dem to distribute Haig & Haig Scotch, Gordon's Dry Gin, Dewar's Scotch. Not only dat. Dey was sittin' on a mountain of booze dat they import during prohibition so dat they could be the first horse out of de gates when prohibition ended."

"Smart training for the booze race," I said.

"Of course. But guess what type of men dey had to do business wit to get that much booze under they belts when dey wasn't supposed to be bringing de stuff into de country?"

"Jockeys?" I said with a smart-ass tone.

"Yea, a jockey named Meyer. And little Meyer got a lot of fucking muscle behind him."

"I bet. Booze was a dirty business in those days."

"Couldn't play in the mud without gettin' your nice Ivy League white gloves dirty. Now, de old man Kennedy had others do his dirty work for him, and got in real good with labor bosses around de country. And you know who dey was?"

"Right," I nodded. "Them," I said, referring to the generic "them" who used to hang in the rear of the Tavern or do business in the back rooms of Brooklyn candy and ice cream shops. The "them" also included Jacky — except he was part of the French — and not the American — "them."

"Yea, dem," Tony said. "And guess whose votes dem got for de president?"

"The labor votes."

"Right, kid," he nodded. "So, as a show of his gratitude, Kennedy, thinking he smarter than them, and his fucking dumb brother, dey go on dis witch hunt. Except dey don't hunt dem witches. They hunt dem. I know from speaking with some of tha lawyers who represent dem dat Kennedy's brother, Robert, hired ten times tha number of Mafia prosecutors as the previous president, and spent 13 times more time presenting dem to grand juries. The lawyers says dat, dis year, it was something like 1,000 days or some shit."

"And before?"

"Let me tink," he paused, "the lawyers said there was only like 100 days in 1960, or something like dat.

"An increase."

"A small one," Tony said sarcastically with his index finger and thumb pinching ever so close. "Plus, Kennedys been fucking with the wrong types of people to be fucking with. One is dis mean fuck named Marcello in New Orleans."

"Never heard of him.

"He and his New Orleans guys is all mean fucks. Word has it that Carolla, the boss befaw Marcello, met Capone at a New Orleans train station. Carolla had his New Orleans cops on de payroll with him. When Capone and his bodyguards got off de train, them cops took they guns, broke dere fingers, told dem to get the fuck back to Chicago."

"Wow," I had just learned a new theorem in physics but it was no theorem. It was an equation of black market power.

"Yea, wow is right, kid. Stay the fuck out of New Orleans, those broken fingers said," Tony continued. "Those fingers also said don't go hitting the bee hive down there unless you ready to get stung."

"And how did the Kennedys hit the bee hive?"

"Brother Kennedy ordered Marcello deported to Guatemala in about 1961. That case been in da courts for some time now. I get de info from speakin' with all of these lawyer types that comin' in here," Tony said from his leaning on the bar position.

It's like he held up the bar. His girth and the bar formed one large powerful mass.

"So these guys helped the Kennedys get into power, and then the Kennedys use that power to go after the very guys that got them there?"

Tony nodded very slowly and subtly.

"You could say dat."

"In the ballpark?" I asked.

"Yea, yea, kid, you in the ballpark."

"Don't bite the hand that feeds you?" I questioned.

"Don't bite the hungry mean connected moneyed don't fuck with us or we kill your first born hand," Tony agreed — in his own way. "Alright, kid, I got to set up shop for tonight. Enjoy your read," he pointed to my satchel.

"Thanks, Tony," I raised my glass to him.

I sat there shocked. I had been following the United States Senate Select Committee on Improper Activities in Labor and Management (also known as the "McClellan Committee"). It started meeting in 1957 and dissolved in 1960.

But I didn't know the backstory about it all. Tony just gave me some of it. And the "it" seemed like the President, or some/all of his family, had made a deal with whatever it is "they" might be called. But then the President broke the deal, from what Tony just told me, with "them."

Like Jacky, some people in the Tavern used the label "public servants" for the folks who make up the "them." The black market entrepreneurs brought desired vices to market even when they were illegal. Women, gambling, marijuana, or what have you. Banning all of this and demonizing it — instead of allowing some of it (women, dope, marijuana, gambling) but regulating it — gave the government the moral high ground — and justification — to tax, pay the judges, lawyers, and cops to make money out of it all. Then there are the prisons. I couldn't forget the prisons. The government doesn't make money off prosecuting child molestation cases in the church. So we don't see commissions on it. But you do see commissions on organized crime — like McClellan.

Dirty money talks — the McClellan commission listens.

Abused kids cry — there is no commission to listen.

Maybe Milton Friedman is right. He is a prominent economist whose classes I took at Chicago. He thinks prostitution and certain drugs should be legal — but regulated by the government, just like booze. I guess that's where the public service thing comes in.

I could see both sides of the coin. Some of the guys in the "them" did business harshly, making a lot of enemies. They'd jaywalk, spit on the cop's shoes, and dare the cop to come after them. Jacky wouldn't spit on the cop's shoes. He might take the cop to lunch, or slip him some cash, but Jacky wouldn't make it obvious. Maybe that was the difference between the rest of them and Jacky's type.

The difference still didn't stop me from being shocked that a sitting president was murdered. I don't think I'll ever get over that. At least I am making some semblance of meaning out of it. That way, I could see how it fit within my action-reaction worldview and I didn't think the world had just been turned upside down. I know the world isn't flat after all, although it seemed it might have been today.

I opened Sophia's diary to a few days after she arrived in New York.

July 5, 1942

When Meyer and his men dropped me and Otis off at our new apartment yesterday, which is located at 1025 Park Avenue, I didn't believe it. The place was fit for a royal family.

Jacky over did it this time.

After Meyer told me the address of the apartment the other day, I went to the New York public library with Otis to do some digging about the place. I always found libraries to calm my nerves in stressful times — and the library on 5th Avenue didn't let me down. I found out that the apartment was constructed in 1911-12. It was made for a well-known composer of light opera and popular music. His name was Reginald DeKoven and his wife's name was Anna.

The apartment is a lovely rare survivor from the period when Park Avenue was being groomed into a grand and exclusive boulevard. At the time, it was bordered by private homes and elegant apartment houses. I also found out it was designed in an unusual urban adaptation of the Jacobean Revival style by John Russell Pope, one of America's leading architects at the time.

"You like the place, doll?" Meyer asked as he closed the door to his Cadillac limousine in front of the apartment.

I looked up at the dominating, symmetrically arranged, bay windows and the solid brick facade with stone trim. The windows reminded me of the late sixteenth and early seventeenth century manor houses that I had seen when I traveled with Richard throughout England.

I was speechless.

"Hey," Meyer lightly brushed my arm to get my attention, "what you think?"

I looked at him with slight tears of joy in my eyes.

"It's beautiful, Meyer, just beautiful," I said shaking my head in disbelief.

"Yea, well, you had better believe it, doll face," as he motioned to his men to take our things upstairs. "This is your new home."

When we got inside, I found vast halls and elegant spaces. I imagined that this was the scene of gatherings and concerts for the DeKovens and their friends from socially elite circles of New York. I found out from my digging that this is exactly what they did when they were there.

"Where should they put your things?" Meyer asked as he walked inside the house with me. Our shoes made that welcome noise they make when you walk on new wooden floors.

I didn't know what to say.

"Put her bags over there, boys," he motioned to what looked like the living room.

I looked over to Meyer and put my hand softly on his forearm.

"I can't believe this," I said.

"Believe it, doll, you done good," he said as he softly put his hand on mine.

"Mommy, mommy, mommy!" I heard Otis say from the other room.

I walked into the living room area. It was flush with light from the bay windows that peaked outside onto Park Avenue.

There was a Lionel train track laid down next to the windows. A ribbon and a note were on the train. Otis's name was scribbled on the note.

"Jacky wanted us to get that for the kid, you know," Meyer said as he watched Otis start playing with the train. "Jacky thought it would make the kid feel more at home."

I felt like I was in a dream.

I looked around. The place had been decorated with wooden furniture made by Frank Lloyd Wright, who was one of my favorite architects. It was simple and yet sophisticated, earthy and yet cosmopolitan, fresh looking and yet old souled. The rest of the place had similar details that made it pop. On the living room wall was a painting by Juan Miro. I think it was an original showing a lovely white hand in blue background catching a red bird. There were colorful Persian rugs strewn about, and leather burgundy sofas in the living room.

"Let me and the boys know if you need anything." Meyer gave me his home phone number on a small ripped piece of paper. He leaned over and gave me a kiss on my check.

"I need Jacky," I said in a kidding but not so kidding tone.

"He'll be in touch with you, but still not by phone."

"Oh?" I asked as though things had changed since when I saw Jacky.

"Sometimes them things have ears of their own, especially where he is," Meyer thumbed in the direction of where he thought France was.

"I get it," I nervously nodded. I remember Jacky telling me about Madeleine listening into phone calls from the Gestapo officers. I am sure they had the same ears listening in on Jacky.

"Everything is going to be fine, missy," he said to reassure me.

The rest of Meyer's men walked out and tipped their straw fedoras in my direction.

"Ding, ding, ding," I heard Otis in the background playing with the train. He didn't seem to be in any pain.

I was.

"So long, fellas," I said to them men walking outside.

The door closed. I stood there. I felt alone. And all I needed would have been hearing Jacky's voice, having a coffee with him, or even puffing a cigarette together. I didn't care about the diamonds, the money, the apartment, the clothes, or the perfume. I would give this all away just to see him again and know that he is alright.

July 25, 1942

I received a letter from Jacky today. Enclosed was the photo that Napoleon took of Jacky and I in Deauville that one night during dinner. The letter was short and to the point. I guess that is what I would have expected from him. This is what the letter said.

"June 14, 1942, Sophia, you just leave and I already miss you. You on the boat right now with the ocean breeze doing the crawling through your hair and the sun spreading her wide warm all over your milk color body, yes? Even if this ocean has the much cold breeze and rain on you and Otis, she is better than France. I coming to New York soon. I writing when I can. Please give kiss to Otis. I finish writing this loving you always, Jacky."

I took the photo out. I am going to get it framed and put it on my piano in the living room.

August 4, 1942

I heard a loud knock this morning.

I opened the front door. There was an envelope on the doormat for me. My name was on it. I opened it up. It read.

"Dear Sophia, you don't know me but I know of you. I am a long time business associate of good ole Jacky. I only hope y'all can visit New Orleans. I also hope y'all is settling into New York just fine. I have had some of my boys up there enclose something in this here envelope that will make y'all's transition easier. If y'all need anything, please call 504.522.0908. Ask for Little Man and give them your number. My boys will get in touch with me. I'll call you as soon as I can. Yours truly, Carlos Marcello, New Orleans, Louisiana."

Enclosed in the envelope were $100 bills totaling what looked like about ten thousand dollars. I didn't know what Jacky did to make all of these people want to help me so much, but I am sure they made a lot of money with them. I get the feeling he was the goose that laid the golden eggs.

Boy does it help to have powerful friends — even if they are in dark places.

August 6, 1942

"I have something to tell you," Meyer said to me over coffee and cigarettes this afternoon. He has been coming on and off to check in on me. He is a nice person to have in the house, but he is no Jacky.

There was cigarette smoke in the middle of the kitchen. Coffee was brewing on the back stove. I looked outside one of the bay windows. There were two black Cadillac sedans waiting outside for him. Meyer didn't seem to get far anywhere outside of his house without his men. They weren't so close you could see them right way, but close enough so they could take care of business if needed. When he walked the streets of New York, the men in black seemed to hover barely in the distance in their Cadillac cars, or on foot not far behind, or ahead, of Meyer.

I guess that's why they called him Clever Meyer.

I tapped my cigarette ash onto the tray.

"Yes, what is this something you have to tell me?" I looked at him with try and surprise me eyes. After all that I have been through lately, I didn't think anything could get a rise out of me.

"Jacky's been framed," he said somberly and paused to smoke and let the "framed" have it's effect. Meyer put some ash into the ashtray, just as I did.

"What?" I held my cigarette tightly in the thunderstorm that I thought I was about to go through.

"Yep," he said nodding his head, "it was some French bastards we used to do business with."

"Auguste?" I remember asking.

"Yes," he looked at me with surprise, "you know him?" He asked.

"Jacky told me about him," I said in a matter of fact way.

"Yea, well, that man and others who been doing tricks with Vichy made it look like Jacky was in it with them."

"What does that mean?" I asked.

"It means the Allies think that Jacky," he adjusted himself in the wooden chair to get more

comfortable. He even took off his suit jacket. Meyer always seemed to be in a suit. It was his trademark, just as Jacky's trademark was his tuxedo at night. "It means the Allies think that Jacky Blacky is a double agent," Meyer said in a disappointing tone.

"How did that happen?"

"Pretty simple," he put some ash down in an about to give a tutorial type of way. "Auguste had the Germans talk about doing deals with Blacky. They knew that the English and Americans would be listening. Right when that happened, Auguste knew that Jacky wouldn't have Allied blessing anymore."

"Leaving him high and dry," I said. I got the point.

But Meyer had to make it sharper than I wanted.

"And now," Meyer looked outside onto Park Avenue, "Jacky is squeezed between the Germans, English, and Americans."

"A lone wolf," I said without hope as I stared at the ash on the table.

"Not quite," he put his hand on mine, which was resting on the table.

"He still has us," he broke a smile.

I knew the "us" didn't mean just Meyer and I. It was an "us" that referred, in reality, to "them." But I didn't really know who "them" included, other than the guys in the clubs where Jacky worked, the guys at the casino, the guys at the pier who picked us up, the Marcello guy, his guys, and then Meyer. I had a feeling there was a more to "them" than met my eye.

"So what does that mean? How are we going to help?" I asked with distrust as tears brewed in my eyes.

"Please don't cry, Sophia," he said as he took out his handkerchief and wiped my eyes. I was coming pretty damn close to wanting to give up and not caring anymore about feeling like I had given up.

What was it all worth anyway?

Otis kept me sane.

"Meyer, Meyer," Otis said when he came into the room and tugged on Meyer's suit jacket. "Let's go play with the train, let's go play with the train," Otis said with excitement.

Meyer had played with Otis before. And I think Otis thought it would happen every time Meyer came over.

"Not now, bubula, but we'll play next time, I swear," Meyer petted Otis on the head. "Good little bubula," he said as Otis went away peacefully — only after Meyer bribed Otis with a candy.

A good hustler is good with kids because kids are the best hustlers of them all. Jacky was like a big kid but with big kid toys. Instead of the train track, the fire engine, and whatever else Otis played with, Jacky the hustler substituted other things as he got older — cars, women, money, homes.

I looked at Meyer.

He looked back at me.

He could tell I was coming to the end of my rope.

He leaned over.

He leaned over in the way I could see him when he leaned over towards someone whose neck he was *about to ring, except it wouldn't be him that did the ringing. The poor guy whose neck was about to be rung wouldn't even know what was coming down the dark road or when it would arrive.*

"Sophia," he said.

I looked away towards the window.

"Look at me," he said again but I kept looking towards the window.

He reached over and softly put his hand on my cheek. Jacky and him must have gone to the same school of thought, the hand on the face to show you grace when you feel like you have lost face school of thought. Meyer slightly directed my attention over his way.

"It's going to be alright," he said softly, firmly, and with certainty that I clung to in the storm of uncertainty.

"It's going to be alright?" I asked him, I asked the swamps in Louisiana, I asked the Fifth Avenue shops, I asked the guys at the casino, I asked the guys from the five families who picked me up when I first arrived off the boat.

"I wouldn't tell you if it weren't." He said with a period at the end of his sentence that made me remember the cherries on top of the ice cream sundaes my grandparents would get me after church on Sundays back in New Orleans. The cherries marked the end of my day at Church. His period marked the end of my suffering — or so I hoped.

August 11, 1942

"How is Jacky?" I asked Meyer over our coffee and cigarettes this afternoon. Meyer was Jacky's surrogate cousin. All of these men seemed like

surrogate cousins to one another. It showed in the way they greeted one another: a kiss on the cheeks, a short hug, and big laughs with pats on the back.

Meyer didn't say anything.

"I haven't received any letters from him," I worried to Meyer. I took a long drag off my cigarette. The nicotine filled smoke gave some temporary relief to my concerned soul. I felt like I was crumbling.

"They found out where he lived," he said with disgust as he put his ash out into the ash tray.

"What?"

"But he is fine," Meyer looked up at me.

"Fine?"

"There were some neighbors who saw him going out on the ledge, and then toeing it until he got to the neighbor's window when they came," Meyer said with a proud tone. "But they eventually got him there when they searched the building later that night."

"The Germans?" I asked.

"Gestapo, yes," Meyer said.

"So where is he now?"

Meyer just sat there silently looking outside the window.

"Meyer," I leaned over in my own tough lady with a hard-core Sammy private investigator type of way, "where is he?"

He looked up at me with sort of sad dog eyes.

"I don't know, Sophia. This is the last note we have from him," and then Meyer handed me a long crumpled up note that Jacky had given someone, who had given it to someone else's nephew, who had given it to someone else's cousin, who then gave it to someone's wife, and then who put it into

Meyer's hands. There were probably 25 degrees of separation between Jacky's hands and where the note now sat in mine.

I read the note and understood what Jacky had done. One night outside a family club, he and his army of thugs slaughtered a slew of the same Nazi officers who had come to get me that one morning at the school. The officers knew that it was Jacky, and only Jacky, who could have given their wives the photos.

"None of you knows where he is now?" I asked again with concern.

Meyer waved his head back and forth. It was a wave that I could have seen on him taking the Fifth Amendment in front of some congressional investigation, or in front of a judge, or in front of a jury denying he knows anyone — or anything — in his dark syndicate. They all seemed to have that talent to wave their heads back and forth like they didn't know anything. It was part of their secret code of conduct.

Of course, sometimes the head nod meant just that — I don't know. But, for the initiated, the nod was done with a wink. The wink means "I act like I don't know, but I do know, and the wink of my right eye means I do know — I'm only doing that with you because you are in the club and they are listening." In this case, the "they" is the McClellan Commission on organized crime. They aren't in the club. So Meyer and his boys just take the Fifth in front of the Commission and behave like they don't know when, in fact, they do.

They — and now I mean Jack and Meyer's "they" — have the same code of secrecy as societies like Skull & Bones at Yale. I should know. Many of my New Orleans friends joined these secret societies. The main difference between the kissing cousin code and the Ivy League society code is the color of the members' collars. Meyer and his cousins have blue collars, whereas the Ivy boys have white ones.

And so part of me believed Meyer — but another of me part didn't believe him at all. Not that I thought he was trying to hide something to hurt me, or for some nasty reason. If anything, he wasn't telling me something to protect me. Perhaps there were wires in the walls? Perhaps all of those cars that I saw parked outside at night weren't just neighbors' but FBI cars?

It was that other part of me, that part which had Jacky's see through the surface of things and into things that are behind the surface, which made me feel like maybe there was something else going on. It's like I saw the wink in Meyer's eye without him actually winking or needing to wink.

The uncertainty made me feel queasy.

I didn't feel easy.

My breasts didn't feel breezy.

I wondered if it was the stress.

What a mess.

And on top of it all I have been missing my period!

If it weren't for Otis, I feel like I could jump off the roof.

"Getting low on your mint julep there, kiddo, you want another fill up?" Tony asked me as I sat at the Tavern bar. I looked up from Sophia's diary.

"That would be great," I raised my close to empty glass up to him.

"Got one right here, son," Tony gave me another julep and took my empty one.

"Swell!" I said as I looked eagerly at this new concoction Tony had made.

"Enjoy, son," Tony said.

"Thanks, T," I said and nodded a thank you to him. I jumped forward in Sophia's diary. The juleps were having their effect on me, and I didn't want to get too plastered before I finished my reading for the day.

> *September 8, 1942*
> *More morning sickness, breasts getting tender, and my appetite has changed. All of this could be because I have been worrying so much lately, waking up at night, and wondering if I would ever be able to hold Jacky again in my arms. The lack of sleep has been catching up with me.*
>
> *Plus, I haven't been able to control the anxious thoughts going through my head. I keep wondering if I would ever be able to have coffee and cigarettes with him again, to laugh at his sarcasm, and to feel like I had found my soul mate — all in the dingy closet of Otis's school.*
>
> *My symptoms remind me of when I was pregnant with Otis. It is probably all because of the trip to New York, and this tortuous stress, but I had better look into it.*
>
> *God only knows.*
>
> *September 14, 1942*
> *I knew something was in the oven. And it wasn't an egg.*

I went to the doctor today. He did his tests. By God almighty — I am pregnant!!!

I know exactly who the daddy is. It isn't the milkman. It is my man. I can't believe my dream has come true. It was the only dream I really cared about when I was with him, other than us getting out of Germany safe. The doctor told me the due date is about February 14 of 1943. I can't believe it!!!

At the same time, I am so sad that this is all happening without Jacky around.

That's why I cried all day today. I cried all day because my dream is coming true. But the dream has been turned upside down. I thought about having a little child who looks like Jacky, talks like Jacky, smells like Jacky, makes me laugh like Jacky, and has the soul of Jacky. But now Jacky isn't around to see him, me, or us.

Except from above.

I am going to keep crying. I am tired of feeling like I need to be perfect. I am tired of denying that little girl inside, telling her to shut up, and to keep quiet while I try to act like all is well. I am the good Protestant girl who doesn't do otherwise — she gets with the right religious man, who has the right degree, and who has the right smile that makes you feel safe and warm at night.

That's until you are shocked that the smile is camouflage for a whole other darker world underneath that you never would have imagined was there. The smile is a new shoebox with old shoes inside. Meanwhile, the scoundrel looking man, with holes in his arms, dirty friends, archangel looking eyes, and without a smile holds up an old and decrepit shoebox to your eyes. He makes you think that there is nothing inside but old dust, cobwebs, and pain.

"Trick is on you," I imagined Jacky telling the whole world when he held up his old box for all to see, including me. Oh yes, we scowled at him. We covered our children's eyes. We didn't want to even look at the wretched vagabond. But now look where I stand? I am about to have that vagabond's child and he isn't around to see it. That's because of me, the upper class, upper crust, top shelf woman from good stock.

I need to get out of town with Otis for a while. I need this. I need to think about my next steps. I know many New Yorkers get away to Maine. I also heard they go to Martha's Vineyard. I have heard of them all. But I am going to do something I have always wanted to do. I am going to California. I am going to take Otis, and the new one inside me, to see what it is like to live in a new place, without history, and without all of the scars that we have in the south and east.

Maybe sometimes leaving the place you think you belong is the only way of knowing whether you truly belong there. Maybe it's good to go to zero, and to strip away all of your comfort to see what really matters.

That's exactly what I am going to do until October.

October 31, 1942

"How you like my costume?" Meyer asked today.

"You look like a butler," I said still gleaming with my California tan. I visited Los Angeles, Santa Barbara, and San Francisco with Otis in September.

"Yeah, yeah, yeah, doll," he said sarcastically. *"But you missing something."*

"Oh?" I asked."

He opened his tuxedo jacket.

I thought he was going to show me a pistol.

"And may I take your order, madam," he said in a playful English accent, which was funny to hear coming from a Lower East Side Jewish boy. He took out a notepad and pen to take my order as though he were working at a hamburger stand.

"You silly goose," I cracked a smile.

"And you the laughing gypsy," he said pleased that he made me chuckle.

I was dressed up as a gypsy, a pregnant one at that, with my own twist on it. I felt that free spirit when I was traveling in California. It was a feeling I imagine the first Americans must have felt when they came to the East Coast, and which maybe they had lost. The cold, sleet, and snow can beat down that free spirit inside so that it becomes a whimper or cower. California's sun, ocean, and energy refreshed me like no place back east could.

Meyer and I stood outside on Park Avenue as Otis did his trick or treat at a nearby apartment.

"Still no word?" I asked.

He looked over at me.

"Still no word," he said as he smoked his cigarette and smashed it into the ground. *"How have you been feeling,"* he asked as he looked down at my belly.

I could tell his concern was sincere. He was not tightlipped and hiding behind the Fifth Amendment.

"I have been feeling better, thank you," I said as I rubbed my stomach. "I just need to know what happened to him."

"I know," he said as he lit up another cigarette, "but you need to take care of that now," he looked over to my belly. "You may never know what happened to him," he looked up at me with grave eyes.

I still didn't believe him for some reason.

December 26, 1942

"We got you a Christmas present," Meyer said to me on Christmas day yesterday. He and the other guys, the ones who first welcomed me off the boat, enjoyed some treats that I had prepared for the holidays. They were buzzing off some martinis that they had put together with homemade gin and vodka.

All of them were dressed in tuxedos. I was wearing a gown, or what I could wear of a gown, made by Chanel New York for me. My belly was pushing outward. It looked like a good old boy belly. Except mine wasn't filled to the brim with moonshine and whatever else those Louisiana country boys used to put in there.

"Oh yea?" I asked as the boys stood joking, smoking, and drinking. "What's the present — Jacky?"

"Not quite doll," Meyer said, looked over at the rest of the men, and paused. "We getting' you a butler to help you and keep you company so that you won't be alone when the baby comes," Meyer

looked down to my belly like the belly could hear him.

"Well, that's a relief," I said with some sarcasm, but with some appreciation, too. I knew Meyer and his crew would be around. But I needed someone to help me when the little one came into the world. Of course, Jacky is what I wanted.

But a butler would do in the meantime.

"Seriously," I said to Meyer with my hand resting on his arm. "Thank you — thank you for everything you have done. I might not show it, I might not say it, but I wanted to let you know ..."

He interrupted me.

"Sophia," he said as he put his martini down. "I understand. Things will get better once you have some help," Meyer said with a smile on his face. "This fancy butler was trained in England. He been servicing some of our friends in France and England for sometime now. The man has gotten rave reviews."

What would Jacky do? I asked myself. How did Jacky deal with these times?

"I hope he wears a monocle so he can fit the part." I tried to slap a good guy slap on Meyer's shoulder but I really couldn't because I'm not a good guy, nor am I really in any mood to joke or play with the dark cloud of Jacky's unknown whereabouts hanging over my head. But I tried my best anyway.

Meyer smiled at me.

Then I thought to myself: Jacky may be gone forever. But he would live on inside me forever. The only way to do that is to remember him for the lesson he taught me: have a sense of humor when you look down the barrel of a gun, cause it isn't going to make it any better to die scared.

"Want another julep?" Tony said to me. I closed Sophia's diary.

"I think I am going to pack it in early for tonight," I said back.

"Early morning tomorrow?" Tony asked.

"Yup." He knew about my meeting with Sophia tomorrow morning, but didn't want to ask. "What do I owe you for that one?"

"It's on the house," Tony said.

"Are you sure?"

"Yeah," he said, "but you be sure to come back tomorrow night. Tony here," he then pulled up his pants, which were drooping below his tight and yet big former boxer belly, "wants to see you after uze done wid Sophia."

He looked directly into my eyes.

And then I wondered if Tony was in the "them" that Sophia talked about in her diaries. Was the "them" the same as the "us" that Meyer used with Sophia? How many kissing cousins were in the "them" and "us?" Just how far did "them" go into, and up, in the world? The more I read Sophia's diaries, the more I understood that I was more like Sophia than I had originally thought.

Oh yea, she was more polished. And, oh yes, she was more moneyed.

But we were cut from the same American cloth.

Like her, maybe I was coming to think that the American cloth was off target about the way we should live and love. The cloth says: go to school, get married to your school sweetheart, get engaged, get the white picket fence, go into debt, pay the mortgage, and have the kids. The cloth also says: your wife's family is your extended family. That's the path the Midwest cloth taught me to walk. Maybe there was another less linear way, and more maze like path, to sincere love.

Those kissing cousins that Sophia met showed me that. They were kissing her. But it was Jacky doing the kissing through that long maze of men from different families, different interests, and different bosses. It was their lips. But Jacky was making their lips move.

CHAPTER 13
Stage Fright To Delight

"Good morning, Hank," Winston said to me with a short nod of his head as I walked up to Sophia's apartment. It was around 7:45 a.m. on a cool November Monday morning. The sun was bright and warm. But I was feeling dark inside because of President Kennedy's death this past Friday.

Winston was standing outside the door. He was in his usual attire. In the corner of his mouth was a cigarette. The right side of lips kept the cigarette there for safe keeping while the left side spoke. A ventriloquist — I thought to myself when I saw how artfully he could talk outside of one part of his mouth and then keep the other so tight. I guess all of Sophia's clan seemed to have this ability. It was a talent of the foregone era.

"Good morning, Winston," the emotionless robot inside me said.

"Cigarette?" He held out a pack of Gauloises, a French cigarette that The Doors had popularized in the States. Winston was awfully hip for an old Englishman.

"No thanks," I put my hand up. "Too early."

"Smart lad," he put the pack back in his jacket. "She is waiting for you," he said as he opened the door to Sophia's apartment building. "I'll be right up, old chap. I'm waiting for a delivery."

I went up to see Sophia. The flowers I had bought for her were in my hand. I wanted to thank her for being so open with me, especially before she left for a long trip later today. I came before work so I could say goodbye.

"Oh Hank," she said when she saw the pink flowers, "you didn't need to." She was wearing what looked like an Hermes scarf — I had seen her wear them before — and a lovely suit, which I think was made by Valentino. I think Sophia was wearing this designer the first time I met her. Mrs. Kennedy usually wore colorful pink versions of the Italian designer, but Sophia's suit was black today. Her scarf was a mix of grey and black. She looked like she was prepared for a funeral. But what did I know?

In the dining room, there was a table full of bagels, salmon, and cream cheese. I could smell fresh coffee in the air. Apparently, Winston had a busy this morning preparing for my arrival.

I was honored.

"I wanted to," I said to her in reference to the flowers.

She smiled.

We hugged.

It was a short hug.

But it felt long.

It felt long the way a stare from someone you connect with on some deeper level feels. You cannot explain why the stare feels so long and substantial — but it does. It's like you have known the person for a long time even though it might only be for a few seconds. And yet you might know that person better than someone you have known for a lifetime.

You get this feeling all from that look.

We are smart monkeys, as Jacky might say.

"Let's have some coffee and food, darling," she said in her understated elegance. She softly put her nicely manicured hand on my back to direct me towards the food. "Let me put these in some water first," she pointed to the flowers. "Please help yourself, Hank."

I went into the dining room. I picked up the pot of coffee. I poured the black sludge into a coffee cup. I guess she liked her coffee thick and dark like the bottom of the East River. Maybe it's because her life had become thick and black. I guess she got her taste in coffee from those mornings with Jacky at the school. She had made her metamorphosis from straight and Oxford smart with Richard to sidewinding and Marseilles smart with Jacky. I wondered, as I poured the coffee, how much this change had ruined any part of her that was sweet and soft, like the one who cried about her parents. Instead, there was, perhaps, a woman who didn't want to take the time to have tears, feel, or touch as much.

"How is the coffee?" She asked.

"Great," I sipped the coffee. "Same type as you guys used to drink at Otis's school?"

"Almost. Without the smoke to impregnate it with its smell," she smiled as she poured some more coffee into her cup.

"Speaking of impregnation, what happened with your daughter?" I smiled and sarcastically looked over to her as I took some bagel and locks.

Suddenly I heard Winston come into the door and quietly close it.

"Need anything?" He asked in his proper English accent. While he sounded the Oxford type, he seemed more like a working class cockney type of guy underneath all of the polish. Maybe it was the way he held his cigarette, his warmth, or his subtle and simple rough around the edges energy.

"No, dear, thank you," Sophia said.

"No thank you," I echoed.

"Very well. I'll be in the other room if you need anything."

"So you want to know about my daughter?" Sophia picked up from where I left off with "speaking of impregnation" — just like I imagined the snoop she hired in Paris picked up on incomplete information, or thoughts, to formulate where they would lead.

"Yes," I smiled.

"Her name is Ella," she said as she put some food onto her plate.

"I love that name. After Fitzgerald?"

"Not F. Scott, and not after Kennedy," she looked over to me.

"After the jazz singer — Ella Fitzgerald?"

"None other," she said. "Let's go into the living room, darling," she said.

We sat on the couch. She ate. I ate. The sun shined in from outside. I was starting to feel a little better from Friday, and from when I first arrived this morning. I felt like I understood Sophia and her place, but I didn't understand what happened in Dallas.

"Ella was born February 15, 1943."

"Here in New York?" I asked.

"Mount Sinai," she said as she ate.

"Music?" Winston came out from nowhere to ask.

"Yes, dear," Sophia said softly. "That would be lovely. Request?" She looked at me and asked.

"I leave it to you."

"Winston?" She asked.

"Little Red Rooster is quite the smash hit now. Sam Cooke sings it. Quite a proper song for today."

"He always seems to have his pulse on the cool," she looked over at me with adoration. "That sounds good, darling," she said as she continued eating.

Winston put on the album. Cooke sang:

> I'm a little red rooster,
> Too lazy to crow for day
> I'm a little red rooster,

Too lazy to crow for day
Keep everything in the barnyard,
Upset in every way
Dogs begin to bark now,
And the hounds begin to howl
Dogs begin to bark now,
And the hounds begin to howl
Watch out stray cat,
The little red rooster's on the prowl.

"Where is Ella now?" I sipped some coffee.

"She is a sophomore at Yale," Sophia said. "She is majoring in politics, political theory, and economics, some fancy program they have over there," she looked over and smiled at me.

"Jacky could have been a Yale professor," I jousted and took a long sip of my coffee.

"Could have founded a program there called 'Making Something Out of Nothing,'" she smiled.

"Was that the last correspondence you got from him, the one from," I put my coffee down and opened up my Moleskin booklet, which I took here and there when I read the diaries. "I think it was June 14th?"

"The last one," she said in a curt tone, "I ever got," she placed her coffee on the coffee table.

I didn't want to pry. I could tell it was a sensitive subject. She paused.

"I didn't mean to be rude, Hank, with my tone," she said after finishing a bite of her food.

"I understand, Sophia. It's sore spot."

"That's why I gave you the diaries," she said endearingly. "You have a sincere curiosity in what happened and don't judge. You haven't said one judgmental thing in this whole time. You remind me of Otis. I think I told you that the first day we met."

"Where is he?"

"Graduated from Princeton and is now at Tulane Law School."

"Dummy, like his mother," I smiled.

She smiled the same.

"Why would I judge?" I asked in reference to her earlier question.

"A lot of people would," she said.

"Because?" I wondered.

"Of the company I have been keeping."

"Doesn't fit the blue blood mold?" I asked.

"Pretty much smashes it against the wall," she said with a devilish smirk.

"And replaces the old mold with a new and improved one," I said quickly to fill in the blank.

"I had to leave France," she said defensively, and without saying whether it was all an improvement — or merely a change from miles per hour to kilometers per hour.

"I would have taken their hand, too, that day at Otis's school," I said.

"I had no choice."

"You could have stayed," I said rhetorically. "But you probably wouldn't be here now speaking to me."

She nodded.

"And I don't know if you knew by taking Jacky's man's hand that one day that you would be getting envelopes by Marcello and others like him on a following day."

"I never would have imagined it," she agreed.

"One domino hits another. Before you know it, you are on Park Avenue talking to some bright eyed Chicago educated kid who is learning more through you than I could have at all of the Ivy schools — plus Chicago and Stanford — put together."

"Thanks, Hank," she blushed.

"I mean it," I said.

"I know it's sincere."

I could tell she was sad. I think she had the same sadness as I did knowing Jacky left behind her and the kids.

"I'm sorry if I am not so talkative today," she said looking reflectively at her coffee.

"It's alright," I touched her hand like I envisioned Jacky would touch her hand to comfort her.

"I feel horrible about what happened to President Kennedy on Friday, Hank," she looked up at me with some tears in her eyes. "I couldn't sleep last night."

I could tell. She had slight bags underneath her eyes. It looked like she was up all night. I was up, too. Yesterday, Sunday, November 24, 1963, Jacky Ruby, a Dallas nightclub owner with suspected ties to the Chicago underworld, killed Harvey Oswald, the sniper who was suspected of killing President Kennedy. This chaos was all so stressful and sad for me. Maybe that's why I just gazed at my apartment ceiling last night.

"I know you read about the men being in this 'them,'" she said. They saved my life. And it's all because of Jacky."

"Exactly Like You," a Louis Armstrong song came on in the background.

"But you aren't exactly like them, Sophia," I said in comforting way. I took a bite of the bagel I had made.

"I know that," she took out her box of Chesterfields. "But I also know I have taken their money. I wouldn't be where I am now in my life if it weren't for them. Nor would my children have been safe if it weren't for them."

"Nor would you be doing good things for people who need it through Veritas without them," my defense lawyer came out. I hated most lawyers. They seemed to cause more problems than they solved. But I liked great ones — about 5% of them.

"Yes, but I feel guilty about what happened on Friday," she said with a trembling grief in her voice.

"You didn't cause it," the metaphysics professor spoke.

"Kennedy didn't deserve that," she said sadly. "Not like it happened. He should have been warned."

I looked outside to think and then looked back through the smoke.

"Tony says..."

"I know what Tony says," she interrupted. "I know it in a way that you know the math in your head. I still feel horrible for Kennedy's family."

She understood the math. She understood that Camelot wasn't perhaps what it seemed to be. Yes, the paper reported the glamour. Yes, it reported on the positive things, the civil rights things, and so on. No, it didn't tell about Marilyn Monroe, how President Kennedy got voted in, his father's — Joseph Kennedy's — booze connections during prohibition, and the way in which that family came to be, it seemed to me. But, what do I know other than what Tony, my street arithmetic professor, told me in the Tavern? Stuff I had never heard of before, nor will likely every hear again.

"But I guess I saw this coming," she looked over at me with some relief as her cigarette drooped out of her mouth. Her relief that she saw it coming came from the bottom of the tub being uncorked for the water to wash through and let you feel all better after the warm bubble bath.

That cork was her temporary denial of the powerful enemies the President and his father had made through the years — especially after the commissions on organized crime in labor, Kennedy's deportation of Marcello to Central America, and the President's reported frolicking with call girls at the White House pool in the afternoons. The President couldn't have arranged for his female entertainment without inching over the line to deal with the "them" in New York, Los Angeles, Chicago, New Orleans, Dallas, Las Vegas, and so on — "dem" and "dose" guys in Tony's talk.

Sophia put some ash into the tray on the table.

"It was like a slow water torture for a lot of them the past few years." She used "them" this time not in reference to Kennedy's Camelot of popular lore, but to the underground Camelot of "them" — the one made up of people like Jacky, Meyer, and their cousins.

"I am going to the funeral anyway," she said as she looked outside the window. "Winston is driving me down to Washington later this morning," she looked over at me. That explained the funeral get up. "And then, as I mentioned to you before, we are taking a long trip . . . overseas."

"For how long?" I asked.

"At least a few months," she said, "but I don't know for sure right now."

Sophia paused as we listened to the music in the background. As she did, I thought about how much I would miss her.

"You remind me a lot of myself when I was younger," Sophia suddenly confided.

"Young and naïve," I said in a self-deprecating tone.

"You may be young," she put her cigarette out in the ash tray, "but you are not naïve. Otherwise, I wouldn't have spent all of this time with you. You understand things are more complex than they seem at the start," she sipped more coffee.

"Just A memory," by Duke Ellington and Johnny Hodges, played in the background. I could see Winston out of the corner of my eye come into the room and switch the albums.

"Thank you, darling," Sophia said over to Winston without looking at him.

"Well, I feel naïve," I said with a let down in myself tone. Oh, I was a reporter at *The New York Times*. I was book smart. I had "made it," as they say. Or so I thought. But I was blinded by so much of what I read that I felt like I didn't really know anything about how the world really worked even though I thought I did. It's like Darwin caught me flat footed with his discovery that we evolved from apes.

That Darwin was Sophia.

"I used to feel the same way, too," as you saw from what I gave you. "Jacky introduced me to a whole other world where many of the things that I thought were important, or powerful, or meaningful were unimportant, not powerful, and meaningless," she said with a cynical tone.

Jacky was Sophia's Copernicus. He showed her the world was not flat.

"Like being the president of the most powerful country in the world means you are untouchable — when, in fact, you are not?" I said as I drank a healthy dose of her black Jacky Sophia brand of coffee.

She nodded a slow hesitant nod.

"The way I was raised to think is, in many ways, in the rear view mirror now, Hank," she said as she lit up another cigarette. "But I am still loyal, still try to love like I have never been hurt, and still cherish family." She paused. "But Jacky helped me change the way I think about the world."

"A lot more nuance?" I asked.

"You could say that." She responded.

"Do you think you'll love like you did with Jacky again?"

"Haley's Comet? Ever hear of it?" She asked sarcastically.

"Is the Vatican in Italy?" I retorted.

She smiled.

"The last time the comet came by was, I think, 1910," she said.

"A long time to wait for a taxi," I said jokingly.

She smiled warmly and sipped her dark coffee.

"And so you understand a man like Jacky doesn't arrive every morning like the sun," she said.

"We are taught to think that way though, aren't we? I mean, that people are replaceable."

"We are. The Ford Assembly line — a part doesn't fit, get another one," Sophia said.

"But there isn't another Haley's Comet," I supported her thought.

She looked content as she puffed her Chesterfield and sipped her coffee looking outside the window.

"I have had my fill of the French Comet," she continued. "It's not like I didn't sufficiently gaze at him in Deauville," she grinned.

I raised my coffee glass to her. After taking a big gulp, I confided: "I don't think I'll ever again see things the same way after meeting you, and reading what you have given me."

"That's a bad thing?" She said with one of her eyebrows raised upward.

"I don't think so. There is a dark side to the moon. To think it is just that bright thing we see at night is foolish."

"Feeling less foolish?" She asked.

"Less, but not completely so," I smiled.

"Why not completely?" She asked.

Part of her face was in a shadow created by the window behind her. They say that shading in photos gives the subject its personality. I thought that was true before I met her. But I only knew it in an abstract way, like how you know a city, say New Orleans, from seeing pictures and reading statistics on it. Sophia started to give me the practical knowledge behind that shadowing, behind that shade, that I only knew in theory before. And I guess it was that shade that I didn't quite know yet the way she knew it — or the way Tony knew it.

"I don't think I could ever love the way you have loved," I said looking outside the window in an ashamed way.

"Want one?" She held out a cigarette for me to light up.

"Thanks," I took it, lit hers up, and then lit my own. We sat on the couch in the now smoky living room. There was a moment of silence. It wasn't an uncomfortable one. It was one where you sit with someone and seem to know that time is fleeting. You sit appreciating that fleetingness with one another without saying a word.

"What makes you think you *can't* love like I have loved?" She asked as she blew some smoke out. She looked at me and waited for my answer. I felt on the spot. But I guess that is a good thing. When you are forced to step up to the plate, you can see what you are made of. Other people can see what you are made of, too.

"Because I am too scared," I admitted.

"Scared of what?" She put some ash into the tray.

These are just a few of the emergency phrases that went through my head when she asked me this — striking out, failing, being a fool, not being good enough, not rich enough, not good looking enough, boring, disappointing.

"Hank?" She put her hand on my knee to get me out of my stuttering Hank inner thoughts.

"Not being worth it," I answered as I put some ash into the tray.

She sat back in the couch. She looked deep in thought for a moment.

Winston played "Walk Like a Man," a song by the Four Seasons, on the record player.

"Winston has a sense of humor," she said softly over in my direction. She leaned forward in her couch, and then said:

"Hank, we all have fears of not being worth it, as you say. How do you think I felt after Richard? I didn't think I'd be able to satisfy any man, especially one that I could love. So I just hid and stayed in my little cave."

"Until Jacky started getting more marks on his arms?" I asked.

"Yes, but that wasn't about me. It was about him. And yet those marks made me come out of my cave. I realized I had been living without electricity — love — for so long in my life when I saw him living without it, too."

"He acted like a mirror?" I asked.

Sophia nodded.

"Even though we were from such different backgrounds," she said and took a long drag.

"So you didn't feel so alone when you were with him?"

"Right, Hank," she sipped some coffee. "That's why I am so happy to have met you. You are a sharp, introverted, and yet curious young man."

We both sat smoking.

"And I suppose I didn't feel alone with him," she broke the silence, "because I didn't feel like all men were like Richard when I was with Jacky. That was my fear. I would see a man on the street and project Richard onto him."

"Not to say a lot of men aren't like Richard," I smirked.

"True," she dropped some cigarette ash into the tray, "but not all."

"But Jacky repulsed you in the start," I said.

"He did. I was scared of what I didn't know or understand. But the deeper I swam, the more comfortable I felt."

"That initial fear goes back to the way you were raised in Louisiana?" I asked.

She nodded with approval.

"We are all from different places Hank, but we are not the places we are from. We have to practice in our lives understanding the difference, and not just becoming an addition of all the things we were brought up with, you see darling?"

"Choice has a part to play," I nodded.

"Yes," she nodded. "I had come to a fork in the road with him. I had a choice to take a road with him that I had never been on before, or I could just stay on the road I was on without him."

"A lot of people would have just stayed alone."

"Status quo," Sophia said.

"That's why I said I don't know if I could love like you did with him. I don't know if I could have taken that road less traveled," I said.

"Hank," she leaned closer to me, "you came to my house initially to write an article about the donation my charity made to MOMA, right?"

I nodded and sipped my coffee.

"And yet you have for the past few weeks been coming back to see me so that you can speak to me and read the diaries."

I nodded again.

"Hasn't our time together, and those diaries, been its own road? Isn't it one that you had never been on before, one that you wouldn't have seen yourself on just a few months ago, sitting in that *New York Times* building of yours?"

She had a point.

"It was very unexpected. I saw that photo and . . ."

"Your heart did the rest," she smiled in my direction. "It reminds me of a quote from Einstein."

"Love that guy," I said.

"I can't believe I am announcing quotes! I guess your Chicago ways are rubbing off on me," she said with an affectionate smile.

"Well, I guess you are learning from me just as much as I am learning from you?" I can't believe I just said that to a woman like Sophia. Maybe reading about a guy like Jacky had given me more unexpected courage than I had originally realized.

She just kept smiling and then continued with her thought.

"I think Einstein said something like, 'the intuitive mind is a sacred gift and the rational mind is a faithful servant,'" she took a long drag of her cigarette, "but 'we have created a world that honors the servant and has forgotten the master.'"

She looked at me and smiled.

"I've been guilty of that," I surrendered with my hands slightly up. "Whatever the problems in my life you are talking about — school, career, love. Whenever they come up, I seem to want to think things through, like it's a big math problem that I am going to solve."

She sat there and nodded for me to go on. She took another drag and sipped her coffee.

"But I often find myself lost in the weeds of my thoughts the more I get to thinking about how to solve the problem."

"I understand," she said softly. "That electrical chord you try to untangle with your mind often only gets knotted even more the harder and harder you try to untangle it."

"Yes!" I slapped my knee. "That's exactly right," I looked around a little embarrassed to see if anybody was looking or listening, like Winston. I don't think I had ever been so open with someone before.

But I guess that's because nobody would understand anyway. For my parents, figuring out things is the way to go. They are practical people and only think about practical things. They don't like talking about anything that is outside of their day in and day out routine, or which they can't see with their own two eyes. Their focus and simplicity is comforting in some ways — but it is also limiting and naïve.

Or maybe they didn't want to see things that they could see if they took their blinders off. Maybe they wouldn't want to meet a guy like Tony who tells them straight about the things their beloved president did. They have this archaic respect for institutions to the point where they don't question things. And yet I concluded from my studies at Chicago that questioning the status quo of authority is what we are supposed to do in a free society like ours. Sometimes, or even oftentimes, we may even agree with the status quo, but it's good to do so consciously, informed, so we know what we are agreeing to — and foregoing by agreeing.

"Well," Sophia put her coffee down and took me out of my head. "Think about this — my young Chicago friend. What about walking away from those electric chords you are trying to untangle and taking a walk to smell some fresh eucalyptus tree bark. Ever smell that stuff?"

"Can't say I have," I puffed my dirty cigarette as I thought about the clean smelling bark.

"The smell is soothing. It's almost like a massage through your nose," she paused. "Not like other things people in this city might put up their nose," she gave me what I imagined to be a prohibition gin grin. "And then, after you have had your smell, you take your walk."

"Or a swim in the ocean?"

"Or a horse back ride," she said playfully. "Whatever it is, you come back to those tangled chords and take a more Zen approach to it, darling. You calmly and slowly take the chords apart without rushing the process. After some time, you'll see that the chords are untangled."

"Or that I found a nice girl?"

"Maybe in the chords," she smiled. "Yes, though," she said as she lit up another cigarette. "That is the way to meet a woman. If you are too in your head, like I gather you have been from speaking with Tony," she looked at me and smiled. "You are never going to get out of that little safe world of yours to approach a woman who **wants** you to approach her."

"And what if she doesn't want me?" I asked with worry.

"That's why you don't approach it with your head. You see, the mind works with abstract symbols — just like how those physicists at Chicago work with abstract concepts like atoms," she nodded me warmly with a smile. "Your mind sees that rejection in a sort of binary way, like yes and no, instead of 'she is not ready to have history of love,' 'she isn't a good fit,' or 'I'm not ready to have a history of love.' But when you approach rejection with love, you won't take it like 'she doesn't want me because I'm worthless.' The love of yourself will say 'she may not want me, and it may just be now, but there is a lock out there that my key will fit. This woman saying 'no' is actually a chance to get closer to it."

I just sat there — listening. She caught my stage fright so accurately it scared me. I knew that she knew Tony, but I didn't know they talked about me like that. It showed me she cared. I was flattered that a woman like her would care about a guy like me. It was empowering.

"Surfer Girl," a popular song by the Beach Boys, came on over the stereo.

"I guess Winston has a hankering for the ocean?" I asked.

"Or maybe he is giving you a hint?" Sophia smiled.

"I should bleach my hair and start surfing?"

She put some ash out into the ashtray.

"Maybe learn from the way the surfers cruise those waves, without trying to figure out at every second where they are going, and what is the next move. They let the wave tell them their next move."

"Like Jacky and you did with your lives?" I said.

"We took heed of the signposts and took the turns we thought we should take when we thought we needed to take them. We didn't have the luxury to sit there and think about so many things in the future because of what was happening in the war. There may not have been a future."

"And yet things worked out between you," I put my cigarette out. "Even though you obviously came from . . ."

"Night and day," Sophia finished my thought.

"It didn't seem to matter, though. You both seemed to react the same way to the same things, like when the Vichy police were rounding up all of those Jewish children in, when was it?" I opened my notes to look. "Yea, sometime in July of 1941."

"That's when I knew that I loved him," she said with a quiet, vulnerable, and yet sweet voice, one that she didn't show me often. "He had his scarred arms, he had his habits, and yet we came from the same place, somehow, where it mattered," she pointed to her heart.

"But I also loved his mind," she said after a pause.

"It wasn't a formally trained one," I noted.

"But a better one, in so many ways," she retorted. "Maybe we get so formally trained that it blinds us to things that aren't in those little lessons we learn in school about how the world and people should work. We are taught in school only to look in certain places for certain things — whether it is love or money. We aren't taught about other secret gardens that can also contain those things we are looking for — and so we don't look in those places because we don't know about them. That's until we meet someone who hasn't been blinded by that formal training like we have. That person takes our hand, tells us to be quiet, and walks us into the garden that only someone like him or her knows about."

"A garden that only someone like Jacky knows about," I said.

"Yes," she nodded.

"And when the Gestapo came that, day, to Otis's school . . . ," I started saying.

"Yes," she sort of interrupted, "that was a turning point."

"If I took my notes right, let me see here," and then I flipped to the part of my notes from that day in her diaries, "I think you said something like, 'Did Jacky set me up? Did he turn me in to get reward money? For some more heroin or coke? For some whore?'"

She looked at me. Surprised eyes. Maybe even deer in headlight eyes.

"You had your doubts," I said as I picked up my coffee to take a sip.

She just sat there for a moment.

"I did. I think I had them all along. I think that is what made me feel so raw with him. I was scared. I was scared from the time that I met him. Yes," she leaned forward to take and light up another cigarette, "I started feeling more at ease as time went on, but I always had that little doubting Thomas inside."

"Asking untrusting questions like you did that day."

"Right," she said. "But that day erased all of my doubts. It was a scary day. It is those dire times, those life or death times, when you see who is in your shovel crew."

"That day showed you that Jacky was in your shovel crew," I smiled.

"He was the chairman of the shovel crew board," she smiled back. "And yet I didn't see that he was an all star until that day. But he was there all along."

"What was there all along?"

"The part of him I saw that day. Loving, loyal, smart, cunning, powerful."

"Maybe you were too caught up in the diamonds?"

"Come again?" She asked with the cigarette resting softly between her index and middle finger of her right hand.

"It's a song in the 1953 film *Gentlemen Prefer Blonds* called, 'Diamonds are a Girl's Best Friend,'" I said in a confident and knowing way. "Maybe you were too brainwashed to think that diamonds — or a man who could give them to you — are your best friend?"

Was that me that just said that or some other person that I hired? Had I changed somehow from the timid boy when I arrived in front of Sophia's eyes to a young man who can grow a respectable mustache that doesn't look like I painted it on? Was the confidence I showed just now that respectable mustache?

"Good point," Sophia said. She seemed to know exactly where I was going with it. That's when I knew that this path I had taken with her and Jacky, learning about their lives, made me more inspired, live more, and feel more — love myself more.

"Ring of Fire" was now playing. It was one of my favorite songs by Johnny Cash.

"That's what most women are brought up on," she took a long drag. "The newspapers, the magazines, the television. It's all about the diamonds. And so men crawl over each other to offer up the shiny goods to the red queen."

"Just like in the movie. There is that one scene where the men are fighting each other to give Marilyn the diamonds."

Sophia leaned forward and focused her stunning blue eyes on mine while she dropped some ash into the tray. Her eyes had seen a lot of bad things and had endured a lot of pain. They were deep, and I don't mean into the eye sockets, but in their stare. It's like they saw through me, into the insides of me, and behind me.

She leaned back in the couch, paused, and then said:

"Meanwhile, there is a man standing off stage who won't buy into her game." She looked outside the window onto Park Avenue and then focused back on me. "He is standing alone, watching the spectacle, with his arms crossed, and wearing all black. He stands there alone baring his teeth in a mischievous and yet knowing grin towards that ring of fire," and then she pointed behind her to the Johnny Cash album playing. "He stands there knowing what happens when another man comes along with more treasures than all of the men on stage put together."

"Their egos would be smashed," I said.

"Why?" She asked rhetorically.

"Their treasures would be worthless to her now," I answered.

"Right," she tapped her index finger on her head.

We finished up our cigarettes and put them into the ashtray as though to put a period on a life-changing chapter in my life. It was one of the first times I had really asserted myself to someone that I thought was above me, better than me, and different than me. Before I met Sophia, I felt like just another cog in the wheel. Just another reporter, just another graduate from the system, and just another Midwestern transplant in the city of Gotham.

Meeting her changed all of that.

As we sat there smashing our cigarettes into the ashtray, I looked at her without her knowing I was looking. I saw the mosaic that was Sophia. I saw her shovel crew in all of the men at the Tavern, I saw all of the children she helped with her charity, and I saw her getting her hands dirty with *Resistance* during the war. And yet you couldn't see all of these parts of her without knowing her layers. All your mind would see is the posh, seemingly stuck up and oblivious, Upper East Side woman. She would look like the rest of them. And I guess that's why I felt like she made me feel better about myself. After reading what I had read, and what I learned about, I wasn't just like the rest of them: the other cogs, the other reporters, the other college graduates, or the other Americans.

No.

Sophia made me feel different about myself. I was a new brand and a new me. Maybe it's because there was a new pathway created in my brain. Maybe I am wrong, but I believe our brains can change. Of course, nature — our parents, our grandparents, or our great grandparents — has an effect on how our brain's pathways are formatted when we are born. But our beliefs — how we think about the world — can also change these pathways as we move along in our lives.

"Hank," she said suddenly through the cloud of smoke with sun light rays running through, "I had better be going." She looked at her fancy watch. I think it was a Tank Oblique by Cartier, I later found out after checking out some advertisements in the paper. "Winston has to drive me to Washington soon."

"Ah, yes," I looked at my Hamilton watch, not French but a good old American standard.

It was about 9:30 in the morning now, and I knew I had to be getting to the office.

We both got up. I started collecting the plates.

"Please," she stopped me with her hand on mine. "Winston will take care of all that."

"Are you sure? It's my pleasure," I said.

"Yes."

We had eaten — but it wasn't enough for me. I was still hungry to learn more. I was eager to hit the Tavern for what seemed like a graduation dinner that evening after work. I had finished all of the diaries, but thankfully Sophia wasn't done with me.

"Don't be a stranger, Hank, just because you have finished what I have given you," she said softly as she walked me to the front door. Her hand was resting softly on my forearm, in a motherly and comforting type of way.

"I won't," I said as I put my satchel around my shoulder.

"Let's arrange for a tea upon my return from my trip, darling. Call my secretary, and she'll call you later when she knows the date of my return. Here is the number." She handed me a business card with the Veritas logo on it along with a New York address and phone number.

"I would love that," I took the card.

We gave one another a big hug. It was short, like the other ones that we gave one another. But it was long enough when it is between two people like us who have shared so much. A minute hug between some is worth an hour hug between others.

We broke our embrace.

"Where is Winston? I want to say good day."

"Oh, he is probably outside having a smoke darling," she said. "He likes to sun bathe when the time is right. You'll find him next to the front door. That's his spot," she said as she walked towards the dining room to start collecting the plates and other things.

"Safe travels, Sophia. I'll see you when you get back."

"That's a deal, Hank," she looked back and smiled.

I closed the door and headed downstairs.

Winston was standing next to the front door just as Sophia had predicted. Balancing very delicately on the right corner of his mouth was his French cigarette.

"Finished up?" He asked with a small vintage smile.

"Yup," I said. "I just finished the last entries she gave me."

"What do you think, old boy?"

"It would take more than a minute for me to tell you," I said as I looked around the street. It was full of mothers walking their strollers and high school kids on their way to school. "I will say that reading the diaries changed my life."

"For the better, I hope," he said as some little flakes of ash dropped from his cigarette onto his black tuxedo jacket.

"No doubt," I nodded as I stood next to him.

"So I was right then?" He asked.

I looked over to him.

"I seem to recall," Winston took a long drag off of his cigarette and then said, "that I told you before you were going to learn something, right?" He softly patted my shoulder with his right hand.

"That was an understatement," I said.

"I suppose old sport," he shrugged his shoulders, "I am an understated type of guy." He grinned a big grin. The guy who is wearing all black, and standing off stage in the *Diamond's Are a Girl's Best Friend* scene, would have the same grin on his face. It was a grin that was knowing and confident, but it was also subtle and stealth about how much wisdom was behind it. I didn't know much about this Englishman. All I did know was that that Meyer brought him here for Sophia.

I suppose I knew something else, too.

I knew Winston was a spirited and humorous guy from listening to the music he played inside. But I got an even clearer picture of him when I was outside Sophia's apartment. I guess Sophia liked men like this. I could tell why. They kept things light — and real.

"I had better be going," he said as he smashed his cigarette with his right foot. "But you remember what you learned up there, and you won't regret it."

"What, I'll win a prize?" I asked sarcastically.

"Yes, son," he said as he looked at me. "That prize will be up here," and then he tapped his head with his index finger, just as Sophia had done.

A car honked loudly on Park Avenue, and I turned around to look. When I looked back, poof! Winston had gone upstairs. He didn't seem to be a quick moving man, but maybe there was more to this Englishman than met the eye.

I made my way to the office. And then, after a full day at the paper, much of which was taken up by the Kennedy story, I took the train to the Tavern in the early evening.

Dirty Quiet Money

"Hey, it's graduation day for junior!" Tony said when I came in. There were a bunch of men wearing nice Italian suits in the back of the Tavern. They all seemed to look over at me when I walked into the door.

Who are those guys? I thought.

"That's right, Tony, graduation day," I said as I ignored my inner nervous Nellie and put my satchel up on the bar. "Where is my Hawaiian lei of flowers?"

"Kid, you ain't gettin nottin like dat here. But you going to get a nice martini and some good eats, on the house," he leaned over and patted me on the shoulder like Winston had just done. "Maybe we'll even put an umbrella in the drink to make it extra special?"

He smiled his big steak eating teeth at me.

There were a few Madison Avenue advertising types at the bar when I looked to the right. When I looked to the left, I could not believe my eyes.

It was that girl I saw before on the subway — here at the Tavern!

Holy shit! Holy shit! Holy fucking shit! I thought to myself.
I couldn't say holy shit enough times to myself.

"Here you go, kid," Tony put the vodka martini back in front of me. I turned from looking at the girl to look at Tony.

"Like the scenery?" He smiled.

"Can't complain," I sipped the drink and ignored my neurotic battle station thoughts inside. The drink was almost all vodka. I had one like this on Easter Sunday one time in New Orleans. I was doing a story there for the paper. I remember having just one and walking through the French Quarter like I had never learned how to walk in my life.

As I sat there at the Tavern bar, I looked like a clumsy CIA agent acting like he is not looking but really looking look over at the girl. She was reading a book. She caught me and smiled. Oh shit! My response was an "I just got caught cheating on my test" type of look in front of me.

And then I thought to myself: why? Would Jacky do that? A guy with holes in his arms, a criminal record, and all that crap, could rap to a gal like Sophia! Why can't I do the same thing? Yet I am sitting here afraid in my little cocoon? So I took another sip of my vodka, got up off my stool, and walked over to her. There were some people sitting on each side of the natural beauty, so I just stood behind her for a moment, and waited for my chance.

Think: Jacky the cat, the smooth cat, Jacky the smooth cat.

Okay, smooth cats aren't usually cranked up on smack and coke like Jacky was. But that is beside the point.

She looked back at me. She was tall, but not taller than me. I stand about six one. She was about two feet shorter. I could smell the hint of patchouli oil coming out from underneath the red bandanna that she had wrapped around her neck.

"Interesting reading?" I boldly asked.

"Who Fears The Devil," she said as she put a placeholder in the book. She put it on the bar next to another book called "Chinese Kung Fu — An Instruction Manual." Her hair was long, brown, and down to the middle of her back. There were little strands of blond in her hair, like she had been in the sun for a long time bathing and reading one of the books.

"Light reading for a light day," I joked.

"If you don't fear the devil, every day is light," she smiled as she turned in her seat to look at me with her green hazel eyes. They peered out at me from her bright freckled face, with droopy eyebrows, high cheekbones, and a chiseled jaw.

I looked her up and down. Not for a long time. It wasn't a doctor's examination. But it was my own type of investigation for a second. She wore skin tight shabby chic Levi's. I loved those on her. They showed off her athletic legs. She sported a pair of worn down brown cowboy boots. They were old but snazzy. Her jeans fit nicely over the boots. On her chair was a worn leather satchel. It looked like it had been to Africa and back to the States a few times.

"I think I saw you on the subway the other day," I said with a smile. I wondered to myself if I was doing the wrong thing talking to a woman I thought was a hippy type who maybe didn't have the same sense of the world as I did, without the center that I had, and without the same Midwestern-type values: God, family, and country.

But where have those Midwest values gotten me? Dates with my hands.

"I know you know you saw me on the subway the other day," she said to me with some punch. "I thought you'd never say hello," she sort of slapped me on my chest with the back of her hand that was on the end of her long arm which came out of a tight fitting V-neck white t-shirt. The shirt was so thin I could tell she wore a fancy looking black bra underneath. It looked like one of the ones I could picture on a woman like Sophia: elegant, provocative, and powerful. Maybe there was more sophistication to this free spirited gypsy looking woman than met my sometimes narrow minded Chicago eyes?

When I felt the back of her hand on my chest, I thought maybe it was a good thing she was the way she was and I was the way I was. Maybe that is what would make our chemistry? Or maybe it is what would puncture our air balloon into little pieces as we fly on a sunny day over the Illinois prairie on the way to a Sunday picnic?

"I move slowly," I said apologetically looking around. "But then I pounce like a hungry cat when I know my prey is there for the taking," and then I formed my hands like a cat pouncing and made a cat sound.

Good God, man, what are you doing acting like some cheesy frat cat from the jungle? Do you think you are some Tarzan with your nerdy stick body that a 3 year-old girl could smash into pieces with a sneeze? You are making a fool of yourself! Why don't you talk to a girl who is more preppy, more college like, like one of those sorority girls at the bar?

There is no future with this one, my inner voice said.

She'll just want to play with you like a cat does with a string, and then leave you for some other guy who is not as boring as you are. How tacky can you be? You are smarter than that.

Oh, that annoying inner voice that I was brought up with. I have had it since I was young. It told me not to look at the black and white photograph of Jacky and Sophia that day in her apartment. It said to me: stick to your job and don't take any detours that they didn't pay you for!

That's when I ignored the inner me. They say you should follow it. But sometimes you have to recalculate it before you can.

Today I am ignoring that voice again. It has been brainwashed into my head by so many: my parents, other men, other women, our institutions (the Churches, the Temples), and, of course, history. History says what worked in the past should be recreated in the now. But, oftentimes, what worked in the past doesn't work in the now. That's because the now is different than the then.

This isn't a bad thing, I tell myself today. This doesn't mean that there is something wrong with me no more than this means there is something wrong with nature. I remember reading "The Bear," by Faulkner. In it, the mighty bear is killed at the end by human kind, even though it was able to survive through bullet wounds and other injuries. Mother nature didn't weep for the bear or judge the humans for killing it. Nature had taken its course. And today, I am taking my course. Mother nature isn't judging me for doing it. If anything, she is clapping for me. Even if the clapping is watching that skinny Chicago boy take a nose-dive into a pool without water.

"Are you a domesticated cat or a wild one?" She asked me in jest and interrupted my nervous insecure mind.

Thank God — or nature or both — for her humor.

"Both," I said. "I try to keep things interesting."

"Ooh, I like that," she nodded her head.

"Kung Fu?" I asked looking at her book on the bar.

She looked over at it and then turned to look back towards me.

"A woman's got to have her tricks of the trade," she smiled at me like she could twist me in two if she wanted to.

"You take Kung Fu classes?"

"At the Wu Mei Kung Fu Association," she pointed over towards the west side of Manhattan with her thumb. "It's over on Lafayette Street."

Initially, I thought she was kidding. But I could tell from the look on her face, and from the book, that she wasn't.

"How long have you been going there?"

"A few months. Before that, I studied it in San Francisco."

"So you know your stuff?" I asked with surprise. "I didn't think patchouli and Kung Fu mixed," I said jokingly. "A contradiction?"

She glared at me with what I imagined Jacky's razor sharp eyes looked like. I never expected them from a woman like this.

"I could knock you off your feet with one punch to your chest," she pointed to where my heart was.

"You give getting knocked off your feet by a gal a whole new meaning!" I smiled.

She giggled and got out of her sting like a bee tone.

"My name is Hank," I held out my hand.

"Este," she said with a smile.

"A pleasure," I said as I shook her hand.

"Totally," she said in her California accent as she smiled.

I could see her martini was almost done.

"Can I get you another?" I pointed to her drink.

"If you are having one, too," she smiled.

"Of course," I said.

I looked over to Tony. He saw me looking. I put two fingers up and pointed to her drink. He nodded.

"Come here a lot?" She asked.

"It's my local haunt," I said.

"A good place to haunt," she smiled. "Where are you from originally?"

"Chicago, and you?"

"San Francisco."

"Never been."

"Never been to Chicago, either, other than through the movies. Own a machine gun?"

"Nope, but I know people who know people who do," I said with the wildness of the undomesticated cat, thinking I would shock her. The statement was true. Sophia knew where to go to find a triggerman if she needed to.

"Well, then, you know some good people to know," she said with a smirk.

"Here are your drinks, kids," Tony came up and put the drinks in front of us. "These on the house, Hank. Compliments of the gents in the back," he pointed to the back room of the restaurant where all of the finely dressed men were sitting.

I looked at Tony shocked. What guys in the back? Why would they buy me a drink? Are they going to expect something from me in return? Ah, the nervous Nellie of Hank's upbringing, always being in fear about the next thing, whether I am doing the right thing, never considering that sometime doing the wrong thing is the right thing. I leaned back in my seat to peer into the back room. The men back there looked like members of the underground board of directors. They raised their glasses to me and smiled. I took my drink and did the same to them.

I had no idea who these men were. I didn't even know why they were raising their glasses to me. I returned the gesture anyway. I made it up as I went along with them, and with Este. I guess that is what you have to do sometimes — make it up as you go along.

"Friends of yours?" Este asked.

"Friends of a friend," I said thinking of Sophia. I handed the drink to Este.

"Cheers," I raised my glass.

"Cheers," she said.

We sipped.

"Must be a powerful man you know," she said as she turned even further around in her chair towards me.

"It's a woman," I said as I sipped my drink.

She looked at me with surprise. I had caught her attention.

"Even better," she slowly nodded.

"Funny that you thought it was a man," I said.

"Funny you thought I didn't know Kung Fu just because of my scent," she said with an "I gotcha" smile. We sat drinking our martini potions quietly for a moment — a calm moment like the ones I had with Sophia.

As we sat there, I thought to myself: Este was right.

She seemed like a butterfly. Her spirit was free, and her clothes kind of screamed that to the world. "I am a world traveler, I have seen far off lands, and I float from place to place," the butterfly part of her would say.

And yet I know she had the ability to sting like a bee. "I have been in many fights, and have knocked many men to their backs, with a mere thrust of one of my long arms," the bee part of her would say. It was in this double meaning that I resonated with her. I felt that she mirrored Sophia in so many ways. By extension, Este was like me, too.

But I wouldn't have known that if it weren't for Sophia. I learned being around her that underneath this button down Chicago boy's exterior is a world traveler. I have it inside me to be a guy who likes to have a healthy amount of adventure and uncertainty in his life. I never would have known that if it weren't for Sophia, though. I never would have continued on the diversion that day if she didn't let me.

"It's none of your business," Sophia could have said when I asked her about the black and white photograph. Or she could have punted: "oh, that's just an old friend of mine from Paris."

She didn't. She seemed to sense my curious soul right when she met me. That is why I knew she was sharp. Sophia could look at a person up and down and measure them up in a second. It would take others research and background checks to do that.

I guess that's why Plato was right when he said like attracts like. I am ambiguous because of my double or dual meaning, and so I am attracted to women like Este who have the same vibrations, like two guitars hitting the same chord.

"You know, there is beauty in uncertainty Hank," Este broke the silence with a smile and her hand on my forearm, just the way Sophia would touch me during our talks. Este then went back to sipping her drink.

Beauty in uncertainty — I love that! Maybe the booze was catching up with me. Or maybe I was catching up with myself.

"Hold that thought," I said, "I have to use the restroom. I'll be right back," I rubbed Este's back in what I thought of as a Jacky type of way.

I walked to the back of the restaurant and past the smoky room where the underground board of directors was sitting. I swung open the bathroom door and then went into a toilet stall. As I relieved my bladder into the toilet water below, I looked up at the old peeling ceiling and thought about how pressure can stifle things in life. If there were some man standing outside the stall right now banging on the door, he would have given me stage fright. But there wasn't. And so I took the piss without feeling remiss about taking too much time while someone waited in line.

While I stood there with my eyes closed, the time grew between now and when I finished the diaries. I started to get more perspective on the forest that was Sophia's story instead of being mired in the details: this Louisiana plantation, that café in Marseille, this jail in Paris, or that Gestapo officer.

That's when it hit me.

I opened my eyes and whispered to myself: could Winston be Jacky? They are the same age. They are the same height. They hold their cigarettes in their mouths the same way. Winston slaps me on the shoulder the same way that Jacky would have. Sophia laughs and speaks to Winston like no regular butler. Lansky and the others got Winston shortly after Sophia was having Ella. She told me that she never received another letter from Jacky. This may have been true. But I never asked her if she had ever seen him again, which is a whole other question that wasn't asked — or answered.

"Enjoy the read, young man, I suspect you are going to learn quite a lot in those," I remember Winston saying to me one day at Sophia's sometime back. How did he know if he wasn't Jacky? He seemed to know the diaries, and he seemed to know Sophia better than just some stranger who is put in her house.

The water stopped splashing in the toilet. I zipped up my zipper.

But then I thought: why continue with the charade now in 1963? The war is over, after all.

I walked over to the sink. I put some soap onto my hands and started washing them. I continued my investigative thinking as I looked into the mirror: I know Jacky had to go into hiding after being framed during the war. I know he was living on the run for a long time. A little plastic surgery, a change in name, and the butler get up would have been perfect hide out for him while the heat was on — and since it has been on. After all, they say that sometimes the best way to hide something is right in front of your face. Maybe that's why Sophia and Winston are taking this long trip overseas right after this fiasco in Dallas?

I finished washing my hands. I pulled some paper out of the dispenser to start drying them. I thought: While I don't think

Jacky's record as being a Nazi collaborator was ever cleared, I also don't think he was a high priority. There were others who the Allies — and the Israelis — wanted more. They caught Adolf Eichmann, the infamous SS officer, in Argentina a few years ago. He was living under an assumed name and, I think, had undergone plastic surgery so as to disguise himself.

As I approached the bathroom door, I concluded: right when I think I had things figured out, like with Este, I was thrown for a loop with her Kung Fu. The same was true with Sophia and Jacky. Right when I thought Jacky was fish food somewhere, I realized maybe he was eating fish at Sophia's.

The uncertainty was beautiful because it led to possibility. Where there is possibility, there is hope. I didn't know for certain that Jacky was gone forever. I was now as uncertain of that as I was certain that every pebble of sand on the beach is just like the next pebble of sand on the beach, and that there are plenty of pebbles to go around. So there is no need to treat any pebble more special than another. The pebbles get in between your toes and you clean them out like useless cockroaches after you leave the beach. The pebbles aren't special.

But Jacky is special. He is special because he knew how to toe that line between being and nothingness, between power and powerlessness, between hope and hopelessness, between good and bad, or between lover and fighter. Right when Sophia thought she had him figured out, he slipped out of her pigeonhole and occupied a different one. When she tried to keep him in that one, he goes back to the first one. Jacky was no pebble.

Nor was Sophia. That is why I felt so inspired by them. They made an art form out of not fitting in. That is why I felt so alive when I was around Sophia, and hearing about Jacky. I was always told to fit in by my parents, and felt bad when I didn't. But Sophia and Jacky made me feel ok about not fitting in all of the time. Sophia's impossible to bottle up and cork energy infused me with the spirit to talk to Este, who was sitting right on the other side of this bathroom door. I knew I would be alright if Este didn't want me, because Sophia and Jacky were able to find one another after so many didn't want them.

But they found each other anyway.

And so I pushed open the wooden bathroom door and walked outside past the underground board. I looked back at them. They were all huddled around their table talking. One of them saw me looking back at them, and he winked at me with a smile. He then went back to their huddle. That wink was like the kisses from the cousins that Sophia's cheeks received when she arrived in New York that day. I received the wink from that director, who got the wink from Tony, who got the wink from Sophia, who got the wink from, perhaps, Jacky, Winston, or whatever his name is now.

I walked back to Este.

"Have a good trip?" Este asked after I tapped her on her shoulder to let her know I was back.

"I thought the trip was just starting?" I asked as I picked up my martini.

She picked up hers.

"I hope so," she said, smirked, and then raised her glass. I did the same with mine. We both smiled a "we are about to get away with something" smile.

It was official. My stage fright had turned into stage delight.

The End